AFTER THE FALL

A FALLEN MEN NOVEL
BOOK FOUR

giana darling

Published by Giana Darling
Edited by Kim Book Junkie and Jenny Sims
Proofread by Michele Ficht and All Ali
Cover Design by Najla Qamber
Cover Model Christopher Mason
Cover Photographer Jorden Keith

License Notes

To my sister, Gracie.

For always believing I'd have a book published to dedicate to her one day.

"Long is the way and hard, that out of Hell leads up to the light."
—John Milton, *Paradise Lost*

A note to my readers:

Please trust me to take you on this journey. It will be rough waters and placid calm in equal parts, but I promise I will get you to shore safely, if a little worse for wear in the end. As you know, there is much beauty to be found in pain.

PLAYLIST

"My Babe"—Whitehorse
"From Eden"—Hozier
"House of the Rising Sun"—The Animals
"Won't Go Down Easy"—Jaxon Gamble
"I Want You, I Need You, I Love You"—Elvis Presley
"Good Times Roll"—The Cars
"Dangerous"—Royal Deluxe
"Devil's Backbone"—The Civil Wars
"East of Eden"—Zella Day
"Glitter & Gold"—Barns Country
"This Is My World"—Esterly ft. Austin Jenckes
"Prisoner"—The Weeknd
"Stairway to Heaven"—Led Zepplin
"I Will Follow You Into The Dark"—Death Cab For Cutie
"All Right Now"—Free
"Heavy Is The Head"—Zac Brown Band ft. Chris Cornell
"The One"— Kodaline
"Love Me Tender"—Elvis acoustic
"Reasons Not To Die"—Ryn Weaver
"Black Sea"—Natasha Blume
"When The Pary's Over"— Lewis Capoldi

"Where's My Love"—SYML
"I miss you"—mxmtoon
"Brother"—Kodaline
"Lost Without You"—Freya Ridings
"Sense of Home"— Harrison Storm
"You And I"—Barns Country
"To Be Alone With You"—Sufjan Stevens
"Only Love"—Ben Howard

PROLOGUE

King

NEVER THOUGHT MUCH 'BOUT DYIN'. I was still a young man by anyone's standards, only twenty-three and healthy with it. My lack of curiosity 'bout death stemmed more from my lifelong exposure to it more than anythin' else. Had a father who killed his uncle in a church parkin' lot when I was a kid, sent to the clink for half a dime. There'd always been guns in my house, in the clubhouse that was home to my dad's motorcycle club, The Fallen, and guns worn on the hips of the men who hung there. Learned to shoot when I was five, how to defend myself usin' the stick limbs of a twelve-year-old boy's body, and how to use a knife like a fuckin' extension of myself when Priest rolled into my life and taught me his deadly craft. Mostly, I knew death 'cause it stole my best friend, my fuckin' brother in everythin' but blood, when we were still kids, still filled with hope and piss and a shit ton'a vinegar.

So yeah, I wasn't unfamiliar with death, but it wasn't somethin' I'd ever worried 'bout for myself. Never thought of it until now, and to be fuckin' honest, I never coulda known I'd be facin' down death's door with no chance to escape it. Suppose some would argue there was a choice, that there's a choice to be had in all things.

Only, I'd counter there was no other decision to be made for me in that moment. Dyin' meant my dad would be free, my girl would be safe, and my family would be whole.

How could I do anythin' else but die?

For them.

Yeah, that's exactly right.

So, I stood on the edge of that cliff that had been my place, a kinda special settin' for so many of the greatest fuckin' moments of my life, and I stared down the craggy wall of rock droppin' into even more sharp rocks and the churnin' ocean below, and I braced myself.

There was pure evil at my back, and 'fore me, only a chasm that represented an empty future without any'a the people I love.

Shoulda been a sad moment, maybe somethin' like a tragedy. But as I heard the cock of the gun and the hard spit of the bullet from the chamber somewhere behind me, I couldn't muster up a tear 'cause I was only filled with hope. I'd found what I loved, and I was only too willin' to let it kill me.

Hope that my sacrifice would ensure the happily ever after I'd once promised my woman.

CHAPTER ONE

King

I SAW HER IN THE PARKIN' lot five years ago when I was sellin' drugs to some preppy college kids. Not the most poetic place to fall in love at first sight, but I believed enough in fate to know you can't choose those things.

She was standin' across the asphalt like a mirage in the heat waves of the midday, late summer sun. The shine caught the long tumble of hair streamin' down her back and turned it to burnished gold, threads of copper glintin' in the curlin' mass of it as if each strand was semi-precious metal. Instantly, I wanted to sink my hands into that silken cloud, fist the locks between my fingers, and *tug* so that those nearly purple red lips, stained like a bruised plum, would bloom open for me to pluck at and plunder. I knew how she would taste just lookin' at her, somethin' hot and heady, potent like whiskey.

Even thinkin' this, I knew she wasn't the kinda woman to succumb to just any man's flashy desires. She walked with a prim elegance across the lot to Mac's Grocer as if she was a debutante 'bout to be presented for her social inauguration, her gait liquid and her posture naturally straight. There was a haughtiness to the tip of her chin, a cultivated class to her sweet, tight pencil skirt and a blouse that shoulda been a male deterrent but wasn't 'cause the material was just sheer enough to promise a glimpse of a dark lace bra beneath.

She was buttoned up, but the promise of more, of what would happen if a man like me got his hands on her and trust from her, stretched me taut as an overextended coil 'bout to snap back.

I wanted that. Her body and, almost inexplicably, her trust.

I knew instinctively with a woman of her caliber, I couldn't have one without the other.

It was her I was thinkin' 'bout when Mute drew my attention to the yuppie as fuck college kids rollin' outta their mint Mustang convertible strollin' over to buy some weed. I was thinkin' 'bout her, so I knew somehow when the hairs at the back of my neck stood on end that she had spotted me.

She watched.

She watched as I dealt with the punks who wanted a cheaper deal on grade fuckin' A marijuana, and she watched as Mute and I waited for them to leave 'fore we busted a gut laughin' at their fear. We were barely eighteen, but we'd been grown in the manner of men since we were boys. We knew how to intimidate, but more, we knew how *not* to be intimidated, especially by things that didn't matter like those guys' generic, expensive ride, and college educations.

We'd been taught young what really mattered in life.

Family, brotherhood, loyalty, freedom.

And love.

Maybe none of the men who'd raised me said it explicitly, but that's what they'd taught me. It was love that made Axe-Man leave his old chapter of the Fallen MC over in Calgary and move to Entrance, B.C., and love that made Bat give up his military career to get home to his wife (even though she ended up bein' a bitch). It was love that made my dad go to jail for years when he shoulda been raisin' my little sister, Harleigh Rose, and me.

Love makes people *do* things.

When I was done laughin', I wondered as I stared across the asphalt, lockin' eyes with a waif of a woman with a fuck ton'a just gorgeous hair, if it was love that made me wanna cross that lot and claim her for my own.

Name unknown, characteristics unchartered.

I knew just by the look of her that she was it for me.

The one.

Romantic thoughts for an eighteen-year-old son of a notorious outlaw motorcycle club Prez, but not unusual for me.

Born that way. Romantic as hell and desperate for a time when the girls 'round me weren't just vapid or clingy bitches to be enjoyed for mutual pleasure 'fore I shoved them off. Desperate for a time when I'd find the right kinda woman and know in my bones, I had to make her mine.

And I felt it, my skeleton hot and too heavy in my body, weighted with lust and words, a destiny I'd never 'fore understood.

Lookin' at Cressida Irons, the woman that would become *my* woman despite all'a the obstacles, I knew she would always be fuckin' mine.

And me, irrevocably, fuckin' ecstatically, hers.

Four years after that fateful day in a grocery store parkin' lot and I still felt electrified with my love for that woman.

But watchin' the professor of American Lit pace back and forth in a short tweed skirt over swayin' hips that drew male eyes like a hypnotist's pendulum, I found myself intrigued with her too.

She was short, slight, but woman in all the ways that counted. The pert breasts pushin' against the cotton button-up would perfectly fill my big hands, just as the little waist would fit under the bracket of my palms like they were made to frame them. I liked this woman's confidence as she spoke 'bout *allegory* and *verisimilitude* as if they were literary diamonds she wanted to collect and polish and ache over. I even liked the way she bit the edge of her lip as she listened to a student's response to her question, as if she had to hold back her excitement physically or it would froth over like uncorked champagne.

She was bright and intelligent, so magnetic with passion for the subject. Every single student in the room was enraptured by her.

I sat in the back row of the lecture hall with my heavy boots propped on the seat below me, a pen between my teeth to satisfy my urge to take *her* between my teeth, and I watched her for the entire three-hour class. When it was over, I wasn't the only one who lingered to speak with her. There were four guys, all muscle and bravado like your typical university hotshots, and an over eager girl who swarmed the professor like moths to a flame.

Still, I waited.

I was good at it. A patient man since birth, which was fuckin' good 'cause I had a sister who would try the patience of a saint and a family who regularly got up in each other's shit in a way that could be irritatin' as fuck.

But I was a man who was born wantin' to meet his soulmate *now,* and I'd waited years for that, so I could wait a while more for this professor with the prim skirt and dirty girl big hair.

At least, I could wait until one of the punk ass kids got too close to her and smiled an inch from her face.

I was up outta my chair, eatin' up the stairs between the stage and me like they were nothin', and then I was there, between the idiot and her.

Her.

My woman.

The one I'd dreamt 'bout since I was a fuckin' kid but never really *believed* was real, 'cause how could God or the universe or anythin' like it create someone so breathtakingly perfect for someone else.

The moment I stepped into play, the air between us went electric with tension. It took strength to decide to scare off the punk ass college kid instead'a takin' the woman I'd been lustin' after for the last three hours into my arms in a ravagin' embrace.

Then I decided, what better way to stake a claim on someone, so that idiot would understand, than to do exactly as I wanted to.

So, I stepped closer, watchin' her pupils blow wide and black as I slipped an arm 'round that little waist, and then I hauled her up against my chest so I could smile down into her face.

"Hey, teach," I said just to watch that blush flare up over her cheeks, but then I was done with teasin' and my mouth was over hers.

She was stiff at first, that split-second hesitation that lingered even after four years of livin' a different kinda life than she had 'fore with a totally different kinda man. Truth was, I fuckin' loved that little hiccough of doubt, of prudishness that would never die. It was like suckin' on an ice cube; at first it stuck to your mouth, intractable as hell, but a second later came the melt.

That was how it happened, the kiss then and the kisses always, especially in public. She went hard then soft in my arms, her breasts pressin' against my chest, her hips curvin' into mine, and her hands slidin' up into the back of my hair where they loved to tangle and pull me closer.

She lost herself in me, in the texture of my hot mouth sealin' hers, in the way our bodies fit together and ignited like perfectly stacked tinder to a flame.

You ask any man, they'll tell you, there's nothin' fuckin' headier than that.

When I finally pulled away, her eyes were still closed, long lashes like fans over her pink cheeks, lips damp and parted, invitin' further plunder.

I refrained, even though I wanted to bend her over that podium and fuck her until her moans echoed in the auditorium.

Instead, I cupped the side'a her face in my big palm and grinned at her until she swam up from lusty depths and once again realized where we were. When the awareness came, she frowned puckishly at me then shoved me away with her little hand.

I laughed but followed her unspoken order and put distance between us, perchin' my ass against her desk with my arms and legs folded as I stared down the four crestfallen assholes lustin' after my girl.

"Woah," the only other girl murmured, her eyes wide and glitterin' behind her glasses as she looked between the prof and me. "Is that your boyfriend?"

The woman I'd just kissed senseless scrunched up her nose in an absurd and adorable expression of displeasure. She waved a hand my way and shrugged. "That's King."

"Like *the* King?" One of the idiots asked, shootin' me a confused glance.

"Drake," she reprimanded kindly. "Does he look like an aristocrat?"

I grinned wolfishly at them and waggled my ring burdened hand at them. "At your fuckin' service."

She flipped her long, thick mane of hair over her shoulder to shoot me an eye roll, but there was a smile on her lips.

Cressida Irons had changed in a lotta ways over the past half-decade, but she had not lost one ounce of her sass.

"I think that's enough for today, boys and girl. If you have any questions, you can email me or visit me during office hours, but I think you are all as prepared as you can be for finals."

"But I had some questions—"

"Professor Irons said enough," I said casually, leanin' back on my hands so that the muscles in my arms popped into relief. "Think you'd better get goin'. Unlike you, apparently, your prof has a life outside the classroom."

The guy stuttered then swallowed his pride and turned with his friends to shuffle up the stairs and outta the room. Only the girl remained, cute, but way too young. She looked up at Cress like she was some kinda superhero.

It was cute as hell, mostly 'cause my girl *was* worthy of such adulation, but my patience was at its end.

"Got an appointment we better get to," I urged Cress.

She cocked a hip and planted a fist on it. My cock twitched at the sight of her so prim and proper like that, buttoned up and polished as if she wasn't secretly the dirtiest girl I knew.

"What kind of appointment?" she demanded with a secret smile that said she was enjoyin' calling me on my bullshit.

"One with our bed, maybe the kitchen floor if we can't make it up the stairs in a timely fuckin' fashion."

I swallowed my laughter as the blush in her cheeks travelled down her neck into the slice of skin revealed by her blouse just over her breasts.

The female student made a noise of distress in her throat and turned big eyes to Cress. "Is he really your boyfriend, Professor Irons?"

I wanted to tell her *no*. Cressida was not my girlfriend.

What a fuckin' paltry term for what she was to me. Our relationship felt as elemental to me as Adam and Eve's, as if we were born of each other *and* meant for each other. As if there was no other choice in the world as inevitable as our decision to be together.

I wanted her to be my wife as well as my life, 'cause then maybe people would have a better chance at fathomin' the depths of my feelings for my woman, but I couldn't propose.

Not now.

Not when I was prospectin' for The Fallen and shit with the Ventura's was so bad, I was thinkin' we'd be mountin' a full-scale gang war against them sometime soon. Couldn't do it when Staff Sergeant Danner was makin' it his mission to take down my father by any means necessary. Even if those means weren't so legal.

How could I ask the best woman I knew to put herself in the line of fire just so I could have the male satisfaction of seein' my ring on her finger?

The only reason I'd waited so long was to give her time to know her new self, the one born of our love that she'd been hidin' inside herself like a second soul for so many years. Wasn't fair to my girl to make her mine 'fore she'd even really had a chance to be *hers*.

So, I didn't like Cress bein' my 'girlfriend' or this kid callin' her Professor Irons instead'a Professor Garro, but I could live with the bad taste in my mouth so long as she was safe.

"Yes, unfortunately sometimes this bossy boy is mine," she said with a frown that she undercut with twitchin' lips. "I'll be in my office next week if you need any help then, Mary. Okay?"

Mary nodded her head, shot me a quick look accompanied by a fierce blush, then hustled up the stairs and outta the room.

"Having fun?" she asked me with a cocked brow and hip at the same time, sass personified.

I smirked at her. "Always, with you."

She shook her head at the ceilin'. "How am I supposed to be irritated with you when you're always romantic as hell?"

"Is hell romantic?" I asked, leanin' forward to tag her hand and pull her between my legs so I could fit my hands 'round her waist.

"For the morbid and the literary."

"Dante might argue that." I ran my nose down the line of her open shirt so I could smell the warm, apple scent of her. "Not sure he found anythin' romantic in the circles of hell."

She shrugged, but a hand found the back of my head and began to comb through my curls. "I think anyone who's read the *Inferno* or *Purgatory* would disagree even with the author himself. An adventure to the bowels of hell is not without its magic and beauty. And isn't that what romance is?"

"You tell me." I softly bit the top inner crest of her breast and looked up at her with my cheek to her chest.

"That's what you make me feel," she whispered as she tipped her head down to feather her lips and her words against my forehead like fairy dust. "Magical and beautiful."

"You are," I agreed easily as I let one hand wander down her outer thigh then back up under the hem of her tweed skirt so I could feel the texture of her thigh high stockin' give way to silky bare skin just 'fore I reached the satin of her panty-covered sex. I traced my index finger along the edge of the fabric and ran my thumb over her clit. "Show you just how much magic and beauty we can make, babe."

She softened slowly, melted warmly like butter poolin' in my palm, but her low-lidded eyes darted toward the door at the top of the stairs. "King…" she breathed, but it wasn't a true protest.

My girl liked the risk, the tang of danger that resonated metallic as blood on the back of the tongue.

I planted my palm on her belly and pushed her backward until her ass hit the desk then farther, until her hips canted and my momentum pushed her on top of the wood. I swallowed her gasp and ate at her sweet mouth until that lost breath turned into a deep moan.

My cock throbbed harder and harder as she sunk deeper into her desire for me. I loved the evolution of this classy, educated woman into a sensual wanton who came alive just for me.

Nothin' else made me feel worthier of my namesake.

More like a fuckin' king.

I slid my fingers under the crotch of those panties, felt her wet against the back of my knuckles and *ripped*. The fabric gave way, and I wasted no time in unzippin' my fly to tug out my hard cock, slottin' it against her openin'. I sunk my other hand in the thick hair at the back of her head and tugged so that her mouth bloomed open for me, pantin' and wet, her gaze clingin' to mine.

"You're mine," I told her. "And I can take you wherever I want, can't I, babe?"

She blinked slowly, lids tremblin' and heavy. "Yes."

I nudged the head of my cock between her silky folds. "I can take you hard."

"Yes," she hissed.

"Fast."

"Yes, yes, yes."

"I can take you any time, any place, any way I want," I growled and then shoved my cock to the hilt in her wet embrace.

Her head tipped back on a low moan, and I pressed my teeth to her flutterin' pulse to feel it race under my tongue as I ground even deeper into her.

As I started to pump my hips against her, holdin' her so close to me there was no space between our bodies, I pulled back to say against her mouth. "You love the idea of bein' found 'cause you want people to know that you're mine and mine alone."

"And you're mine," she said fiercely, bitin' into my lower lip and fistin' a hand in the back of my shirt to draw me even closer. "Your cock, your beautiful body, your heart, and your soul."

"Fuck yeah," I groaned as she moved her mouth across my stubbled jaw and down my neck to suck at my skin.

Four years with this woman and I still couldn't get enough, be deep enough, love hard enough to satiate my fuckin' burnin' need for her. She rippled 'round me, and her breath stuttered as she started to fall apart 'round my cock.

"That's it, babe. Come all over me."

And she did, as if my words were the key to unlockin' her pleasure. She shuddered in my arms as I plunged harder into her clutchin' heat, chasin' my pleasure and heightenin' her climax.

My balls were heavy, and the base of my spine tightened as I thought 'bout comin' inside her bare, as I wished for the hundredth time that I could plant my seed inside her and create life with our love.

The thought blazed a flamin' trail down my back and exploded in my groin. I groaned into her mouth as I spilled inside her, and she took my cock, my tongue, my cum eagerly, like she couldn't get enough.

After, our damp foreheads pressed together, our pantin' breath slowin' between our relaxed mouths, I wrapped my hand 'round her slender neck just to feel her pulse return to normal.

"Love you," I told her, 'cause I liked to tell her in moments like this, times that didn't matter so much, and also in moments that did.

Straight up, I liked to tell my girl I loved her 'cause life had taught me not to take a fuckin' thing for granted.

Speakin' of... "Gotta get to the compound, babe. Shit's hit the fan, that's why I came to getcha."

Her sigh fanned over my face, but when I pulled back to

look at her it was to see her eyes alight with fire. "'Course it has. Well, whatever it is, we'll be ready for it."

"That's my babe." I cupped the back of her neck with my hand and planted a hard kiss on her mouth. "Let's do it."

CHAPTER TWO

King

THE COMPOUND HAD BEEN my home since I was old enough to cogitate. Knew every inch of the asphalt, the number of bricks that made up the clubhouse and how many tools we kept in the garage. Lost my virginity in one of the older brother's rooms at twelve to a biker bitch ten years older and drank my first pint in the bar with the club members like I was of age even though I wasn't even old enough to drive.

The club was my home, but I'd grown up thinkin' it wouldn't be my life.

For all the things I loved 'bout the life, I also hated a fuck ton too.

Most of all, it was the thing that had taken my dad from me too young. Imprisoned for killin' the son of a bitch who shot through a little girl to get at him, he'd been absent from my life and my little sister, Harleigh Rose's, for way too fuckin' long.

I watched him now, quiet as he sat in church, the room we held club meetings in, his big head propped on a fist, the other hand scratchin' absently at his beard. There was somethin' in his face I didn't like, somethin' like a warnin'.

"Gonna stand there all day lookin' pretty, or are you gonna get your ass in here?" he growled without movin' his stare from the middle of the table where The Fallen MC insignia was burned into the wood.

"Gonna sit there all day gettin' older than you already are while we got real problems to address?" I countered, but I pushed off the doorframe with my hip and strolled over to him.

I waited a beat, towerin' over him, but not by much 'cause my dad was a big motherfucker even seated, and then finally pulled out the chair to his left and sat down.

"Learnin' new tricks of intimidation?" Zeus drawled. "'S cute, King."

"And your broodin' is so swoony. Want me to call up Lou and get her in here to properly appreciate it?"

"Enough," he said, finally anglin' his body to face me, a smile in his beard.

I grinned back at him as we clasped hands and tugged each other in for a hug and a slap on the back.

"How'd I raise two mouthy kids?" he muttered, but it wasn't a condemnation.

His twitchin' mouth made it a compliment.

"Pretty sure snarky is the Garro family language. Now stop beatin' 'round the bush, have you heard from Harleigh Rose?"

The humour tamped outta his face like a snuffed candle. "Says she 'needs space', as if that wasn't the whole fuckin' reason she got into this mess in the first fuckin' place."

The brother in me agreed with him. My little sister had

been abused by her boyfriend without our knowledge for the past couple'a years without tellin' us, and 'cause she lived down in Vancouver, it was all too easy for her to hide it from us. Still, guilt burned in my gut like an unbanked fire 'cause I was just that kinda man. The kinda man that needed to take care of his loved ones, and when they hurt, it fuckin' killed me I couldn't save them from that pain.

And H.R. was in pain, there was no denyin'. She'd been forced to kill the sack of rancid shit who had no right to call himself a man after he'd sexually and physically assaulted her two months ago, and now she was like a ghost livin' among ghosts.

She didn't want help. Even when we'd forced her back to Entrance in the aftermath so Cress and Dad's wife, Loulou, could comfort her and the club could protect her, she'd been an unreachable island.

It was rough for men who were used to control, to gettin' their way and enforcin' their protection, to have one of their women refuse to let them do as their hearts and instincts demanded.

So, as a brother and a man, I was bitter with frustration and unrealized revenge, angry with her for scornin' our care.

But as the kinda human I'd been born, one with a heart that sometimes felt too acutely, understood others too emotionally, fuck me if I didn't understand it.

Since we were kids born into a home with a shit mum and a dad who went to prison, Harleigh Rose had always been my responsibility. Maybe that's why I got that she needed space in order to process 'fore she could come to us. She needed space to find her strength again, 'cause she wouldn't be weak for anyone, not even herself.

I got it.

I didn't like it, but I respected the hell outta it, 'cause no one was stronger than that girl, except for maybe Dad's girl, or mine.

"She'll come back," I told Zeus. "In the meantime, got anythin' you wanna share with me?"

There was an edge to my question, but it was justified. I'd been prospectin' for The Fallen MC for months now, and Zeus still told me dick all 'bout the issues plaguin' the club. Technically, I got it. Prospects were kept in the dark until they had an opportunity to earn their patch. But I wasn't just any prospect. I was born King, raised to be king by the current fuckin' king of our club.

If there was any time for fuckin' nepotism it was now.

But Zeus wouldn't crack, and my patience was wearin' real fuckin' thin.

He stared at me for a moment, somethin' workin' behind his silver eyes. Ransom and you got that custom job for that Lombardi actor needs doin'. He's comin' for it in a month, and you gotta fuckuva lotta work to do."

"Don't be a dick." I leaned back in my chair and crossed my arms, facin' off with the devil. "I want in on real shit. Why'd you think I joined up after so many fuckin' years? To wear grease on my jeans and a cool patch on my back? I'm not some newbie that needs vettin' here, dad. I'm the fuckin' son you raised for this shit."

"And who says I'm done raisin' ya?" he countered. "You think you're ready for the kinda pressure I get every fuckin' day as Prez? Let me tell you somethin', King, you could be born with a crown on your head, raised every fuckin' day on the kinda shit you need to know 'bout power and keepin' it, and you still wouldn't know shit all 'bout the mantle passed to your shoulders. Heavy is the fuckin' head that wears the crown, even if it's made of grease, leather, and iron."

"Maybe I'd be better prepared if you actually discussed shit with me as it went down? You want me to be like Harry Truman when he took over from FDR? He didn't know fuck all 'bout the atomic bomb, and then he was being told to drop it on a goddamn city. You want that kinda devastation in your wake?"

"Seein' as we don't gotta fuckin' bomb in our back lot, I'm thinkin' you're bein' overly dramatic. Told you all those books would go to your head."

"Yeah, well, they did. I graduated from one'a the top universities in this country with an honours degree in business. At least let me put it to good use. I'm wastin' away in the garage every day."

The fact that I loved havin' my hands on an engine meant dick all if I couldn't expend my brain too.

"Don't plan on goin' anywhere for a long time, boy. Got two more kids on the way and a young wife, trust me, I'm here to stay."

"Trust *me*," I urged him, leanin' forward to bare my teeth at him in a way he would understand. Sometimes, we were less men than wolves in a pack, the young males always testin' and tryin' to outdo the alpha. "You never know what could happen. Don't want to spend a single day on this earth without ya, old man. You're my dad, my Prez, and my goddamn hero. But life happens, and we sure as hell know by now that sometimes it happens *bad*."

Unconsciously, Zeus rubbed at the spot on his chest where a bullet had once ripped through a little girl and into him. Years later, that little girl was his wife. If anyone could understand fate and its convolutions, it was him.

Yet, his eyes hardened as they focused on me, and his mouth went tight. "Listen to me. You gotta good woman, a woman that's been waitin' for you to pop the motherfuckin' question. If you can tell me why you're hesitatin' on that when you haven't paused even once in your life for anythin' you wanted and you want Cress more than any'a that, then you got me. I'll bring you into the fold in a serious way, and don't get me wrong, I'll be happy to do it."

There was a trap there, layin' poorly hidden in the grass.

He'd landed on the one reason he coulda used against me in this argument.

'Cause the reason I wasn't married to the love'a my fuckin' life yet was a direct result of my participation in the club. Oh, Cress had encouraged me to do whatever the fuck I wanted to do, not 'cause she didn't care, but 'cause she did. A woman like her, that class and caliber, never would've thought she'd end up hitched to a man with a bike and an ironclad association with a criminal outfit. But there she was, and even though she said she loved it and me, part of me hated that I'd brought all that she was into the shadows.

So, I waited. What I was waitin' for exactly, I wasn't sure. Maybe some idea of what my role would be in the club, how much danger she would be in as a direct correlation of my position.

I'd spent the past three years watchin' first Lou and then Harleigh Rose bein' targeted 'cause of their association with Zeus, and after what Cress had been through already, nails hammered through her palms, abducted and tortured 'cause of me, I wasn't sure I could live with myself if somethin' else happened to her 'cause of the club. 'Cause of me.

I looked at the skull and wings burned into the table, drew my thumb over the rough edge of a tattered angel's wing, and tried to figure out how to outwit Zeus.

"Thought so," he finally said into the silence, but he didn't sound triumphant. Only sad. "You think I'm bein' a dick. I can live with it if it means you got time to figure things out in a way you can live with. Can't keep your woman and this world separate, son. When you figure out how to reconcile that, I'll be happy as fuck to swear you in real like, you get me?"

Even if I didn't know him enough to read between the lines, I knew it was the end of the conversation. Dad had a way of doin' that, leavin' things open ended on the surface so you didn't feel he'd actually turned you away when he had.

I blew a deep breath out of my mouth and ran agitated fingers through my hair. "You think Cress has noticed?"

"Think you got yourself a damn smart woman, so my guess? Hell yeah. Know she's also a good woman, which is why she hasn't read you the riot act yet."

My lips twitched even though I was irritated. Thoughts of Cress did that to me. "Not so far behind as you think. Started designin' the ring six months ago."

"No shit?" His brows shot up, and he scraped his chair closer. "Pull it up on your phone, I wanna see that shit."

"What are we, women?" I asked, even though I did as he asked and pulled up the specs I'd worked out with the jeweler in Vancouver.

Zeus snorted. "Gotta good eye for the pretty stuff. Hell, just look at my wife."

We both laughed at the same time in the same way, heads thrown back to chuckle at the heavens. When I looked back down, Nova was walkin' in followed by Curtains and Boner.

Nova grinned his pretty boy grin and dipped his head over my shoulder to look at the phone screen. He let out a low whistle. "Jesus, brother, that's for Cress?"

"Fuckin' finally," Boner hooted, slammin' his hand on the table. "Seriously dude, I was like one second away from sweepin' her away from ya."

"Only person, fictional or not, Cress would leave me for is Satan from *Paradise Lost*." I scraped my eyes over Boner and clicked my tongue. "Don't think I got anythin' to worry 'bout far's you're concerned."

Boner cupped his prolific bulge in retaliation and winked. "What I lack in looks and smarts, I more than make up for in size. Just ask any'a the biker bitches hangin' 'round here."

Nova hit him on the side'a the head. "Don't think I've ever escaped a conversation with you where you didn't mention your huge ass cock."

"If you got it, flaunt it," he replied with a one-shouldered shrug.

"Bunch'a idiots," Zeus muttered, but he couldn't keep the smile from his voice.

More brothers started to file into the room and take their places 'round the table, readyin' themselves for the biker version of 'church' we held there every Sunday and whenever there was news to share.

"Shit, boy, that's some ring," Buck, our VP and one of the older members of our chapter, said as he clamped a hand down on my shoulder. "Maja's been on me for info 'bout you gettin' your head outta your ass and askin' Cress to marry ya, so thank fuck you're finally doin' it. Got good news to report to the Old Lady, she'll be hankerin' to give me somethin' good herself."

There were a few chuckles and whistles at his comment, but it was Priest who took a seat beside me and leaned over to look at the photo of the emerald ring 'fore sayin', "Fallen colours, classic cut, pricey as fuck…decent ring, brother."

I smirked at the club's enforcer, a man of few words who would rather cut a man to pieces than gossip with the rest of the guys. "I can die happy with your approval then."

"When're you askin' her?" Curtains asked as he flopped his ginger ass into the chair at the other end of the table and pulled out his deluxe laptop. "You want, I can get that shit on tape with my new drone? I've been dyin' to test it out on somethin' other than surveillance."

"Bought you that fancy ass drone so ya'd use it for the grow-ops, not for spyin' on a private moment 'tween King and his woman," Zeus reminded him. "Now, let's shut the fuck up 'bout King's business and focus on the club. We gotta problem."

"Don't we always," Nova muttered, makin' Boner and Curtains both snicker.

"You're in a position of power, people'll always want what

you've got," I said as I leaned back in my chair and steepled my fingers to get comfortable for what was sure to be a long ass meetin'.

"King's right. Told ya weeks ago the Berserkers wanted to meet up to discuss patchin' over—"

"Pieces'a shit, the lot of 'em," Axe-Man grumbled as he shoved on a pair of glasses that were completely at odds with his tatted, biker aesthetic, readyin' himself to take notes of the meeting. There was a ripple of agreement.

Far's MC's went, there was definitely a spectrum. The Fallen'd always been outlaws. We peddled in marijuana, and sometimes arms traffickin', but we didn't mess with any'a the fucked-up shit like narcotics or human traffickin'. We got our own system of belief and codes of fuckin' honour, whereas clubs like the 'serkers only had straight up greed and nothin' but shady morals and a fuck ton'a mean to back it up.

As a club, we hated them. As a man, I wished every single piece of shit with the wolf head patch on his cut would burn in hell. The tension between the two clubs had nearly exploded when we found out Harleigh Rose's long-term Old Man, a Berserker, had beat her for the past few years, and none of the brothers there did fuck all 'bout it.

And they'd wanted to parlay.

It was straight up stupid, and we would've been just as dumb to assume the overture was genuine.

"They want somethin'," I muttered.

It was easy enough to draw that conclusion, but I knew more than most of the brothers sittin' at the table with me 'cause I had an in with one of their members.

The only one I didn't actively want to kill and the only one with any shred of morality. Probably 'cause of the girl I was secretly harborin' for him while he made sure he could keep her safe.

"The way I figure it, they're makin' nice to lull us into some false ass state of security while they try to pull the rug out from under us," Zeus agreed. "Reaper had nothin' real to say 'bout crossin' over, and the whole time he sat there with a motherfuckin' grin like he knew somethin' I didn't." He paused and tugged on his bottom lip the way I did. "Turns out, he's fuckin' Farrah."

My eyebrows shot into my hair as everyone went on alert. "You're fuckin' kidding?"

"Wish I was, but the bitch has shacked up with the jackal. Seems the only real reason Reaper had for meetin' me was to introduce me to his new Old Lady and let her ask me for a little fuckin' favour."

"No shit." Bat shook his head and cracked his bat tattooed knuckles. "Motherfucker has a set'a balls on him."

"It's Farrah with the balls," Buck grunted. "She always was a piece of fuckin' work."

"Thank God, you traded up, Prez," Nova said with an eyebrow waggle. "Lou's a fuckuva lot easier on the eyes, and she's a sweetheart."

"Farah didn't use to be such a bitch," Zeus protested, but even he didn't seem convinced of it.

There must've been a time when my mother wasn't a ragin' bitch, but I certainly couldn't remember it. From the time I was a kid, my only priority was takin' care of Harleigh Rose and keeping her as far from Farrah's influence as possible. Our mother had an unhealthy obsession with being a bitch to H.R. while groomin' her at the same time. Me, she just ignored.

As hard as it was to believe my dad, my fuckin' hero, coulda made as massive of a mistake as he did marryin' a woman like that, I had to be thankful he did, or I wouldn't fuckin' be here.

"What'd she want?" I asked over the chatter.

"Leads into our next problem," he growled, eyes flashin' bright as lightning. "Apparently, the Ventura outfit has seen fit to start up a fuckin' underage pornography gig outside'a

Entrance. That drug ring we busted in the high school a while back? Part'a that was hookin' the teenage girls on drugs and gettin' them in too deep with the cartel so they'd have to work it off with Irina in her studio."

"That's just..." Curtains swallowed hard, his Adam's apple bobbin' in his thin throat. "I've seen the kinda places shit like that is posted, and it's... it's not good, and it's definitely not fuckin' safe for those girls."

"No shit. Seems Javier had been tryin' to set up a human traffickin' circuit along the coast from here down to Mexico, but it was too much of a hassle, so Irina started to recruit locally. Now, you're probably wonderin', those'a you who had the displeasure of meetin' my cunt ex-wife, why she would offer up that info all sweet and easy. She didn't. Apparently, Honey's involved."

My heart spasmed at the name of my half-sister. Hadn't seen the girl since she was a baby, the first year she was born to Farrah and the man who had moved in 'bout thirty seconds after Zeus was incarcerated. We'd all lived together like one fucked up family. Farrah had taken her when she'd fucked off over a decade ago, and I hadn't seen her since.

But I'd always thought, in those quiet moments 'fore bed when your conscience is most acute, 'bout what happened to that pretty little girl with the unfortunate name.

Knowin' Farrah, she couldn't have grown up good.

And evidently, she hadn't.

"What're we gonna do 'bout it?" It wasn't a question of doin' somethin' or not. There was no way The Fallen would let somethin' like this lie. We were the only outlaws allowed in Entrance, and we'd gone to greater lengths to see that enforced than savin' some poor girl from prostitution.

Zeus scrubbed a hand over his face. "Gotta lot on our plate right now. The fuckin' PD won't lay off for a second. We need to make sure our shit is tight and not jump headfirst into somethin' that might lead to gang warfare, you get me?"

"Well yeah, but the girls…" Curtains protested, paler than I'd ever seen him. "Boss, you don't got the right idea of what's happenin' to those girls."

"And you do?" he asked with a raised brow.

The redhead licked his lips, quick and reptilian. "I—fuck, I used to work for a man who did some dark net dabblin'. He liked…those kinds of things. Took me a while to figure it, but once I did, I was outta there."

"No one's judgin' ya, man," I said, tippin' my chin up. "Brothers here have done a whole lot worse than that."

"Never get those photos outta my head," he muttered, lookin' down at his computer and peelin' at the edge of the Hephaestus Auto sticker there. "Don't like the thought'a girls bein' forced to do that shit."

"None'a us do," Zeus assured him. "So, we got three issues to tackle. One: how the fuck do we shore up our shit so the pigs don't find a way to end us while we're expandin'? Two: how the hell do we get the Ventura fuckers to close up shop? And three… how do we get Honey outta that shit stat?"

"I've been lookin' into some things," I said, even though I knew 'fore I even opened my mouth that I'd be met with protests. "Coupla things we could do as I see it. Openin' up a few legit weed stores now that shit's legal just makes straight up sense." The murmurs of dissent started, people mutterin' 'bout the government cuttin' into our profits etc. I held up a hand to quiet them. "I'm sayin' we open up a few. It's not gonna cut into our profits or your cut of those. We gotta put up some money to start this shit up, but trust me, your average housewife is blazin' Mary Jane these days in Canada. We'll get a shit ton'a business, and any association with The Fallen and marijuana can prettily be tied into the new gig."

"'S a clean idea," Priest muttered beside me.

"It's fuckin' *horseshit*," Skell objected loudly, just like I knew he would. "I didn't join a fuckin' Fortune 500 company where

I gotta pay into a fuckin' 401K. I'm a bonafide member of an *outlaw* biker club so I can fuck the man, not blow him."

"Fine distinction, that," Nova said under his breath with a smirk.

"It makes sense, brother," Axe-Man, surprisingly, pitched in. He was what I considered the 'old guard', the generation of bikers that grew up in the era of my father. The man wasn't that old, but he'd been patched in since I was a boy, and he wasn't the kinda guy to rock the boat.

He tipped his chin at me as if he knew what I was thinkin', and I returned the gesture in thanks.

"No sense to me," Skell retorted, his ugly mug screwed up with disgust. "We never done shit like that, and I don't see no reason to start."

"Entrance PD has never been so up in our shit 'fore," Nova countered, his affable smile meltin' clean off his face. "King's tryin' to protect us, you dumbass."

"Dumbass?" Skell shoved back from the table and loomed over it with a sneer. "You wanna take this outside, and we'll see just what this 'dumbass' can do to rearrange that pretty face'a yours, Casanova?"

"Fuckin' sit down, Skell," Zeus barked in a way that defied disobedience.

Skell didn't even hesitate.

"That's it, sit like a good little doggie," Priest praised in his cold as a blade voice.

Skell made to stand up again, but Zeus's voice cut through the tension. "Enough!"

"He's not even fully patched in," Skell objected, pointin' a bony finger at me. "He's not even old enough to wipe his own ass without help from his teacher."

It was my turn to shove back from the table. I planted my fists on the surface and leaned across it close enough to breath the same air as the hotheaded biker. "You speak one more word against my woman, I shit you not, Skell, brother or not, I'll beat your face in."

"I'd like to see you try."

"Not eighteen anymore," I reminded him, flexin' the thick muscles coiled like ropes beneath the skin of my arms and chest. "Haven't been a kid since Z went to prison, haven't been a boy since I met the woman who made me understand what it means to be a man. Sorry you don't have a woman to help you understand that the only type of man to be is one who *listens* instead'a judgin'." I glared down at him, noting the sheen of sweat poppin' out over his brow and the way his body hunched away from mine in instinctive fear. "You wanna fuck with me, brother? I'm down. But you fuck with my woman, I kid you not, it'll be the last thing you fuckin' do."

Thick quiet followed my words, vibratin' the air like a struck gong. No one stepped in to pull me away from Skell 'cause no one liked the way the fucker talked 'bout Old Ladies. His was, regrettably, a grade A bitch, but that didn't mean the rest of us stomached it when he spewed that crap 'bout our women.

Especially me.

And Zeus.

"And when my boy's done beatin' your face in, Skell," he said, an echo of my thoughts as he stared down at his scarred hand and clenched it into a ham-sized fist. "I'll be there to beat the leftovers."

Skell's beady gaze shot between my dad and me for a tense moment 'fore he scowled and leaned back in his chair to cross his arms like a petulant child.

"But King?" Zeus said idly. "Skell's gotta point. You're not a full member of this club, so when we take the vote 'bout the legit businesses, Ransom and you won't be included. You wanna head out to the bar, and we'll meet ya there?"

A muscle in my jaw ticked away as I ground my teeth against the frustration of my situation. I was *born* Fallen, but even if I wasn't, I'd worked my ass off my whole life to better myself so I could better the club. I'd graduated with honours from one of the top universities in the country so I could bring that knowledge to this exact table and make a difference. Only now, the old guard wouldn't have it.

I locked eyes with Zeus, readin' his resolve and also his disappointment in some of our brothers for not acceptin' all that I had to give. He wanted them to, but he wouldn't force it, and I hated that that made him a good leader.

"Fine," I said, standin'. "But know this, brothers. I'm here to stay, and I'm here to take the club to even greater heights than we've seen 'fore. All you have to do is trust my intent and give me a fuckin' chance."

I met each of their gazes 'fore I turned on my boot and walked out the door, Ransom at my heels. And not for the first time that week, or even that day, I wished like hell my best friend, Mute, could'a been beside me.

Even so, when I sat at the bar and Ransom rounded it to grab us both a beer, I knew I had support in the club. And half an hour later when Nova, Curtains, Boner, Axe-Man, Kodiak, Lab-Rat, and even Priest took up seats 'round me after church, I knew it was only a matter of time 'fore I'd get a real spot at the table and a real say in the game.

CHAPTER THREE

Cressida

SPRING WAS BREAKING through the perpetual grey ceiling we lived under in the winter months, the light turning from creamed to liquid honey as it streamed through the porous clouds over my upturned face. I sat on the top of one of the picnic tables toward the front side of the clubhouse, my hands braced behind me so I could soak up the rays. There was the distant hum of machinery and male chatter from the garage bays at Hephaestus Auto to the left of the lot and the soft brushing swish of sea breeze in the evergreens standing before the high chain-link fence like sentries. Ares sat on the bench beside me, but his entire side was pressed against my leg, an arm looped around my calf as he read in his hoarse, Latin-accented English from John Milton's *Paradise Lost.*

"How can I live without thee, how forego
Thy sweet converse, and love so dearly joined,
To live again in these wild woods forlorn?
Should God create another Eve, and I
Another rib afford, yet loss of thee
Would never from my heart; no, no, I feel
The link of nature draw me: flesh of flesh,
Bone of my bone thou art, and from thy state
Mine never shall be parted, bliss or woe."

Ares stopped reading, his thumb sweeping over the text as if he could feel the words like the texture of a flower petal on his skin, in his soul. I smiled as I watched him, because I recognized a poetic heart when I saw it, and I loved that he was being raised by a biker club who would protect him so that his heart could further flourish.

"What do you think?" I asked.

I wanted to brush my hand through his hair, but Ares had rules about how he liked to interact with people. No touching, not unless he instigated it. He was incredibly affectionate when the mood struck him, especially with Loulou and me, but if he was touched without consent, frankly, he turned terrifying.

He angled his head up and back to look at me, the sun catching his depthless brown eyes, turning them liquid and warm as maple syrup. "I think Milton gets this story better than those idiots that wrote the Bible."

I clucked my tongue at him, even though I agreed. "We might not believe in that kind of religion, but that doesn't mean we talk crap about it, Ares. What would you do if someone said something like that about the club?"

The arm around my leg constricted, and his jaw clenched.

"Exactly," I agreed. "So, it's good practice not to condemn what someone else believes in. It took me a very long time to realize that, and judging that way almost kept me from some of the greatest treasures in my life."

"Don't get why you stopped teachin' kids," he muttered, looking back down at the book. "You're good at it and shit."

I swallowed my laugh because Ares was only nine, and he did *not* like to be laughed at. "Thanks, babe. It was fun while it lasted and I got King out of it, so I'd make that trade any day."

My decision to give up teaching for the student who had gotten me fired in the first place was both the craziest and best choice I'd ever made.

"Yeah, he's the shit too," he muttered, and I couldn't help laughing because he was right, and his admiration was adorable.

"Agreed. Besides, it's books that I love most, and opening Paradise Found excites me a lot more than teaching ever did."

I'd grown up with parents who raised me like a marionette instead of a person. They puppeteered me through the entire first twenty-six years of my life, and it took meeting King to make me realize just how weak I'd been. Now, four years after I'd broken my mold and started an affair with my high school student, I was finally woman enough, *me* enough, to pursue my real goals.

Currently, I had two.

One, open a bookstore in Entrance, fill it with gorgeous books, comfy chairs, youth programs, and book clubs.

Second, marry the love of my life.

My gaze cut back to the clubhouse where I knew King was having a chat with Zeus about club business, and I wondered for the hundredth time when King might propose.

It wasn't that I was in a hurry, but I'd been divorced from my scumbag ex for four years, and King and I had been living together all that time.

I was ready and more, I didn't get why he wasn't.

This was the same man who had spotted me across a

crowded bar and demanded to take me out on a date that very moment. The same man who basically moved in with me the minute we started sleeping together, and the same man who wrote me love poems every week since the first week we went out.

He was the kind of man who took what he wanted and did what he needed without hesitation.

I stared down at my bare hand and brushed the skin over my left ringer finger.

Ares's hand slid over mine, and when I looked over at him, his face was soft with understanding. "Wasn't it you who told me family is in the heart, not in the blood or papers that make it so in the eyes of the fuckin' law?"

I rolled my eyes at his curse word because he was too young to curse, but then again, he was too young for most of the trauma his young self had endured, so I didn't chastise him for it.

"That's smart. It does sound like me," I agreed, just to see his small smile.

"Fuck *off*!" A shout suddenly tore across the asphalt.

Ares went rigid, and I was on my feet in an instant, stepping in front of him to obscure the view of him from the street. We didn't know exactly what had brought Ares to Zeus's cabin outside of Whistler last year, but we did know that whatever he had run away from was the kind of bad even outlaw bikers considered *bad*, so we were all protective of him.

There was no need for it, though. The woman, still shouting, who had startled us was a short thing in a mini skirt with a strip of fabric across her straining breasts. Her masses of strawberry blond hair went flying as she whipped around to snarl at the man following her slowly in an old Buick.

"Fuck you, Cisco," she screamed at him, hitting her big, slouchy purse against the car. "You want me to call the fucking cops? Because I will!"

"What're you going to tell them, slut?" he demanded

coarsely. "You want to make peace with Rina, you get your ass in this car and come with me."

"Make me," she bit out.

But I had seen enough.

"Stay here. If things get hairy, call for the men," I told Ares as I moved quickly across the lot to the chain link fence.

I was through the gate and behind the girl by the time the man named Cisco reached through the open window to grab at her.

I intercepted his hand and twisted it into a fierce lock that Bat, our veteran brother, had spent years trying to teach me to master.

It seemed, based on Cisco's shocked cry, that I'd finally mastered it.

"I think this girl has told you to leave one too many times," I said with false cheer, my smile more like a sneer on my face. "It's time you listened to her."

"You fucking bitch," he groaned, his surprisingly handsome face crumpled with pain and hatred. "You don't know who the fuck you're dealing with here."

"No," I disagreed politely and leaned close so he could see the resolve in my eyes. "You don't know who *you're* dealing with. This is Fallen territory, so if you want to harass some girl right outside our gates, it *is* our problem."

There was a flash of recognition chased hard on the heels by fear. "Fuck."

"Fuck is right," I agreed. "Now, fuck off."

I held eye contact with him for a long beat, just to reinforce my threat, and then let go, stepping back immediately with my arm moving around the girl to bring her out of reach with me.

"When I find you again, you're in deep fucking shit," he spat at the red head before gunning the engine and roaring off down the street.

I watched the car turn the corner before looking at the girl beside me. She was absolutely lovely. Exactly that word. I took in her heart-shaped face with delicately winged brows, a perfectly formed mouth, and a small nose topped with large, pale brown eyes the colour of sunlight on syrup. She was so beautifully feminine she almost looked like a cartoon, but the glaze in her eyes and the jitter in her thin frame made her something all too human.

A drug addict about to come down from her high.

What a tragedy.

"Hey, honey," I started to say softly, the way one would talk to a stray cat, but she looked startled and then angry with me for addressing her like that.

"How do you know my name?" she demanded.

Her eyes cut to the garage and the emblem of The Fallen MC Nova had spray painted on the side of the clubhouse.

"Fuck me, fuck," she cursed viciously then took a huge step away from me as if I was infected with the plague. "Listen, bitch, you keep you and yours the hell away from me. You hear me? I don't need to be messed up in biker drama."

"Your name is Honey," I said slowly, less a question than a memory dredged up from the banks of my brain.

Honey Yves was the daughter of Farrah, the ex-wife of Zeus and ex-mother of Harleigh Rose and my King.

I'd never heard of anyone else named Honey, and I very much doubted it was a common name, so…

"Honey Yves?" I asked, vaguely aware of movement in my periphery.

She shivered and clutched her stained hobo bag to her chest as she started to back away from me. "You don't know me. And listen, I didn't need your help with Cisco, and I don't need your help now, you get me? I'm a grown ass woman."

Lies. She wasn't a day over fifteen, *maybe* sixteen. I'd taught teenagers for enough years to be able to peg their age.

"I'm not trying to take you anywhere or force you to do

anything," I told her with my hands open to the heavens. "I just wanted to get that creep away from you."

"Yeah, well don't expect a thanks or anything."

"I don't." I bit my lip, warring with myself. "Listen, I'm starving, do you want to grab a bite to eat with me?"

I wasn't hungry. I'd made Ares and myself grilled cheese sandwiches in the clubhouse kitchen before we went outside to read, but Honey looked frail, as if she hadn't eaten more than a candy bar in days.

I knew she didn't have a relationship with King or Harleigh Rose, that they hadn't even seen her since she was a baby, but I still felt compelled to do something. It was just human decency.

She peered at me suspiciously and licked her lips almost convulsively, a high tick I recognized from years ago when my own brother had partied too hard and too often.

"Why?" she asked, the single word an accusation.

I shrugged. "I'm hungry, as I said. I also believe in the sisterhood. You were basically just accosted on the street, and I'm feeling like you could use a girl friend to chat to."

She snorted and whatever tenuous relationship I'd been trying to form between us dissolved like sugar in water. "Yeah, right. For all I know, you and your Fallen bastards work for Cisco and the lot of them too. No way I'm going anywhere with you, bitch."

"Wait," I urged, reaching out to stop her with a hand on her arm.

She went berserk at my touch, whipping her bag around to slam it savagely into my chest, robbing the air from my chest.

I bent over with a loud exhalation, clutching my belly as I tried to breathe.

"Fuck," a familiar voice exclaimed as the gate jangled open and then motorcycle boots appeared in my limited view.

A hand went to my back, slid up my spine, and cradled the

back of my head before King dropped into a squat beside me. His pale blue eyes were glacial with anger as he studied me for further injury.

"Who the fuck did this to you?" he demanded.

I sucked in a shaky breath, tipped my head to find Honey long gone, and said, "Your sister."

CHAPTER FOUR

Cressida

"I CAN'T BELIEVE IT," I said, still shocked by the news hours later. "How could they have the balls to set something like that up in Entrance of all places? This is Fallen territory."

King chuckled as he brushed a hand across my lower back, leaning over me to open the fridge and grab the butter for me. I stared at it as he pressed it into my hands and then retrieved the flour from the cupboard. It took me a moment to realize he was prompting me to make his favourite, salted caramel apple pie.

"King!" I protested, before giving into a giggle. "Why is it that whenever I'm getting anxious, you always force me to make pie?"

He shrugged a shoulder, a lopsided grin tucked into one cheek as he hopped up onto the counter beside me. "Settles that busy, beautiful brain a beat, and I like pie. Two birds, one stone."

I shook my head as if I was exasperated, but the truth was, I loved that he knew me that well. All the little ways we loved each other and looked after one another that no one else would notice but us. It was those small miracles and mercies of love that I found most beautiful.

"Seriously though, the gall!" I continued, even as I chopped the cold butter into cubes. "They obviously don't know who they're messing with, even after we took down Javier's disgusting high school drug ring."

"Babe, you gotta start swearin'. There you are, actin' all biker tough like any seasoned Old Lady, and then you bust out, 'messing with'."

I shrugged as I started to work the butter into the flour. "I'm still a work in progress."

"Aren't we all? I mean, everyone but me seein' as I'm perfect already." He took a huge bite out of one of the apples I had set aside for the pie.

I rolled my eyes. "No one's perfect, not even you."

"Funny you say that now. I gotta distinct memory of just this morning after I made you come all over my dick, you sayin' the words, 'King, *God*, you are perfect.'"

I blushed madly, feeling the heat sluice down my neck and over my chest. "Actually, if *I* remember correctly, I said 'King, *God*, your cock is perfect.'"

"Ah," he nodded somberly, as if he hadn't been playing me the whole time just to get me to say it again. "That musta been it."

I laughed despite myself and flicked my flour coated fingers at him. "You're lucky I love you enough to ignore your arrogance."

"Lucky you love me, straight up, babe," he agreed easily, in that way he had of making our love seem even more epic because he was so matter of fact about it. "Lucky you make sweet ass pies too."

"You owe me an apple. Can you go grab one for me?"

"On it," he said, jumping off the counter and smacking my ass as he moved by me to the side door.

I watched him leave, hands covered in flour, eyes wide as I appreciated the way his form had changed in the past four years. The tall, somewhat lanky body of the eighteen-year-old student I'd fallen in love with had morphed into the body of a Greek god. He spent a lot of time at the club's gym lifting weights with the guys, and his broad shouldered, narrow hipped body was testament to that. I loved tracing the lines of his muscles under all that golden skin, my tongue sliding down the trough of his obliques to the muscles that arrowed into his groin, rippling my fingers over the symmetrical boxes in his abdominals. I knew and worshipped every inch of that body, and I felt no shame in checking out his tight butt as he swaggered out the door to the apple trees he'd planted on the side of the house for me years ago.

It was one of a thousand ways King had helped me to make this little ramshackle cottage a home. When I'd bought it four years ago, it was dilapidated to say the least, with a list of issues as long as my arm. Fixing it up had been part of King's courtship, wooing me by bringing the brothers by to spruce things up, and over the years, we'd made it our mission to turn the neglected house into a home.

Now, the old wood floors were sanded down and re-glazed so they gleamed in the pools of honeyed sunlight spilling in from the double paned windows lining the entire back of the house. At one point, we'd moved out for a few months so the kitchen could be remodeled, and now the lower cabinets were painted a warm, dark green and the open shelves were stained to match the dark wood paneling installed throughout the rest of the house. I had a huge butcher block slab over my island with stools on one side with a stove in the middle and a huge dining room table to match for when we had the Garro clan or the brothers over to eat.

King had helped Eugene make some custom furniture for our sunken living room so that everything felt rustic and mismatched in a way that worked with the space.

From the bookshelves taking up every spare inch of wall space in the small home to the painting Nova had done for us of a girl holding an apple falling into a waiting palm to the massive print we hung in the hallway of King and me on our trip to Graceland, this home screamed *us*.

And I loved it more than I could ever say.

I'd been married to a man for seven years before I'd met King. We'd lived in a big, expensive house in Vancouver next to other big, expensive houses filled with beautiful, expensive things, and I'd never once felt at home there the way I did in Shamble Wood Cottage with King.

It made me understand, in a way I never could have before, that it was people who make a home.

I was a girl living a dream I'd never before thought possible to dream, and I didn't feel any shame for glorying in it.

Softly, I sang along with Elvis as he crooned over the speakers, swaying my hips as I put the dough to chill in the fridge and started in on making the caramel sauce. I smiled when the door opened quietly but quickly stilled when the air didn't charge with King's presence.

Trying to be discreet, I carefully moved my hand along the counter to grip the handle of the butcher knife I'd used to cut through the apples and called out easily, "Thanks, honey. Did you get them, okay?"

The old wood floors creaked behind me. Before I could even make a conscious decision, I was dipping low and sweeping in a circle to bring up the knife to the groin of the unknown assailant. Less than a second later, a gun was pointed at my temple, a cold, hard kiss of metal with a deadly mouth.

We froze, suspended in a stalemate for one long breath.

Then the man relaxed his grip on his gun and chuckled, "Fuck me, Cress. That how you always greet visitors?"

I peered up through my dishevelled hair to see Wrath grinning down at me from his awesome height. The adrenaline flooding my system ebbed and was replaced with hyper relief.

I laughed as I dropped the knife, and he offered me a huge, tattooed hand to help me stand up. I brushed the flour off the handle and dropped the weapon to the counter before I wrapped the biker in my arms.

"Blame Priest," I explained into his rock-hard torso, used to hugging men that felt like slabs of marble. "He and King made it their mission to educate me in the finer arts of brutality should I ever need them."

He patted my back, a bit too hard even though I knew he tried to temper his strength. "Glad to hear it. How's it hangin', Queenie?"

"Like you care," I teased as I pulled away. "You just want to know how Kylie is."

His smile was beautiful because everything about Wrath was beauty incarnate. If I wasn't so head over heels in love with my own biker, I might've been struck dumb by the perfection of Wrath Marsden's features. Combined with his looming height and quilted abundance of muscles, he had to be one of the most intimidating men I'd ever seen.

Yet, I couldn't think of him as anything but a great big teddy bear after seeing the lengths he'd gone to in order to protect the woman he loved. The smile carved into his face, lighting his luminescent, blue gray eyes and creasing his bearded cheeks was a prime example of that.

When we'd first met Kylie's beloved boyfriend after King befriended her in a psychology class at UBC, we hadn't been expecting to meet a man wearing the patch of The Fallen's rival MC, the Berserkers. At first, I thought Wrath and King would come to blows over their divided loyalties, but then Kylie had stepped up to place a soothing hand on Wrath's shoulder much the way I did with King, and they'd calmed enough to reluctantly share a beer.

One beer turned into four, and by the end of the night, we'd become fast friends.

We hadn't looked back since, despite our differences.

"She good?" he asked, instead of protesting my comment.

Nothing meant more to him than Kylie.

I wiped my hands on a tea towel and stirred the melting sugar in the pot on the stove. "She misses you and her mum, but whenever I see her, she seems good. I think Eugene's got a soft spot for her, and she's become great friends with Lila."

"Good," he grunted, leaning his six-foot six-inch frame against the counter. "Called Eugene and he's bringin' her over now. I'll take her out for a bit, bring her back and we can all grab some grub together?"

"Don't worry about us, if you want that time with her, take it."

"We don't gotta lotta people we can be ourselves with… it'd be nice to hang with King and ya," he admitted.

If he'd been anyone else, I would have hugged him again. Wrath had brought his girlfriend Kylie to us a few weeks ago to protect her, of all people, from her father, Reaper Holt, the President of the Berserkers MC, who would rather see her killed than see her with any of his brothers.

It was fucked up, and we'd been only too happy to help them out. After all, if anyone knew what it was like to have the world against them, it was King and me.

So, I grinned at him and asked, "You like pie?"

His answering smile wasn't as vibrant as the one saved for Kylie, but it was stunning all the same. "Doesn't everyone?"

Wrath was sitting at my pretty island drinking a beer when King returned with a crate of apples and ink stains on his fingers. He clocked Wrath right away but ignored him as he dropped the apples to the counter and reached around me to wrap his hand over my throat and tip my face for his kiss.

He tasted as crisp and sweet as the apples he'd just picked.

"Caramel smells good," he murmured, even though it was me he was smelling, running his nose down the line of my neck before biting into the junction of my throat and shoulder. "Save some separate, yeah? I gotta mind to test a theory and see what's sweeter, you or the sugar."

A shiver ripped through me and my lids fluttered closed as he licked at my pulse then lightly sucked at the skin there. He could reduce me to ashes and embers with a single kiss and he had no qualms about wielding his power, even in front of guests.

Actually, *especially* in front of guests if they were of the male variety.

"Stop being such a caveman." I laughed, slightly breathlessly before playfully shoving him away. "Get out of my kitchen and catch up with Wrath while you can. Eugene should be here any minute to reunite the lovers."

"Good," he said as he retrieved his beer. "Fuckin' hungry and not just for that pie."

Wrath laughed, a rusty, almost painful sounding chuckle that spoke of disuse. "This from a man who writes poetry?"

King shrugged and pulled his folded, worn leather notebook from the back pocket of his jeans before tossing it on the table so he could sit down. "How do you think I got her in my bed? Dirty poetry's the way to a woman's heart *and* into her bed."

"King!" I laughed, tossing an apple at his head which he caught all too easily. "Why do you always have to embarrass me?"

"'Cause I like the way you blush for me, babe," he grinned, unabashed, and then abruptly sobered. "And I like braggin' 'bout the fact that all that's you is *mine*."

I pinked as rosy as the Ambrosia apples on the counter

beside me and ducked behind a sheave of my hair as I poured the caramel over the apple mixture in the pie pan.

"Good to see ya though, brother," King said, clinking beers with Wrath. "What's the news?"

"You should know, Farrah's been hangin' 'round Reaper," he started off. "He's callin' her his Old Lady, so you know it's serious for now, even if it's temporary."

"Yeah, got the knowledge from Zeus 'bout two hours ago. How's that play out for you?"

"He's distracted, which would normally be good. Problem is, he and his new woman are distracted by your sister."

"Fuck."

I locked eyes with King over the counter and read the anger and helplessness in his eyes. I just knew he wanted to get on his bike and roar down to Vancouver in a blaze of gasoline and smoking tires, throw Harleigh Rose on the back, and steal her away to Entrance where we could keep her safe.

Only H.R. didn't want that.

She wasn't the kind of woman who waited for a man to save her. She was the kind of woman who stormed the battlefield herself, damn the consequences.

Even though she'd just killed the man who had been abusing her for years, she was reluctant to accept any help, even from the brother who loved her and semi-raised her, or me, the woman she considered her friend and almost mother figure.

It killed me, but I knew it absolutely slayed King. He was just that kind of man.

"You keepin' an eye on that situation?" he asked Wrath, voice calm but hands fisted.

"You know it. H.R.'s keepin' an eye on me while I keep one on her, though. She's a smart one, even though she's dumb as shit for hookin' up with Lion."

"Lion?" I squeaked. "As in Lionel Danner?"

"One and the same," Wrath confirmed grimly. "Motherfucker doesn't know I'm in with ya, so he thinks he's got everyone fooled. Playin' the biker part, tryin' to take down the club, obviously. Thing is, he's a good man, and I'm inclined to like 'im despite 'im bleeding blue."

"That's because he is a good man," I admitted begrudgingly. So many years with The Fallen, under the corrupted thumb of Staff Sargent Danner, had turned my bias against the men in blue, but there was no doubt in my mind Danner Junior was one of the good ones.

He had to be, he had practically raised King during the years Zeus was incarcerated.

King seemed to think so, too, if his pensive expression was anything to go off of. He stared into the middle distance, thumb rubbing over his lower lip as he did when he was contemplating something.

"Fuckin' Danner," he finally said with his boyish grin. "Always stickin' his neck in where it doesn't belong. Gotta say I'm grateful he's takin' care of H.R., though, God knows she needs watchin' over."

"Don't let her hear you say that." I winked at him as I opened the oven and slotted the pie onto the top rack. "She'd have your balls."

"She would," he agreed proudly. "Still, I'm tellin' you, Wrath, riskin' my balls and all 'cause my sister is my responsibility, and now, I'm hopin' she's yours too."

Wrath and King locked eyes, sharing something between them that only two men with a code of honour built on brotherhood and masculinity could fully understand.

"'S already done to tell you the truth of it," he finally said with that rusty chuckle. "She and Lion were bein' idiots moonin' over each other, so I stepped up. You hear talk she's my woman now, don't be surprised."

King groaned and knocked his forehead against the table dramatically, making me laugh as I made my way toward him. Instantly, he pushed back his chair and made room for me to sit on his lap. "In bed with a cop and a rival MC biker…fuck me, if Zeus hears of this, he'll come down on H.R. like the hammer of God."

"We won't let it come to that," Wrath assured. "I got that situation under control so long as you keep takin' care of my girl."

We weren't really taking care of her, but we had arranged for her to live with Eugene up in his secluded mountain cabin so that she would be out of sight and out of mind of her filicide inclined father. Eugene wasn't officially affiliated with the club, so if for some reason one of the Berserkers went looking for Kylie, they'd only find her visiting a friend of her family or shacked up with some random older guy. Only King and Eugene knew of the arrangement with Wrath, and I knew King planned to keep it that way, both for Kylie's protection and as an ace up his sleeve should he need to use Wrath's info to deepen his position in The Fallen.

Just because he was the son of the Prez didn't mean King was exempt from earning his spot in the club.

There was the sound of tires on the gravel outside and instantly, Wrath's face transformed from his normally taciturn expression to one of absolute ecstasy.

"She's here," he said, almost to himself, and then he was up and stalking across the kitchen to the front door.

King buried his nose in my hair and chuckled softly. "Should we leave them to it?"

"We could…but this is my favourite part," I admitted, wriggling off his lap even though he playfully tried to grab me.

"My hopeless romantic," he teased as he followed me to the door.

"Hopeless 'fore you," I agreed as we halted in the door and he wrapped his arms around my waist, chin perched on my shoulder so we could watch the separated lovers greet each other. "Not so much now."

He pressed a kiss to my ear in silent acknowledgement of my sappiness.

And we watched.

Kylie was out of the car like a shot, slamming the door in her haste before sprinting toward Wrath, curling black hair flying behind her, long dark legs churning, arms outstretched.

"Wes," she cried out seconds before she launched herself into the air like a pole vaulter and was caught in the large bracket of Wrath's embrace.

Instantly, he brought her tight to his body, her limbs wrapping around him like ivy, their faces tucked into each other's necks as if they needed to feel the other's pulse beat against their cheeks. Reassurance, after so long apart, that they were both alive and well.

It made my heart ache to watch them, as it did every time they reunited since Wrath brought her to us for protection months ago. I couldn't imagine being separated from King. The longest we'd ever gone without physical contact was when he went on runs down the coast with the club, and that was never for longer than two weeks. He felt too elemental to me to be parted with for long.

As if sensing my thoughts, King used his nose to push my hair away from my neck and kissed my pulse point. "You know, sometimes, even when I hold you like this, bein' with you feels like a dream I've got no business dreamin'."

"I pinch myself every day," I admitted. "Who would have known the prissy schoolteacher would be so happy with the gorgeous rebel?"

"I didn't doubt it."

I rolled my eyes and shoved my hips back into him. "Born to be king, doesn't doubt a thing."

He laughed, and the warm waft of his breath on my neck made me shiver with longing. "Everyone's got doubts. Even I'm not exempt from that. Just never doubt my longing for you, Cress babe. Not for a single fuckin' second."

His tongue flashed out to lick a sultry path down the side of my throat, and I practically melted back into his embrace.

"Now, come inside. Got a hunger only the taste of you will satisfy," he whispered in my ear before sinking his teeth firmly into my neck.

I moaned, tipping my head instantly to give him better access even though we were in full view of the embracing lovers and Eugene.

"Gonna invite me in for a spot'a tea?" Eugene bellowed from down the drive, laughter rich in his rough voice.

"Only thing I'm drinkin' down is my woman," King called back even as he moved us backward into the house. "Fuck off and find your own refreshment."

He closed the door on their laughter, and I opened my mouth to protest his brazenness even though I was used to it, but his mouth stole the words on my tongue as he sealed it with a searing kiss.

When he pulled back, it was with that smug, lazy half smile tucked into his left cheek. My lips tingled, and my nipples ached as I pushed my breasts into his chest in a physical entreaty for *more*.

"You wanted to say something?" he asked as he swiped his thumb over my kiss-swollen lower lip and dipped the pad over my tongue. He tasted of apples and the salt of man.

I tried to kiss him again, eager for the feel of his mouth on mine, but his hand at my throat, squeezing just enough to be felt, stopped me.

"No, babe, wanna hear you ask for what you want from me," he demanded huskily.

I strained against his hand, loving the way it arrowed heat straight down my throat to pool in my gut like a shot of whiskey.

"You," I gasped as his grip tensed tighter and his other hand flattened on my lower back to push me into his groin where I could feel his hard cock throb against my hip. "I want you, always."

"Yeah," he agreed gruffly, dipping down to lick my lower lip then tug it between his teeth. "My woman is always greedy for me."

And God, I was. I'd spent half my mature life thinking I'd been some deviant woman, some unenviable slut for craving sex the way I always had. My ex-husband had degraded me for those desires, consenting to make love to me only when he hoped it would produce a baby.

But not King. He took pleasure in my body the way a painter does his art, every curve and dip of my surface a delight to revel in, every movement of my form a different temptation to chase after. He made me feel ripe and wanton with the way he gorged on me, loving his mouth on my sex, his fingers playing at my skin, his lips sealed over mine as he drank long and deeply from the well of my mouth.

Sex with King was nothing short of sumptuous. And as he backed me farther into the kitchen, lifting me onto the counter beside the stove, I tangled my fingers in his hair, eager to discover more ways he could teach me his lessons in corruption.

I watched as his big hands made quick work of my buttons and fly then tugged off my jeans and panties, loving the way his King of Hearts tattoo peeked at me from the side of his middle finger. I had the matching one, with a Queen, on the inside of mine, and I loved the reminder of me he wore on his skin.

"Gonna feast, babe," King said as he tugged my hips sharply to the edge of the counter. "Brace your feet against the edge and open that beautiful pussy for me."

I blushed because his filthy mouth never failed to smoke under my skin. Cool air wafted over my exposed sex as I brace my hands behind me and tucked up my feet, not feeling insecure because King was between my thighs, his thumb rubbing over my bare pubic bone as if I was a work of priceless art.

"Fuck me, but I get so hard just lookin' at this pretty pussy." His thumb dipped down the edge of my lips then swirled at my entrance, playing in the wetness that pooled there. "Love feelin' you get wet for me, all swollen and aching for my cock. Is that what you want, babe?"

I groaned, trying to jerk my hips up to get more of his thumb inside of me. "Yes, King, please, stop teasing me."

"Stop?" He laughed, eyes sparking like glass in sunlight. "Babe, I'm just gettin' started."

I moaned, this time in protest as he moved away just long enough to pull the bowl of cooled caramel into reach. His grin was wicked as he dipped a finger in the sugar and twirled some around his thumb before offering it to me. I sucked hard then lapped my tongue around the tip in a way that made his eyes go black with want.

"Good?" he asked roughly as he went back for more then smeared it over my bottom lip. He didn't give me time to answer. Instead, he leaned over to suck the sweetness from my mouth.

I was panting when he finished kissing me, and I could feel myself leak from my sex, pooling over the counter like spilled caramel.

"King, please."

"I love the way you say my name. Like a zealot reveres the name of her deity." He dropped to his knees, still tall enough that he was eye level with my dripping wet pussy. "Fuck me, what a sight. What do you think is sweeter? You or the caramel?"

I gasped as he painted warm candy on top of my clit then laved it with his tongue. It felt electric, as if he was rubbing raw energy over my sensitive flesh. I bucked up into the heat of his mouth, needing him to shock my clit until I burst open into that elusive orgasm, but he only played with me, adding caramel to my outer lips and sucking them into his mouth, swirling his tongue as if licking droplets from a leaking faucet.

"Sweet and salty," he rumbled against my inner thigh as he used his caramel-free hand to sink two fingers inside me and *twist* in a way that made my back arch and my toes curl.

He folded my legs farther back, pressing me open like a book for him to read, to study and dedicate to memory so that he could recite the taste of me, the smell of me, anytime he wanted.

"Oh my God," I chanted as he worked his fingers and his tongue in perfect harmony, playing me so easily it was almost degrading how quickly I needed to come. But it was exactly that edge of shame that made me cry out and spasm around his fingers, shouting to the ceiling as I released the wild ecstasy coursing from my core.

He lapped at my cum, running his tongue from my taint all the way up and over my clit. I shuddered as he moved over my sensitive nub, but I still ached for something more.

"Please, I need you inside me," I told him, using my hands in his hair to drag him up to standing so I could hook my legs around his back and bring him close.

I reached down with one hand to undo his jeans and take his hot, steely flesh into my hand. A groan escaped me before I could think to stop it, and my mouth watered at the feel of him as I notched his leaking crown against my entrance.

He ran his clean hand through my hair then rubbed his thumb over my cheekbone. "You want me inside you, babe?"

I nodded, tipping my head back as he worked his mouth over my ear and across my jaw.

"You want to feel me stretch open this beautiful pussy?"

I whimpered as I felt myself grow even wetter.

"Want me to show you with my body just how much I fuckin' worship you?"

"Yes," I cried out as he surged into me, seating himself completely inside me.

I writhed against him, wrapping my arms around his shoulders to hold on as he clasped one hand on my ass and kept the other in my hair to hold me still while he pumped into me. It seemed almost unnatural, how much I craved the connection between us, how feeling him inside me felt like a key fitting into a lock, letting the real me burst through, darkly, maddeningly greedy and possessive for every drop of King he could possibly give me.

"Come in me," I urged, clawing at his back, feeling a moan move through him. "I want to feel you spill hot and deep inside me."

"Fuck," he cursed viciously, head tossed back, eyes squeezed shut in a motif of exquisite pain. And then he groaned so deeply it moved through both of us like a roll of thunder and he was coming inside of me, cock thumping, hips grinding, and I was coming with him.

I gasped into his feasting mouth on mine, shuddering and shattering against his body, waves breaking open on an intractable shore. It felt so natural to give in to those desires, to ride them all the way to completion, and then, because I was obsessed with him, with *us*, to dreamily imagine the next time we could come together like that again.

King pulled away and brushed a damp lock of hair off my forehead. He was so utterly lovely, so deeply beautiful, the sight of him almost made me believe in God again, because only a divine hand could have made a face like this.

"You have this way of lookin' at me," he murmured huskily as he continued to thread his fingers through my hair. "Lookin' at me like I'm the sun and your fuckin' dazzled by me."

"I do," I agreed easily. "I am."

"Just a man, babe. Don't forget it," he reminded me, uncharacteristically somber.

I frowned and reached up to smooth the little furrow

between his brows. "You're far from *just* a man, King. You're *my* man."

"Sap," he accused laughingly, nipping at my fingers.

"So says the man who writes me love poems nearly every day."

"So says the woman who thinks Satan is literature's greatest man."

"He is." I linked my arms around his neck and smiled. "Should we name our firstborn son after him, do you think?"

King burst out laughing, and even though it was like looking into a supernova, I kept right on watching him.

CHAPTER FIVE

Cressida

BEFORE I FOUND King and he changed my life, I lived for the written word. I meant that in an almost literal way. My life during the years before meeting King was so dull, so incredibly uninspired, that a far better alternative could always be found between the bound pages of a favourite book. By extension, bookstores became my second home, perhaps my *real* home, because there I could be exactly who I was meant to be as a reader. I could be the wild, fierce heroine in Tamara Pierce novels or the witty, well-meaning star of Jane Austen's love stories. I could travel the world the way I'd always wanted through the narratives of Bill Bryson and luxuriate in the lives of sensational men like the ones found in F. Scott Fitzgerald's fictional universes.

Bookstores were a home for my troubled mind in a time when I had no safe harbour to develop who I truly wished myself to be.

So, it was no wonder it had always been a dream of mine to open my own.

But it was a dream in the way I'd always imagined all my dreams to be; unattainable. A pretty thing to look at but up in the clouds so high it could never possibly rain down to earth.

Of course, that was all before I met my biker poet.

The first time I mentioned opening a bookstore to King, he'd cocked his head and said, "Cool. Let's do it."

And he hadn't meant that in a condescending way, as if it was inconceivable that I hadn't pursued that goal before, or in a domineering way like my parents or my ex, William, might have acted. King said it easy as you please, because for him, it was just that simple.

If he wanted something, he took it.

Which meant, in his beautiful brain, that if I wanted something, he would make it happen for me.

So, even though I made the decision to go back to university with him to earn my Master's in English Literature, he still urged me every day to consider opening my store.

And then, when we graduated and I wasn't sure if I should continue as a professor at the University of British Columbia, he took the step I'd been too afraid to take.

He bought me a storefront.

It was on Main Street itself, just a few blocks down from Entrance Bay Academy where we'd met, and right beside Honey Bear Café, my absolute favourite coffee shop in the province. Before we owned it, it had been an antique shop run by an elderly woman who'd passed away. It was dirty, rundown, and needed a whack ton of TLC.

I loved it.

Together, with help from the brothers, my old colleagues Rainbow and Tay from EBA, and our friends, Benny and

Carson, we transformed the tired space into an absolutely beautiful literary oasis.

Paradise Found was dark and moody in the way I imagined 18th century literary cafes to be, with deep leather chairs, brass sconces and exposed brick. The only natural light came from the two enormous floor to ceiling windows in the front left corner of the shop, and the black trim beautifully highlighted all the warm red brick. It was broody and moody and absolutely, if I did say so myself, fabulous.

And we were due to open next week.

"Stop fussing, you're giving me a headache," Rainbow called out to me as I wiped a smudge off the huge windows in the corner of the store. "Seriously, woman, I'm tired just looking at you."

"You don't want to go home too tired to have sex with King," Tayline chimed in, popping her head around the corner of a bookcase to waggle her black brows at me. "Now, that would be a *crying* shame."

She and Rainbow snickered and then devolved into full blown belly laughter when Benny sighed dreamily and added, "Totally."

Carson rolled his eyes at his boyfriend and tugged him hard into his front. "You sayin' I don't keep you satisfied, Benny Benito?"

The blush that coursed over his pale olive skin was vermillion, but he still leaned heavily into the taller man and batted his lashes at him. "Satisfied has nothing to do with it. King Kyle Garro is beauty incarnate, and you know even if you won't admit it in front of Cress." He dipped his head back to make eye contact with me. "Seriously, he's told me before. He's a gay man with eyes, so of course he thinks King's hot as hell."

It was Carson's turn to look uncomfortable, but we all laughed because it was rare we got one up on the ex-football star.

I smiled at them as they ducked their heads close and whispered to each other. I'd taught them both as a teacher at EBA years ago, when Carson had been the run-of-the-mill bully and Benny the fairly obviously closeted gay boy who bore the brunt of his negative attention. The whole situation had been a mess of miscommunications complicated by Carson's bigoted father, a drug dealing teacher, and Benny nearly dying from an overdose. So, seeing them together and happy now was a gift I knew they both cherished.

I turned back to the windows and adjusted the pillows at the base of one window seat, surprised again at the turn my life had taken. If you had told me I'd ever be best friends with former students, let alone dating one of them, I'd have called you crazy.

"You are so cute I could gag," Rainbow informed them testily as she shoved a stack of books into the display by the cash register.

"You're just becoming a bitter old shrew because you're not getting any," Tayline countered, sticking out her tongue at her best friend. "Seriously, when was the last time you got laid?"

"None of your business, sprite."

"Only because you don't have any business to share," she countered.

I laughed at them over the low rumble of "Good Times Roll" by The Cars playing over the surround sound speakers, and Rainbow shot me a withering glare for siding with Tay.

I shrugged. "I'm sorry, Rainbow, she has a point."

The beautiful Korean woman sighed and slumped against the cash desk dramatically. "Don't I know it. Why can't one of your delicious alpha bikers take an interest in me, huh?"

"Probably because you catch more flies with honey than with vinegar," I pointed out, thinking of all the times I'd brought Rainbow to one of the club BBQs or hang outs at Eugene's and she'd deliver sass upon heaping layer of sass.

She blew her bangs out of her face and winced. "I know. I get bitchy when I'm nervous, and those big, beautiful bikers? Who the hell wouldn't be nervous around them?"

"That's fair," Benny added as he moved away from Carson to finish sweeping the aisles. "I still stammer like a freak when one of them first starts talking to me."

"It's adorable," Carson assured him with a grin.

"It's lame." Benny muttered, suddenly interested in his shoes.

"Anyone who thinks it's lame can fuck off with it," Carson countered with an easy shrug. "I think it's cute as fuck."

"It is," I agreed, just for the record, because Carson wasn't the only voice Benny needed to hear.

Benny blushed a beautiful red and ducked his head behind a bookcase.

"I get bitchy when I'm hungry," Tay admitted, getting back to Rainbow. "Cy thinks it's adorable too."

"Cyclops actually said the word 'adorable'?" Rainbow asked dubiously.

Her skepticism was warranted. Matthew Broderick, aka Cyclops or Cy, which he was called because he'd lost an eye saving Tayline years ago from human traffickers, was not the kind of man one would assume had words like 'cute,' 'cuddly,' or 'adorable' in his lexicon.

But I was a woman claimed by a biker, so I knew the secret of all alpha men. If they found a woman worthy of their wild hearts, for that woman and that woman alone, he would be sweeter than any other kind of man.

"He did." Tay proved my point with a secret little smile.

"Hard to believe since he almost ripped the head off of Officer Ormand the other day," Rainbow muttered.

"What?" I asked, always alert to the goings-on of the police force in Entrance since they were always *ultra*-aware of us.

Tay shot Rainbow a glare and then sighed. "It's not that big a deal...Cy already reported in to Zeus about it."

"Yeah, well, you didn't tell *me*," I pointed out, fisting a hand on one hip while cocking the other. "What went down?"

She rolled her eyes. "You know, you've gotten a whole lot bossier since being with King."

"Yeah," I agreed. "If he's going to be king one day, I've got to be queen. What else would you expect?"

"You've always looked more like a Disney princess than a biker queen."

"Looks can be deceiving," I countered, because I'd learned that the hard way back in my stupider days when I'd almost given up a shot at King just because he was involved with the club. "Now, fess up."

Collectively, we grouped around the little living room set up I had in front of the windows, sinking into the big, comfy leather couches and the twin armchairs to listen to Tay.

"You know Ormand? He's mid-forties, divorced, and a Canadian redneck if I ever saw one. He still lives next door to me because he didn't let his wife keep the house in the separation. Anyway, he's always been a bit of a nosey parker, obviously because Cy comes and goes a lot and any Entrance PD officer is going to keep an eye on that. Recently, he kind of upped his game. He now has binoculars he uses from his bedroom to peer into my house, and he always comes out onto his porch whenever Cy shows up... At first, it was all just male posturing nonsense, but I was driving home from school the other day and the fucker pulled me over for no reason. He was super aggressive with me, leaning into my open window and kind of berating me for being involved with The Fallen."

She shrugged, but I noticed the shaky quality of the breath she dragged into her lungs and knew the incident had unsettled her.

"He pestered me for ten minutes, until I threatened to call

Cy and the boys to come pick me up if he wouldn't stop harassing me. He was visibly angry, but he let me go."

"Woah," Benny said, his big eyes wrenched wide. "That had to be kind of scary."

"They're upping the ante," Carson noted grimly, looking at me.

He'd started hanging around The Fallen, the first step before anyone was ever considered to prospect for them. I wasn't sure if he hung out with the brothers just because he got on with them or if he honestly desired to patch in to the club. He had a degree in business from UBC, but so far, he hadn't been able to get much work, and I worried he would join up for the wrong reasons.

I nodded though, biting my lip. The police had been inserting themselves more and more into our lives over the last few years. Ever since Javier Ventura became mayor.

It seemed nearly impossible, but he was actually *worse* than our former mayor, Loulou Garro's deceased father who was in bed with Javier's Mexican cartel, Danner's corrupt police force, and Warren's high school drug ring.

Somehow, the villain had become the town leader, and things continued to spiral out of control, as evidenced by the fact his wife Irina had set up an illegal pornography business outside of Entrance.

"Be careful, okay?" I told Tayline, taking her hand in mine as she sat next to me. "Do what Cy says."

She snorted. "You sound like one of them."

I shrugged because I did, but it was for good reason. "We're involved in a world where abductions, murders, and battery actually do happen to the people we love…I just want you to be careful. Everyone knows you and Cy are tight, and if the police are going to give the brothers any more trouble..."

"Then that should go doubly for you," she countered.

I reached over to the end of the couch and produced the

Sig Sauer handgun Zeus had given me for Christmas last year. It was identical to the guns he'd given Harleigh Rose and Loulou. "Don't worry, I'm always prepared."

"Mrs. Irons carries a gun," Carson teased. "Colour me surprised."

"*Miss* Irons," Benny corrected automatically and then giggled. "Soon to be Mrs. Garro, I hope."

Everyone looked at me expectantly. There was a niggle of unease in my belly like a worm burrowing into the earth, tunneling through my foundation of confidence. I shrugged and laughed lightly, awkwardly. "Don't look at me like that. We're in no rush to get married."

And we weren't. Our lives were beautiful just as they were. I reminded myself of this every day, especially when I saw old friends from my past life in Vancouver getting married and having babies. There was always a pang in the base of my gut when I saw the gorgeous wedding dresses and celebrations or those plump, wrinkled faces and little fists.

As much as I had changed over the course of the last few years, I was still a romantic traditionalist at heart, and I yearned for those things with a fierceness that sometimes took my breath away.

"I call bullshit," Rainbow announced as she rearranged her long, boney limbs in her chair. "I've seen your face every time we walk past a baby, and there's no denying your womb basically melts at the sight. Plus, hate to break it to you, babe, but you're not getting any younger."

"Hey!" Both Tayline and I protested because we were the same age.

"Thirty is hardly ancient," I argued, even though I'd found a grey hair at my crown just last week and thrown a bit of a fit about it to King. I was lucky I had the kind of man who'd let me rant, then pressed a kiss to the top of my head, declaring me beautiful in all of my iterations.

"Have you talked about it at all?" Benny ventured, trying

to keep his eyes on me and failing as they slipped to the side where Caron sat in his own chair with a furrowed brow, flipping through a non-fiction book called *Vagina.*

I smiled at him because we were in the same tough spot. "Not really…I mean, we speak about the future all the time in an abstract kind of way. We want to name our daughter Eve if we have one, and we want a cat someday soon. We've always dreamed about going on our honeymoon to Alaska and driving up the coast on the bike together." I sighed gustily and leaned my head back on the couch cushion to look at the beams in the ceiling, searching for answers. "At what point is it my responsibility to talk to him about it? Isn't he supposed to be the one to ask me when he's ready?"

Everyone was quiet for a beat. None of us was married, and therefore, none of us really knew the answer to that question. I decided I would call Maja, Buck's Old Lady and resident biker bitch guru, to hash things out.

"I think no matter what, it's important to remember the obvious. King loves you. Never seen a man love a woman so much and so openly as that boy loves his Queenie," Tayline stated, curled up like a kitten with her head on Benny's lap while he stroked her short hair. "You have a man who isn't afraid to let you know every day how much you're loved, and I think that's even better than a marriage certificate."

"Preach," Benny agreed softly.

I had to agree with them, which was why, as I got back to work shelving the last of the books in the many rows of dark oak bookshelves, I felt ill at ease and almost ashamed of my lingering desire for more. Was I being greedy and ungrateful for wanting a ring and a ceremony when I already had more love than any one person should ever be entitled to?

I was still mulling this over as I trailed my hand over the spines of the books in the non-fiction section, letting the soft bindings and beautiful covers calm me. Lost in my thoughts, I was not prepared when I pushed a book into the shelf, and something caught my sleeve on the other side.

I gasped, then tugged to free it, thinking the fabric must have caught on a book, but then fingers wrapped around my wrist, tugging back so that the front of my body was forced up against the shelf. Before I could struggle again, the hand was gone, and a low chuckle wound around the corner of the stacks like tendrils of smoke.

Seconds later, a long, hard body was pressing me to the bookcase.

"'S your prince charming come to life," King murmured, voice light and full with laughter as he nuzzled into my neck.

"You scared me!" I scolded, but I was already losing breath to the desire burning up my core, my voice was weak because of it. "What are you doing here?"

"Was in the neighborhood and missed my woman, so I thought I'd drop in and steal a kiss…or two."

King's rough fingertips skimmed along the side of my jaw and moved my thick sheet of hair over my shoulder to leave my neck bare to his questing kisses.

"Fuck, always smell so good," he moaned as he dragged his nose down my throat and the other hand wrapped around my opposite side to dive beneath my jeans and play at the top of my satin panties. "Feel so fuckin' good too. Can't ever take my hands off ya."

"I don't want you to," I admitted. "The second you touch me, I want more."

"I know. Can feel it in the skip of your pulse just here." He tongued my neck where my heart beat like a percussion drum. "Feel it in the furl of your nipples." His hand skated up my belly to my breast where he tweaked the peak with strong, relentless fingers then arrowed it back down my jeans to frame my swollen clit between two fingers. "Feel it in the way you throb for me so damn quick. Tell me, babe, if I dipped a finger beneath these pretty satin panties, would you be soaked through with want for me?"

My head fell back to his shoulder, lips parted on a long exhale as if there wasn't any more room in my body for air, only the hot weight of heady desire.

"Yes, but, honey, everyone is up front helping out. We can't play back here."

I knew the moment I said it, it was the wrong way to handle the situation.

You see, it never did any good to say 'no' to a biker when he wanted you. They always found a way to sway your opinion in the end.

King nipped my earlobe then trailed love bites down my neck until he reached the delicate junction between my neck and shoulder, biting me and holding on with his teeth as his fingers skated down the placket of my underwear and swept underneath. I moaned despite myself as two long fingers sunk inside me and curled, pressing against my tight walls, making me ache and wriggle in his intractable hold.

"King," I breathed, half-protest, half-plea.

"You want me to stop, babe? 'Cause I can feel you ripplin' 'round my fingers and soakin' my palm. I don't think you care that anyone's in the store. I know my dirty girl likes the thrill of gettin' found out."

I panted, too focused on the way his thumb began to strum my clit to protest, especially because what he said was true. It was exhilarating to think that someone might stumble upon us, me pressed between the books and King's body like a drying flower, his big hand palming my pussy, making obscene wet noises as he played with me, and I moaned for him. I loved the idea of people knowing how quickly I succumbed to him.

"You want people to see how beautiful you are when I make you come for me," King practically purred, his voice a raspy texture that abraded my skin wonderfully.

"I want you to see it," I told him, bucking back my hips, desperate enough to demand what I wanted, consequences be damned. "But I won't come unless you're inside me, so I guess now, the decision is yours."

King pressed his smile into my neck then pulled away to drag my jeans down my legs, leaving them circled around my calves while he did the same to his own. His big palms framed my hips and tipped them so my ass jutted back.

"Love this ass." He dragged his rough fingers over one cheek before giving it a short, sharp slap that made me gasp and press my face into the books so I wouldn't be heard. "Hold on to the shelves, Cress, I'm gonna take you there hard and fast."

A moment later, the hot crest of his cock was at my entrance.

"Brace," he warned on a growl that made a violent shudder roll down my spine.

And then he gave me every inch in one smooth, brutal glide that compressed everything in my body toward the apex of my sex. I couldn't focus on the way my sweating hands slipped over the shelves as I grappled for purchase to push back against his every thrust, or how the heels of my leather booties slipped against the glossy wood floors. Everything was centered between my legs, at the gorgeous feel of King's cock sliding thick and unyielding as a blunt edged weapon in and out of my clasping folds.

The wet sound of our joining made my ears burn, but I loved it, just as I loved the dirty words King said in his raspy, breathless voice as he took me.

I loved it even more when he wrapped my hair around his fist, once, twice, until it was tightly wound and my head was craned backwards, using it to tip me toward his hot, waiting mouth. My groan rumbled through our kiss, echoing back to me over his tongue.

"Like a fuckin' vice 'round me. Love this tight pussy, love

this sweet, hot mouth," King praised before sealing his lips over mine once more.

It was the praise that did me in. After a lifetime of feeling deeply ashamed of my libido and the sinful, rough fantasies I harboured in the dark, it was the pleasure of King bringing them into the light, into *fruition,* as if they were some gift for him to unearth, that broke open my pleasure.

"God, King," I gasped as my sex clamped down over him and my womb cramped with the force of my orgasm.

I could feel it wrack through me, shaking every thought out of my head, every iota of shame from the fabric of my being. And when he grunted, planting his cock so deep inside of me I could feel him at the entrance to my womb, and he came, it felt fitting in a way that was hard to explain.

Because that was what King did for me. He sucked the poison out of me with his lips, his teeth, and tongue. He made sure that whatever bad thoughts or feelings I secretly concealed were eradicated and replaced by the sheer immensity of his vivacious, laughing love.

I rolled my forehead over the books so that I could watch as he stepped away from me to use a clean, folded bandana from his back pocket to gently wipe his cum away from between my legs.

This was almost my favourite part, the cherished routine of post-coital lovers. How he cleaned me, always, unless he wanted me to sleep with his cum inside me, and how the first kiss after sex was an achingly tender punctuation mark to end our intimacy.

I hummed into the kiss as he leaned forward to offer it to me after righting my jeans, and then I held him close so I could turn and wrap my arms around his neck. He smelled so good, like man and sweat and the faint salty musk of *me,* which I took a moment to breathe in.

"I love you, you know?" I whispered to him. "Sometimes it

terrifies me how much I love you and how deeply happy we are."

His hands came up to wrap over my wrists as I held his face. "No fear, Queenie. There's nothin' we got comin' that we can't handle together."

"That's sweet."

"Fuck sweet, babe. It's the motherfuckin' truth." He lowered his forehead to mine so that those incredible, pale as the dawn sky blue eyes were all I could see. "Told you once, and I meant it. I'd tear the fuckin' world apart if it wronged you."

"Same." And in a way, I already had. I'd torn the small, comfortable world I'd lived into pieces in order to be with King in his all-consuming world of loose morals, intense loyalty, and rough rituals.

"Good."

For a moment we just stood there, breathing each other's breath. I wrapped one of his curls around my finger just because I could and relished in our closeness.

"Can't believe I fucked you up against the religious texts," King finally said.

"What?" I pulled back and whipped around to see the poorly arranged books in the case.

They were, in fact, religious texts.

"We are so going to hell." I groaned and thumped my hand against my forehead.

The sound of King's deep belly laugh prompted me to spin around again so I could watch him tip that glorious mane of blond waves and curls back, corded throat exposed, face tipped to the sky as if offering his humour to the heavens.

Before he was even done laughing, he looped a long arm around my waist and tugged me into him so that I could feel it vibrate through me.

When he was finished, he looked down at me again, tears

of mirth caught in his thick lashes and a lopsided grin in his cheek.

"Hate to break it to you, babe, but I'm thinkin' that ship sailed when you agreed to fuck your student."

"King!" I shouted as I shoved at him.

"No denyin' it."

"Well…no, but still," I said primly. "You didn't have to say it."

"Love sayin' it. Love that you came over to the dark side for me. Says a lot 'bout my powers of corruption."

"It says a lot about my *lack* of control and your over inflated ego," I corrected.

"Potato, po-tah-to," he said with another low laugh. "Point is, you're mine."

I sighed as if the idea didn't delight me. "If I write it on my body, will you stop saying it so much?"

He brightened. "No, but like the idea of that. We'll go see Nova at Street Ink and getcha a nice little tatt right here." He hooked a finger under my jeans and brushed at the skin near my hip.

A shiver rushed through me before I could curb it.

"It can be your present to me," King went on as he used that finger to pull me forward and around the corner to the back lounge where a few leather chairs were set up for reading.

"Present?"

"Happy four-year anniversary, babe," he said with a wink, before taking me by the shoulders and swiveling me to face one of the chairs.

In it lay a box filled with a fluffy blue blanket, and in the folds of that blanket lay an even fluffier tuft of grey.

"I forgot?" I gasped, momentarily distracted from the box of fluff. "Oh my gosh, King, I'm the worst girlfriend ever."

He laughed, hands in his pockets as he rocked back onto the heels of his motorcycle boots as he did when he was uncharacteristically shy. "Nah, you got lots goin' on here at the moment. Honestly, considered not even bringin' it up, but then I did that run down to Vancouver the other day and saw this guy…and I knew he was yours the second I saw him at the SPCA. Can't have a real literary bookshop without one."

King moved forward to kneel by the chair and burrowed his hands in the blanket to reveal an absolutely tiny, little ball of fur.

It was grey with darker striations rippling out from between its big yellow eyes like waves in a pond. The moment it wrapped a little white paw around King's wrist and looked up at him to meow this little, rusty mewl, I was a goner.

"Oh." My hands flew to my cheeks to bracket my smiling mouth. "Oh my gosh, King. You got us a cat."

"Half cat, half shadow," he grumbled good-naturedly as it meowed at him again and rubbed its little cheek over his knuckles. "Cries for me whenever I leave him alone and followed me 'round the house this mornin' like my shadow."

I bent over to put my nose near his face so he could sniff it delicately before he uncurled a paw to place it on my cheek and kind of pat at me gently.

My eyes were shining when I turned them up to look at King through my lashes. "Shadow seems like a good name then."

"Welcome to the Garro clan, little Shadow," I told the cat. "It's the best freaking family there is."

CHAPTER SIX

Cressida

I PEERED at Ares as we waited at the one traffic light leading out of town on Main Street, trying to discern from his usual quiet state how he was feeling after school that day. He was an absolutely beautiful boy, thickly lashed, rich brown eyes, a generous mouth, strong jaw, and this tangle of fabulous black hair that spiraled into thick curls and waves. But his beauty didn't seem to have much bearing on his fellow nine-year-old schoolmates. Instead, they noticed the thickness of his Spanish accent, the unusual, adult-like reserve of his personality. At first, they'd peppered him with questions: where was he from, who were his parents, did he like living with the infamous

Garro family? But when he never answered, their curiosity calcified into bitterness, and the bullying began in earnest.

He didn't like to talk about it with us. We knew because Loulou and I had gone in for numerous student/teacher interviews at the elementary school, and his teachers had expressed their concern, but Ares wouldn't speak about it. Once, he returned home with a black eye, and I thought the entire brotherhood of The Fallen would roll into the elementary school parking lot and take out whoever had hurt one of their own.

But Ares had stopped Zeus with a hand on his arm, looking up at him with those beautiful brown eyes that were more soulful than most men thrice his age. "Don't worry, Z. They're the ones who will regret it in the end."

What Ares said that day was so unspeakably wise yet sad at the same time. What life had Ares lived before we found him, orphaned and alone, squatting in Zeus's Whistler cabin last Christmas that made bullying so very trivial?

None of us forced him to speak about his life before because most of us knew what it was like to have another life. We respected it, even if it made us uneasy to give that much psychological freedom to a child.

"You're quiet," I noted finally, because he'd yet to say a word since I'd picked him up at school.

He rolled his head against the seat to shoot me a look that said, 'aren't I always?'

"Especially quiet," I corrected. "If something is bothering you, I hope you'll tell me."

His silence continued for a few minutes as he stared at me and mulled over whatever dark things lurked in the deepest caves of his mind. I hummed along to the song on the radio while I waited, taking note of the police car that pulled onto the road behind us.

"What am I to you?"

"Excuse me?" I asked, distracted by the cop car that was quickly gaining on us.

"What am I to you?"

I glanced at him sidelong to determine where he was coming from but found only a blank canvas in his expression. "Well, you're my family. Why are you asking?"

He hesitated, gaze dropping to his hands where long, thin scars marred the olive skin. We all wondered about them, but after I tried asking once, no one did again.

"What do I call you then? And Zeus and Loulou and H.R. and King? What are you to me?"

"Family," I repeated firmly, because I was starting to understand the problem. "If anyone asks about where you come from or who you belong to, that's what you tell them. You're Ares Garro. That's what it says on all your official documents, isn't it? And that's what we know to be true."

"But no one is like…my *papá* or *mamá*?"

"No," I paused, trying to give him something concrete, because I knew that was what he wanted and what others would expect. "If you want a mother and father, I guess Zeus and Lou could be considered your parents, because you live with them most of the time. But King and I love you, and you live with us just like sometimes you stay with Lila and the Booth family or with Bat and his boys…I think you're rather lucky actually, Ares. We'd all fight to be the ones you consider your parents, although I hope it doesn't have to come to that. The best thing about being part of The Fallen is that labels cease to matter. Everything boils down to love and family. You get that from an entire club filled with men and women with massive hearts. I know it's not a perfect answer to your question, but I hope it's enough."

Ares looked away from me quickly, but not before I could see the relief and hope shining in his eyes. A moment later, his hand reached across the console to tug on a lock of my hair in quiet thanks. "It's more than I ever had before."

"Same," I assured him. "It can be overwhelming at first, but you'll get used to it."

A loud *bleep* startled me before the flash of red and blue lights drew my gaze to the police car that was suddenly tailgating me.

I turned on my blinker, indicating that I was going to pull over to the shoulder, trying to keep calm even though my heart was in my throat.

"Be calm, okay?" I told Ares, who's eyes were wide with panic. "Everything's okay. Stay in the car, and be quiet unless I tell you otherwise. I'm sure it's nothing."

But I knew it wasn't.

I hadn't been speeding or doing anything else unlawful, and as the cop car pulled to a stop behind me and Office McDougal stepped out of the car, I knew things were *not* going to go smoothly. His partner stayed in the car. I couldn't tell who it was at the distance, but he fidgeted nervously, as if he wasn't sure about what his partner intended to do.

McDougal was a short, squat man, as if God had pinched him at the head and feet, so his proportions were horribly off. He wore a constant sneer around town, as if everything about Entrance personally offended him. Coming from the much more conservative Alberta, I was sure it did.

He stalked slowly toward my open window, his strut timed perfectly as if some invisible spaghetti western soundtrack played in his head.

"Good afternoon, Ms. Irons," he drawled as he stopped in front of me and squared his hips to the window. He didn't lean down, so I was forced to make eye contact with his groin and holstered weapons. It was a power move, and a pathetic one at that.

"Good afternoon, Officer," I greeted sunnily. "Is there something amiss with my car?"

I knew there wasn't. My pimped out, pale pink Honda Civic was personally serviced by King at Hephaestus Auto every six months and drove better than a Honda had any right to.

"Might be," he prevaricated, finally deigning to lean down, bracing an arm on my window ledge so that I was forced to back up farther into the car to get some personal space.

His eyes wandered down my body, noting with some surprise that I wasn't decked out in biker bitch finery. Instead, I was wearing black jeans and a lace and silk blouse that showed only a shadow at the top of my breasts. He scowled at them as if offended I wasn't showing more skin.

"What brings you out to this ritzy neck of our woods?" he asked suspiciously.

I ground my teeth. Back Bay road was prime real estate in Entrance, a long ribbon of asphalt decorated with sweeping acreages and million-dollar homes. I'd bought Shamble Wood Cottage for a steal years ago because it had been a dilapidated dump, but I supposed Officer McDougal didn't know that.

"I live out this way." My smile forced my lips apart uncomfortably like a dental retractor.

"Hmph. With that felon? The Garro kid?"

I watched as he spit on my front tire and tried not to give in to the urge to throttle him.

"King isn't a felon, but, yes, I live with him there."

"Seems to me a woman like you shouldn't be shacking up with a sort such as him," he noted as his beady eyes once against lingered over my breasts. "If I were you, I'd get out while I could."

"Oh? Do you know something I don't, Officer?" I asked politely even though his breath reeked of onions, and he was leaning too close.

"Know a lot of things you don't, Ms. Irons. Just a friendly warning to you."

"Thank you, but it's unnecessary. Is that all?"

McDougal narrowed his eyes. "No, I don't imagine it is. Why don't you get out of the car for me?"

"Why?" I asked, even though I knew why. The moment I'd seen his police car tailgating me, I'd known he would find a way to manufacture an altercation just to poke at The Fallen.

"Because I damn well told you to," he snarled, moving back so he could wrench my door open and pull me out roughly by the arm.

Adrenaline now fully kicked in, I craned my head back to make eye contact with Ares who sat petrified in the passenger seat, trying to relay with my eyes that everything was going to be okay.

McDougal hauled me clear of the car then used the arm he held as a lever to push my front up against the side of my car. His booted feet kicked my legs apart, and his other hand planted on my low back to pin me to the hot metal.

"Now, I'm checking you out 'cause the company you keep, I suspect you got drugs or weapons on your person."

"That's complete bullshit, and you know it," I snapped, struggling out of his hold. "You pulled me over to start something."

McDougal pressed his groin into my ass and ground into me, his weight crushing me against the car so that I couldn't wriggle. I shivered in revulsion as his voice wafted damply over my ear. "You want me to start something, that can be arranged, biker whore. I know you're just gagging for dick."

Fuck this.

Letting anger and my training at the hands of Priest and King fuel me, I carefully lifted one foot off the ground and angled it at McDougal's foot. The spiked heel rammed into the tender inside of his leather encased foot, and he cursed loudly in my ear before relinquishing his tight hold on me.

"You fucking bitch—" he started to holler, but Ares was suddenly there using his momentum as he burst out of the car to push the officer to his ass in the dirt.

"Get the hell away from her," he growled, small chest heaving, fists clenched at his side.

McDougal lunged at him before I could move, shoving him brutally into the side mirror. I gasped as Ares fell to the ground with a quiet grunt of pain.

Before I could think, I was on McDougal. Using all of my weight, I shoved him to the ground and straddled him, pining his arms to the ground with my knees so I could land a brutal punch to his right cheekbone.

Pain exploded in my knuckles, but I bore down on the yelling cop and prepared to make him pay for fucking with me and mine. Vaguely, I heard Ares yelling encouragement at me in the background.

Before I could do so, hands were wrenching me off of McDougal and dragging me to the ground beside him where I was flipped on my belly to have my hands roughly shackled in handcuffs.

"Cressida Irons, you are under arrest for assaulting an officer of the law," the other cop, the one who had been waiting in the car, kneeled over me and clicked the bitingly tight cuffs around each of my wrists. "If I were you, I'd remain silent."

King

NO. FUCKIN'. Way.

I turned off the engine of my Dyna Low Rider and swung off the bike 'fore any'a the brothers followin' me could even park their rides. My boots ate up the asphalt as I prowled up the stairs to the Entrance Police Department and shoved through the glass doors.

"Where *the fuck* is my woman?" I demanded from the center of the reception area.

The woman mannin' the desk went pale as her eyes raked over my windswept hair, leather cut sportin' The Fallen skull and tattered wings, and the wicked lookin' knife holstered at my hip.

"Um…" she hummed, but then interrupted herself with a squeak as the door burst open behind me and the stomp of motorcycle boots filled the suddenly dead quiet police hall.

My brothers had arrived.

"You want me to ask again?" I cocked my head and smiled at the woman, but it wasn't a pretty thing. It was a threat.

"King, Jesus, man, calm down," Officer Gibson said as he appeared from down the hall, hands open and raised to the heavens in surrender. "We got her."

"Yeah, you fuckin' do. I want to know why the hell she was pulled over in the first place?" I stalked forward, gettin' in Gibson's face. He was tall, but I was taller, and the gym had been good to me, packin' me with muscles so I was built stronger than most men, too, him included.

He didn't let me intimidate him, not really, but I saw the

flash of apprehension in his eyes, and it stoked the fire of my vengeful fury higher. If he thought his friendship and ex-partnership with Lionel Danner meant I wouldn't nail him to the wall for keepin' me from Cress, he would be sadly fuckin' mistaken.

"King, calm down. McDougal pulled her over for a broken taillight, and things got a little out of control."

"Yeah? Thinkin' things have been out of control here for a fuck of a while now, Gibson. Only half-decent copper left seems to be *you*. So, excuse me if I don't buy your brand of bullshit. Now, bring out McDougal, or I'll go back there and find himself."

"I'll have to arrest you if you manhandle an officer," he warned me.

I sneered down into his face, lettin' him see a side'a me that few ever saw. One that lived to dominate and subdue, one that yearned for chaos and rebellion against the fuckin' man. I let him see that barely leashed animal in my eyes and then smiled my weaponized smile.

"You don't take me to see my woman or that motherfucker in the next two seconds, I guarantee it'll be more than just me you gotta arrest for manhandlin' an officer," I said with a jerk of my head to indicate the handful of brothers at my back.

Zeus was there, too, lettin' me handle things my way 'cause it was *my* girl they'd done wrong.

Gibson swallowed thickly, searchin' my face for somethin' he wouldn't find, then sighed. He rubbed a hand over his buzzed head then stepped slightly to the side in physical capitulation.

"I'll take you to see her," he said resignedly.

I nodded, lookin' back at my brothers in a silent bid for them to stay there, then followed Gibson down the hall.

"I *am* sorry about this," Gibson muttered quietly as he led me through the maze of the station. "Things are…getting difficult around here for those of us who don't agree with SS

Danner. The cop with McDougal wasn't okay with what went down, but he couldn't very well side against him."

"He damn well coulda," I countered. "That's the thing 'bout you pigs, your blind loyalty means you don't take care of business in your ranks. Your shit stinks to high fuckin' heaven 'cause you never deign to take out the trash."

Gibson sighed again as we stopped in front of a holding room door. "Not arguing with you, King. Cress is a good woman, and I hate to see her in here…'course, maybe it was only a matter of time since she hitched her cart to you."

I stepped forward threateningly. "Whatever you think of me and the club, keep Cress out of it. You got any honour at all, you'll leave all our women out of this grudge match."

"It doesn't have to be a grudge match."

I laughed coldly. "Should'a thought of that 'fore you arrested my woman."

Gibson hesitated, fear ripe on his face for me to pluck and devour. But I was done playin' games with him. I just wanted to see my girl.

So, I slapped a hand on the door and arched my brows.

With a quiet sigh, he opened it.

As soon as the door swung open, somethin' came flyin' at me.

I braced on my back foot and opened my arms just in time to catch Cressida as she wrapped her limbs 'round me and stuffed her face in my hair.

"King, King, King," she chanted as she clutched at me. "Thank God."

I could feel the anger cracklin' in my belly, the inferno of my wrath lickin' flames up the walls of my gut until they burned and smoked in my throat. Bein' smart enough to give us privacy, Gibson closed the door behind us as I moved into the room and perched her ass on the metal table so I could pry her gently off'a me and check her over.

Those whiskey eyes I loved so much were blown black with

anxiety and too dark in her pale face. I cupped her cold cheek and gathered her hands in one of mine to inspect them too. The knuckles on her right hand were red and abraded from violence.

A shock of mirth pulsed through my anger, and I barked out a laugh as I looked up into her suddenly sparklin' eyes. "Please tell me you fucked that motherfucker up."

She laughed, but it was breathy, and I could see just how shaken up she was. "I got one good punch in, but I did have him pinned for a hot minute. Got him in the foot with my heel, too, when he had me pressed against the car."

A low grumble worked its way loose from my gut. "He fuckin' touched you?"

She bit her lip and placed both hands on my chest as if attemptin' to soothe a rabid bear. In that moment, I felt like one too.

"He pulled me over with some bullshit excuse then made me get out of the car so he could 'check me' for weapons and drugs. Tayline told me in the shop yesterday that Officer Ormand had done basically the same thing to her recently."

"They're askin' for it," I growled.

There was no easier way to earn the wrath of The Fallen then to fuck with our women and families.

"I think they are," she agreed, wrappin' my waist with her legs to pull me in tight. "They know you're more likely to mess up and commit an actual punishable offense if they can get to us. But you're smarter than that…right?"

My woman was clever playin' on my ego like that, but still, I knew better than to rashly agree. My blood ran too hot in my veins, ignitin' an anger that I didn't know how to bank. McDougal had fucked with my woman. Put his goddamn *hands* on my woman. I had to show him what happened to a man who wronged Cress.

I had to show him just what would happen if he did it again.

"King," Cress called, hands framin' my face so she could pull my gaze down to her. "Please, don't play into this game. They want you to blow a gasket and screw up."

"Knew what kinda man I was when you started datin' me, babe, and that is *not* the kinda man that stands idly by while his woman is harassed."

"He also shoved Ares," she admitted, wincin' when I cursed viciously and slammed a palm loudly against the table. "But he's okay, really. He's with a case worker drinking juice."

"The point is not that you and Ares are okay. You need to get this, Cress, 'cause you signed on for me prospectin' with the club just as much as I did. We do not let things like this go unchecked." She opened her mouth to protest, but I pressed a finger to her lips and ducked my head low so I could speak just for her and not the cameras recordin' us. "We *will* fuck up McDougal for fuckin' with you and Ares. And we'll do it in a way there's zero blow back. You get me?"

She sank her fingers into the hair over my ears and curled them in, holdin' me tight, eyes wide and so trusting it made my heart clench. "Whatever you have to do, honey."

"My rough and tumble queen," I praised 'fore I kissed her 'cause kissin' her was my only option.

I needed to taste that trust and feel that love on my tongue. She moaned into me, chest archin' so her breasts could press against my chest.

"Proud of ya," I told her when we broke for breath. "My badass biker girl."

"You know it," she said, beamin'.

"H.R. is probably gonna make you some kinda biker bitch reward," I teased. "Maja and Hannah will get you drunk on tequila to celebrate, and I'll have a drunk and horny Cress on my hands."

She laughed, her entire face so filled with light I felt the warmth of it in my chest.

"Only you could make me laugh at a time like this."

I shrugged with faux modesty which prompted another giggle as someone knocked on the door. We broke apart to watch Mr. White, the club's lawyer shove past officers McDougal and Gibson.

I started toward the McDougal fucker with a snarl, but Mr. White held up a stayin' hand. "Just a moment before you slug him, please, Mr. Garro. I think you'll be satisfied with the way I handle this, and I do prefer to get one Garro out at a time, so let's focus on Miss Irons, hmm?"

I swallowed the harsh burn of rage like cheap whiskey and moved 'round the table to sit beside Cress and Mr. White while the two officers took seats on the other side. Mr. White cleared his throat repeatedly, like an opera singer preparin' for the stage, as he sifted through his briefcase, producin' a folder of documents and an iPhone which he laid on the table.

After removin' them from the folder, he crossed his hands over the pages and looked at the officers. "We seem to have a bit of an issue here. By all accounts, it seems Officer McDougal," he indicated the pig, who sneered in response. I flexed my hands under the table and bared my teeth at him. "pulled over Miss Cressida Irons because he thought she had a faulty taillight. Officer Hutchinson was kind enough to go to the scene just now, and he sent a few photos that show her taillight was smashed *after* this incident."

McDougal opened his twisted mouth to protest, but Mr. White kept on.

"So, not only did you illegally pull over my client without cause, but you then proceeded to drag her from her vehicle where you then manhandled her against her car. When her nephew, a minor by the name of Ares Garro, tried to intervene, you then shoved him to the ground."

"That's horseshit," the cop spewed, spittle flyin' over the table. "You got nothing but your word to prove that nonsense. The word of a biker's bitch against the word of a policeman."

"Ah, I wouldn't be so quick to smear the Garro name any

further, Mr. McDougal," White cautioned with his small, polite smile that I knew well enough to know meant he had an ace up his sleeve.

"They're criminals and scum. Everyone in this town knows it," the asshole retorted.

"McDougal, shut *up*," Gibson warned.

"Do as you're told," I muttered under my breath just so McDougal would look at me as I cracked my knuckles and leered menacingly at him.

I wanted him to feel the force of hatred emanatin' off me like radioactive waves from a nuclear blast site. I wanted him infected with fear for me so that when I finally stalked him and captured him like a predator does his unworthy prey, he'd reek of panic and stink with remorse.

Mr. White swiped open his phone, clickin' on a few things 'fore he swivelled to face the two cops.

"This is a video Ares Garro was clever enough to take of the incident before he became involved. In it, you'll see Officer McDougal drag Miss Irons from her car and clearly assault her against said vehicle. While it's true that Miss Irons used force to subdue Officer McDougal and then later pushed the officer to the ground, the video proves that this was done in an act of self defense against the attack first leveled against her person and then that of young Mr. Garro. Coupled with the irrefutable fact that you pulled her over without cause, I do believe we have reason to press charges against the Entrance Police Department. Would you like to bring your Staff Sergeant in to speak with us, or would you like us to wait while you call your lawyer, Officer McDougal?"

The silence that followed was tenuous as a book held too close to a flame. A moment passed, and then it caught on fire when a little snort of humour escaped my throat. McDougal was up and outta his chair in a heartbeat, leanin' over the table to take a swing at me.

Fuck *yeah*. That was exactly what I had been hopin' for.

'Fore McDougal could right himself from his missed swing at me, I was on him, pushin' him to the back wall in one huge shove then holding him up against the wall so that I could smile into his ugly face.

I loved to smile. I'd learned that it was a valuable tool of intimidation when I was angry 'cause it spoke to somethin' that wanted to unhinge itself inside me, somethin' dark and crazy that wouldn't obey my rules.

"You fucked with my woman," I growled under the chaos of noise behind me as people reacted to my move. "And now, motherfucker, I'm gonna fuck with you."

I dropped my hold on him and stood back before Gibson could pry me off him. Cress was already waitin', purse in hand, for me to reach for her so we could walk together from the holding room.

Mr. White followed close behind, his short legs strugglin' to keep up.

"Normally, I wouldn't advise brutality against the police, King."

"I'm a biker, White. What else did you expect?" I countered with a cheeky grin.

"You're a good man, too," he said quietly, pushin' his glasses up his nose. "I sincerely hope you don't lose that now that you've joined your father's business."

I slung an arm 'round Cress and curled her into me so I could kiss her forehead, maintainin' eye contact with the lawyer over her head. "I've got my North star, if that's what you're worried 'bout. She will always right my course, even when I might do wrong."

"Always," she agreed proudly as we walked 'round the corner into the front hall.

My brothers were still there, determined faces, arms crossed, like men ready to go to war at the whim of their commander. It was the first time they'd done that for me, held position while they waited for my orders, and it was a heady thing to realize men like that, dangerous, intelligent, fuckin' incredible men, respected me enough to do as I asked of them.

Zeus stepped forward, his face set to stone, eyes flashin' like a lightning strike. "Good?" he asked Mr. White.

The man must have nodded 'cause his face softened slightly, and he continued forward to kiss Cressida's head and clap me on the shoulder.

"You okay, teach?" he asked my girl, dippin' down so he could look her in the eyes and read what she might be hidin' there.

"Unfortunately, it's not my first time in the police station, and it probably won't be my last," she quipped with an easy, one-shouldered shrug.

I chuckled and tucked her farther into my side. "Don't you know, Dad? Cress is a biker babe now."

Zeus's smile was a slow, wide evolution across his face, and then finally, he laughed. "Gotta thank God or whatever else for puttin' women like Cress Irons and Loulou Garro on this earth, eh, son?"

"Every fuckin' day," I agreed.

The air in the room went static suddenly, and I knew without even turnin' 'round who would be standin' behind me just by lookin' at the expression mirrored on Nova, Bat, Buck, Curtains and Axe-Man's faces.

Staff Sergeant Danner stood at the mouth of the hallway, hands fisted at his sides, mouth screwed up like a twist cap over shaken soda. He looked 'bout ready to explode, which surprised me 'cause SS Danner had always been more of a cold, edge of the blade kinda crazy than a hothead. I'd heard from H.R. that his wife was divorcin' him, and I knew despite whatever cold heart lay in his chest, that man had a soft spot for his wife. Apparently, the pain'a the divorce was just more kindlin' in the fire of his hatred for The Fallen.

It was hard to believe the man standin' in front of me,

painted red with loathin' for me and mine, coulda ever opened up his home to H.R. and me as kids when Lion had taken us in after Zeus went to prison. There was no trace of that man left in the villain that faced us now, so there'd be no trace of remorse in my heart for the ways in which we'd end him.

"That woman is under arrest. You can't leave with her," Harold demanded.

"I believe Mr. White already proved that you really don't wanna be playin' that card given what went down today," I argued, my voice a long, low drawl just to piss him off.

"The entire lot of you are criminals. Don't think that just because my father and his father 'fore him couldn't bring The Fallen to their knees that I will fail too."

Objectively speakin', Harold looked a fuckuva lot like his son, Lion, but the two Danners couldn't have been more different if they tried.

SS Danner was all 'bout power at any cost and the things he felt were right and wrong despite what he mighta otherwise known in his heart to be true.

Lion Danner was everythin' moral, courageous, and good. He'd read the Harry Potter books with me when I'd lived with him, and he had always seemed to be the definition of a Gryffindor, a hero through to his very bones.

It was both sad and ironic that he had such a shitty father.

"You gotta vendetta that'll burn you up faster than you can aim that fire at us," I told him, calm, cool, and so collected I could see it infuriatin' him further by the tick at his jaw. "This isn't 'bout justice for you, Danner. It's 'bout wantin' to be the biggest man in town. Hate to break it to you, but you're in bed with a bigger man. When Javier Ventura's done with you, he'll stomp you out. And as for us?"

I stepped into line with my brothers who broke apart to let Cress, Zeus, and me slide into place between them.

"You've got nothin' on us, and you won't ever get the best

of us 'cause we're straight up better men than you could ever dream of bein'."

"But, Danner," Zeus added, his voice just as weaponized as mine. "You come for more Fallen women or our families, I'm tellin' ya now, straight up, The Fallen will come for you."

CHAPTER SEVEN

King

THERE WAS someone in the house.

I woke up with a start and that knowledge, as if the intruder had triggered some invisible alarm in my head. Cress was in her habitual place, sprawled half on top of me, her silky hair fanned over my chest, an arm curled 'round my waist. Carefully, I dislodged her and rolled silently off the bed to crouch at its side. I had a shotgun under the bed, a knife on the bedside table, and a Walther P99 gun under the mattress.

I opted for the knife and the handgun, tuckin' the latter into my waistband as I crept from the bedroom onto the landing then down the stairs. It was only when I reached the bottom that I heard the fierce whispers of men arguin' by the slidin' doors off the livin' room.

When I pushed the backdoor fully open, it was to find Wrath and Cressida's brother, Lysander, locked together. Wrath had his gun at Sander's gut, but Sander had him in a headlock with his own weapon trained on his temple.

"What the fuck is goin' on?" I asked, unable to hide the humour in my voice.

"Claims he knows you," Wrath growled.

"I fuckin' well do," Sander snapped. "My fuckin' sister lives here. If you'd given me half a bloody second to talk, I would'a told ya that."

"Cress?" Wrath asked, though he didn't release his hold.

"Let him go," I told them both through my laughter. "Bunch'a idiots, the both of you. Why the hell are you tryin' to break in our house this time?"

They hesitated then swiftly broke apart, both takin' enormous steps away from the other, plantin' me in the middle of them. They were both huge ass men with more muscle than sense sometimes, but I wasn't concerned. I'd grown up watchin' Zeus mediate between men like these, and I knew all his tricks.

"Came to tell you the 'serkers are lookin' to pull off a highway robbery when you lot do your run down the coast tomorrow. They were pissed as fuck when Zeus turned down a meetin' and this is retribution. Seems they gotta tip off from someone," Wrath told me as he leaned against the railin' and crossed his arms, grimly eyein' down Lysander. "Wonder who that could'a been?"

"Like hell it was me," Sander spat, lookin' nothin' like his pretty sister and everythin' like an ex-con.

I slapped a palm on his chest before he could lunge across the deck and kill Wrath. "Yeah, we believe you. Still don't know why you're here, though. Cress said she hasn't seen or heard from you in a fuckin' age. Why now?"

Sander glared at Wrath then back at me. "Maybe we could talk 'bout this after fuckin' Goliath over there fucks off."

"Or maybe I should stay to make sure you aren't a lyin' sack'a shit tryin' to get back with the sister who basically excommunicated you already," Wrath countered.

Sander stared at me in shocked horror, obviously surprised Wrath was a good enough friend to know 'bout our history.

I shrugged, not at all sorry 'cause truth be told, I still held a wicked grudge against him for puttin' Cress in the spot he did with the Nightstalker fuckers who abducted her and hammered nails through her palms.

"He's a member of the Berserkers," Sander pointed out. "You really think you can trust him?"

"You were a member of Cress's family, and you betrayed her, so you tell me how much loyalty means?" I responded, leavin' no room for argument.

The older man cut his eyes to the ground and chewed on his cheek, apparently tryin' to level out his shamed anger.

It was the middle of the night, and I didn't have the energy or desire to baby him, so I left him to it. It'd become shockingly normal for Wrath or Sander to show up in the dark hours and either call or 'let themselves in' to update me or check on things. Didn't mean I didn't find it damned annoyin' sometimes.

"When're they aimin' to come at us?" I asked Wrath, after shootin' Sander a look. Cress's brother would rather put a bullet in his own brain than betray her or hers again, so I felt relatively comfortable speakin' in front of him.

"Off Exit 78 on the Sea to Sky highway."

I nodded, pullin' up the image of that stretch of road in my memory easily 'cause I'd been ridin' it since I was a boy.

"Right. Let 'em, there's no way you can convince Reaper not to go through with it, not without givin' yourself away. We'll put a tracker in the bags, stuff half of them with nonsense and track them back to their warehouse. Assumin' that's where they'd take the loot?"

Wrath nodded.

"Right. We'll have a second group of brothers go down the mountain earlier and wait to follow your crew to the warehouse. We'll hijack them there, get our shit and *theirs,* then show them what it is to fuck with The Fallen."

Wrath started at me for a long second, brows cocked, tatted arms flexed as he stroked his short beard.

"Comin' into your own," he said finally. "See what they say 'bout you bein' a smart motherfucker."

I shrugged, but my grin was wicked with arrogance. "Thanks for givin' us the heads up. Make it convincin' when you see me, yeah? If this goes off without a hitch, maybe I'll finally get patched in."

"And when you do, you'll nominate me to patch over," he reminded me of the deal we'd struck over a year ago when we'd first started shootin' the shit after Kylie and I'd made friends in our psychology and business seminars at UBC.

"Yeah, brother," I agreed, steppin' forward to clasp his hand and bring him in for a hug punctuated by a thump on the back. "I got you."

"Got you, brother," Wrath promised 'fore steppin' back. "See ya tomorrow night."

I flicked my fingers at him in goodbye and rounded on Sander. "So, what brings you here in the dead of fuckin' night this time? Cress is sleepin'."

"I figured."

He looked up at the window to our bedroom and sighed in a way I felt in my gut. He might not have been the best brother in the world, but we all make mistakes, and I got that more than most. I hadn't been there to protect Harleigh Rose from her abusive, piece of shit boyfriend, and Sander hadn't been there for Cress for most of her trials 'cause of his own failin's. Didn't mean he didn't wish it was different.

"Heard she was hauled into the police station today. I just wanted to check in with you, see if she was all good, if I could do anythin' to help."

"Sander…" I blew out an exasperated breath and tugged my hands through my knotted curls. "Listen, man, you know I'm happy to let you know how she is when you drop in or give me a call, but you can't just show up like this. She'll reach out when she's fuckin' ready."

He kicked the toe of his motorcycle boot against a loose stone and watched it pitch off the deck into the night. Despite bein' born into the same middle class, conservative family as Cress, Lysander had started down a different path a long fuckin' time ago. Now, that wild lifestyle played out in the wrinkles beside his eyes from squintin' and the grooves 'round his mouth. He'd played the part of a biker back when the Nightstalkers were still in town, but he hadn't dropped the style; he still wore a leather jacket and shit kickers as if he was just waitin' for a club to reach out and take him in.

I wanted to hate the man for the ways he'd fucked up with Cress, but it was hard to hate the how when you understood the why of somethin'. And I got why he'd fucked up. Parents like theirs that didn't give a shit 'bout them would turn pretty much anyone into a less than wholesome version of themselves.

"She means everythin' to me," he said quietly, in his hoarse voice. "Can't tell ya how many nights I can't sleep just thinkin' 'bout if she's doin' okay."

"She's with me," I said. "Of course, she's fuckin' okay."

"Yeah." He nodded curtly, but the moonlight highlighted the way he grimaced. "Know you do a better job of protectin' her than I ever could. Doesn't mean I don't wish I still had a part to play."

"Fuck, listen, I'll talk to her, but I'm not makin' any promises. I've tried 'fore, and she's had none of it. Hate to break it to you, but she's gotta whole club full'a brothers who would die for her in a heartbeat. Not so sure she'll forgive you just 'cause she misses havin' a sibling."

Sander nodded, still lookin' off over the railin' into the

ocean, wet and black as spilled ink under the silver moon. His knuckles were white as he gripped the wood, and I knew he was sufferin'.

"Appreciate it, man."

Never known a man so alone in the world and so wishin' he wasn't.

"Only bein' I loved my whole life," he admitted quietly. "My princess since I first held her, and she was just this tiny little thing, but every part'a that was so perfect it made my chest so tight, honest to Christ, I couldn't breathe."

Which was why this happened, the late-night break-ins to get updates about Cress, because he was the kinda man who revolved like the earth around the sun that was his family. A man like me.

Only Lysander Irons didn't have a kickass dad and a wicked sister, a group of men like uncles and brothers and a fuckuva best friend like Mute.

He only had a sister he'd hurt who'd cut him outta her life in a way she might not ever let him back, but that was the only hope he had left.

Hence the midnight chats.

"Wouldn't be talkin' to you if I didn't get that, man. Our sisters, our responsibility. It's somethin' that doesn't ever end."

"No," he agreed. "I'm guessin' not."

I hesitated, unsure if I wanted to give it to him. "We all make mistakes. Worry every fuckin' day 'bout the choices I make knowin' they'll affect my woman. It's the only reason she doesn't have my ring on her finger yet. I'm as much to blame for her bein' out in danger as you and William were, and I still put her in danger—as the fuckin' PD proved today—just by bein' with her. The trick of it is to make it worthwhile every day. If you want back in with her, you just gotta find a way to prove that you love her in a way that'll never die. 'Cause of the men we are, the day might come when we unintentionally put her in a position where she might be without her brother or her man, or we might be without her."

"So, you're sayin' make the danger of lovin' a wild animal somehow appealin'" Lysander asked with a wry grin.

I chuckled, slappin' a hand against his shoulder then squeezin' him in camaraderie. "Yeah, man, that's exactly what I'm sayin'. Now, we 'bout done? I gotta woman in bed I've gotta get back to."

"Yeah."

I moved back into the house, but 'fore I could close the slidin' door, Sander's tattooed fingers curled 'round it to stop me. When I met his gaze, I realized for the first time that he had the same whiskey eyes as my woman.

"For the record, haven't known her like I'd want to for the last four years, but I've never seen my sister happier than she is now she's with you. You wanna marry her? Do it. If I know anythin' 'bout her anymore, it's that she loved bein' a wife, would'a loved bein' a mother, she was just doin' it with the wrong guy."

I swallowed the possessive pain in my throat that always cropped up when I thought of my Cress with that asshole, William, and nodded. "I'll keep that in mind."

I hesitated in the doorframe of our bedroom after I'd locked up, unable to keep myself from admirin' my woman in our bed. She laid sprawled across the length of it as if she'd been searchin' for me in her sleep. The light poolin' in through the window like molten silver cast a shine on the sweep of her thick hair, turnin' her skin into hills and valleys of semi-precious metal. Our little cat, Shadow, had found his way onto the bed and was now curled up on Cress's outstretched hand, eager for her warmth.

The sight of her like that, comfortable and vulnerable in our bed, hit me in the chest like a struck gong, the vibration of it echoin' through my blood.

I loved her so much, it frequently took my breath away, and in that moment, somehow, it stunned me yet again.

When I got back into bed, skin cold against the incredible warmth of Cressida's bare flesh as I gently hauled her back over my body, I wondered 'bout Sander and the part he'd played in our lives. He wasn't a bad man, just a good man that'd gotten lost on his way and made some poor as fuck choices. I didn't think he deserved to be cut outta our lives, not after helpin' save Loulou, Bea, Harleigh Rose, and Mute from an ambush up at Zeus's cabin three years ago, but that wasn't my choice to make.

The only choice I did have to make was whether or not to get my head outta my ass and marry the woman of my dreams.

I'd always been the kinda man, even in the body of a boy, who knew what he wanted and fuckin' took it. So, why the hell was I actin' like a scared little boy when I was faced with somethin' that would make me happier than anythin' ever had? Unfortunately, the answer to that question wasn't obvious. All I knew for sure was that it *did* mean more to me than anythin' else ever had, but that didn't make my hesitation any less cowardly.

When it came down to it, I had to trust her.

Last year when I'd been unsure what to do after graduation, it was my Cress who had suggested I prospect for The Fallen and combine my love'a business with our family enterprises. I'd been shocked as fuck, but she'd only laughed her high, bell-like giggle and told me that it was 'bout time I started on the path that had been my birthright.

She'd stood by me through thick and thin, legal and illegal activities, without really battin' an eye, and I hadn't realized until then just how little tangible credit I'd given her for that.

It wasn't that she was unready or unwillin' to be the iron queen to my Fallen king… it was that I hadn't been ready for the responsibility of draggin' her entirely over to the dark side'a life.

I thought of her today, holdin' her own against that pig, McDougal, defendin' Ares like a wrathful mama bear, and I knew she was already gracefully sittin' on that chrome throne in our underworld, ready and *wantin'* to rule by my side.

She had always been mine. Since that first moment we locked eyes across the parkin' lot at Mac's Grocer, but now I understood that she was also *ours*, intractably Fallen.

I ducked my head to press a kiss to her fragrant hair and ran some of the silken strands over my fingers just to feel her, like pinchin' yourself when you think you're dreamin'.

"Mmm," she hummed sleepily, stirrin' enough to rub her cheek sweetly against my chest. "Where'd you go?"

"A stray cat," I explained, just like I had 'fore when Sander came callin' to check on her.

"You know he'll just keep coming if you keep feeding him," she mumbled.

I swallowed my laughter. "Yeah, babe, I know."

CHAPTER EIGHT

King

EVERY BIKER HAS a love affair with the road. It's the rush of the wind kissin' love bites into your cheeks, the pull of it in your hair like a lover's familiar fingers, the thrum of the bike between you and the rushin' asphalt; akin to ridin' a chargin' horse into battle, both dangerous and heady. I hooted into the cold night air just to taste the ocean brine on my tongue. Nova cried out behind me, ridin' gunner in our formation with me as road captain at the lead for the first time since I started prospectin'. We were all high on the ride, eatin' up miles under our treads and still yearnin' for more. We would never be satisfied with a life off a bike, and that, more than the leather and the cussin' and the clubhouse, was what made a man a biker.

My euphoria over the ride was tempered, though, by the fight that had broken out earlier when I'd told the brothers in church 'bout my plan to offset the ambush.

The old guard were vehemently opposed to what they called my 'dumbass, arrogant' plan. They wanted to vote to call off the drug run entirely.

Safe, easy, obvious.

The prerequisites for any decision they made.

I was not, as a rule, a fan of any'a those things.

Yeah, my plan was reckless and ballsy, but it was also damned clever.

If we could follow the Berserkers after they grabbed our herb, we could discover their warehouse and get an even bigger payout while also deliverin' a valuable fuckin' lesson in not messin' with The Fallen MC.

I wasn't a fully patched-in member, so I wasn't allowed to witness the vote let alone cast my own. So, while I'd waited in the bar with Ransom yet again, like some kids in timeout, I'd been frustrated and angry thinkin' my plan wouldn't pass.

I was fuckin' thrilled when Zeus opened the carved chapel doors to announce they'd voted in my favour. It didn't take a genius to figure out he and Axe-Man had been the two to flip on the older contingent.

Still, winnin' was sour grapes 'cause Skell, Heckler, Buck, and Wiseguy were not fuckin' happy with me when they walked out to straddle their hogs to get down the mountain as part of the faction that would follow the Berserkers to their store house.

Zeus had slapped me on the back and ordered Ransom to pour me a beer. "Wanna be callin' shots, you gotta be prepared to get the odd stray bullet to your gut."

"Great," I'd muttered into my beer, unused to havin' people be angry with me.

"You get used to it. 'Sides, those old motherfuckers got short memories."

I grinned as I accelerated, rememberin' the way my old man had winked and laughed. Joinin' up with The Fallen had been the right decision, and I knew it every time I gotta sit with my dad and shoot the shit with him like it was part of my job. 'Cause it *was*. If I'd gotten employment outside'a the club, he woulda loved me just the same, but I woulda missed out on talkin' to him in any kinda real way, 'cause even the Prez's son was exempt from club business if he wasn't a member, and that club was Zeus's life, after Lou.

I was sick and fuckin' tired of bein' left outta the decision makin', though, which was why tonight was a massive gamble that absolutely fuckin' had to pay off.

There was a discernable shift in the energy of the crew as we neared Exit 78 and the scene of the ambush. We'd decided to go down real easy, lull 'em into a false sense of security so they wouldn't be hyper vigilant, checkin' their tails on the way back to Vancouver.

It went against the grain for us. In a sense, we were a pack of animals, loyal to our brothers, but vicious as hell when outsiders intruded on our territory. Only the least temperamental men rode with me tonight—Axe-Man, Curtains, Nova, and Cyclops—'cause it took a special breed of man to take a hit and roll with it instead'a fightin' back.

Just 'fore we hit the exit, I held up a fist and called out, "Live free, die hard!"

Our club motto was echoed back to me over the howl of the wind, and moments later, they were on us.

It was a dark night, the moon obscured by filmy clouds, the ocean refractin' the anemic light like a dull mirror so that we could see the grainy outline of the sheer cliffs to our left and the drop to the water below on our right.

Perfect weather to stage an ambush.

The Berserkers were suddenly in front of us, a dozen men

appearin' like demons outta the shadows, forcin' us to come to sudden, grindin' halts that sent our bikes careenin' into the asphalt. The road tore up my right side, rippin' through the denim like sharp teeth, scrapin' up my side with burnin' claws. I gritted my teeth as I kicked free of my Harley 'fore it could crush me and rolled with my momentum until I landed in a kneelin' position.

The fightin' at my back had already started, the dull *thwack* of fists against flesh and grunts of exertion as my brothers fought our enemy.

I braced on my torn-up knee and pushed to my feet, hissin' at the fiery burn of road rash down my side. The base of my spine tingled with premonition, and I spun 'round in a crouch, knife in hand, to face the two men who were creepin' up on me.

One, thank fuck, was Wrath.

He stared at me with the cold eyes of a killer, his face filled with savagery as if the taste of fightin' in the air had infected him with rabid intent.

For a second, I thought maybe he'd fuckin' turned on me.

In the next, I shifted slightly so my left side was visible only to him, and I winked.

Even in the dark, even with adrenaline fuzzin' the edges of my vision, I saw his lips twitch.

Yeah, Wrath Marsden was with me.

So, I angled my body toward the other biker, readyin' for anythin' 'cause the 'serkers were fuckin' crazy.

Only, it wasn't a Berserker wearin' a leather cut and motorcycle boots, but the one man other than my father I could say had a hand in raisin' me.

Lionel Danner.

I blinked, tryin' to right the palimpsest my vision made of him three years ago when I'd last locked eyes on the man and he'd been as he always was, stern, decked out in western Canadian style denim on denim with aviators tucked forever in his shirt, to the guy wearin' a leather cut and steel-toed motorcycle boots as if he was born in 'em.

I'd known logically that there was a chance'a seein' Lion, given he was undercover with the 'serkers, but I was still shocked as shit by the sight'a him as rough and tumble as any biker I'd ever seen and totally at ease with it.

He looked shell shocked by the sight of me, too, and when Wrath stepped forward to attack me, Lion took a step, too, as if to stop him.

I kept an eye on Lion as Wrath swung and connected *hard* with my right cheek. Pain blasted through my eye and sinuses sendin' explosive, bright and colourful bursts behind my closed lids. Forcin' my eyes open against the ache, I launched myself at Wrath, pushin' down the laughter tryin' to escape my chest as we grappled. It reminded me of bein' a boy, wrestlin' with Mute, tusslin' and inflictin' pain but only enough to score a point.

That was what Wrath and I did for a few minutes, exchangin' blows, aimin' away from the tender places, but givin' it good when we landed a punch. At some point, Lion moved away to join the fight, and it was only us battlin' at the edge of the fray.

"Quit fuckin' smilin' like a goon," Wrath grumbled as I connected with his chin and sent him stumblin' backward. "You wanna give us away?"

I swallowed the metallic taste of adrenaline off my tongue and bit the corner of my lip to halt my smile 'fore it could form again.

"Now, you fuckin' get *down* and stay down. Grease and Mutt're leadin' this pack, and they're crazy ass motherfuckers," Wrath ordered.

Obligingly, I took his next hit on the chin and went down like a ton'a bricks. Just so happened the hand I had flopped over my chest was arranged so that my middle finger was raised to Wrath.

My blood went hot then cold with dread when a gunshot sliced through the silent night, reverberatin' off the cliffs and out over the ocean.

Who the hell had they shot?

If they'd killed one'a my brothers, this plan would be dead in the water and I'd murder every last one'a those motherfuckers.

"Down," Wrath growled, shovin' me to the ground then turnin' on his boot to run toward the rest of his club who were huddled 'round a moanin' body.

I'd never been happier to hear moans of pain, 'cause it meant no one was dead.

Not yet, at least.

Still on the ground, I watched as Grease, the Berserkers VP, rallied his guys together along with three bags of our shit, ordered Wrath and Lion to do the clean-up, then took off as the sound of sirens began to wail faintly from up north.

As soon as the grumble of bikes receded to a low purr, I shot to my feet despite the ache in my body and jogged over to my fallen brother.

Wrath intercepted me 'fore I could reach him with a strong grip on my arm.

"That went off without a hitch."

"You call a brother of mine gettin' hit, goin' off without a hitch?" I asked, my raised brows cuttin' lines in my forehead. "You forget if things go your way, that man moanin' on the ground will be your brother too?"

"Didn't forget," Wrath said with an eye roll. "You're just bein' overprotective. So, he got a little bullet wound. He'll live."

I shoved past him, eager to make sure everythin' was gonna be fine with my Fallen brethren.

Lion was already crouched over Axe-Man, slappin' lightly at his face to rouse him from his pain-induced stupor.

"Fuck," the massive blond man wheezed as he came to. "Fuck you, ya fuckin' 'serker."

"Shut the fuck up, and put pressure on your damn shoulder. The cops are comin', and they'll getcha to the hospital," Lion ordered in that stern voice I recognized, but with the slang of a biker.

"Fuck you," Axe-Man repeated 'fore launchin' a wet missile of spit at Lion's shocked face. "Not goin' to the hospital for a fuckin' flesh wound."

Lion wiped his cheek roughly then cursed under his breath and turned toward us, carefully rearrangin' his features when we locked eyes. The man'd always been private, reserved to the point of coldness and unflappably polite.

It would've been fair to say few people really knew the man he was beneath the good guy, gentleman cop persona, but I did.

And so did Harleigh Rose.

In fact, if anyone knew Lionel Danner, it was my little sister, and if anyone loved him better than anyone else, it would've been her too.

"Thanks, man," I grumbled to Wrath, pissed Axe-Man was hurt even though it wasn't his fault. "Did you have to hit me so fuckin' hard, though?"

The mammoth masqueradin' as Axe-Man shrugged, shoulders 'bout ready to rip through his tee. "Had to look the part."

"Yeah, well don't think anyone's gonna be the wiser the way you clocked me. Jesus, gonna have a headache for a week after this. Cress is *not* gonna be happy with the shiner." Which wasn't exactly true. My girl hated to see me hurt, but she also gotta helluva rush from takin' a fuckin' from me after I'd been out on a run and the animalistic side'a me was pushed to the forefront.

"What the fuck is goin' on here?" Lion finally asked after watchin' us like a novice at his first tennis match.

I swallowed my laughter, but it still coloured my tone when I said, "Good to see ya, man. Gotta say, like the leather better than the Canadian cowboy look you usually got goin' on."

"What the fuck?" he repeated, confusion evident in his expression.

This time, it couldn't be helped. Laughter coiled in my belly and sprung forth so loudly, I had to tip my head back and clutch my side to keep upright.

Recovered, I wiped a tear from my eye and grinned at him, tryin' not to chuckle again at the irritated bewilderment stamped on his face. "Yeah, I bet you're thinkin' what the fuck right 'bout now, but we don't got time to clue you in. I gotta see if Axe-Man's gonna make it, and you two gotta get the fuck outta here."

Wrath grunted in affirmation and stalked off. I made to do the same but stopped shoulder to shoulder beside Lion first, lockin' eyes with him.

"Good to see ya, Danny," I murmured, usin' the nickname my twelve-year old self had given him. "Stay safe, yeah?"

"Lion, get movin'!" Wrath hollered from down the hill where they'd stashed their rides, and I took it as my cue to get a move on too.

Axe-Man was fine. The bullet had gone through and through, just under his lat muscle, and after we tied his bad arm down to the handle, he was able to ride back to Entrance on his own bike.

We took the back roads up the mountain, passin' the cops racin' down to the scene just through a copse of trees, makin' it safely back to the clubhouse in no time. As soon as I walked through the door, Ransom was handin' me his cell.

"Sup?" I asked, pinnin' it between my ear and my shoulder as I reached over the bar to grab the cold beer waitin' for someone else on the counter.

"We got 'em," Bat pronounced, dark glee evident in his voice. "We fuckin' got 'em."

I cracked open the beer usin' the side'a the counter and lifted it into the air 'fore cryin' out to the boys in the clubhouse. "We got 'em!"

A rally of cheers rose from the dozen men surroundin' me as beers were quickly handed out and someone turned up the music, Esterly's "This Is My World" screamin' through the air.

"How much?" I shouted over the noise 'fore takin' a pull of my beer.

Energy coursed through me, jerkin' my knee as I sat on the stool, vitality thrummin' through my fingers as I drummed them against the bar top. This was why the club always had women on hand, biker bunnies who hung 'round 'cause they liked the taste of men in leather and the feel of all the rough and wild between their thighs. The brothers could plug that excess energy after a ride or a fight into their outlet and finally come down from the high.

Needed somethin' to take my mind off shit, so I could focus on what needed to be done next then get back home to my woman.

One'a the girls, a gorgeous red head I'd once messed 'round with named Tempest Riley, caught my eye from across the room and jerked her head up in question.

Cell still to my ear, I looked away, not botherin' to acknowledge her.

Everyone knew Cress was it for me, but it didn't stop some of 'em from tryin'.

"Near three hundred pounds of green and a motherfuckin' arsenal of guns. Seems the rumours are true, and they got an in with the Port Authority to smuggle this shit through the harbour."

"Fuck." The Fallen didn't deal in anythin' but primo marijuana. We grew it, sold it, and distributed it from sea to shinin' fuckin' sea. They were apeshit for it over in China, and it was even in hot demand across the world in Australia. Zeus started this gig when he cleaned up the club after his uncle Crux got our club involved in some fucked up enterprises, and it was a gig we were all good with. We made cake, and we didn't have to deal with the moral or physical fallout associated with the harder stuff.

But weapons… those could be sold for a tidy profit or, even better maybe, stockpiled in case'a Armageddon.

"What's Z say 'bout the guns?" I asked.

"We'll take some, not all. We don't got the kinda apparatus to deal arms."

"True, and I gotta feelin' the Vancouver PD are lurkin' 'round the 'serkers. Best leave somethin' to be found, yeah?"

Bat was quiet for a beat, readin' into what I wasn't sayin' in the way he could. He was a former SEAL and one'a the smartest men I knew. Had no doubt in my mind he knew I was keepin' secrets, he just respected me enough to let me hold 'em close for now.

"Wrappin' things up. Be back 'round three in the mornin', Z wants everyone at church for 10am."

"Will do, brother. Stay safe."

"Yeah. And King? Well done, brother. A gamble, but well fuckin' worth it. Wish I'd been the one to think it up," he praised.

And I felt that, the praise like water and sunlight on the small tree of pride growin' up my spine. I was learnin' my place, *earnin'* my place in the club with men who had raised me, inspired me, and fuckin' loved me since I was a boy. It felt good. No, it felt like comin' home to have that kinda respect from men I'd always seen as leather backed heroes.

"Thanks, man," I murmured, tryin' to keep the ache outta my voice then decidin' I didn't give a shit if he knew how much I cared, 'cause he deserved to know I loved him. "Means a lot."

"Means a lot you came home in the end," he countered and then, as was his way, abruptly hung up.

"Hey, brothers!" Curtains hollered from near the pool

tables as red and blue lights started to flash against the walls. "Think we got some company."

"Fuck," I muttered as I slammed my beer down and prowled to the door, Nova and Cy followin' into step on either side'a me.

There were two police cars parked at angles in the driveway behind the chain-link gates that separated our compound from the road, and Staff Sergeant Danner stood 'fore them, hands on his hips, eyes hot on me even from across the yards of pavement.

"Need somethin' Harold?" I called out, stayin' on the doorstep instead'a goin' to him like he woulda wanted.

"Got a call about a turf war out near Exit-78. Reports of shots fired and motorbikes. You know anything about that?"

"Hmm," I rubbed my hand over my stubbled chin as I faux-pondered. "Nah, not likely. We've been holed up here celebratin' Nova finally sleepin' with a girl from Nigeria."

"Doin' the 'round the world challenge," Nova drawled as he took a seat on the stairs and sprawled out. "Hit ninety-seven countries so far. Gotta taste for somethin' Nordic next."

One'a the officers waitin' with Danner choked on his laugh as he swallowed it down.

"Cut the crap," Danner shouted. "We're checking hospitals. There was blood found at the scene, so I'm guessing one of yours or the other was hurt badly. When we find the hit biker, we'll know the truth."

"You do that, Danner," I agreed easily, 'cause Axe-Man was currently in one'a the closed garage bays bein' seen to by Dr. Ross who'd been on Fallen payroll for decades. Doc was losin' his eyesight, but it was better than nothin'. "Give us a call, you need help with your investigation."

The fumes of anger between us turned the air waxy with the heat of his hatred. Danner stood there, braced, itchin' so fiercely for a fight I wondered if he'd break down the gate and come at me.

Finally, he turned and got back into his cruiser.

The other car lingered as Danner drove away, and I realized why when Gibson emerged from the car with Hutchinson, the only two cops left that were even mildly friendly to The Fallen.

For them, I got my ass in gear and went to meet 'em at the gates. Gibson's face was contoured with turmoil, and Hutchinson looked close to panic as he pressed his cheek to the fence.

"Danner's got a tip on one of your locations," Hutchinson hissed. "Apparently, someone called in about a suspected grow-op in the mountains near Squamish."

Gibson held a hand up before I could say a thing. "I don't want to know whether or not that place is real or yours or what. I don't even want to be here to tell you this …this goes against everything I've previously believed in, but, fuck, I don't sanction the way SS Danner is coming after you, and I don't think you're all as evil as you might seem. You especially, not if Lion raised you."

I peered through the shadows at Riley Gibson, really seein' him for the first time ever. His skin was pale and crumpled like used waxed paper, unhealthy and exhausted, no doubt from sleepless nights ponderin' his morality. He was the kinda man, like Lion, who's conscience weighed heavy on his soul, and I knew whatever Danner was plannin' for the club had to be fuckin' *dark* to get Gibson on our side.

I nodded curtly and stuck my hands in my pockets as I rocked back on my heels. "Appreciate the call, boys.

Hutchinson tipped his chin, knowin' he'd wake up in the mornin' to a shit ton'a grade A weed on his doorstep, like a gift from the fuckin' tooth fairy. Payment for his aid.

But Gibson hesitated, so conflicted I could see war clashin' in his eyes despite the night's darkness.

"You gonna be good to handle it?" he questioned quietly,

eyes dartin' over my shoulder to the brothers who waited on the stoop of the clubhouse.

I waited until his gaze locked with mine so he could see straight down through to my soul. "Nothin' is all black or all white, Gibson. Mighta hurt you to come give me the knowledge, but you gotta know, this place and these people here aren't 'bout chaos and murder and wrongness. Yeah, we got our own code, but the cornerstones of that are loyalty and brotherhood. You just helped us out? Means one day, somehow, we'll repay the debt. Don't worry 'bout bein' found in bed with us, either. Not one'a us is a nark, least of all me, not to a man like you, not to a friend of Lion's, yeah?"

The cop let out a shaky breath then gave me a smirk like a twisted wire, mangled and wrong. "Trying to stop a war, you know?"

My hard chuckle was as brutal as the cockin' of a barrel. "Yeah, man. Though, gotta feelin' it'll happen whether we want it to or not."

CHAPTER NINE

King

THERE'S A TIME DURIN' the earliest hours of the mornin' when the night's at its darkest and the stars begin to dim, when only the wicked and the rebels are awake. It was that hour at The Fallen compound, chapel was full to burstin' with all twenty-two men of the Entrance Chapter squeezed into the long room, sittin' in hand carved chairs with wings at their backs, or standin' against the wood paneled walls. A lone yellow light swayed over the oak slab table, castin' shadows that obscured the brothers' faces like masks, lendin' an eerie, demonic quality to the meetin' as if Zeus was Satan leadin' a meetin' of hell's lords.

I dragged in a deep lungful of the tobacco, leather, and pine-scented air, feelin' the nostalgia of it in my chest.

"We plannin' on tellin' those fuckers exactly who stole their loot?" Skell asked, leanin' forward to make eye contact with Zeus. "They should know what happens to those who cross The Fallen."

Zeus snorted. "Don't ya worry 'bout that. Priest left their lookouts nasty little reminders right across their damned foreheads."

Priest's grin sliced across his face, teeth shinin' in the light cast by the blade he twirled in his tattooed fingers. "Carved it right into their skin."

"Buck, you'll take Wiseguy, Heckler, and Boner to organize the new product in the Grouse warehouse tomorrow. Brace for retaliation, boys, but I'm thinkin' the Berserker bastards have a lot on their hands right fuckin' now, and we won't see shit all from 'em."

"And the fuckin' pigs sniffin' 'round the grow-op?" Heckler mumbled 'round the cigarette clamped between his teeth.

My smile was just as sharp as the knife Priest played between his hands as I said, "Got the Porter boys up there now pourin' concrete over the hatch in the shed. That'll keep 'em out. The workers can make their way outta the underground on the other side'a the mountain through an old minin' cave."

"It'll have time to set?" Bat asked.

Jerkin' my chin up, I answered. "It's a Friday, and they just got the tip this mornin'. Danner'll still have to wrangle a warrant and dot all his fuckin' I's 'fore he can get up there. It'll dry by Monday."

"Criminal prodigy over here," Boner crowed, wigglin' his fingers over me like a magician workin' magic.

"If ya'd put it to the club, anyone could'a come up with that idea," Buck reasoned, and I tried not to take it personal.

He was an old guy, mired in old ways, but I knew he still thought of me like a grandson.

"Or a better one," Wiseguy muttered, livin' up to his name in ways I did not fuckin' like.

"'S a good idea, and it's rollin' out," Zeus said, stoppin' the grumblin' 'fore it could roll into somethin' bigger. "Keep in touch with the Porter boys, and go up with Axe-Man to see it's done right 'fore the weekend's over, yeah?" I nodded. "Now, I got a woman keepin' my bed warm at home, so let's wrap it up."

There was a rumble of agreement as everyone shifted, readyin' to leave, but I stood up 'fore they got the chance and cleared my throat.

"Prez, wanna chance to say somethin', it's cool with you?" I addressed Zeus, who didn't look even a little surprised.

He inclined his head, rings clinkin' as he linked his hands and sank back in his chair. "Let's 'ear it."

"Mean no disrespect by sayin' it, but I gotta. This was my plan tonight. Plan that landed us over three hundred pounds'a weed and a fuck ton'a guns, not to mention providin' a serious blow to those motherfuckers. Near on half of you wanted to toss it 'fore even considerin' the idea, and I get it, I bring some radical notions to this club. Might not make you comfortable, but I just proved sure as shit that they can work. Been prospectin' for well over a year now, and yeah, I know there's no time limit on provin' loyalty, but fuck me, brothers. I was born with Fallen blood, raised by a man who'd give his life for the club, and I've grown into a man who knows without the shadow of a fuckin' doubt that my life is here with the club."

I took a deep breath, fisted my hands and leaned into them over the table so I could look each of the men in the eye. "Now, I'm thinkin' it's time you proved me right and patched me in as a full member."

Priest grinned manically at me, Axe-Man crossed his arms and sat back in his seat with a small grin in his beard, Boner started slow clappin' like the lovable idiot he was, and Nova thumped his hand on the table 'fore hootin', "Damn straight!"

Zeus cleared his throat, and the room went quiet as they waited for him to pass judgement on my speech. It was a gutsy move, makin' a speech like that to men who didn't like to be told what to do or when to do it by anyone other than their Prez, but it had to be done.

I was chompin' at the bit, and I needed this shit sorted so I could move on with my life.

With my plans for Cress and me.

Zeus steepled his hands, eyes on his weddin' band then up at me, the grey opaque as concrete. "You gonna marry your woman?"

Seemed like a non-sequitur, but it was the one reason he hadn't brought me in sooner, and I respected the question.

I couldn't keep my girl separate or shielded from my life choices. She was my partner, and she'd been my rough and tumble queen for a lot longer than I'd originally given her credit for.

Jerked my chin up, pulled the ring box outta my pocket, and tossed it over the table to him. "That pass inspection?"

His eyes stayed on me as he scooped it up and flipped it open, then they caught on the bright shine of the massive square cut emerald framed by two rectangular diamonds. He touched it gently with his thumb then looked back up at me.

"Bein' an outlaw doesn't work out well for ya, you should go into jewelry," he deadpanned.

The joke shattered the tension like a fist through glass, and everyone laughed as he tossed the box back to me, and I put it in my pocket.

"Alright, King, you wanted it, you got it. Unless anyone's got an objection, brothers, prepare the garage."

Half hour later, the club was crowded into one'a the garage bays that had been cleaned out to make room for the ceremony. I say ceremony, but that was too religious and organized a word for the way The Fallen recognized a new brother.

I was on my knees, shirtless and waitin' while the brothers formed a circle 'round me. Even Axe-Man was there, cleaned up and bandaged tight by Doc, because the ceremony couldn't be done without all'a the brothers present. The cement was cold and hard, uncomfortable, but I didn't even think of complainin' 'cause this, right here, was what I'd always wanted.

"King Kyle Garro, prospect of The Fallen brotherhood, do you pledge your body, blood, and life to this club?"

There was a solemnity to Zeus's voice, a gravity I could feel tyin' me to the floor, keepin' me on my knees even if I had wanted to stand.

"Yeah," I said, my voice comin' from my gut.

"You swear to live free, die hard, and act in the best interest of this club 'fore all else?"

My head was bent, gaze trained on the grease stains in the brushed concrete floor, but I was thinkin' 'bout the knife I knew Z was palmin' and readyin' over his exposed palm. The rituals of initiation were sacred, not spoken 'bout, even between brothers, outside'a these moments. But I knew this part 'cause I'd been curious 'bout the slanted scar across Dad's palm as a kid, and he'd told me 'bout it.

"Yeah," I agreed again and felt a surge of energy crackle through the room, sparkin' from brother to brother as they encircled me.

"Does each man standin' agree to take King into the fold and see him as a brother from 'ere on in?"

There was a stompin' of motorcycle boots against the ground, the vibration travellin' through my bones until I reverberated with it.

In answer, Zeus sliced his palm open with the wicked end of his knife and squeezed until blood ran down his wrist into a waitin' metal cup branded with The Fallen emblem. One by one, the brothers passed the cup along, addin' their blood, their life to it, until it reached Zeus again. I tipped my head up when he stepped in front of me and watched as his fingers dipped in the blood.

"The Fallen is for life," he reminded me as his red, wet fingers smeared over my cheekbones, across my nose, then down from my forehead to my chin in a bloody desecration of a cross. Finished annoitin' me, he moved back and said, pride blastin' through his voice, "King Kyle Garro, awake, arise, and be forever Fallen."

I got to one knee then stood at the center of my brothers, my family, finally and irrevocably one'a them.

"Welcome to the fold," Zeus said with a wide, almost manic grin.

"'Bout fuckin' time," Nova called out then set the hose on me, cold water blastin' into my chest.

I laughed as it cleansed me the way it was supposed to, a biker baptism of blood and water in a house of iron.

Shakin' my wet hair outta my eyes like a dog, I grinned at my brothers and yelled, "Live free, die hard."

"Fuck yeah!" they roared and then they were on me, punchin' me, huggin' me, shakin' me, hands on me in the final step of acceptance, in a show of love and loyalty I felt like was carved into my bones.

Fuckin' finally, I was truly Fallen.

CHAPTER TEN

Cressida

"CRESS, BABE, WAKE UP."

I moaned, still caught in the tendrils of a fragrant dream and unwilling to embrace wakefulness. Shadow meowed quietly near my face, and I realized my cheek was pressed into his fur.

"Cress, do as your man says," King's voice said against my ear, and then I registered the feel of his hands sliding up his oversized tee against my back. "I've got somethin' to show you."

Even half-asleep the sweet call of King's voice was too irresistible to ignore. I rolled languidly onto my back, tangled up in the soft bedclothes, Shadow hissing in protest as I dislodged him. I was arrested at the sight of King sitting over me.

His chaos of blond kinks and curls hung in his face, partially shading those extraordinary glacial water eyes, crinkled at the corners with pleasure as he looked down on me, the sentiment echoed in the curled set of his full mouth.

"Gosh, you're beautiful," I breathed, because I couldn't help it.

My hand went to his cheek, fingers sliding through his silky hair, just to feel the realness of him. He smiled as he grabbed my hand and brought my palm to his mouth to kiss.

"Come, I don't wanna miss it."

"Miss what? It's got to be the middle of the night."

"Not quite, and that's all I'm gonna say. Get dressed."

I grumbled but did as he asked, shivering at the cold nip in the air as I shed my tee and slipped on an easy pleated dress. King whistled as I quickly ran a comb through my hair and brushed my teeth.

"You're awfully cheery for so early in the morning," I mumbled through my toothpaste before I leaned over and rinsed.

King's hands found my hips, and he pressed his groin to my bent behind. "Got a good woman, the *best* woman, in my bed, a club of brothers at my back, and a house we made together into a home. How can you doubt my cheer?"

I met his gaze in the mirror, sass softening under his warm regard. "I'll remind you of that whenever you get grumpy."

"Never grumpy," he countered, scowling at the use of the word. "When the fuck have I been grumpy?"

"Um, maybe right now?"

He chuckled and landed a swat on my ass. "Will be if you don't hurry this fine ass up. Meet you downstairs in one minute, or I'm comin' up and takin' you over my shoulder."

I tipped my chin. "Maybe I need two minutes."

He dropped his head back between his shoulders as if

beseeching God for patience and then ducked quickly, wrapping his long arms around my legs and lifting me up over his shoulder as if I weighed no more than a sack of rice.

"King!" I protested through my laughter as he moved out of the bathroom and onto the landing at the top of the stairs. "Put me down!"

He spanked me once, twice, and then hooted as he pounded down the stairs, straight out the door of the cottage. He dumped me in my Honda, to my surprise, closed the door before I could say a word, then jogged back to the house.

I touched my face just to feel the breadth of the smile there then sighed as I leaned my head back and closed my eyes.

"This is your life," I told myself. "This is real."

Because sometimes I needed to hear it aloud. I needed to remember that this man and the family that'd adopted me through him were real, alive, and mine.

I started as the backdoor opened, King swinging a bag onto the seat before he rounded to the driver's seat. It never ceased to amaze me how delicious he looked driving my girly pink car. It seemed to emphasize his sheer size and manliness instead of undercutting it.

I smiled at him as he adjusted the seat and brought up the song 'You and I" by Barns Courtney. He tinkered with the rear-view mirror then turned his gaze to me.

"Ya ready, babe?"

"Honestly, why do you even ask? You know I'd follow you anywhere," I admitted, blushing because I couldn't seem to quit the habit.

King chuckled, planting a hand on my thigh as he began to drive us through the dark, empty streets of Entrance. We were quiet for a time, but my curiosity eventually got the better of me. As an Old Lady, I wasn't entitled to know much about the goings-on in the club, but King was the type of man who didn't mind sharing with me most of the time, and I felt lucky for it.

"Did you sleep at all?"

"Nah, but for good reason. Dealt with the Berserker problem fuckin' beautifully, and now you're lookin' at the newest fully patched member of The Fallen MC Entrance Chapter."

Instantly, I squealed, drawing my legs onto the seat so I could sit on my knees and lean across the console to wrap my arms around his neck and pepper his cheek with kisses.

"King, this is *fab*! Like holy freaking *wow*! I am just so thrilled and beyond proud of you! It's like a promotion at work only so much better because this is like…the family business, and I am just. So. Flipping. Happy!"

He chuckled, bracing against my attack. "Sit your ass back down, or at least get outta my face, babe. Can't see to drive, and not crashin' this cage with precious cargo in it."

"Oh, fine. But you should know, I think this is deserving of something special," I announced as I flounced back down in my seat. "What do you want?"

"What do I always want?" he asked with a salacious grin as he parked the car in the shadows of a dead end.

"Sex."

"Mmm." He crossed his arms over the steering wheel and waggled his brows. "So, what's on offer exactly?"

Heat sluiced over me like a bucket of warm water. I wriggled in my seat some and bit my lip. "Whatever you want."

"Givin' me a lot to think 'bout, babe," he teased. "Now, c'mon."

I followed him out of the car, waited for him to retrieve the bag from the back, and then snagged his hand as he led us off the road through a barely trodden path in the bushes until we emerged in a clearing.

I knew the cliff we stood on because King had spoken of it often. It overlooked the caramel sanded half-moon of

Entrance Bay from its farthest right corner and offered spectacular views of the snow-capped, towering mountains across the ocean.

I'd never been there before. We had talked about it a few times, but I respected that this was King's special place with Mute, their haven away from home where they could hang out and do whatever it was boys did as they grew older. I could easily picture them there at the horrifying edge of earth, legs dangling over the abyss, shoving at each other when they laughed as if they weren't suspended from a terrifying height.

The grass was long and slightly damp in the weak light of the pre-dawn washing across the sky, but King led us through it to nearly the very edge before he let go of my hand to unearth a large blanket from the bag. He spread it out for us then dropped to his knees to retrieve my well-worn copy of *Paradise Lost*, a thermos, a container of berries, and his current brown leather notebook.

"Sit," he urged with that boyish smile I'd first caved into temptation for. "Watch the sunrise with me."

I folded to the ground beside him then giggled when he flopped down on top of me, wrapping me up in his limbs as if I was a present and he the ribbon. I curled my legs around his narrow hips and smiled into his face as he drew his thumb gently over my brows.

"What are you looking at?" I asked, as his eyes tracked over my face. I counted the dips and craters of vivid blue in his irises, wondering if I had the topography of them memorized yet.

"Only girl I ever wanted," he said somberly.

"I've never really been a girl to you." I laughed. "I'm still eight years older than you, even if it doesn't seem like such a difference now that I don't actually teach you."

"Still teach me every day, babe. One'a the reasons I love you. 'Cause I gotta curious mind that needs stimulatin', and you've gotta mind like a vortex, no matter how far down I go, you never end, and I getta keep on learnin'."

"I'll never get used to you so easily saying things like that. Such beautiful words spoken so confidently when you're so young and such a man in every other way."

His eyes narrowed and one thick golden brow arched. "Tellin' you the ways I love you isn't manly?"

"I shouldn't have said it that way. What I meant was, it takes so much courage and self-confidence to give people pieces of your mind and soul the way you do, and you make it look so natural. Most men, alpha men especially I think, have trouble articulating their emotions because they worry it will make them look weak."

King considered my words as he played his fingers over my hairline and down the side of my face. He was a tactile man, almost as expressive with his touch as he was with his poetry.

"It's ironic, then, for men to let themselves get caught up in what people could think, robbin' themselves of love and praise, the gift of givin' it and havin' it given back. That's the real weakness."

"I used to be like that," I admitted, thinking of the woman I'd been. The woman who'd been terrified of dating a rebel, of being involved in anything that might be perceived as wrong or risqué.

Now I couldn't imagine a life colouring within the lines. Where was the fun or individual identity in that?

"Did you?" he argued casually, as if his words didn't fundamentally shift my self-perception. "You were reluctant, babe, I'll give ya that. But you still explored your curiosity with me, still took a chance on a man who coulda fucked you over, and then when he didn't, you gave yourself over to me in a way that was a promise. A pledge as solemn as the vow a dogmatist gives his god."

"I didn't really have a choice in it. You utterly beguiled me."

"There's a choice in everythin' we do."

And this was one of the many ways King proved to me every day that he was the most brilliant man I'd ever know. He had the soul of an ancient philosopher, a somber wisdom that didn't seem borne of experience, but birthed from some inner peace he'd been inherently gifted with from some god or fate.

"Roll over," he demanded, already flipping me onto my stomach.

I didn't protest as his hands, rough from working at the garage, moved up my thighs, taking my dress with them until I was forced to lift up so he could take it off over my head. Naked, but for the pale pink, ruffled panties I wore, I lay in the cool air as the sun began to peek over the horizon and hummed as King trailed kisses up my spine, pressing one to each vertebra.

"Speaking of choice," he said as he moved away and collected something else from the bag. I was too content to watch what he was doing, stretching lazily across the cashmere blanket to stretch my fingers in the cool, damp grass. "There's been a decision weighin' on me for a long time, now. A decision I shoulda made a long fuckin' time ago."

"Mmm?" I asked, eyes trained on the meeting of sun and sea as gold began to seep across the water, heralding the sunrise.

King leaned into my side, one hand braced on the other side of my bottom, the other suddenly pressing something faintly wet against my skin. I started to rise, startled by the sensation, but he hushed me and pressed me back down.

"Still remember the first day I met ya. How could I not? Even remember what I ate for breakfast, how the hot air, waxy and chemical from the asphalt and the heat, felt against my face. 'Course, it was the most important day of my fuckin' life. A man doesn't forget shit like that. Not ever."

He continued to move the wet tip against the delicate skin of my back, only now I realized what he was doing. King was often lightning struck with inspiration, grabbing a receipt, a napkin, or the leg of his jeans to use as a canvas for the felt pen he always kept on his person for the poems that rushed to his brain like a spring river bursting from its bank.

He was doing that now, using me as a blank page to carry his beautiful words. I already carried one of his poems tattooed on my ribcage, but I loved this spontaneity, loved feeling like both his muse and his art simultaneously.

"There are only two days as I see it, that could ever top that," he continued, and I closed my eyes to better feel the texture of his lovely voice on my skin. "The day you become my wife and the day you give me our babies."

My body went stiff, overly starched from the shock of his words. We'd spoken idly about marriage and babies, but nothing like this, nothing that opened a new door for our relationship to enter.

A hand stroked down my side while he continued to write, as if he was soothing a spooked horse. Accordingly, his voice gentled.

"Wanna get married at our house, babe. In the clearin' through the trees so when you come to me in your weddin' dress it'll look like just as much of a dream as it'll feel to me gettin' to marry a woman like you."

"Okay," I whispered, afraid to break the tenuous sanctity of the conversation by speaking any louder. "I've thought about that too."

I could hear the answering smile in his voice. "'Course you have, 'cause my girl gets me."

"Are you asking me to marry you?" I ventured, because my heart was a rabid animal trying to break through my chest, and asking was the only way to appease it.

King chuckled lowly as he manhandled me until I was seated in his lap, knees on either side of him and his hands were framing my face. I was practically naked, and he was completely clothed, but the discrepancy felt right somehow. I'd only ever wanted to be bare and vulnerable with this man because he was the only person who'd ever viewed everything I was as a gift.

"Babe, for the last four years, that question has been branded on the edge'a my tongue, and every time I look at you, I get a little more tempted to say it."

"So, why wait?" I tipped my forehead against his and twisted my fingers in his hair while one of his hands found and cupped the back of my neck to hold me to him.

"'Cause you'd only just found the kinda woman you wanted to be and the kinda life you wanted to live. Didn't wanna make either of those all 'bout me, not 'fore you gotta chance to live for yourself."

"I don't think you understand." And I was shocked that he didn't. "But it was through the prism of your love that I found myself and my life in the first place."

"Yeah, I'm gettin' that now," he murmured through a wry smile.

"Not like you to be so slow," I teased, nipping at his lower lip.

"No, so why don't we rectify that right fuckin' now," he suggested.

I shivered as he moved the hand on my neck down my back to trace the words he'd written on my skin as he spoke them to me.

"She was a queen
Raised to sit on a golden throne
In a kingdom of crystal and ice

All I had to offer was my sword of smoke and world of gasoline
With soldiers shielded by leather and coated in tatts

My currency was love and loyalty
In a market that traded in diamonds and class

I would do anything to convince her
That she might have been raised to sit on a golden throne
But she belonged on the seat of iron with a crown of steel
At my side."

I was crying, my entire body moving like the sea with the force of my tremors, but I blinked away the wet so I wouldn't miss a moment of seeing King's handsome face broken open with love for me.

"Cress, you've been my teacher, my lover, my best friend, and my Old Lady. Now, I'm askin' you with everythin' I am to be my wife and queen."

Words drowned in the tidal wave of emotion swamping my belly and throat. I felt almost sick with love, every particle and atom infected with absolute adoration. Dizzying, crying, swooning, I could only cling closer to the strong, beautiful body against me and breathe in the laundry clean, fresh cut grass scent of him.

His hand found the back of my neck in that familiar, possessive hold that anchored me to him, and his hot breath wafted over my ear as he burrowed his nose in my hair. "Takin' that as a yes, Cress, babe."

I pulled my face out of his neck, tears streaming, cheeks flushed, hair tangled by the ocean breeze, as raw on the outside as I was internally. My hands framed his face, those strong planes, cut-glass cheekbones, and plush mouth I'd been immediately seduced by, and I dragged in a steadying breath so I could say what I needed to say and say it strong.

"Not yes, King." A smile tattooed itself between my cheeks in a way that felt permanent, as if the happiness of this moment would be worn on my face for eternity. "*Fuck yeah.*"

I watched light shine through the crust of his tundra blue eyes, absorbing the way they crinkled at the corners, savoring how his pale pink mouth bloomed open into a smile that took my breath away. And then he was tipping his head back to the sky the way he did, throat strong and bronzed as it moved with his delighted laughter.

He crushed me closer, his humour moving through me as profoundly as his proposal, and then he yelled, "Fuck *yeah*!" to the sky as if thanking God for shunning us from Eden so we could find this slice of our heaven on earth together.

"Gonna be my wife," he growled possessively, wrapping his hand around my neck and tugging so I was pinned for his mouth to devour and feast at, slow, intense sweeps of his tongue against mine that left me boneless.

My hands curled in his kinky, silken mass of hair, and I held on tight, along for the ride, always ready to follow King into whatever adventure moved his rebel soul.

I'd been proposed to before, married for seven years to another man, yet I'd never felt even a drop of the passion and overwhelming ardor I harbored for this young, vibrant man I was somehow lucky enough to call mine.

"I've loved you since the moment I saw you," I told him, mouths brushing, tongue swiping against the lush curve of his bottom lip. "And I'll go on loving you forever."

"There's no end to my love for you. It's woven into the very fabric of my soul, so even when our bodies die, we'll still never stop lovin'."

King captured my sob between his lips and kissed me savagely, as if the ruthlessness of our love could eradicate any doubts or any obstacles that might ever cross our path. I tugged him closer still and moaned when he lay me gently on my back to press his weight between my legs. He propped himself up on a bulging forearm and trailed his hot hands between my breasts, over my quivering belly, to dip in the well between my legs where he drew wet circles over my clit.

"Gonna marry you," he murmured, eyes glazed with desire as if he was mesmerized by the sight of me naked and laid out for him. "Gonna marry my girl, and then I'm gonna plant my babies in you."

I moaned, neck arching as he pressed two fingers inside me, preparing me for the large cock lying hard and hot against my thigh.

"Yes," I hissed, clutching his iron shoulders, writhing against his hand. "God, King, please."

"Please what?" he teased cruelly, dipping down to press scalding, open-mouthed kisses to my breasts. "What does my woman need?"

"You, inside me," I begged, tugging at his big belt buckle, diving beneath to undo his fly just enough so I could shove my hand down his pants and palm his dick, giving it a hard squeeze that made him groan.

He moved over me, not taking off his jeans, just tugging out his mouth-watering dick so I could watch as he slotted against my damp center. He braced his forearms on either side of my head and played his fingers over my hair, just resting at my center, his eyes filled with love so tangible that my breath caught in my throat.

"Could spend my life inside ya and never get enough," he admitted then impaled me in a long, smooth stroke that made every inch of me quake. "Love this sweet, snug cunt."

"Yes," I agreed as he started pumping slowly, achingly tender inside me. "Love the feel of you inside me."

And then we were just hushed, stuttering breath, jagged moans, and the soft, wet slide of flesh against damp flesh. The ocean air felt warm between our arching bodies, skin steaming in the cold morning light. The sun finally burst over the edge of the horizon, dousing us in champagne gold as if nature herself was blessing our union.

A coil in the base of my belly twisted tighter, tension higher, until I felt taut as a wire held over a flame, about to fray apart.

"Come for me," King urged, face twisted into painful pleasure as he moved quicker, harder inside me, tugging my leg up and over his shoulder so I was utterly exposed to the ferocity of his movements. "You come for me, Cress, and I'll come deep inside this tight pussy."

"Fuck," I cried, back bowing as pleasure arrowed down my spine and burst through my tender sex, pulsing through so hard that tears leaked from my eyes, mumbled words of thanks and broken prayers tumbling from my slack mouth as I came and came and came for my King.

"Mine, mine, mine," he chanted on each thrust as he wrung every ounce of pleasure from me in search of his own. Fuck yeah, Cress, givin' you my cum."

And then he groaned, head tipped back, throat exposed for me to nibble and suck on as his cock kicked inside me and the hot flood of his cum warmed my insides. I held him close, felt the climax move through him like a tsunami, like the tension before the flood, the devastation wrought on his body until he was limp and satiated, damp and panting in my arms. He gave me his full weight, knowing I loved the gentle crush, as he pressed lazy, easy kisses against my cheek. As we spiraled down from the heights of our pleasure, I felt conjoined with him, flesh fused, hearts tangled so tight I couldn't dream of there being even an inch between our chests. I coveted the closeness because my whole life I'd yearned for someone to know me, from the darkest corners of my sexed brain and morally ambiguous heart, to the brightest echelons of my wisest thoughts and deepest dreams. There wasn't a part of me this man didn't know and love, and to be so wholly consumed by someone as beautiful straight through to the soul as King was, was better than anything else.

When he shifted to the side, I murmured in protest, half-asleep, half-drunk on the warming sunlight and the new satisfaction in my previously restless soul.

He hushed me, reaching for his back, then hauling me over his chest so that I could watch as he slid something onto the base of my left ring finger.

I gaped at the huge emerald, square cut and regal between a frame of diamonds as clear as mirrors flashing in the sun.

"Fallen colours for my Fallen girl," he explained, kissing the ring before resting our tangled hands against his heart.

"It's perfect. You're perfect."

"Nah, not really. But don't care much for perfection, in general. Only gotta be perfect for you."

I rubbed my cheek into his sternum like a cat and arched under the hand that stroked down my back.

"I didn't realize how much I needed this," I admitted. "Not that I wasn't happy, but I was so ready to take the next step."

King made a grunting noise of distress. "Sorry, babe, it took me a beat to work my way 'round to it. Didn't want you to feel like you were makin' a mistake."

"How could you ever believe I'd think that?"

"Worried, I guess. I'm Fallen now, and don't much like the thought'a my woman with a husband in jail or dead."

And there it was, that secret sliver of insecurity that pierced King straight through to his heart. I blamed his evil mother for never loving him the way she should have, and it made me want to weep to know he'd bear those scars for life.

"You're not your mother or your father, King. Even if you don't believe you'll make good choices, *I* do. And I hope you know by now, I've grown into the type of woman that wouldn't blink at visiting you in prison if I had to, that wouldn't ever turn her back on you just because *we* decided on a life of freedom and rebellion. Remember, it was Eve who made the decision to leave Eden, not Adam."

He chuckled as he twisted my hair between his fingers,

watching the strands catch the light. "*I form'd them free, and free they must remain*," I quoted from Paradise Lost.

"Free together," I agreed.

"We have a girl first," King told me, "namin' her Eve."

My heart turned over in my chest at the beauty of that. "Okay."

"Boy, it's Lucien."

"Our little Satan?" I laughed.

"Our little morning star," he corrected.

"I was thinking Prince," I admitted. "I've got a collector's edition of *The Prince* at the shop I was waiting to give you once you were patched in. The art of manipulation should come in handy with all those alpha males you've got to round up."

He laughed, forcing me to hang on to his chest so I wouldn't fall off. "Prince, son of King, you know Zeus'll love that."

I did. It was one of the reasons I loved it so much.

"Okay, babe, Prince it is."

"I like Lucien too, though."

His grin was wicked as he rolled me back over and spread my legs, a hand sliding down to play in his cum as it leaked out of me. "Don't worry, babe, gotta feelin' we'll have a fuckin' baseball team'a kids by the time I get tired'a plantin' my babies inside ya."

I laughed as he kissed my neck, clutching him to me, accepting him into my body again and thinking with absolute certainty that he was right.

CHAPTER ELEVEN

King

HE TIMED IT.

The motherfucker.

SS Danner purposely raided our storehouse so it'd interfere with the openin' of Cressida's bookstore, assumin' all the brothers would be preoccupied, feel conflicted 'bout leavin' when they found out.

Only we weren't conflicted 'cause my woman wasn't.

"Go," she said instantly when Zeus relayed the phone call from Gibson, explainin' that the police had just pulled up to our storehouse outside Squamish. "Go and show that bastard how much smarter you are than him."

It was a big fuckin' day for my woman. Paradise Found was a symbol of all the growth she'd made and all the ways she'd flourished since she changed her life to live it free of her family's expectations. The store was fuckin' perfect from the bottom of the glossed floor to the waxed beams gleamin' on the ceilin'. And it was finally time, after months of hard work, for Entrance to see exactly how special my Cress was. This place wasn't meant to be just a store to buy books, but a home for anyone with a sense of loss that needed to be found, whether that was in the pages of a book, a chat sittin' on leather with friends, or talkin' to Cress who could soothe a troubled soul better than a shot of whiskey or an hour with some fancy therapist. She'd been talkin' to one when I'd interrupted, a young guy who didn't look down on his luck so much as up on my woman.

Couldn't blame him, way she looked that day. Spent a fuckuva lotta time in the bathroom, dancin' 'round in one'a her bookish tees—*The Great Gatsby*—while she did stuff to her face that made her lashes look even longer and her lips the kinda red a man absolutely had a solemn duty to kiss off. The pencil skirt was a leather so fine it hugged every inch of her curves, and the white, starched blouse, unbuttoned just a little too low, remindin' me of the days I'd sat in high school English class lustin' after her, writin' poem after poem to leave on her desk in an effort to woo her.

So, couldn't blame the man for tryin', but I still put an end to it. And did it in a way he wouldn't think to come back for a second effort, even if I wasn't 'round to block him.

All of that beauty was heightened by the sheer fuckin' joy and pride that radiated from her, so much it took serious effort not to stare at her and lose my train of thought when I was talkin' to the people millin' in and outta the store drinkin' champagne and beer. Everyone in town was there, even the ones that looked sidelong at the dozen bikers shootin' the shit like it was our backyard, and we were all makin' an effort 'cause we got it.

Not often you see a dream come true, so we were savourin' it just as much as Cress.

Only the fucker Staff Sergeant had decided to ruin the fuckin' day by bein' an asshole and raidin' one'a our warehouses.

"King," Cressida said, bringin' me back from the anger threatenin' to consume me. Her hand went to my cheek, and I tried to focus on the way all that hair moved over her breasts as she shook her head instead'a the ways I'd kill SS Danner for this. "Honey, look at me."

"See you," I grunted, 'cause I did, fuckin' every day I looked my fill, like a glutton, shamelessly gorgin' myself on her beauty and grace, tryin' to be the kinda man that deserved it.

"Go," she urged with a soft smile. "Seriously, I am not going to be mad at you for going. I assume they need you there?"

"It'd be good," I said at the same time Nova said, "Fuck yeah."

Cress laughed. "Of course, they need you and your big brain. Get out of here, and be safe."

"Get gone," Tayline ordered, popping up behind Cress like the little sprite she was, puckish and fuckin' adorable. "I got your girl. We'll go for some drinks after it's all said and done."

"Make it tequila," I said with a slight sneer 'cause my girl got loose and heated on the Mexican booze.

"Done."

Zeus stepped forward to squeeze my woman's shoulder and bent low to look her in the eyes. "Sorry to go, Cress. Real proud of you, ya know? Takes a big set'a balls startin' your own business, but if anyone can make it succeed, it's you."

Cress blossomed under his praise. Not afraid to say it moved me, the friendship between my Old Lady and my dad. Different as oil and vinegar, but they got each other, respected each other in a way I didn't even fully understand. It hurt, too, though, watchin' Cress with him, sometimes, eatin' up the almost paternal affection 'cause her own parents had abandoned her over her choice to be with me. It stung, knowin' I'd caused that deficiency and simultaneously felt fuckin' great I had the kinda family that could more than fill the gap.

"We'll celebrate this and the engagement proper with a party at the clubhouse, yeah? Wanna toast to the fact we're addin' another kickass female to the Garro family."

Cress beamed. "That'd be good."

Z nodded, patted her shoulder, then turned to stalk off over to Lou and haul her—mid-conversation with EBA's librarian—into his arms to thoroughly kiss her goodbye.

"One last thing," I told Cress, even though the rest of the brothers had already rolled out, straddlin' their bikes out front.

She frowned as I tugged her hand and led her to the couches so I could hop up on the coffee table and lift her up there with me. She made an adorable noise in the back of her throat, but let me haul her up and pull her close as everyone went silent.

"Just wanna say one thing 'fore I jet here, but it's important, so I'm glad you're listenin'. This woman's been my woman since the day I clapped eyes on her, but two days ago, she agreed to be my wife. So, cheers to her fulfillin' her dream of opening a bookstore, and cheers to me for fulfillin' my dream of gettin' her to marry me."

Then 'fore anyone could say anythin', I kissed her.

Nothin' romantic like a dip or some shit.

No.

I was a biker, and this wasn't an announcement.

This was a claimin'.

So, as people started to shout and clap in congratulations, I picked her up, one hand to her luscious ass, the other at the back of her neck to hold her still while I plundered the sweetest mouth I'd ever kissed. And just as she always did, she softened into me by degrees until everyone else was forgotten and the only two beings in the entire world was us.

When I pulled away, her eyes stayed closed, flutterin' like in a dream. Couldn't resist brushin' my lips against her red, kiss bruised mouth until she came back 'round from her daze. Her eyes flashed opened, sass floodin' right back in, and she asked, voice wry, "Was the alpha display entirely necessary?"

"Most things worth havin' are." I grinned nice and easy as I let her slip through my hands, slidin' down my body so I could feel every inch of those soft curves against the hard planes of mine. "And trust me, this was worthier than most."

"Heathen," she teased, but she was happy.

It shone in those wide brown eyes, stretched that sinful mouth into a broad smile, and just fuckin' glowed from her, makin' her even prettier than she already was.

"Your heathen. Your man. Soon to be your husband. Better get used to it, babe," I said with a wink as I jumped back off the table and helped her down. Watched her straighten that fine, little pencil skirt over the sweet curve of her ass then gave it a slap as I turned to walk away. "Any fucker hits on you again, you tell 'em just how heathen your man can get."

IT WAS A SHIT SHOW.

Cops fuckin' swarmed the treed hill like ants, cop cars and SUVs parked at all angles, throwin' lights across the grass gone gold with the sudden spring heat.

It was a fuckuva lotta fanfare for what looked like a tiny shack on an isolated track of wilderness, but someone, and I'd fuckin' find out who it was, had tipped off the corrupted coppers to our grow-op here, and they were now goin' over it with a fine-tooth comb.

Ignorin' the men in blue, I swung off my Harley and ambled over to Zeus who was talkin' to Walter Townsend, the local we'd hired as the front man for the Christmas tree farm that ostensibly owned and operated the property.

"Told 'em they wouldn't find nothin'," he was sayin', wringin' a ballcap between his hands. "Just disruptin' my day for nothin'."

"Sorry 'bout the trouble," I said, offerin' my hand so we could exchange a shake and back slap. "You know how it is."

"Fuckin' joke is what it is," he grumbled, glarin' at the cops as they hauled shit outta the little storehouse and ripped it apart in their search. "Gonna have a massive clean-up on my hands."

"Ransom'll help ya," Zeus promised. "Now, I'd suggest takin' a seat and settlin' in for some fireworks when they find fuck all that they're searchin' for."

So, we did. The six of us who'd rode down leaned against our bikes, smokin' and talkin' like we didn't have a care in the world, 'cause we didn't, while the cops did their work.

Was obvious two hours later that they'd reached the end of their search 'cause the air went hot with frustration.

"Good men, those Porter boys," Buck muttered 'round his cigar, tippin' his chin to me in deference of my strategy even though he'd been one of the ones to protest it.

"The best," I agreed with a wink, because the new concrete was smooth and set like it'd always been the office floorin'.

"'Bout done, boys?" Zeus called as they started filin' back into their cars. "Can we check out the damage now that you've come up with shit all?"

"Fuck you, Garro," Officer McDougal said, his left eye still purple and yellow, lip scabbin' over.

We'd tracked him down after he'd pulled over Cress and tried to fuckin' assault her, and we'd dealt with him accordingly. Funny how a simple ski mask could hide your identity well enough to jump a man and get away with it in the dark of night.

Unconsciously, I flexed my fists, eager for the ache in them again if it meant clockin' the motherfucker out cold.

Sensin' my aggression, McDougal frowned then skittered farther away.

Nova laughed at his fear and clapped me on the back as we walked up the hill to the buildin'. "He's not gonna forget ya in his lifetime, that's for damned sure."

"Good. Wanna be his only nightmare after how he scared Cress and Ares," I grumbled, then stopped and whistled long and low at the devastation the cops had wreaked on the place.

Wallpaper was ripped off the walls, some places the dry wall was even cut off to check behind the panelin' for hidden shit. The furniture was trashed, desk broke up, chair cushions torn out, and even the (newly) poured cement floor had been hammered into a bit at either end.

"Thorough motherfuckers," Zeus grunted, kickin' over a piece of wood.

"Still found fuck all." I picked up a cracked photo of Townsend's wife and kids, carefully rightin' it on the only surface still standin'. "They want us bad."

"No shit." Zeus stared at the floor under his foot, the exact place a hatch had been a week ago, leadin' down to two acres of greenhouses filled with Mary Jane. He stomped on it with a heavy boot and grinned at me. "Gotta smart kid."

"You're just gettin' that? Knew you were gettin' older, but…" I whistled and rocked back on my heels.

Zeus laughed over the sudden clatter outside and moments later, Staff Sergeant Harold Danner appeared in the doorway, backlit like a villain makin' his first appearance in a country western.

"You're laughing."

Zeus chuckled again and crossed his massive arms. "Got good ears, Danner."

"You know we got a tip off about illegal activity tied to The Fallen going on here," Harold snarled as he stalked farther inside. There was an ugly curl to his lip like plastic warped from the heat. "You got anything to say about this serious allegation?"

"Yeah." Z stroked his beard and cocked an eyebrow. "That's why I was laughin'."

Danner snarled. "You think you're so above the law you can't be caught? Don't know how the hell you covered this shit up, but I'm coming for you and yours. And I won't stop until I'm dead in the ground."

"That can be arranged," Priest muttered from the corner where he leaned against the wall in the shadows of the door.

Danner whipped 'round to glare at him, clearly startled, a little afraid. Priest was like an animal; he could smell fear, and it turned his crank. A red slash of lips crossed his face that was meant to be a grin but was really only a threat.

Danner stepped away from him and closer to Zeus, not noticin' when Priest adjusted his position to be at the cop's back.

We surrounded him.

Even though there were officers outside, it was just Danner and us alone in the small office.

I moved, closin' in.

"You threaten me all ya want," Zeus drawled. "Been doin' it all our lives, don't think you get it doesn't scare me."

"It should scare you." Danner stepped forward, so locked on Z, he didn't notice the way we tightened around him, a loose noose around his neck. "Limited resources in this Podunk town had me scrambling for years, but now I have real power and money at my back."

"Javier Ventura treatin' ya good?" I asked, noticin' the way Danner checked out the new patch on my cut, the shock and faint disappointment he had at findin' me fully Fallen when he'd tried so hard to influence me to be a different man when I'd briefly lived in his home. "Must give it to you good in bed, you keep crawlin' back in there with him even after what happened to Benjamin Lafayette and the Nightstalkers."

"Watch yourself, boy," he growled. "I taught you to respect your elders."

My laugh was so hard it hurt comin' up. "You taught me dick all. Even your son doesn't respect you. Had to leave town 'cause he was embarrassed to work for his corrupt daddy. I learned from him and Z what it is to be a man."

"You're a criminal, and your sister is a biker slut who murdered her own boyfriend," Danner barked.

And that was it.

The elastic band of tension holdin' us all back snapped, and we flooded over him like the cops had over this hill. Zeus got there first, though. Hauled Danner up by the neck with one massive hand and kept him danglin' in the air like a human piñata for us to take a crack at.

Harleigh Rose was the hot button, especially now after weeks of silence, after Dad had returned only days ago from visitin' her with a scowl darker than a starless night over his face, claimin' H.R. wasn't welcome home until she got her head outta her ass and realized where her loyalties really lay.

No matter her momentary isolation from our lives, Garros

didn't let *anyone* say shit 'bout their family, and The Fallen sure as fuck didn't let somethin' like that pass without retribution.

"You speak'a my daughter like that one more time, don't care who you are, don't care if I go down for the rest'a my life, I'll rip you apart with my bare fuckin' hands."

Cops pushed the door open, weapons drawn, presumably compelled to check on us 'cause they heard Zeus's roar. But he didn't stop holdin' Danner aloft, and we didn't stand down.

"You're filth," Danner managed to wheeze. "To make matters worse, the underage girls you're using for your prostitution ring are dying from that shit you're getting them hooked on. Good luck living with yourself, Garro."

Zeus squeezed once, so tight it seemed Danner's head would pop off, clean and easy like a cork from a bottle. Shakin' his head, he tossed him to the ground and loomed over him.

"Do your fuckin' research. 'S not us leadin' that ring, it's your fuckin' buddy Ventura and his wife. For once in your small, pathetic life, get your head outta your ass," I growled, steppin' up beside Zeus to leer down at the villain who'd somehow given half his DNA to one'a my heroes. "And clear out. You got nothin' here, and this is private property."

Priest leaned down and hauled the Staff Sergeant to his feet 'fore he could move, but Danner pushed him off as soon as he was standin'. He straightened his uniform and tipped his chin like the haughty piece of shit he was.

Only, there was real threat in his eyes, an edge of demented anger that had no rules or boundaries. He wanted us bad, and I wondered if he wouldn't go to new and extreme lengths to pin us with somethin'.

Ominous premonition rolled down my spine like the warnin' of thunder 'fore a storm.

"Enjoy your time as free men," he said smoothly, easily, as if he knew somethin' we didn't. "It won't be long now."

CHAPTER TWELVE

Cressida

"MUM?"

I hadn't said the word in so long, it felt foreign to me, a dead language I wasn't quite sure how to pronounce.

There was a long silence on the other end of the phone, and then Phoebe Irons cleared her throat delicately and asked her only daughter, "Who is this?"

Not a harbinger of good things to come.

But it had been weighing on me in the weeks since the proposal. Not the radio silence that had existed between my parents and I since I divorced William and took up with King, but that fact that I was getting married again and they didn't know. There was a lingering sense of familial obligation, of daughterly guilt, that prompted me to pick up my cell one quiet afternoon at Paradise Found and call them.

"Your daughter, Cressida."

"Ah, well, yes…hello."

A shocked laugh, a single *ha* of disappointment, burst from my lips. "Is that really all you have to say to me after four years? *Hello*?"

There was a weary sigh from the other end of the line, and I was reminded where I got my predilection for that from. How odd it was to know that I shared DNA and mannerisms with a person who would never and could never understand who I truly was aside from those commonalities.

"What would you prefer me to say, Cressida? Hello, I haven't seen hide nor hair from you in half a decade, but I am so thrilled you picked up the phone now? Because I don't feel that way. You made your bed, if you're in trouble yet again because of the degenerates you've decided to associate yourself with then I am sorry, but you must lie in it."

It was surprising how much it hurt to hear her apathy. It surprised me because I hadn't expected to care. My parents had groomed me to be married to their best friend, pressured me to be a stay-at-home wife, and basically belittled every dream I'd ever had. Then, when I'd finally found happiness, they had turned their backs on me just because that happiness took a different form than they'd expected.

How could I care about the opinion of people like that?

What did it matter when I had people in my life who respected me, supported me, and loved me unconditionally? When King had given me a family of my own, greater than any I could have previously imagined?

I decided it must've been biological. Something intrinsic in me that needed the approval of my parents, maybe even at the price of my own contentment.

At least now I knew it was a price I wasn't willing to pay.

"No," I said slowly, rubbing at the sore spot in my chest. "I'm not exactly sure what I thought, but I wanted to reach out to tell you something."

"Unless it's that you've finally overcome this mid-life crisis, boy-toy phase you are in, then I doubt I want to hear it."

I winced, ignoring Benny who frowned over at the cash register as he helped a customer gift wrap one of our special editions. If he knew who I was talking to, sweet, passivist Benny Benito would rip the phone from my hands and stomp on it if it meant getting me out of this toxic conversation.

"It's not a phase. I'm only thirty. And King is the farthest thing from a boy toy you could ever imagine. He graduated from UBC with honours, and he's the kindest man I've ever known."

Mum—or Phoebe, really, not Mum anymore—laughed her classy, tinkling laugh, being a bitch the way women like her were; passive aggressive, backstabbing, and manipulative.

I found I much preferred biker bitches. They said it outright, fought about it hard (sometimes with fists), and then let sleeping dogs lie after it was aired properly.

"He's a good-looking boy you took advantage of as his teacher. I'm honestly surprised you weren't prosecuted properly for it."

Freaking frack, but it hurt to have my mother think I was some scheming seductress, and it hurt even more that she refused to see my relationship for what it was. Anger sparked in my belly, and the savageness that normally lay dormant like a sleeping dragon in the pit of my gut stirred slowly into wakefulness.

"Well, Mother, you should know that good-looking *man* has asked me to marry him, and I've agreed. We're getting married in three months, and for one crazy moment, I thought I should let you know."

The plans had come together like a dream. King and I weren't flashy people, we didn't need an orchestra or fancy food and a ton of bling to make our wedding special. Instead, we were having a massive potluck with all the Old Ladies bringing the food, Eugene playing the piano for the processional, and Curtains DJing the reception. We would get married on our property, amid the hundred-year-old trees thick as castle spires and just as magical.

Three months. It was a quick engagement, but honestly, I would have married King tomorrow at Vancouver's city hall. I'd even stopped taking birth control, because we wanted babies, and we wanted a lot of them. I was only thirty, but I wanted to be a young mum, and King was only too happy to spend countless hours in bed with me endeavouring to give me exactly that. Those babies would probably never know their maternal grandparents, and that thought did strange alchemy to my feelings about Phoebe and Peter Garrison. It changed my guilt-ridden disappointment into calcified anger.

"I hope you aren't expecting your father and I to attend." Phoebe's voice was filled with mild revulsion, and I could picture her as she was, standing with her hand on her chest like some 18th century ingénue who had been shocked to her core by scandal. "He just received an award at the university, you know, for his commitment to education, and it would *not* do to have his name associated with those…animals."

"I guess it depends on your definition of animal, doesn't it?" I asked, tone saccharine, belly burning. "To me, an animal is someone without the intelligence to discern right from wrong, truth from fiction. Someone who is unevolved and cruel for the sake of cruelty. Someone like *you*."

"Are you quite done?" Phoebe asked with a wan sigh as if I was being some ridiculous teenager acting out because she wouldn't extend my curfew.

"Yeah," I said, suddenly filled with bone-deep weariness because I knew whatever love she'd ever harboured for me was based on a sense of societal obligation, the way she felt a mother must love a daughter, and not on anything real like who I was as a person. "Yeah, Phoebe, we're done. I won't bother you again."

"I'd prefer it. We both consider ourselves childless now. It's for the best."

Agony blew straight through me like a cold wind off the coastal cliffs, and I shivered violently as I hung up the phone and tossed it, a little too forcefully, to the window seat beside me. I closed my eyes, hugged my knees to my chest, and let my head drop back against the wall, trying to breathe through the pain as I compartmentalized it.

I took a moment to text King, who was working at Hephaestus Auto that day, to tell him what happened, and in typical fashion, he sent me back something both simple and profound.

King: *Family isn't in the blood.*

It's the echo of each name

That sounds with the beat of your heart.

I closed my eyes again, clutching the poem on my phone to my chest as I exhaled all the poison my mother had sown in my mind so I could replace it with the beauty of King and his words.

"Appreciate now's a fuckin' bad moment, but I've been waitin' awhile, and I can't stand here and watch her do that to ya without makin' myself known."

Instantly, my eyes flared open because I would recognize that voice even in a deafening rock concert, even in gale force winds.

My brother.

A sob bloomed in my bruised heart and clogged my throat.

I hadn't seen him in ages, and he looked so much the same.

Lysander had always been so handsome, almost too handsome once, but time and prison had worn away that edge like waves on rocks so that he seemed weathered now, smoothed into something more manly than pretty. He was even bigger than he'd been after getting out of prison, so wide across the chest I doubted I could wrap my arms around him if I tried. The muscles bulging out of his tight grey tee were tatted from shoulder to fingertips in a series of images I knew depicted Greek myths, our favourites like Apollo and Adonis, Paris with his gold apple, and the three goddesses, Hera, Aphrodite, and Artemis. I'd helped him pick each one, once upon a time, and to see them again made the duality of my reaction all the more intense.

I missed him acutely. He had been my one constant growing up with my parents and then when I was with William. The one person who always tried to put me first even when he wasn't in a position to do so. He cared for me so much that he'd even gone to prison for me after killing the man who'd tried to rape me.

He'd been my hero and my saviour until he wasn't. Until he'd gotten in so deep with the Nightstalkers MC that he'd used my position with King to get an in with The Fallen in order to inform on them to the rival club. Until his actions had perpetuated my abduction by that club and my torture at their hands. The center of my palms still burned sometimes when I remembered the agony of being impaled by inch wide nails.

Yes, he'd helped save me in the end.

Yes, a year later he'd shown up out of the blue and helped to save Loulou, Bea, and Harleigh Rose from an ambush.

But there was so much water under the bridge, the structure had collapsed, and I wasn't sure it could ever be rebuilt.

"Sander," I said, noting the way he shoved a hand through his masses of hair the exact same honeyed brown as my own. "What are you doing here?"

"I come here." He cleared his throat awkwardly, shifting from one big foot to the other in a way I didn't want to think was adorable, but was. "Come 'ere a lot since you opened, but I try to stay outta the way."

"So…you stalk me?"

"No, fuck!" His eyes, green swirling through the brown, widened comically. "Jesus, Cress, I just wanted to see ya. It's been years, and now I'm back in town, I couldn't resist."

"Back in town?" I couldn't help my curiosity. "You got a job?"

His lips twisted in his short beard, and I knew it was the kind of job that didn't require a resume. The same kind of job he'd always had.

"Somethin' like that. Listen, I just came 'cause I heard 'bout the engagement, and I wanted to say congrats. Like King a helluva lot more than that fucker William, and I'm glad as fuck you got a man like that at your side."

"A man like what?" I was being combative and waspish, but I was tired of judgement and disappointment after speaking with my mother. I didn't need more family drama to get me through the day.

"A man that'd lay down his life 'fore he ever let somethin' happen to ya."

This was true. King wouldn't let a bee sting me if he could help it, and that overprotective, alpha instinct was one of the many reasons I loved him.

I bit my lip, studying Sander closely, noting the strain and the slack skin beneath his eyes that said he didn't sleep much or very well.

"How are you?" I inquired, even though I was nervous, afraid to give him an inch when my heart yearned for a mile, my brain knowing better than to give him either.

He seemed just as disconcerted by my kindness and I was reminded by how utterly *sweet* Lysander could be beneath all that gruff toughness.

He perched his ass on the edge of the coffee table so there was still a decent distance between us and braced his arms on his thighs. "I'm doin' better. Sober five years now. It's been…a weird year. Got into some stuff I never thought I'd enjoy or even be good at, but guess life's good that way. At surprisin' you when you least expect it."

"Preach," I agreed, and a small part of me knew it was just to see him grin at me. "Can you tell me about it? Is it…legal?"

His lips twisted, and I knew that even though he wanted to answer me, he wouldn't.

"Never mind." I held up a hand. "I would rather you not lie."

"Okay."

We were quiet for a moment, and my eye caught on a rare shade of reddish blond hair the colour of melted down rose gold. It niggled at something in the back of my memory, and before the girl in question scuttled down the A-C fiction aisle, I realized it was Honey Yves.

King and H.R.'s half-sister.

I stood up before I could think and followed her, Sander behind me. She was in a dark corner at the end of the row slipping a book into the back waistband of her jeans.

Stealing from me.

Before I could do anything about it, Sander was striding past me, straight to her. She let out a truncated scream as he caught her arm and wrenched the book from its hiding place. He was so much bigger than her, dark and foreboding, whereas Honey was slight and utterly feminine. I was worried for one terrible moment that he would hit her.

And then to my shock, after a moment of locked eyes, *she* hit *him*. A hard punch straight to the solar plexus that expelled a loud grunt from his chest, and then she was turning, running toward me, hair flying like a pennant in her haste for escape.

"Wait," I called, trying to catch her arm only to have her fling me off.

In the light at the end of the row spilling in from the windows, I could see bruising crawling up the side of her left cheek and jaw up into her hairline.

Someone was clearly abusing her.

My heart clenched with empathy and I knew I needed to do something. Whether that desire stemmed from Honey being related to King and H.R., or from some more general sympathy, I didn't know or care about it. She was clearly in trouble, and I wondered if she'd come to the bookstore as some subtle cry for help.

"Wait!" I yelled after her. "Please, wait. You can have the book, just please come back."

She didn't stop to listen to me.

In fact, she tore through the front doors so blindly, she almost ran over the two cops strolling in as if they owned the place.

They shouted at her to watch herself, but she was gone before they could even finish their sentences.

"Freak," I faux-cursed under my breath, dragging a hand through my waves to try to settle myself from the calamity of the day before I faced the officers. "What can I do for you, gentlemen?"

Officer Ormand and a cop I'd never met but knew to be Officer Peters ambled over to me in tandem. I wondered idly, cruelly, if they'd practiced that.

"Just checking out your new place of business," Ormand drawled as he picked up *The Prince* by Machiavelli from the recommendations display and flipped through it before deliberately dropping it to the floor.

There was a lot I could forgive. I was a loving person, an understanding person now, if not before I'd met King, and I allowed for a lot of wrongdoings before I drew the line.

But I could not and would not *ever* forgive flagrantly desecrating a book.

I crossed my arms, cocked my hip, and raised a brow. "Well, here it is. My little corner of the literary world."

"Yeah." Ormand sniffed and scratched at the razor burn on his neck as he surveyed it, noting Benny working behind the cash desk and two customers quietly talking in a corner near the cookbooks. "Your idea to start this, was it?"

"Yes, whose else would it be?"

I could feel Sander at my back, lingering hidden in the shelves, and noticed Benny frantically texting on his phone, knowing he was calling in the guys.

If the cops were here, it couldn't be good.

"The Garros, maybe?" he suggested as Peters made his way around the store, sliding books off their shelves so they tumbled to the ground, cracking spines and bending pages.

I started forward to stop him, but suddenly Ormand was in my space, an iron hand shackled around my wrist.

"He's just doing his job. You wouldn't want to obstruct justice now, would you, Ms. Irons?" He sneered. "See, I was thinking, if this wasn't your idea, it'd be a damn good way for The Fallen to launder money. Lots of cash moving through a quaint little bookstore like this, huh?"

"We only just opened, it's too soon to tell," I said stiffly, not giving him the satisfaction of my struggle. "I assume you brought a warrant, if you're going to search the premise?"

"Sure, sure," he nodded and dragged me to the front desk. He leaned over to rip off a piece of paper from the receipt machine then grabbed a pen.

I watched as he wrote 'WARRANT' in block letters across the paper then tucked it quickly into my cleavage.

"Fuck you," I growled, about to launch myself at him because how dare he invade my space and bully me like that.

Then Sander was there, his hand planted on Ormand's chest, shoving so he fell back against the front counter.

"Fuck off, Jon," he snapped, looming over him. "This ain't right, and ya know it."

"I know shit all about it," Ormand retorted, shoving off the counter to stand and straighten himself. "And you'd do yourself a favor by getting out of here while you can. Danner won't be happy to see his pet off its leash."

"Fuck you. This is my sister's store, and I'm not lettin' you vandalize it."

"Vandalize? We're the police," Ormand yelled in his face, spittle flying.

"Vandalize?" Peters echoed from over by the couches as he produced a Swiss Army knife and stabbed it into one of the cushions, carving it open until the stuffing spilled out. "Why, we're just doing our jobs. This place is a suspected front for a criminal *gang*."

Sander stepped forward menacingly, but Ormand only laughed. "Don't make me collar you, Garrison."

I didn't need Sander to help me anyway. Instead, I stalked to the front counter, rounded it, dropped to my ass on my high heels, and opened the locked box I kept under the register. When I popped back up, it was with my Sig Sauer leveled at Ormand.

"What're you going to do with that, bitch? I'm a cop."

"Yeah? Well I'm a Garro," I retorted. "And if you don't get the *fuck* out of my store, I'm well within my right to shoot you for trespassing because that worthless piece of paper you arrogantly shoved at me was *not* a legal document and will absolutely *not* hold up in court."

There was a static silence, the hum of potential energy low and throbbing in the store. I could hear the two customers breathing heavily, panicking in the back, and Benny was now beside me, his own hand on a knife Carson had given him for his last birthday.

Then, Peters had the audacity to kick over an entire display while grinning wickedly at me. "Oops."

Well, if he wanted to call my bluff, I was all too happy to prove my worth.

I cocked the gun, aimed it high at the top box of the window on the wall across the store and fired.

Glass shattered and rained down over the seating area. The cops looked almost comically shocked by my action. I pressed my advantage as soon as I heard the familiar purr of Harleys approaching.

"Get the fuck out before I shoot you, or worse, the guys get here and deal with you their way," I threatened.

Ormand growled like a rabid dog denied a meal and shoved past Lysander on his way out the door, Peters followed slowly, kicking at a book he'd thrown to the floor earlier.

"We're watching you, all of you. Just waiting for you to make one stupid move and all the cards will come tumbling down," he sneered as pushed open the door, slamming it shut behind him.

The air felt thick and as impenetrable as amber, Sander, Benny and I suspended in it like bugs for a long moment before Sander broke it by turning to face me. His expression was guarded; locked, and alarmed as a safe house.

"Y'okay?" he grumbled.

"I will be if you tell me you are *not* working for Staff Sergeant Harold Danner," I told him as I put the safety on my gun and started to lock it back up.

He hesitated. "Can't do that exactly."

"Then I can't tell you I'm okay. You keep pitting yourself against my family, I can't consider you a part of it," I said honestly.

His sigh was ragged as he drew both hands through his shoulder length hair then let them drop into an open palmed shrug. "Not doin' it to hurt you. Never do anythin' to hurt you, and honest to Christ, Cress, I've only ever tried to save you."

"I get that you mean well…and I miss you, Sander," I promised. "Something changes, you know where I am. But I will not associate with a man that's actively against The Fallen."

"Glad you got that. A family worthy of you," he said over the increased roar of motorbike engines pulling up in front of the store, parking illegally in their haste to get to me to make sure everything was okay.

"Sorry you don't," I said softly as I turned my back on him and ran out the store toward King who was already running toward me, face creased with worry and anger, arms open for me to jump into without hesitation when I started for him.

When I thought to look around for Lysander again after kissing King and explaining what had happened to Zeus, Nova, and Bat, he was gone.

"I'm gonna fuckin' kill them," King growled as he stalked around the bookstore surveying the damage. "God fuckin' dammit, but they're gettin' ballsy. This shit needs to end, and it needs to end fuckin' *now*."

Zeus cursed under his breath. "Babies comin', cops diggin', 'serkers circlin'… fuck me, but can't we have a goddamn minute'a peace for once in our lives?"

"Not the life you chose," I said softly as he righted a heavy display case like it weighed nothing. "Not the life *we* chose," I corrected.

"Nah, but still, gotta hot as fuck woman at home and babies to prep for. Rather be there than here cleanin' up the pig's mess."

"Rather be takin' you for dinner at Donavon's like we planned, now I gotta find a way to send those fuckers a message not to fuck with my woman," King grumbled, stalkin' to me with a look in his eye that I recognized from nights he came home from riding or fighting, when that pale blue went near white with banked savagery he could only expend between my legs.

"The boys like to go to The Lotus," Nova said, referring to the strip club The Fallen purchased a few years ago, around the time Zeus and Lou found each other again. "Think we can sort somethin' out."

It was hours later, after King had returned home from 'deliverin' a message' to Ormand and Peters that left his knuckles bruised and split over the bone. After he'd taken out his lingering savagery on my body in ways I couldn't innumerate or speak about without blushing, my pussy sore, ass pleasantly aching, his body crushed onto mine like a paperweight to hold me in place so he could love me even while he slept.

But I couldn't sleep.

There was something tangling in my gut, twisting and mangled that set my belly to aching.

Harleigh Rose.

The situation with her was distressing me. She had been my friend and family for almost half a decade and now, yet when I wanted to share the news that I would finally be her sister-in-law, she was absent, so removed from our lives it was almost as if she didn't exist anymore.

I strained to reach my phone on the bedside table from under King's warm weight and used my finger to pull it closer so I could pull up my text messages.

Cressida: Okay, remind me why I love tequila again? I went out with the brothers to celebrate Bat's birthday, and now it's the morning after, and I couldn't tell you anything that happened. We missed you by the way.

Cressida: H.R. honey, please call me back or even text. I've got something exciting to tell you, and I don't want to do it over the phone. Can I come visit?

Cressida: It's the opening of Paradise Found today, and I wish you were here. I know you've got a lot to deal with, so don't worry…just thinking of you, wishing I had your sass and spirit to light up my day and erase my nerves. Hope you're doing well, my love.

Cressida: I love you.

Cressida: Still love you. Here if you need me for anything, even if you don't want me to tell King about it. I've got you, girl, if you'll let me.

Each message was sent days apart without a response. I couldn't even tell if she'd read them, which was somehow worse because I wanted her to at least know how much she was on my mind.

Then, as if I'd conjured the devil himself by saying his name, a text appeared from an unknown number and I knew, even before I opened it, who it would be.

Harleigh Rose: Cress, I need you to come, and do it fast. 4195 Spruce Road in Vancouver. Come alone. I need to explain things to you. I'm worried something might happen to me or Lionel Danner.

My heart lurched into a sprint, trying to hurdle over my ribs and out my chest.

"King," I said, pushing back the soft tangle of his hair and shaking his shoulder. "Get up, get up now."

His eyes slowly peeled open revealing that blue I loved so much, and the moment he saw my face, he was alert.

"What's up?"

I sucked in a deep breath through my teeth and said, "Follow me down the mountain. Harleigh Rose just texted, and I think she's in some serious crap."

CHAPTER THIRTEEN

Cressida

A LOT HAD HAPPENED in the last few weeks, and by a lot, I meant a whack ton in the way only biker lives could. Harleigh Rose had stabbed Lionel Danner in the chest. It was a truth that felt wrong in my head, like I'd been hypnotized to think that way when my gut said different. But it was true. When I'd gone down the mountain to the address she'd texted, I didn't find Harleigh Rose in the suburban home. Instead, through the wide-open door, laying sprawled on the kitchen floor in a pool of warm blood, I'd found Danner, barely conscious and bleeding savagely from a large wound in his upper left chest.

I'd called 911, and then King, who was waiting around the corner so I could at least give the illusion that I'd obeyed Harleigh Rose's orders, set about trying to save Danner's life.

We got the story from Lion days later when he'd come to enough to talk about the tragedy. Apparently, after Reaper Holt, the Prez of the Berserkers MC, had threatened to kidnap, rape, and possibly kill Loulou in order to cut Zeus off at the knees, H.R. had decided to take it upon herself to help Danner and Wrath take down the club. Danner didn't know why she'd stabbed him, only that she *must* have had a damn good reason for doing so because they were madly in love with each other.

I didn't know who was more surprised, him or the club, when Zeus decided that Danner was worthy of not only our respect, but his daughter's love. Shockingly, there hadn't been any drama or fallout. Just a quiet talk between the two men who had raised Harleigh Rose and King followed by a mutual, warm kind of acceptance. With everything going on, I think they all realized drama over a happy relationship was small potatoes.

We'd also made the fairly natural decision to start calling Danner Lion instead of his surname, because he didn't want to be associated with his father any more than he already was. Besides, if he was going to be one of our own—the way it seemed he might be given his relationship with Harleigh Rose—he needed a kickass name to fit in.

Though, spending time with Lion as he recovered, it was easy to see that the knife might not have pierced his heart, but his separation from Harleigh Rose certainly had. She was in deep with the Berserkers in a way that meant she would either end their organization entirely or end up dead.

It was a strange and horrible thing to watch men of action who felt duty-bound to protect their women at all costs be forced to do nothing. At this point, all they could do was watch closely and wait to see what the outcome would be so they could swoop in to pick up the pieces where they fell if need be.

Zeus was irritable, a bear woken from hibernation but unable to hunt. And Loulou was even worse, the hormones raging inside her as she neared her due date, laughing or crying at the drop of a hat. I'd never felt the club so on edge before. Brothers bickered with brothers, Old Ladies were essentially banned from the compound, and Ares was forced to stay with Nova's family, the Booths, just in case a full scale gang war broke out at a moment's notice.

To make matters so much more heartbreaking, Kylie had been killed for Wrath's duplicity, and upon learning about her murder, Wrath had soon followed, killed by the very men who had sworn brotherhood to him. Danner said there was a slim chance Wrath wasn't dead, that the Berserkers had kept him barely alive somewhere to torture, but King and I weren't holding our breaths. No one had known about King's connection with him, and we kept it that way, only Eugene, King, and I planting two markers in the ground at Eugene's cabin so they could metaphorically be laid to rest together. I hoped that they found their peace in the afterlife because they had been so brutally robbed of it on earth.

They were dark weeks, bleak like the winter sky, a low ceiling that hung too close to our heads. Not all was bad, though. Paradise Found was thriving, Shadow was a constant source of delight and had taken to draping himself over my shoulders as I read or puttered around the house, and Ares, as always, brought a level of happiness to our lives with his quiet intensity and tenderness.

But it felt like the calm before a tropical storm was about to roll through Entrance and raze it to the ground.

Today was the only day in over a month that everyone seemed to be in good spirits and that was because it was the night of our engagement party.

I still remembered my first biker party, down to every little detail. It was the moment I embraced the woman I wanted to be and the man I wanted to be with for the rest of my life. The club's Old Ladies and Harleigh Rose with her best friend, Lila, had taken me to the mecca of biker stores, Revved & Ready, to pick out new, wicked cool clothes. Now, those clothes were a staple of my closet, one side filled with the feminine, almost old-fashioned clothes I loved to wear to work, the other a mix of denim, leather, and graphic tees. That's who I truly was, I'd found out. Leather and lace, badass and romantic.

It was a duality that worked for me and worked for King, because that paradox was echoed in his own soul.

Now, four years later, I was an old hat at being an Old Lady, and the party that raged around me felt right and normal. Heckler was making out with two women in the corner near the dart board while Boner hustled people playing pool for cash. Lou was there, so massively pregnant just three weeks out from her due date that I worried she would pop them out given the slightest prevacation. Her mother was there, too, not an infrequent visitor to the club, wearing pearls and a leather jacket like a lady gone bad. She was laughing at Smoke as he mocked shooting a shotgun for some story he was telling.

Old Sam, the owner of the record shop King and Harleigh Rose loved, was there with his wife, Rainbow and Tayline were there arguing with Benny, Carson, and Wiseguy over darts, and even Susan Hobbs, Danner's estranged wife and the woman who had taken in the Garro siblings when Zeus was in prison, sat at the bar talking to the Fallen cop, Officer Hutchinson.

Riley Gibson was also there, looking faintly awkward and out of place, but smiling as he drank with Axe-Man and the biker showed him the hatchet he always kept dangling from his belt. King had insisted on inviting him as a show of faith and gratitude for a supposed tip-off he'd given the club. I was surprised by that, knowing Gisbon was the kind of clean-cut man who seemed hard-nosed about the law and abiding it, but I knew how the club had a way of flipping people's perceptions.

Lila was there, too, with Cleo, looking absolutely gorgeous as she always did these days, caramel skin exposed at her taut belly, tattooed flowers blooming all over her hips and up under the bared skin beneath her breasts. She wasn't smiling, and I knew it was because her fiancé refused to be there, hating the club as he did, and more because Nova was sitting at the bar with a biker bunny on the counter, doing shots out of her belly button with Ransom.

It was funny to sit on King's lap, idly listening to him chat with Curtains, Lab-Rat, and Bat, feeling happier than anyone had a right to be, living my happily-ever-after, while watching the women I loved struggling after their own leather clad Prince Charming.

I doubted Nova and Lila would end up together, even though they were thick as thieves and so perfectly suited it seemed almost ignominious that they wouldn't. Lila was engaged to a civilian, someone outside of the club who hated the club, and Nova was Nova. Aside from King, he was the most beautiful man any of us had met in real life, and also the most afraid of real commitment.

The pair that seemed more likely to engage in some kind of relationship was, of all people, Bea and Priest.

She followed him. It was just something she did. Something she'd done since she was fourteen and introduced to the dark side of life through her sister's love for the ex-con president of another outlaw motorcycle club. It was an odd sight, a pretty little slip of a blonde girl who looked more angel than human, shadowing a stone-cold killer as if he was the god she was born to revere.

Priest pretended not to notice, and he was good at it. He was good at everything I'd ever seen him do, including endeavoring to be the least human man on the planet. But there were these glimpses, like sunlight through storm clouds, that broke apart his stoic features and turned him into something still not quite human, but otherworldly, demonic perhaps, while Bea was angelic. They were an odd sort of yin and yang, and to me, at least, now well versed in the areas between black and white, they seemed well suited.

Not that Priest would ever give in to those flashes of desire I saw like lightning streaks across his face. Not that Loulou or Zeus would allow the overly protected Bea to engage in anything whatsoever with the barely leashed beast.

But I understood Bea. I saw how she could be so compelled by the darkness and mysteries of Priest, and I felt sorry for her that nothing would ever come of her unrequited affections.

Zeus and Lion were both absent, on a trip to Vancouver to check in, of all people, with Honey Yves's uncle, who apparently might have had a tip on the Berserkers. It sucked not to have Harleigh Rose and Zeus there, the two who had adopted me as soon as King had even batted an eye my way, but Zeus had more than made up for it by giving King and I our engagement present before he left: King's new cut replete with the patch 'Road Captain' the full Fallen colours on the back, and a leather jacket for me, too, only this one said 'Property of King.'

"She'll come out on top. It's H.R., if anyone can take on an entire MC, it's my sister. Trust me," King murmured in my ear, using his nose to push the hair back so he could nibble on my lobe. Of course, he'd been able to read my mind in the way only he could. "Sorry it's weighin' on you, babe. Gotta know, it's doin' the same to me."

"I just miss her, you know? And I'm worried about her. I've only ever heard bad things about The Berserkers, they aren't like The Fallen. Even Wrath hated them."

"Not many clubs like The Fallen, Cress. The 'serkers are scum, but we gotta trust that H.R. can handle it."

"I still can't believe we let Kylie go down the mountain," I said, switching gears so I could air all my grievances at one. "What were we thinking? We knew the Berserkers were crazy bad."

"We were thinkin' that Wrath would'a been there with her the entire time and that when he wasn't, he'd have a man on her. What happened to them isn't our fault, babe. You gotta get that outta your head right fuckin' now. Fuckin' tragic, their deaths, but it's toxic to think you coulda saved them or changed their fate."

I bit my lower lip, noting the severity in King's expression. If there was anything my man hated, it was when I blamed myself for things beyond my control. So, I nodded, even though I knew I would secretly harbour guilt and despair over Kylie and Wrath's murders for years to come.

"Good. Now, can you try to relax and enjoy the party? I'm thinkin' it's time for tequila so you'll be amenable when I drag you to the back room and have my way with ya."

Heat instantly sparked between my legs and sent desire curling up my spine. I wrapped my arms around his neck to press closer. "You don't need tequila to seduce me."

"Nah, don't reckon I do," he agreed before taking my mouth.

A flash of tossed black hair caught my eye, dragging my gaze to the woman who'd just passed me, ass swaying in tiny cut-off shorts that displayed the bottom half of her butt cheeks. I could tell she was pretty, even from behind, but there was something about her that resonated with me like a bad note poorly struck. She looked, for a moment, like Paula. The crazy ass biker bitch I'd had a cat fight with in the clubhouse at my first biker party here four years ago. It still burned that she'd been the one to take King's virginity, and I knew I must've been seeing things because after that night, she'd been banished from the club forever.

The thought of seeing her felt like a straight shot of poison to my veins, and I shivered as I tried to purge her from my mind while King's attention was distracted by Lab-Rat who was making a cocktail of rum, tequila, fireball, and cough syrup.

There was a loud clearing of a throat and then someone started pounding on the bar. It was Nova, who, once he got everyone's attention, preened like a peacock and climbed on top of the wooden bar with his beer held aloft.

"We're here tonight to celebrate King, our newborn Fallen brother, and his beautiful Queenie, who in my humble opinion is way too good for that guy's ugly mug." Everyone laughed drunkenly, even King whose laughter was only stopped by my kiss. "Not a man who believes in love and fairy-tale bullshit, but I am a man that believes in the love'a those two. Never seen anythin' like it, outside'a Lou and Z, and doubt I will again. 'Bout time you put a fuckin' ring on her finger 'fore she ran off with Boner." The biker in question hooted, jumped up on the pool table, and cupped his crotch to an audience of laughter. "Nah, but really, it's gotta be said, and I can't believe I'm the one doin' it, but here goes. To King and Cress, the future King and Queen of The Fallen MC."

The roar of cheers rattled the windows and shook the floor as everyone shouted, jeered, and stomped their feet for us.

King stood up, keeping me in his arms, hands under my ass even as he addressed the club. "Seein' as y'all were part of me wooin' Cress by fixin' up that dump that used to be Shamble Wood Cottage, thank you, brothers, for helpin' me convince this woman to take a chance on a guy she never would'a thought she'd wanna keep."

"Guy?" Boner called out. "You were a fuckin' boy back then!"

A blush fired my cheeks as everyone laughed, including King.

"What can I say, saw her, wanted her, took her, and that was the end of that," King declared arrogantly then chuckled into my scowling face. "Just lucky she agreed to be my wife."

"Here, fuckin' here!" Bat called. "Now, fuckin' kiss her so we can get back to drinkin'!"

King's laughter tasted sweet in my mouth as he took mine,

kissing me so thoroughly I forgot we were being watched by a group of bikers until a few of them hooted and wolf-whistled.

I broke away, but King only let me go so far, his hand firm on the back of my neck. "Not a long engagement, babe. Hope you're cool with that."

I grinned, buzzed on the maple syrup bourbon sours Eugene had made especially for me. "Tomorrow couldn't be too soon."

"I'm so happy for you two," Loulou said, waddling over with her big belly bared by a black cropped tee that read 'Biker Mama' in red script over her swollen breasts. She looked so ready to pop; it was a wonder she could stand. Also, she was crying. Big, pretty tears that freely rolled down her face as she leaned over her belly to hug me.

"I'm sorry, I'm a mess," she complained, dashing at her wet cheeks as King wrapped an arm around her and tucked her into his side. "These damned babies put pressure on all of my insides, so I swear, I even feel it in my tear ducts."

"Sure," King agreed easily even though he rolled his eyes at me over her head. "It's just the pressure you're feelin'."

"Exactly."

I giggled behind my hand then palmed the skin stretched tight as a drum over her warm belly. "How are my little niece and nephew doing?"

There was a ripple like a current sucking out the tide under my hand, and I gasped at the same time Loulou winced.

"What was that?"

Lou's gorgeous, almost angelic face, collapsed into a stubborn frown. "Nothing."

"Loulou…that felt like a contraction."

"No."

"Um, *yes*," I argued, looking up at King with wide eyes.

"No. It wasn't. What do you know about contractions?" she snapped.

I recoiled as if she'd slapped me, because if anyone knew how much I yearned for King's baby, it was my girl, Lou.

"Not cool," King growled softly. "Don't snap at my woman just 'cause you're scared. Now, tell me the truth here, Foxy. You havin' contractions?"

Sweat beaded on the top of her brow, and she wriggled on her swollen feet, hand to her belly, eyes glazed as another contraction rolled through her.

She sighed. "Maybe."

"You need to go to the hospital," I demanded instantly. "Why the hell didn't you tell anyone?"

"I didn't want to steal your thunder! It's a big night for you guys. King finally manned up and put a ring on it."

I couldn't help but laugh at the sassiness of my former student. Much like me, she'd changed so much over the years, it was crazy to look back and see the old Louise as the same woman now carrying Zeus Garro's babies.

"Honey, seriously, that's whacked," I said gently. "You having these babies is about as exciting as it gets for every single person here, even and especially King and me. I've been waiting nearly nine months to meet Angel and Walker."

"Zeus isn't here," she whispered, and I saw that fear germinating in her gaze.

She didn't want to do this without him.

King and I locked eyes over her head, and he gently uncurled her from under his arm to walk away, already pulling out his cell to call Zeus.

I wrapped my arms around Lou and felt her tremble as she clung to me.

Instantly, Ares was at our side. He was too young to be at the party so late. It was well after midnight on a Thursday, and things were devolving as only biker parties could, into a series of erotic and illegal tableaus. But Ares wasn't a normal kid, and his eyes said he'd seen a lot worse than a man going at it with a woman on a pool table in the middle of a party.

His big eyes were dark and solemn as he took Loulou's hand and gently put his other one on her belly. "Are they okay?"

Lou smiled tremulously and put a hand in his thicket of curls. "Yeah, Ares baby, they're going to be okay. Just a little early it seems."

"Cool. I can't wait to meet them," he admitted with a little smile as he stared at his hand on her belly then gave it a little pat.

"Cool," Loulou agreed, relaxing a bit in my arms as I stroked her hair and Ares worked his particular kind of calming magic. "They're going to love you."

"Probably be the most loved babies in the world," Ares said with a shrug, completely oblivious to the profound way his words moved through Loulou.

She hissed as another contraction hit.

I let out a relieved sigh when King stalked back into the room, until he got close enough for me to see the stricken expression stamped on his face.

"Z called," he said hollowly. "Apparently, Reaper's got Harleigh Rose, and he wants to make a trade for Zeus."

My heart dropped to the floor at my feet. "Oh, my God."

Lou straightened, her little teeth bared. "Like hell that's going to happen."

"Calm down, Lou," King hushed, gently squeezing her arm. "We got this. Parties over though, babe, I'm sorry."

"Don't be absurd, *go*," I ordered, leaning over Lou to grasp his face and kiss him hard because you never knew, even though I refused to think about it, what might happen in a situation like this. "Go and bring them back to us. I'll take Lou to the hospital."

She whimpered and clenched her teeth against the pain as another contraction hit. "No, no. I'm fine, and I am so *not* giving birth to these babies in the middle of a fucking crisis."

"You so are," I demanded then turned to Ares. "Go get her coat, her mum, and Bea, okay?"

He took off like a shot, leaving King who stared at me like he was memorizing the lines of my face.

"Go," I said softly, "It's okay, baby."

"Love you," he said, gruffly, like the words were torn right from his heart, bloody and raw. "Love you, too, Lou. You both be strong for me, okay?" I nodded, but when Lou didn't respond, he crouched down to pinch her chin and lift her gaze to his. "Hey, Mama, you gotta be the little warrior again right now, yeah? My little sister and brother need you to be strong."

"I don't want to do this without Z," she admitted in a wobbly voice that broke my heart.

"I know, Lou, but you also know he's gotta take care of this so when these babies come, we can all greet them together. The whole Garro clan includin' Harleigh Rose."

"Okay," she whispered, pale and obviously distressed. "Just take care of him, okay? I need…I need him."

"Gotcha," he said, eyes tipping to mine because he knew the feeling. "Love you, Lou, okay? Love you, and I'm gonna love you even more, you bring these babies into the world nice and healthy, all three of you."

"Okay," she agreed, leaning into the palm he used to cup her face. She breathed deeply, steadying herself, then pulled away, blue fire flashing in her eyes. "Okay, let's get these babies out of me. I'm tired of not being able to see my toes."

King grinned. "Atta, babe."

Gibson appeared then, face creased with genuine concern. "Seems things are going down…anything I can do to help?"

King stared at the man, taking his measure slowly, making it obvious but not insulting. Finally, he reached out and clapped the off-duty cop on the shoulder.

"Sure, man. It'd be good if you'd call down to Van PD and let them know there's shit goin' down at the Port Authority. The Prez of Berserkers MC might or might not be committin' a crime there."

Gibson's grin was a slow spread, honey sweet but slightly wicked. "Think I can do that. Thanks for the anonymous tip."

"Just bein' a good citizen," King quipped with a wink then clapped him on the shoulder to send him on his way. "And thanks for the support, Gibson, means a lot. Can see why Lion likes you so much."

"Yeah, yeah." He waved it off. "No need to brown nose me, I'm already doing you the favour."

King chuckled as Phillipa and Bea both swarmed Lou. I passed her over to their coddling so I could wrap my arms around King and give him a hug. There was something about feeling him so strong and solid in my hold that made me believe no matter what happened, he'd survive because he was the strongest man I knew.

"My queen," he murmured into my hair.

"Bring them back to us, honey," I told him as he moved away, keeping hold of my hand until the last second, then turning on his booted heel to rally the men.

I moved back to Lou just as her water broke, splashing against the ground and the two women supporting her.

Bea screamed, "Ew! Jesus, Lou, did you really have to do that on my feet?"

And as Lou and her mother, Phillipa, laughed, I had to believe everything was going to be alright.

If I'd known then, what I did now, I would have taken another moment to let it all sink in.

CHAPTER FOURTEEN

King

IT WAS all over by the time we got to Vancouver. So, instead'a the brothers rollin' over to a crime scene we didn't need to get messed up in, we headed to the hospital where Lou had been admitted and took up sentry in the waitin' area. Over the course of the night, seemed everyone showed. Buck and Maja tucked together in a chair too small for the burly ass biker, Nova on the ground holdin' Lila and Cleo on either side as they slept, Bea curled up half on Lila, half on Priest's feet where he stood beside the swinging doors for hours on end. Smoke arrived with Tempest Riley dragging his asthma machine, and he quickly took a seat next to Phillipa who blushed then shot the shit with him all night long.

I sat there, talkin' to whoever sat beside me to chat or readin' from the first edition copy of *The Prince* Cress had given me, even though my mind was on Cressida who was in the room with Lou, supportin' her through givin' birth.

I'd peeked in on them in the early stages, just leaned in the doorway and watched as Cress fed a sweatin', obviously uncomfortable Loulou some ice chips while tellin' her stories 'bout Zeus and the club from 'fore Lou and Dad had gotten together. I loved the way they interacted, as if there was an invisible force field 'round them, as if their love was a barrier against all the wrongness in the world, insulatin' 'em from it, warmin' them against it. They treated each other like sisters and best friends when really, Lou would technically be Cress's mother-in-law, weird as it was given Cress was ten years older and her former teacher. Luckily, nothing mattered between them but the love they had for one another.

We gave 'em that, Zeus and me. A place in The Fallen family. We'd shown them what it was to love against all odds, to strip the bullshit away 'cause it was what laid at the heart of a person that meant everythin'.

Thinkin' 'bout it made my throat tight and my heart pump slow, my blood weighted with pride and so much affection. If I'd been less of a man, I might'a cried.

The time for visits was over, though. Lou was officially givin' birth, and Zeus, done with the police and the Berserker drama, was on his way to meet his babies.

Heard him 'fore I saw him, the early hours of the mornin' makin' his voice even coarser, his laugh like a lion roarin' through the halls of the hospital.

He rounded the corner, and it struck me like it sometimes did how much larger than life he was. Big man, packed like a powerhouse with dense muscle, thick, dark beard, and eyes as light as mine but silver. Hair like mine, too, crazy and tousled all 'round his angel wing tatted shoulders, brown dipped in honey at the ends. He was beautiful to me, and it might'a been weird to say that as his son, but I felt the beauty of him in my gut because he was the best man I'd ever known. There was nothin' bad in him, not at all, not an ounce. He was love and laughter and family.

He'd sacrificed for the people he loved, and he'd taught me to do the same. He'd shown me that nothin' was more important than protectin' the ones you loved, and it was a philosophy that was carved into my fuckin' bones.

Everythin' good in me I got from him.

Not Farrah, the bitch who carried me in her toxic womb then continued to spit poison at me each of the years of my life she was a part of.

Not the grandparents or ancestors we never knew.

Just Zeus.

One parent; as if H.R. and me had sprung from him fully formed, Athena from the head of Zeus.

Might'a been the day, knowin' I was welcomin' two new siblin's into the world, knowin' they'd have two parents, the *best* parents, kids could probably ever have save Cress and myself, but I felt honest to Christ moved by the sight of my dad in the hall, beamin', proud and strong, even after dealin' with yet another shit show.

Then Harleigh Rose was there, her smile droppin' with an almost audible crash to the linoleum as her eyes, melted down aquamarine, swept over the crew of us waitin' there. A deer caught in the headlights, she froze and looked like she was itchin' to run until Danner approached her, hand to her back, the tiny action holdin' her completely in his thrall.

I moved without thinkin', just needin' to have my little sister in my arms again after weeks of not seein' her. I was walkin, then joggin' when her eyes widened. I thought she'd bolt, so I started runnin', snaggin' her up in my arms so tight she gasped in my ear.

She smelled the same. Somehow it struck me as fuckin' crazy and beautiful that her whole life, she'd smelled the very same. Floral, some kinda barely sweet, slightly earthy flower that made me think of untended fields where wild horses roamed. Pretty and wild, just like my sister.

"H.R." I said into her streaky hair, voice coarse, arms banded too tight 'round her. "Fuckin' welcome home."

Like a key in a lock, she broke open in my arms, clingin' and sobbin' like she'd been separated from me for years and had gone through unmentionable tragedies.

I didn't doubt the tragedies part, and it broke my fuckin' heart that it seemed like years since I'd been able to care for her properly. It was hard, bein' the older one, the one who'd always taken care of her, knowin' that she was old enough now not to need me, at least not in the way she once had.

Felt good, like pressure on a knotted muscle, that she gave me her tears, that she could still feel safe enough with me to drop the thorns and be that sweet, little girl she'd once been.

"My sweet Harleigh Rose," I soothed, draggin' my hand down her upper back like soothin' a cat. "Hush now."

She only cried louder, and I realized it was 'cause Cress was there, wrappin' her arms 'round us both, pressin' kisses to H.R.'s wet cheeks. And Lila, bracketin' us from the other side, whisperin' to her best friend.

"Can I get in on this action?" Nova asked with a leer in his voice. "You know I love a group hug."

"God, don't be gross," Lila admonished, but she opened her arm so Nova could join our huddle.

"Ah fuck me. If there's one reason I became a fuckin' biker, it was to avoid this shit," Buck grumbled from behind me, then he was there, too, proppin' his white beard up on H.R.'s head. "But fuck it, not every day we get our princess back."

Then everyone was there, our hug four people deep, some fuckin' biker kumbaya shit that we'd all pretend didn't happen as soon as we disbanded.

Noticed Lion Danner leanin' in a corner with a small smile watchin' H.R., and I chuckled, thinkin' of all the times they'd look at each other like that, thinkin' the other didn't notice.

"Danny," I said, walkin' over with a grin. "Fuck man, it's good to have ya back."

"Yeah, I recall you not liking me much when Cress and Lou went through their shit."

I shrugged a shoulder, grin still in place 'cause fuckin' with Lion had always been a hoot. "Water under the bridge, you were conflicted back then. You're on the right side'a things now."

Cress laughed as she held H.R. to her, strokin' her hair, lovin' on her without any bitterness at her absence, just happy to have her home.

Fuck, I loved my woman.

"You tell him I was leaving the force?" Lion asked my sister.

She shook her head, but I whooped loudly, fuckin' thrilled to have corrupted another copper to the dark side.

I was gettin' good at that shit.

"Fuck yeah, you did! Wasn't talkin' 'bout the right or wrong side'a the law, though. Was talkin' 'bout bein' on our side again, mine and H.R.'s. We missed you there."

Somethin' in his stoic face moved, like shadows over concrete. "Yeah, King, I missed you, too."

"Here to stay, I'm thinkin'." I winked at him as I went to collect Cress and Harleigh Rose went to him.

It was good to see that, the way she smiled at him like nothin' bad would ever happen again so long as she was with him.

If H.R. didn't need me anymore, I was glad it was him who'd bear the brunt of responsibility for her. She was a fuckin' handful.

"*Fuck, yeah!*" Zeus hollered, havin' raced back to the delivery room as soon as he'd arrived, now back at the entrance of the hall, arms raised, fists tight like a rocker at a concert. "We got two healthy kids and a healthy Lou. Walker and Angel Garro."

Maja climbed on a chair, spun her fist in the air, and started whoopin'.

Everyone else followed, shakin' the thin hospital walls with our celebratin', drawin' nurses out to shush us only for them to start laughin' and cheerin', too, as we thumped Z's chest and let him roar.

"Zeus Garro," a cold voice called out, hammerin' through the noise, leavin' our ears ringin' with the sudden silence.

Danner frowned, steppin' between Zeus and the newly arrived Vancouver cops. "Robson, Hatley, what's going on?"

They stopped, surprised probably, to see a cop with a crew of bikers in 1%er cuts.

"Good to see you, Danner, but this is official business."

"The fuck?" I demanded, pushin' through the crowd so I could get between 'em and Dad.

They got to him first.

"Zeus Garro, you're under arrest for the murder of Officer Gibson. You have the right to remain silent. An attorney will be provided to you by the province…"

"Fuck *that*." I pushed through, stoppin' one'a them from slappin' cuffs on his wrists. "Our lawyer will fuckin' roast you for this. What the hell are you talkin' 'bout?"

"Riley Gibson was found dead, shot through the head."

"Was nowhere fuckin' near Entrance," Zeus argued, calm as a fuckin' monk. "Ask Danner, was down 'ere all night, half'a that spent with 'im."

They paused, but the one named Robson held up a pair of handcuffs. "You can put your hands behind your back, or my partner can do it for you. The murder weapon was found a hundred yards away in a creek bed with your fingerprints on it, registered to you. You've got a problem with that, I suggest you get one of your biker buddies to call you a lawyer."

"My wife just had twins," Zeus said in a dead voice. "Lemme say goodbye."

"You wanted time with your wife and kids, you should've thought twice before murdering again," Robson snapped before the other guy shoved him against the wall and wrenched his hands back.

I lunged forward, but Buck held me back and whispered, "Calm the fuck down. We'll get 'im out, and we don't need to be splittin' resource on you."

"Dad, no," Harleigh Rose cried, tryin' to hug Zeus as he reluctantly let them cuff his hands.

He made eye contact with me as they turned him 'round and started to frog march him down the hall, expression blank but eyes grey fire. "Call White. Meet me at the station. I'll be home with my woman and my babies by tonight. You tell 'em that."

"I will. No way you're goin' back there," I promised, and I felt it take root in my fuckin' soul. He had almost lost his soul to prison 'fore, no way I'd let that happen again.

CHAPTER FIFTEEN

King

"IT WAS THE FUCKIN' pigs," Skell shouted, leanin' over the table in The Fallen chapel, yellin' like everyone had been yellin' since church commenced an hour ago.

It was two days after my baby bro and sister had been born, and Zeus was still in custody.

White had been down there for hours tryin' to get him out on bail, but 'cause he was an ex-con with one murder charge already on his rap sheet, the judge wouldn't set bail.

It'd been like a bomb had gone off in that hospital, a land-mine explodin' underfoot just when we'd thought we were safe, blowin' off limbs, tearin' us to bloody pieces.

The women went to work instantly, led by Cress and Maja, to be there for Lou and the babies. Loulou, needless to fuckin' say, was not doin' so good. She was pissed as a caged wild cat, unable to do anythin' but care for the babies and wait. There were a lotta tears and shoutin', a vase thrown against a wall, but through the meltdown, she was still a new mum and a good one. Walker and Angel were never far from her, always tended to with a gentleness that was so at odds with the fire in her eyes that wouldn't die until Z was free.

And the men, we were tryin' to get our shit tight, 'cause our Prez had just been incarcerated for the second fuckin' time, and there was a fuck ton'a crap that needed to be worked through. But goddamn, it was like heardin' cats.

Everyone was alpha, everyone was mad as a hatter at the injustice of it all, and the meetin' had gone to hell 'cause of it.

"'Course, it's the goddamn cops," I growled, shovin' back from my chair so violently, it tipped over. The brother's eyes went to me, shocked 'cause I wasn't one for shoutin' or outbursts. "We know the why of it, brothers. Staff Sergeant Danner got tired of waitin' for a legit reason to take us down, so he created one. He had to know Gibson'd been helpin' us out, that he'd been at the party that night. Only answer to the fuckin' question. So, let's be smart enough to move on and ask another. What the hell are we gonna do 'bout it?"

A short silence came outta habit, 'cause normally, Zeus'd be the one to stand up and say somethin'.

Finally, Buck leaned forward and slammed a meaty fist on the table. "First things first. We gotta vote."

My skin itched, too hot and tight. It was the anger barely contained in me, but also the desire to step up into the vacant place and be interim Prez while my dad was in the clink. No way it'd happen, though. I'd been fully patched in for a hot fuckin' second, and there was a hierarchy to the club. It was the way it'd always worked.

Buck was VP, so naturally, we'd vote him in as leader.

"'Fore we vote, what's the plan exactly?" Nova asked, eyein' down Buck.

"Drive by shootin', scare that motherfucker outta his skin

with fear. Show 'em The Fallen won't be fucked with or intimidated."

"They'll arrest some of us on reasonable suspicion," I pointed out, even though I'd known that's what he'd suggest.

"So fuckin' be it," he declared, slappin' the table again.

I hesitated, but the rage had blown the lid off my reservations. "We don't need more brothers behind bars. We need to be smart 'bout this, or they'll pick us off one by one. Might be better to let 'em think we're crushed by the blow and need time to lick our wounds. Use that time to make a plan to take that fucker down."

"Kill 'im? Yeah, fuck yeah, I'm down," Lab-Rat growled.

"Can't kill him," I said, watchin' every single brother scowl. "If we want Zeus outta jail, we can't kill the man who knows how Gibson was done or who may even have done the deed himself. We figure this shit out, then we fuck him."

"How the fuck we gonna do that?" Heckler demanded. "We're not fuckin' pigs."

"Man has a point, King," Axe-Man said, calm and slow as he always was. "Not investigators."

"No, but we're goddamn criminals. We can intimidate someone into confessin', stalk a copper to find out his filthy secrets, and blackmail him into tellin' us more. I'm tellin' ya, we got options. Smart ones if we reign in the fury."

"Not reignin' in shit, and I'm shocked as hell you'd be such a fuckin' pansy 'bout this shit when it's not just your Prez, but your *dad* locked away," Wiseguy grunted.

"Hey, man, not cool," Bat chastised, but I was already seein' red.

I leaned over the table so far, my boots almost left the ground, a snarl affixed to my face as I stared Wiseguy down. "You think I'm not 'bout to go apeshit, you're fuckin' *wrong*. Gotta dad better than any other damn man locked away for the second time. New babies at home, fragile wife goin' through that shit alone, even though he didn't do anything.

I'm fuckin' livid, Wiseguy, and you say shit 'bout it again, I'll knock your fuckin' teeth in. I'm tryin' to be *smart* here so we can get him the fuck outta there."

"Somethin' needs to be done *now* to show that motherfucker who he's dealin' with," Skell shouted.

"They know who they're dealin' with. He's made it his life's mission to take down the club, you don't think he's bracin' for an attack and makin' plans to fire back at us? Listen, Machiavelli said, "if you need to injure someone, do it in such a way that you do not have to fear their vengeance."'" I pounded my fist against the table. "'If you do them minor damage, they will get their revenge; but if you cripple them, there is nothing they can do.'"

"Pretty words," Heckler spat. "Don't mean shit."

"You're not listenin'. Danner did this, and we need to end him. I'm just sayin' we need to end him in a way he doesn't come back to try and rip apart more lives. Gotta woman I'm 'bout to marry, you think I wanna to spend my honeymoon in the hole? Bat, you got kids, you want them growin' up without a father? Buck, you want Maja growin' old without you?" The silence was precarious, each brother a stick of dynamite held perilously over a fire. "We target the cops separately, see if we can get one'a 'em to flip. Doubt Hutchinson knows anythin' that could help seein' as he's been in our pocket for years. Take 'em in pairs, bring 'em in, let Priest have his special way with them, and see what we can get on Danner and the rest."

"Zeus was fuckin' framed for murder," Buck said, and as soon as he did, I knew my tactic was over 'fore it'd even begun. "Danner needs to feel the wrath of biker fury, and he needs to feel it now."

"Hear, fuckin' hear!" A few of the brothers shouted.

Nova kicked his foot against mine under the table like an apology.

"Let's get to the vote," Buck ordered.

And it was no surprise, twenty minutes later, when Buck was announced interim Prez.

Cress was asleep in my bed at the clubhouse, passed out after another day lendin' her services to Loulou. Wanted to join her there, get sunk deep in the oblivion of sleep, but Boner, Lab-Rat, and Heckler were out on a ride by Danner's house, doin' that drive-by Buck'd been so hot on.

Didn't sit right with me. Felt like walkin' straight into a trap Danner'd spent months makin' just right. He knew bikers well, watchin' us enough over the years to know how we'd react. He'd expect exactly that.

I sighed into my Blue Buck 'fore suckin' back a gulp of cold brew and knockin' my fist against the hardcover of *The Prince* sittin' on the bar in front of me. Sometimes, there was a barrier between me and my brothers 'cause they disregarded anythin' they couldn't immediately understand. There were a few exceptions, like Priest who'd memorized nearly every religious text he could get his hands on, and Bat who'd been in the military long enough to question things even if they'd stood for eons unchanged. But on the whole, bikers were not the kinda men that liked to be told things from a book, however worthy.

And I was that man, exactly that man, who lusted after

knowledge with a palpable kinda thirst. One'a the many reasons I'd fallen for Cress so fuckin' hard was 'cause she had a brain like the Delian problem, a brain I'd never be able to fully understand no matter how long I puzzled over it.

Words and prose made sense to me in a way that I thought if I cut open a vein, ink would run down my arm and populate a page with verse.

So, I got *The Prince* and wondered how it could apply to my life, to this situation.

We had to be cleverer than our natures, unpredictable in a way bikers never really were. We had to be *more* if we wanted to get Z outta that stinkin' fuckin' hole and Danner dead. Or in there instead'a him.

Frustration boiled in my gut, barely doused by the second beer I was slammin' back at an alarmin' rate.

"You know," Nova said as he dropped into the stool beside me. "Got your point in there."

I cocked a brow, too tired to play games with the club's Casanova.

"Serious as shit, brother, I feel ya. Buck's been in the life a long fuckin' time, sometimes the man gets stuck in the sixties, 'fore the headache and hassle'a technology made bein' a rebel a fuckuva lot more complicated."

"Could still do it," Priest said from my other side, silent as a ghost creepin' up on us. "Take 'em one by one and force them to give us what they know."

"Gotta know, brother." Bat slapped his tattooed hands on my shoulders and squeezed, 'Hell' across one set of fingers and 'Bound' across the other. "We got your back."

A sigh rushed through me then made me chuckle 'cause I sounded like my woman. "Appreciate it, serious as fuck."

There was a loud screech of tires outside, alertin' every single one'a us, guns outta waistbands, knives in hands in a fuckin' flash.

Seconds later, the clubhouse door pushed open and a small figure appeared in the doorframe.

"Hello," Susan Danner, soon-to-be Susan Hobbs again, greeted shakily as she stood clutchin' the string of pearls she was always wearin'. "I was wondering if King Kyle Garro might be here."

I was up outta my seat 'fore she'd even finished speakin'.

"Susan," I said gently as I went to her and wrapped her up in a hug. "What's goin' on? Are you confused?"

Susan had early onset Alzheimer's disease, and I'd seen her 'round town sometimes starin' blankly into space or holdin' a can at Mac's Grocer as if searchin' for the answers to life's questions. I always helped her home in those cases, and I knew those episodes were becomin' more and more frequent.

Still, she had it together enough to divorce Harold Danner before she could be declared incompetent and get stuck with him the rest of her life.

Her shakin' hands found my back and patted at me like little birds afraid to land. "King, oh, honey, are you okay?"

I pulled back and bent at the knee to look her in the eye. This was the one woman in my life who had ever given me a modicum of maternal love, and even though we'd grown distant like Lion and me over the years, I still loved her and always would.

"Worried more 'bout you, Suse. What brings you out here?"

Her pretty green eyes filled with tears, and she brought her hand to her mouth as if to disguise the ugliness of her words. "I went to visit Harold because, well, it was stormy out on the ranch, and I got a bit frightened. He normally doesn't mind because, well, I think he'd like to come home to me. Anyway, well, I let myself into his apartment, and he was speaking with this woman." She made a face of distaste. "Trashy, from what I could see, you know? And they were arguing very loudly so I could hear them even at the base of the stairs."

My heart stopped beatin' for one long forebodin' beat. "What'd they say?"

Her lower lip trembled, and her hands were flutterin' through the air. "She was angry with him 'cause he'd asked her to steal something from your father, and I suppose she didn't like what he would do with it when she did..."

"What did she steal?" I bit out, tryin' to stay calm, tryin' not to scare her even though there was a howl in my throat and the urge to run down prey runnin' rampant in my blood.

She sucked a breath in through her teeth. "I think it was a gun."

Fuck, fuck, *fuck*.

"Okay," I said slowly, steerin' her over to the couches, movin' an empty beer can so she could take a seat, aware that Nova, Bat, and Priest were at my back. "Did they see you?"

"No, no. I was so, well, overwhelmed by the whole thing. You know, Harold has always been so stern 'bout the law, but over the last few years...well, he hasn't been the same. I'm worried, King," she admitted, tears fallin' as she looked at me with the wide, confused eyes of a child set in an older woman's face. "I'm worried he did something truly awful."

He did, I wanted to rage, he did! He put Zeus Garro in prison for a crime he didn't commit.

"Yeah, Suse," I said instead, surprised by the cold, calculated calm of my voice, like ice cubes slotted into a glass. "He did."

"I'm so sorry," she whispered, before droppin' her head in her hands to cry. "You always were such a good boy, and Rosie too. He just doesn't know how to stop once he starts something. Really, I thought, well, I thought he was a good man, but...I guess I was wrong."

The sobs rolled through her like crashin' waves, heavin' her slight shoulders, explodin' from her mouth where they spilled into her palms. I rubbed her back and winced as I comforted her, needin' to get the brothers back into the chapel so we could talk 'bout this latest development.

"Can…" she asked after a few moments. "Can I stay here with you until Lion comes home from Vancouver?"

"Of course," I agreed with a little smile. "You took me in once, it's my turn to repay the favour."

Her smile was tremulous but pure as she looked at me. I hoped she'd never know I'd have to ruthlessly use the information she gave me to put a noose 'round her ex-husband's neck.

CHAPTER SIXTEEN

King

ONCE WAS one time too many for a kid to see their father in prison. The first time Zeus'd gone down, I'd got why he'd done it, even as just a young boy. He'd killed a man to save the life of a little girl, the same girl that a decade later would be his wife. Didn't like it, stuck with Farrah, without my dad and hero, but I got it, and that was important in me learnin' how to deal with it.

There was nothin' to get now. Zeus hadn't done shit all aside from momentarily disappearin' to save Harleigh Rose from a shit situation. Yet, once again, the hero was bein' punished like a villain.

He sat in the bank of phone booths behind warped, dirty plexiglass, wearin' an orange jumpsuit that barely fit his massive frame. The brackets 'round his mouth had become troughs, the creases beside his eyes heavy fans, and when he locked eyes with me, I saw the beatin' his soul had taken by bein' in the slammer again, this time separated from babies he didn't even know yet.

"Dad," I grunted through the pressure in my chest as I took a seat and adjusted Walker on my lap. "Both of your sons are here to see ya."

Dad's face crumpled as he looked between us, eyes chartin' every inch of Walker's tiny body where I held him up for observation, then switchin' to track my own. One tatted hand reached out as if he could touch us then dropped uselessly to the table.

"My boys," he said, voice dry and rough as gravel. "Fuck me, got the most beautiful kids on the planet."

My nose itched as emotion welled in my throat, but I gave him an easy grin 'cause he didn't need to be worryin' 'bout me along with everythin' else.

"Lou says he's already got a mouth on him," I relayed, adjustin' my baby brother so his sleepy blue eyes, already pale in a way indicatin' they'd go silver, were trained on his dad. "Sucks like a Hoover."

He laughed, not the belly rumble I was used to, but a chuckle that brightened him all the same. "Fuck me for missin' that."

"You seen Angel?" I asked, even though I knew Lou had been visitin' every day with the babies.

"Heartbreaker already," he claimed with pride. "Gonna have my hands full with 'er, can already tell."

"If Harleigh Rose is anythin' to go by, you breed fierce women. Thinkin' she'll be okay no matter what."

"Yeah," he agreed. "Got lucky with my kids."

"Nah, we got lucky with you, old man."

His eyes flashed like light reflectin' off the tip of a blade, an almost violent surge of love slicin' across his face.

I got that—a depth of love that was almost agonizin' in its intensity—from him.

"Cress and you will be lucky as fuck too," he said, lookin' at the way I held Walker. "Gonna make me the youngest, best lookin' grandfather we know anytime soon?"

I laughed with him then laughed even harder when Walker whacked me with his little fist as if my laughter offended his grumpy self.

"Yeah, workin' on it, old man," I admitted, lovin' the crazy set of his happy grin.

"Glad to fuckin' hear it. Like the thought'a our kids growin' up together."

I shook my head at the thought, my dad and I havin' kids the same age, but we were bikers, and we were Fallen. We didn't care much for social mores.

"Brothers voted Buck in," I told him even though he'd already know.

Zeus sat back and crossed his arms, eyes still swivelin' from me to Walker and back every few seconds. "Thought you'd wanna talk 'bout that."

I shrugged a shoulder. "It is what it is. Susan Hobbs showed up at the club the other day, worried Danner'd got some bitch to steal your gun for him. Made sense, seein' as you haven't used that piece in years."

"Sat in the bottom'a that desk drawer for 'bout a decade," he agreed.

"Suse gave us the alarm code to his apartment. Goin' with some of the brothers tonight to see what we find."

"What exactly are you hopin' to find? And if you find it, what the hell are you gonna do with it? You're not a cop, King, you find somethin', it won't be admissible in court."

"No, but Lion's been talkin' to Internal Affairs in Vancouver, they got an eye on Harold now, and if they get an anonymous tip off, they might act on it."

He looked skeptical, but I couldn't blame him. It wasn't much to hang our fuckin' hopes on.

"Careful, boy. Don't need you in 'ere with me, not when you got a weddin' comin' soon."

"Cress and I were thinkin' we'd postpone that," I admitted.

"Like fuck you will." He scowled, leanin' forward so his nose was near pressed to the glass. "You listen to me, King. Why do ya think I married Lou while she was almost dyin' in a hospital bed? 'Cause life proves to us again and again it's too fuckin' short, and we can't account for shit that might happen to us. You love that woman the way you do, the way I love mine, like you'll die if you don't have her in your sight, under your touch, then you fuckin' marry her like you planned. Don't punish yourself just 'cause I'm bein' punished in 'ere. The time for your sacrifice will come one day, though, fuck me, I hope it doesn't, and when it does, you want people to stop livin' just 'cause you got dealt a shit hand? Solidarity like that means shit. Don't need you to suffer 'cause I suffer. Need you to *live* and *love* 'cause I don't got the means. Ya hear me?"

Fuck, if I didn't. "Yeah, I getcha. Thing you don't get is, won't be much of a celebration without you there with us."

I looked down at Walker who was now sound asleep. I smoothed a hand over his tiny, downy head. Loved the weight of him in my arms, loved his namesake, and loved knowin' if anyone could live up to the hype of my lost Fallen brother Mute, it'd be my baby brother.

"Look at you with him," Zeus croaked, then cleared his throat of emotion. "Ready to be a husband and a dad, King. Don't take that away from yourself, and don't take it away from me. You think there's anythin' more rewardin' for a father than seein' his kids happy? I gotta be in 'ere? That's what'll keep me goin', knowin' you're livin' free and livin' good."

"Wish I'd done like I wanted and dragged us all down the

mountain to get married the day I proposed in City Hall," I grumbled.

He laughed again, just a hard exclamation of sound. "Fuck, you take after your father, boy. Do it now and do it well. Wanna hear all 'bout it if I'm still in 'ere when it happens."

"White suggested against gettin' the trial moved up. Said we only have evidence against you right now, and they'd move you farther away to a more secure prison if they found you guilty. Harder to overturn a sentence from a jury than pre-trial incarceration."

"Yeah," he said, as if it wasn't whacked he was in there in the first place. "You know what it's like, Ford Mountain Correctional's basically a holiday."

I bit my lip against sayin' shit, 'cause I did know. I'd been kept there briefly in my senior year of high school after Warren, a high school teacher who was now dead, had planted drugs in my locker. In my opinion, Ford Mountain was *not* a fuckin' vacation.

Z must've read the tension in my face 'cause he leaned forward again, hooked my eyes on the silver bait in his gaze, and spoke serious, "Day you met Cressida Irons, you came home with fuckin' stars in your eyes. You remember what you told me?"

Of course, I remembered. It was the day I found myself just as much as the day I found Cress. Man didn't forget anythin' 'bout a day like that.

"Told you I'd met my woman."

"Yeah. Told me point blank you'd met your woman, and when I asked what the fuck you meant, you said you'd dreamed of a woman all your life and didn't know 'er face 'til you saw *her* 'cross Mac's parking lot."

I swallowed thickly, rememberin' it all.

There wasn't a moment that I fell in love, the tumblin' sensation that turns the stomach and has you graspin' at thin air to brace yourself against somethin' that will not recede. No, that came later.

At first, there was a loss.

Of breath through my nose and air in my mouth. Of the metronome beat of my pulse and the strength in my spine.

It was disorientin' for only long enough to shock me like icy water, and then everythin' returned to normal.

I breathed, I spoke, I beat, and stood strong.

But everythin' had shifted an infinitesimal bit. The cadence of my breath, my speech, and heart had shifted from a perfunctory tone to somethin' deeper, somethin' rhythmic that moved more than my body.

Whatever force had moved me through life 'fore had shifted, and it had shifted to her.

A tilt of gravity that indicated a future fall, but for the moment, only left me slightly changed. But changed enough to note it and note the cause for it.

Her.

"Yeah," I finally said, voice thick in my throat. "I remember."

"You marry that woman, King," he warned me. "You marry her for you, and you marry her for me, 'cause I love that woman, and I love 'er for you, and nothin' would make me happier, even stuck in 'ere, than you givin' 'er our Garro name."

"She might not go for it," I said 'cause it was true.

Cress loved my dad nearly as much as me.

"You bring her in, I'll talk to 'er." He leaned back in his chair and crossed his arms, lookin' every inch the biker Prez, even locked up and decked out in orange.

"Hear ya."

"And 'bout the vote, I get what you're not sayin', and I get why you wanted the position for yourself. It'll make sense one day, it's meant to *be* one day, but the club is a democracy, and I'm not gonna interfere in that. If brothers voted Buck, he's it." He paused, devilry sparkin' in his. "But a man's gotta do what he thinks best, yeah?"

"Yeah," I agreed with a satanic smile. "And there's nothin' I won't do for this family and for you. Hope you get that."

"Not a day goes by I don't."

APPLES.

The entire cabin smelled of apples and cinnamon when I dragged my tired ass through the door of Shamble Wood Cottage later that day after droppin' Lou and the kids off at home. The scent revived me like smellin' salts, and even though a minute 'fore, I would'a said nothin' could make me smile after visitin' my dad in prison, the sight of Cress rockin' out to Zac Brown Band, singin' into a wooden spoon to Shadow who looked incredibly unimpressed from where he sat on the counter, made me burst straight through to laughter.

When I finished, she was standin' in the middle of the kitchen with that smile of hers she wore just for me, somethin' like exaltation in the curve of that pretty, pouty mouth.

"Babe," I said, still chucklin' as I moved forward to take her in my arms. "You are such a dork."

She tossed her hair and scowled at me, but the hands that

wrapped ’round my waist said she wasn’t mad ’bout my gentle teasin’.

“I’m a biker babe, King, I’ve got to rock out when the spirit moves me,” she corrected primly.

“Whatever you say.”

Her mouth tasted sweet and hot with fruit and spice, so I ate at it until the sweetness faded on my tongue. When I pulled back, she swayed, eyes closed, lips swollen, and I went hard instantly at the sight of her eagerness for more.

“Made me some pie?” I asked her, kissin’ the tip of her nose ’cause the spring sun had brought out the freckles on it, and they were cute as fuck.

“Mhmm, for a picnic.”

“Babe, got so much shit to do…you know how much chaos is goin’ down at the club. Got plans to use Paula to our advantage tonight.”

“Okay, but after our picnic. We need to have some *fun*, King. You’re not Atlas, you don’t need to bear the entire weight of our world on your shoulders. Let someone else take up the mantle for the afternoon, and come away with me. You taught me what happiness was, and now it’s my turn to give it back to you.”

“My girl’s sweet,” I muttered, feelin’ it like a toothache. “But you want me to have some fun, why don’t you lose the dress, and I’ll fuck you right here on the floor. We can have a picnic right on the carpet after to recuperate.”

Her eyes flared, desire catchin’ the brown and turnin’ it gold, but she shook her head. “I want to be on the back of your bike with you, and I want to go back to the cliff, if that’s okay? It’s gorgeous and it’s been a minute since we just let ourselves experience some beauty.”

“Experience it every mornin’ I wake up next to you,” I argued, kissin’ down her neck, palmin’ her ass through the silk of her white polka dot dress.

“Stop trying to seduce me and put the food in the saddlebags. I'll grab the pie." She shoved me back and flounced over to the fridge, bendin' low so I gotta glimpse of the little white panties coverin' her sex.

"Fine, but I'm eatin' dessert first," I growled, landin' my palm on the curve of her ass. "And I don't mean the pie."

She was right 'bout needin' to let go of all the chaos for a beat and just fuckin' live again. Felt the relief as soon as my Harley rumbled to life beneath me and Cress's arms twined 'round my belly, her sweet form pressed against my leather cut.

This was it, peace found amongst the chaos, havin' the road under my tires, my woman at my back, and the fresh, ocean air whippin' through my hair.

I hollered as we drove down the windin' road just to feel the noise catch in the wind. Cress mimicked me, unwrappin' her arms to toss them up for a moment just to feel the edge of danger and know she was alive.

When we pulled up to the dead-end road and the path to the cliff, I felt lighter than I had in weeks. I snagged an arm 'round my woman's waist as she got off the bike and tugged her to me, kissin' the smile off her face.

"Thank you," I told her, nuzzlin' into the soft valley between her breasts. "Needed this more than I knew. Needed you."

"That's what I'm here for," she quipped easily, runnin' her hands through my hair. "I can't help much with the strategy talk and the biker stuff, but I can make you smile."

"That's the damn truth."

She tugged her fingers in my mane so I was forced to look up into her wicked smile.

"What was it you once said? Happiness is streaking bare-assed naked down the wet sand, drinking too much, and laughing too loud? Well…" She stepped back with a cheeky giggle and started to undo the buttons on her dress. "There's beer and champagne in the bags, and I thought, wouldn't it be fun…" She toed off her shoes and let the opened torso of her dress fall to her waist, baring her sweet tits, nipples taut in the cool breeze. "If we played a little game."

"Yeah?" I asked, the word a growl as my eyes tracked over her. She shimmied her hips, and the dress slipped off, poolin' at her feet to reveal she wasn't wearin' any underwear.

"When did you have time to take off those little panties I saw you wearin' in the kitchen?"

She tossed the scrap of cotton at me then came forward to brace her hands on my thighs and speak against my lips. "If you get naked, too, and catch me before I make it to the cliffs, you can have me any way you want to take me."

And with a nip at my bottom lip, she was off, hair flyin', plump ass jigglin' as she took off toward the cliffs, her laughter followin' like an invitation.

One I took without hesitation.

Shucked my clothes in thirty seconds flat, grabbed the bag of food in one hand, and charged after her, catchin' a glimpse of sun-kissed hair through the greenery. The ground was soft and verdant beneath my feet, the air so sweet it tasted like melted saltwater taffy on my tongue as I drank it down.

It felt fuckin' good to rip across the earth after her, so good I started laughin' even 'fore I gained on her, even 'fore I growled just to hear her scream, even 'fore I snatched her little waist right in the middle of the cliff top and sent us both tumblin' down.

We were both laughin' too hard to kiss, rollin' in the silken grass for a minute 'fore we calmed down, me on top of her, hands pinned to the ground above her head.

She giggled up at me, eyes so bright with ardent adoration it hit me like a punch to the chest.

"Hey, honey," she said softly. "Good to see that smile again."

I dipped down to run my nose along hers. "What would I do without you?"

"You'll never have to know," she promised, then squirmed a little, rubbin' the points of her breasts through my chest hair. "Now, what're you gonna do to me?"

I sat back on my heels and reached over for the bag I'd dropped in my pursuit of her. I dragged it into my lap and dug out the bottle of champagne.

"Think we should make a toast to our wedding first," I announced as I started to unwind the wrappin'.

Cress writhed in anticipation as I popped the cork and held the bottle to her lips as it frothed over, lettin' the sweet liquid slide down her throat.

I moved, straddlin' her chest so that my cock loomed over her face. Fistin' the base, I drew the wet tip across her lips, watchin' as her greedy tongue darted out, tryin' to catch a taste of me. I cupped the back of her head in one hand to better the angle 'fore pressin' the head to her lips.

"Open up, babe," I urged. "Remind me how much you love to take me down your throat."

She hummed long and low, vibratin' 'round me as she sucked my crown, swirlin' her tongue like I was an ice cream cone.

The sight of her like that, the lady gone to harlot just for me, set my blood to boilin'. It was heady, the power of it, to see a woman step beyond her inhibitions to please me and please herself.

"Touch yourself while you suck me," I ordered huskily as she laved my shaft with her pink tongue. "Want you drippin' in the grass by the time I'm ready to fuck you."

She moaned 'cause my woman loved my filthy mouth.

I tipped the champagne again, carefully pourin' it down my cock so it spilled into her mouth. The carbonation buzzed against my skin, and I cursed viciously as she sucked harder, wanton slurpin' sounds comin' from her eager mouth.

"So gorgeous, suckin' my cock like that," I told her, thrustin' now, in and out shallowly just to watch her cheeks hollow and fill with my flesh. "Love it when you worship my dick like that."

"I do, too," she panted, pullin' off to press a kiss to the tip then lick it hard with the flat of her tongue. "Sometimes I feel like a fanatic. When I get my hands on you, your taste in my mouth, my name on your lips, I could overdose on devout ecstasy."

I pressed my cock back into her mouth, guidin' it in and out, forcin' her to keep it open wantonly, lovin' the power she gave me by lettin' me use her like that.

The base of my spine tingled, and my balls drew up, warnin' me I was gonna spill more than champagne in her mouth if I indulged any longer. So, I pulled out and off her, leanin' on my forearms in the grass between her legs.

"Spread those pretty legs wider," I ordered as I tipped the heavy bottle over her beautiful belly. "I have a thirst for somethin' sweeter than champagne."

She shivered at the cold then gasped at the feel of my warm tongue lappin' it up, followin' a drop all the way down to her sex where I baptized her with more sparklin' wine.

"Smell like flowers and taste like honey," I rasped as I moved my tongue down the seam of her groin then up the other side. She squirmed, so I banded a hand over her hips. "Keep still while I drink my fill."

She came almost as soon as I wrapped my lips 'round her clit and *sucked*, buckin' her hips and tearin' out the grass between her clenchin' fingers. I surged up 'fore she was done, thrustin' into her still ripplin' sex, drivin' her climax higher.

The feel of her in my arms like that, completely givin' herself over to the pleasure that I gave her was better than any artificial high or drink, richer than ambrosia.

"Love comin' inside you knowin' there's no protection against makin' a baby together," I whispered in her ear as she spasmed 'round me. "Wanna come in you so deep, you feel it in your womb."

"God, King, *yes*," she screamed, her throat strainin', head thrown back, hair spillin' over the grass as she came again right on the heels of the first orgasm, tremors wrackin' through her and into me so I had no choice but to join her.

I burrowed my head in her neck, tongue to her flutterin' pulse, and spilled myself inside her with a savage growl.

I flopped to my back and dragged her over me, our skin slick with sweat and sticky with the dregs of champagne, the rest of the bottle abandoned, liquid lost to the earth. I didn't care for or need the drunk of booze after experiencin' the intoxication of fuckin' my woman in the grass as elemental as Adam and Eve.

Tangled together, naked and free in the clearin' over the ocean, only the sound of sea birds and water shatterin' on rock to punctuate the silence, I wondered if this was paradise or as close to it as a human could get.

Cress nuzzled into my chest, peelin' open her heavy eyes to look at me. "Being pure is so overrated."

Laughter coursed through me so hard, I shouted it to the sky. "Jesus, babe, you are too fuckin' cute."

"It's true. Why would you ever forgo pleasure like that?"

"Beats me, but didn't grow up the way you did with God watchin' your every step."

She pursed her lips. "This is true. I guess, now, I just don't care if God is watching. If I were him, I'd rip open the sky to get a peek at what goes on between us in bed."

"Corrupted through and through. From pious good girl to thinkin' God's a big ole perv."

She laughed, and the sound moved over me, warmer than the sun.

We lay there for a long time, chattin' and then readin' from *The Prince*, arguin' playfully over the semantics of power and possession, but eventually the conversation turned, as it was probably always gonna, to the club and SS Danner.

"I can't help feeling so badly for Susan," she murmured,

drawing imaginary illustrations over the raised topography of my abs. "Can you imagine what it must be like to realize the man you once loved has turned into a man only worthy of hate?"

"Couldn't have happened to a better woman too. She used to treat us just like her grandkids. Remember H.R.'s first birthday with them like it was yesterday, Susan bakin' the cake in the middle of the night so she wouldn't see it, the smile on her face when Harleigh Rose actually gave her a hug in thanks. She's always been a good woman."

"And she's sick to top it all off."

We sighed in tandem, one'a those little intimacies of bein' so in sync with each other after so long that I revelled in.

"Goods things happen to bad people all the time, Cress. Just the way'a the world."

She was quiet, the quality of her silence like an extra weight on my chest so I propped a hand behind my head, dropped the book in the grass, and palmed her cheek. "What's goin' on in that crazy beautiful head?"

"We have to find a way to prove Danner killed Gibson, and failing that, what? At least get him put away for police corruption?"

"Somethin' like that," I agreed.

She bit her lip, starin' at the ring I'd put on her finger, the emerald catchin' the light. "I just have this bad feeling. Like you're going to do something outrageous."

I tried not to still, consciously draggin' air through my lungs in a nice, easy rhythm of breath.

'Cause I'd considered doin' somethin'.

Somethin' outrageous.

How else could I ensure Zeus'd be free to see his kids grow old, so he wouldn't have to miss even one more moment of their lives the way he'd had to miss years of mine.

In fact, there was a seed of an idea germinatin' in the dark, fertile soil at the back of my brain. I didn't know the shape or size of the bloom it'd produce, but that didn't stop its growth.

My first thought every mornin' was Cress.

My second, my family.

So, it was no wonder I was willin' to do whatever the fuck it took to see them all happy and safe.

But I couldn't tell that to my Cress.

If she thought there was a sacrifice to be made, my girl would demand to be the one to make it.

And that would never fuckin' do.

So, I did the only thing a man could ever really do to take his woman's mind off somethin'.

I rolled her back onto the grass and closed her mouth and the conversation with a searin' kiss.

CHAPTER SEVENTEEN

Cressida

"I CAN'T BELIEVE you and King have sex in public so much," Benny whispered, his hand to his mouth. "You're such animals!"

Loulou laughed as she bounced a fussing Angel in her arms. "Public sex is hot as fuck."

Harleigh Rose shuddered. "What have we talked about? No sex talk about my dad and brother, okay? It weirds me out."

I patted her on the head as I stepped over her legs which were propped up on the coffee table in Paradise Found, folding into the couch beside her.

"I told you that you'd find a man who felt the same way about you, and now that you have Lion, you can't tell me you guys don't have crazy hot, monkey sex," I teased.

She tossed her hair flippantly and crossed her combat booted feet as if she couldn't be fussed to talk about it, but there was a blush in her cheeks she wore just for him.

She and Lion had officially moved back to Entrance, staying in an apartment off Main Street while they did some minor renovations of Lion's ranch property. They had only been back a short time, but already they had reintegrated themselves into our lives seamlessly. Harleigh Rose had a job at a north Vancouver hospital, but when she wasn't working, she was often hanging out with me in the shop, or glued to Loulou's side helping with Angel and Walker. Lion was in the process of starting up his own private investigations company and while it wasn't all that different than being a police officer, it afforded him the license to hang out with The Fallen without worry, something he did a lot of now that he was H.R.'s man.

"Apparently, I'm more of a lady than you two," she accused, pointing a finger at Lou and me. "Seriously, the amount you talk about bangin' should be criminal."

"Some of the things we do are illegal in some countries," Loulou agreed, a gorgeous smile lighting up her face in a way none of us had seen in a while.

She was a new mum to twins, which would have been hard under any circumstances, but having a husband wrongly imprisoned and taking care of two newborn babies would have tested the patience of a saint.

It was a good thing Loulou was about as close to one of those as I knew.

"Did he really drink champagne off you?" Benny asked, his voice dreamy as he propped his head in his hands. "It's like something out of a book."

H.R. snorted. "More like a porno."

All of us laughed, and it felt so good to hear the harmony of our humour. It had been such a long time since I'd been able to hang out with both my Garro girls, and I'd missed the sisterhood.

"Benny, you can't tell me Carson doesn't get wicked with you in the sack," Harleigh Rose said as she picked at a hole in her skin-tight jeans and then started to draw on the skin through it with black sharpie. "Boy looks like he'd fuckin' rock a guy's world, if you know what I mean."

A blush rushed over Benny's skin like wildfire, but his smile was secretive and proud when he leaned back in the chair and crossed his arms. "I'm more of a lady than all of you. I don't kiss and tell."

I laughed so hard my belly ached. "So true. Touché, Benito."

"I still can't get over the beauty of your dress, Cress," Loulou sighed as she swung Angel up on her chest, patting her back to burp her. "Here I am, with spit up on my clothes, and there you are, looking like something straight out of a dream."

It was true, the dress was something from a fantasy, a confection of webbed lace over nearly sheer chiffon that hinted tantalizingly at my body beneath. It was sexy and whimsical, the perfect, slightly contrary pairing I'd been searching for to marry King in.

We'd gone dress hunting, just us three girls, that morning while Benny manned the store, then we all met to have lunch at Stella's Diner. We'd closed the bookstore early but hadn't left yet because it had become a kind of clubhouse for The Fallen women.

"Two weeks." I shook my head, shocked that after nearly five years, I'd finally be King's wife. "I can't really believe it."

I held my hands out for Lou to pass me Angel and beamed when she passed the perfect little parcel of pink, plump baby over to me. She was the sweetest, prettiest baby I'd ever laid eyes on, a thicket of white blond hair on her head the exact same shade as her mama's, her pink lips as pale as the inside of a seashell and just as smooth. I brushed my thumb down her silken skin as I tucked her against my breast and cooed down into her smiling blue eyes. My womb was hot inside me, achingly empty as I held another woman's baby in my arms.

"Zeus and I've been married for three, and it still feels

surreal," Loulou admitted as she stretched dramatically, working the kinks out of her back from hauling around one or two babies at a time.

"Maybe because you got married when you were seventeen?" H.R. offered with a sweet and sour smile.

"Oh, fuck off."

"You're too easy."

"You're a brat."

H.R. shrugged. "Sure, but a lovable one."

"I'm just so glad you're home," I told her, falling carefully to the side so that I could rest my head on her shoulder while keeping a sleeping Angel tucked safely to my chest. "I missed you like crazy."

"Same, Cress. But I'm home now, and I'm here to stay. Thank you, by the way, for asking Lion to play at the wedding. You didn't have to do that."

It was so good to have them home that I'd immediately brought Lion into the fold by asking him to play the guitar at our wedding.

He'd been so touched, I think I'd rendered him speechless.

It felt right to include him when he was so obviously going to be with Harleigh Rose for the rest of their lives.

Everything was finally falling into place, outside of Zeus's absence and one other component.

"Do you think I should invite Lysander to the wedding?"

Lou paused in checking on a sleeping Walker in his basinet, whipping around to stare open mouthed at me. "I thought you were hard lined on your stance about him."

I sighed. "He's my brother, and even though I have you guys now, he was the only person who really cared about me for most of my life. He's made some horrible mistakes, and I don't know if he's exactly on the side of The Fallen, but…he used to be my hero."

"I say invite him," Harleigh Rose declared, shrugging when I pulled back to frown at her. "What? If it wasn't for him, Loulou, Bea, and I would have died that day with Mute. No matter what else has happened, I think he deserves to at least witness his little sister gettin' married as reward for that."

It was a valid point, one that made me feel like crap for not inviting him before now even though I was still, and maybe always would be, suspicious of his motives.

"Okay." I stood up and carefully handed Angel over to her sister. "Let me just take out the garbage and close down the back office then we can head out?"

They all nodded, Harleigh Rose and Loulou launching right back into their interrogation about Benny's love life with Carson.

I laughed softly as I moved through the shelves, fingers to the book spines as I walked by, loving the scent of parchment and the feel of the glossy covers. I made quick work of wrapping up the massive garbage bag filled with the week's detritus then pushed through the back door into the alley.

Immediately, I crashed into someone, falling back thanks to the weight of the bag. Whoever it was reached out to steady me with a firm grip on my arm, their face obscured by the bulk of the bag.

"Thanks," I mumbled, righting myself and heaving the garbage into the dumpster beside me.

"No problem, Ms. Irons."

I froze, trying to swallow the scream lodged halfway up my throat.

"Danner," I said coolly, surprised by my composure. "What can I help you with? Do you need a book? Perhaps one on ethics?"

He was actually a handsome man, a lot like his son Lion, beautiful in the way of classic movie stars like Robert Redford and Paul Newman, right down to the squint and swagger. But all that goodness was stained with hatred as he glared at me, his hands in his gun belt, legs braced and slightly bent as if ready to attack.

"You've got my wife."

"Excuse me?"

"You sons of bitches took my wife. Is there any line you won't cross? She's *ill*, and you take her to make some kind of threat against me?" he stepped forward so I was pretty much pinned between the dumpster and him.

"What are you talking about? Susan came to King. She said she didn't feel safe with you anymore, and she stayed with us for a week until Lionel moved up here with H.R. She's living with your son," I said reasonably.

But there was no reasoning to be had. I could see the manic hatred in his eyes, how it had corroded his soul after so many years. He was a corrupt cop, which I thought might be the most dangerous kind of criminal, a man convinced he was doing right just because he wore a badge and blue when really, he would do anything solely to better himself.

"You listen to me," he said, voice so low I felt it like excess gravity. "You let your dogs know I've got eyes on you. Cops following each and every one of you across town, not just the bikers, but their families. We're watching Louise Garro and those little babies walk across the street. Seeing Tayline Brooks get on her knees for that one-eyed freak in their bedroom late at night. Following you as you try on pretty dresses and eat cake." His smile was like a gun held to my temple, aimed to frighten me to my core. Unsurprisingly, it worked. "Entrance is my town. Not the Garros', not the fucking Fallen's. Mine. And if you think for one moment I won't end each and every single one of you, you're wrong."

"We haven't done anything," I said, because it was true.

Sure, The Fallen were criminals. It was basically Canadian lore at this point, how the club produced the best weed in the nation and owned more territory than the next largest clubs or gangs totalled together, but that didn't mean they deserved this.

To be stalked by a crazy man with a vendetta.

"Two unidentified bikers shot three bullets through the door of my apartment. You're saying that wasn't the work of The Fallen?" he sneered.

"Are you saying you didn't ask two of your cops to illegally search my bookstore for evidence of criminal activity by the club?" I countered coldly. "Besides," I said, playing on a sudden hunch, remembering that slash of dark hair I'd seen at our engagement party, conjoining it with the fact that Susan had said he'd been arguing with a trashy woman with the same features. "Why are you so upset about your soon-to-be ex-wife? Haven't you moved on from Susan? I heard Paula's been keeping your bed warm lately."

Danner's face flashed white then red like police lights with shock and rage. "You shut your mouth. Susan's ill, and she doesn't need you filling her head with lies."

"They aren't lies, though, are they?" I pressed. "You even asked Paula to go to our engagement party and steal Zeus's gun so you could frame him for Riley Gibson's murder. What was it like taking the life of one of your brothers in blue just to see Zeus Garro hang for it?"

"You shut the fuck up," he roared, slamming me up against the dumpster, causing the breath to expel from my lungs like a shot. "You don't know what the fuck you're talking about."

"You took King and H.R. into your home once," I reminded him breathlessly, searching his features for some kind of crack in the ice. "How can you threaten them now?"

"Thought for a moment they could learn better, but I should have known criminals breed criminals. It's in their blood. That biker bitch even corrupted my son and almost got him killed."

"I'm done with this conversation," I announced, moving sideways to the door. "You call us scum, but you're the one that's corrupted your badge and put a good man, a new father, behind bars."

I'd gotten my fingers on the handle before he was there, hand to my throat, squeezing. I gasped around the pressure, suddenly filled with cold dread because there was nothing humane left in Danner's eyes, only hatred and fury.

"You tell them that if they don't bring my wife back to me, I'll start by taking you and Louise. The Ventura's can always use pretty girls for their enterprise."

"You fucking bastard," I wheezed, clutching at his hand, prying his fingers off my throat.

He released me so abruptly I fell back against the door. "You want to go to war with me? You tell your kind I'm ready."

CHAPTER EIGHTEEN

King

"SKELL'S BEEN ARRESTED," Buck announced after Bat closed the door to the chapel and everyone had taken a seat.

There was a low series of curses.

"Are you fuckin' kiddin' me?" I growled. "What the fuck did he do?"

Buck ran a weary hand over his face, and I noticed how much the leadership role had been robbin' him of his health, skin ashen, eyes red with exhaustion. "Decided we weren't doin' enough and confronted Danner in Mac's Grocer… ended up throwin' him into a canned goods display."

"Fuck," Bat groused, rubbin' his temples. "We need brothers outta the big house, not fuckin' goin' in."

"Such an asshole," Curtains muttered, which said somethin' 'cause the kid was not one to judge or talk shit 'bout anyone.

But Skell was an asshole. Buryin' the club deeper in shit just to have an outlet for his vehemence? What 'bout the rest of us marinatin' in our own goddamn fury?

I sighed and pulled at my lower lip so hard I wondered if it'd bruise. "Staff Sargent Danner went by Paradise Found today. Fuckin' threatened Cress when she was takin' out the garage." My words scored like dragon's breath as they left my throat. I'd seen red when Cress told me, even though she'd driven over to the garage herself just to tell me in person so I could see she was unhurt. "Motherfucker put his hands on her. Shit is gettin' outta hand, brothers. We need to do somethin' 'bout it."

"Yeah, fuckin' end Danner properly," Heckler demanded.

"*No*. That is exactly what got Skell arrested," Bat retorted, slidin' Heckler a look that no man could misconstrue, a look that called him a fuckin' dumbass.

Heckler was outta his seat, loomin' over Bat in an instant. "You got somethin' to say?"

"Think I just said it." Calm, cold, ruthless. The Bat trifecta.

"Settle down," Buck ordered.

No one listened.

"You think endin' the man that put our Prez in the can is fuckin' stupid?" Heckler argued, slappin' at Wiseguy's shoulder 'cause the pair of 'em were tight, and both, it had to be said, could be dense as bricks. "You hearin' this?"

"Did the drive-by you clowns went on make any difference?" Axe-Man asked, leanin' back in his chair, arms crossed, biceps bigger than Christmas hams. "You keep goin' after Danner like that, it's just what he wants. Like shootin' fish in a barrel."

"Listen, Cress said the woman Danner's been shackin' up with is fuckin' *Paula*," I cut in, standin' up to lend my voice without raisin' it. There was an art, I'd learned over the years, of talkin' to bikers that included talkin' low and talkin' slow so they didn't think you were orderin' 'em 'round and they could process your words without their own biases interferin'. "Paula, same woman who basically stalked me my entire teenager years. Apparently, she snuck in the night of my engagement party and took the gun. We get to Paula, we got an in. We start targetin' some'a the cops, we find dirt on 'em, and blackmail 'em to flip on Danner. We. Get. An. In. Killin' Danner isn't gonna get Z outta jail, and isn't that the priority here?"

"Sit down, boy," Buck commanded wearily. "Let the men who've been here longer than you've been alive talk 'bout things in a reasonable fuckin' way."

"How is this not reasonable?" I countered. When he didn't answer, I cocked a brow and studied the dissatisfied looks on every single member's face 'fore takin' a serious gamble.

"Callin' for a vote of no confidence."

There was a pause that felt lethal, then Wise-guy broke it to grunt, "The fuck?"

"A re-vote," Bat offered, eyein' me in a way I couldn't tell if it was respect or skepticism. "King wants us to re-vote on who's actin' Prez while Zeus's behind bars."

"Let me guess, you're nominatin' yourself," Buck said, not soundin' combative or seemin' insulted, just mildly shocked and maybe even a little disappointed.

"If anyone will stand with me," I proposed. "Mean no offense, Buck, but this is not the way to handle the situation, and you're not providin' any answers when we've got a real fuckin' need for 'em. This club is under fuckin' attack, and we need to *move*."

There was a pause like the thick, buzzin' quiet after a bomb strikes, and then they started movin'. My brothers splittin' into two factions across an invisible, impenetrable line. Us and them.

It shocked the shit outta me that Bat moved first, standin' up and crossin' 'round the back of Buck at the head of the table to stand by me, startin' a domino effect that included Boner, Curtains, Priest, Cyclops, Lab-Rat, Kodiak, Axe-Man, and finally, Nova, who hopped his ass up on the table and swung over the other side. My side.

It meant I had the majority by two votes.

"Not feelin' too hot today," Smoke rasped from the far corner where he sat with his oxygen machine. "But I'd move to King's side if I could."

"Fuck," Buck grumbled, scrubbin' a hand over his face. "Hope you're prepared to carry the full weight of this responsibility, boy."

I tipped my chin. "Watched Z do it my whole life, and I only intend to fill his fuckin' mammoth shoes while he's gone."

"Now what?" Boner asked, scratchin' his balls noisily through his jeans. "I mean that was an epic stand-off, but are we good to roll out like this? Club divided?"

"Family are the ones you love and the people you'd die for," Nova said, surprisingly somber. "Fallen's a family tighter than most. We got this, brothers. King's at the head of the hydra, and we got a fuck ton'a talkin' heads to put together to figure somethin' out."

"Let's get to it," I suggested as everyone re-took their seats and even the Old Guard quit their grumblin'.

IN THE DAYS FOLLOWIN', it became obvious every brother had a tail. The Entrance PD wasn't huge, but it seemed most've 'em were corrupt, 'cause whenever any'a the guys left the compound, a cop sittin' in plain sight in a vehicle emblazoned with Entrance PD, would tear out after 'em, another one in its place within the hour.

The brothers could shake a tail and laugh doin' it, but when Ormand, McDougal, and Peters made it their mission to follow Loulou, H.R., and Cressida, and a handful of the other Old Ladies, we knew somethin' had to change and immediately.

So, even though Cress and me were supposed to spend the night at Donovan's Steak House celebratin' a week until we said 'I do,' we were at Entrance's resident strip club, The Wet Lotus instead.

Wasn't there to eye fuck the ladies, barely able to tear my eyes off my own woman, decked out in biker babe finery. She sat beside me on a black velvet booth, leather pants up to her belly button, slicked to every inch of her curves, while the little top, just an oversized red bandana she'd found in the depths of my sock drawer, was practically beggin' to be tugged off. She had the dark eyes, big hair, and red lips that made me want to drag her to the floor and take her right there and then, but we had business to take care of 'fore I could take care of her.

The Lotus was Fallen owned, and we had a history with the place given Zeus had met and been seduced by Lou there. But I hadn't been through the lacquered black doors in years, and I was surprised again by what a classy joint it was.

The only black spot on the club was the fact it was frequented often and drunkenly, by a large contingent of the Entrance police force. Includin' but not limited to, Staff Sergeant Harold Danner.

He occupied a back booth, sittin' dead center like some kinda kingpin wantin' to be seen and revered. There were two plainclothes cops at the table with him, their buzz cuts and posture givin' 'em away as coppers, and four barely clothed women.

One'a those bein' Paula.

It was hard to think back on all my interactions with the man over the years and not wonder how he'd turned out this way. In my youth, he'd be such a taciturn man, a stickler for the rules, and devoted to his wife, even if he had been hard on his son.

Where did a greed like his stem from? Was it inherent to his DNA, an extra chromosome, a genetic disease? Didn't think so given the way Lion was the exact opposite of that.

Was evil—like Shakespeare hypothesized about greatness—born, bred, or earned?

He'd noticed us, Cress and me at one table, ostensibly on a date, Nova, Kodiak, Boner, and Cyclops at another drinkin' beers loudly, makin' enough of a ruckus that eyes would go to them.

"Got no reservations 'bout takin' part in this?" I said low to my woman.

Cress smiled 'round the rim of her bourbon sour and winked. "Are you kidding? Paula and Cressida cat fight take two? I should be selling tickets."

I laughed, rememberin' how my woman had once cut Paula and her bitchiness straight off at the knees for the entire clubhouse to see. If any'a the brothers had doubted my choice to date an older woman, and my teacher at that, they'd said dick all 'bout it after that.

"You know, there's not a single fuckin' thing I'd change 'bout you?" I murmured, leanin' over to wrap my hand 'round the back of her neck 'fore kissin' her red mouth. "Proud to be your man, babe."

She smiled against my mouth. "Ditto, honey."

I squeezed her thigh. “They’re both watchin’. Let’s get this done so I can getcha home to our bed.”

Her giggle was more breath than sound as I suddenly hauled her clear across the booth, hand tangled in the back of all that gorgeous hair so I could pin her to my mouth. She moaned then crawled on top of me, straddlin’ me in the booth like she was one’a the dancers who worked there.

Only none’a those women were worth a fuckin’ damn next to Cress.

I slid my hands under her ass, liftin’ her with me as I stood up, then droppin’ her down my body slow, like the trickle of molasses so I could feel her every curve.

When we parted after another minute of long, wet kisses that would’a made me hard as steel if I hadn’t been so aware of our plan, Cress pulled away with a seductive little smile and strutted on her sexy as fuck red heels to the bathroom.

After waitin’ a beat, watchin’ her curvy ass sway, I took off after her when she rounded the corner to the back hall.

There was no way I was leavin’ her alone in the club, not when Danner had flat-out threatened her. Put his goddamn hands on her.

And when I started walkin’, I noticed from the corner of my eye, Paula gettin’ up to follow.

I strolled nice and easy across the room, makin’ my way to the men’s toilets, pretendin’ to take a piss at one’a the urinals while I waited.

Wasn’t waitin’ for long.

The door pushed open with a breath of air behind me ’fore I heard the click of heels and smelled the somewhat familiar scent of cheap perfume. Seconds later, two hands smoothed down the back of my cut.

“King, baby,” Paula purred. “Long time no see, and what a shame that is.”

I tried not to stiffen against her repulsive touch, knowin’ she’d just had her hands on SS Danner.

"Paula," I rumbled, turnin' 'round. She didn't step back, our bodies brushin' together, her big tits against my chest, offered up in her low top like overripe fruit. "What the fuck're you doin' in here?"

"Couldn't help myself," she admitted with a low chuckle, movin' her hands onto my chest, fingers smoothin' over the patches on my cut, lingerin' on 1%ers and the burnin' winged skull. "Man like you's hard to resist. Most beautiful guy I've ever laid my damn eyes on, you know that?"

I grabbed her questin' hands in one'a mine and grinned wickedly when the door sighed open behind her.

"Matter of fact, I do. My woman tells me nearly every damn day."

And then Paula was ripped away from me, the momentum carryin' her straight back into the door of a toilet stall. She tripped over her feet and fell to her ass. Cress stood over her, fists clenched, eyes wild like a mustang on the run.

"I already told you once before, you lay hands on my man again, we'll have a problem."

Paula swallowed thickly, eyes swingin' between the two of us. "Listen, no harm done, bitch. I barely got my hands on him!"

Cress squatted in front of her with an easy nod, but there was coiled tension in every line of her slim form.

"You're right," she agreed, but then a hand went flashin' out, crashin' with a sharp *crack* against Paula's cheek. "That's for bitch slapping me back in the day and for trying to touch my fiancé now."

Paula tried to lurch off her ass to launch herself at Cress, and as much as I loved a good cat fight like any other red-blooded male, that was not the purpose of tonight. So, I stepped between the girls and clamped my arms 'round Paula, pinnin' hers down at her sides.

"Listen up," I told her. "Not personally into violence against women, but gotta few friends who don't care 'bout gender that're mighty fuckin' excited to meet Staff Sergeant Danner's sweet piece. Now, nothin' bad has to happen, Paula, long as you go nice and easy, and answer our questions 'bout your man and what you might'a been doin', uninvited, in The Fallen clubhouse the night of Riley Gibson's unfortunate passin'."

The woman stopped strugglin' in my hold instantly, and I could actually feel a cold dread sweep through her, the way she shuddered and balked.

"Wasn't there," she insisted, but her voice was threadbare with panic.

"Like hell you weren't," Cress snapped, steppin' up to point a finger in her face. "I saw you myself."

Paula didn't breathe for a long second, and then, when she did, she screamed.

I wrapped a hand 'round her mouth 'fore she could get much sound out, but we moved quickly all the same. I dragged her to the door while Cress peeked her head out to check for customers or staff, then I hauled her down the hall out the back-service door to the alley.

Priest was waitin' with a smile like an open wound, red and ugly, as he took Paula from me and made quick work of tapin' her mouth shut, bindin' her hands and feet. He laid her gently in the back of the van then rounded to the driver's seat, takin' off without sayin' a word.

'Fore I could even look over at Cress, my phone vibrated in my jeans, a text from Nova.

Nova: Curtains will be there in a minute.

I grabbed Cress and kissed her hand. "Goin' back in to talk to the Staff Sergeant. You get home now, yeah?"

"Yeah," she agreed. "That was fun as heck, though."

I grinned at her, slappin' her ass just to feel it move under the leather, then kissed her once more like a stamp of possession to her lips. "Want this on you when I get home."

"Yes, sir," she said with a sassy mock-salute I felt in my balls. "Be safe."

I nodded and watched her walk out the mouth of the alley straight across the street to her parked car.

A moment later, Curtains drew up in his obnoxious red Dodge Challenger, Bat already in the passenger seat.

"Good?" he asked immediately as I slid in the back.

I nodded. "Priest's got her. How're the other crews doin'?"

"Heckler, Wiseguy, and Lab-Rat got that rookie Officer Windham, takin''im back to Angelwood Farm now."

It was a simple plan really, divide and conquer the weakest links in Danner's armour. He was goin' after our women, so we had no compulsion 'bout targetin' him and his. Priest would work his dark magic, and I had no doubt that by the mornin', we'd have two turncoats in Danner's rotten to the core operation.

I wanted it to be enough, but the word of a biker bitch and a rookie against the word of an RCMP officer wasn't ironclad, not even a little, so we were on our way to Danner's house to break in usin' the alarm code Susan Hobbs had so kindly given us.

B & E wasn't somethin' I'd added to my resume, but I'd been good with a set of lock picks since I was a kid the way most children were good at baseball or card games. There was somethin' satisfyin' 'bout findin' the right combination of tools to open a locked door, a box filled with potential treasures. Zeus had locked up everythin' when we were kids, his guns, his cash, his fuckin' porn, and I'd made it a habit to get to all of it.

So, it was easy enough to break in to the swanky apartment Danner was renting downtown. The place had a killer view of the water, but what I was focused on was the office space, its door locked, a desk with three locked drawers, and lock box hidden in a bench seat.

Bat, Curtains, and I worked through everythin' carefully.

If we found somethin' it had to be tangible enough to offer to the Internal Affairs Department in Vancouver, which Lion and Officer Hutchinson were currently tryin' to convince to look into the Staff Sergeant.

We found fuck all.

I cursed viciously under my breath as I packed Danner and Susan's divorce papers back into their folder and shuffled a list of seemingly random women's names into another. My gaze nearly slid straight off the page again until I caught sight of two familiar names.

Honey Yves.

Lila Meadows.

"Fuckin' fuck," Bat cursed as he peered out the drapes into the front drive. "We got company."

Adrenaline sluiced through me, but I swallowed the metallic surge of it on the back of my tongue and finished puttin' the shit away, lookin' to Bat for a plan.

He pointed at the bench then back at me, then turned to Curtains and motioned toward one'a the two large gun cabinets on either side'a the desk against the back wall.

Silently, heart poundin' so loud and strong in my throat I thought I'd gag, we moved into hidin'.

It took a few minutes for the door to unlock at the base of the stairs and the sound of feet clompin' up 'em, so I used the time to regulate the harshness of my breathin' and get as comfortable as I could crushed down in the bench.

"You and your husband made me promises," Danner was sayin' when he finally got close enough to hear his murmur. "I expect you to deliver."

"Ah well, Sergeant, I could say the same of you," Irina Ventura drawled.

A shiver ripped viciously down my spine.

If one'a the brothers so much as fuckin' breathed wrong, we were all dead.

Irina was the wife of Javier Ventura, the Canadian representative of the biggest Mexican cartel on the west coast. She was fuckin' beautiful, but she was also goddamn poison, the woman behind the man, the one runnin' an underage porn ring outside Entrance.

"Staff Sergeant," Danner corrected automatically, voice louder as he came into the office. "And I've delivered on all of my promises, Irina. You've been left alone to your disgusting devices for years. I'm only asking you now to rein it in or relocate because you're drawing notice from other task forces."

"You let me worry about those, hmm? You just focus on keeping your lovely boys away from my site and keeping The Fallen occupied."

There was a long pause, but no movement. Finally, Danner sighed. "You said there'd be a bonus for me if I got rid of Garro."

"Yes, I did, didn't I? I thought it would cut the head off the snake so to speak, but I think not. You better take care of a few more of those men, Sergeant, or their wives. Whatever will break them the fastest."

Fuck.

My heart thundered against my ribs, a caged man locked up in a burnin' room beggin' to get free. But I had to lay there, lay there and listen as they spoke 'bout offin' one'a my brothers, one'a our women.

Danner hesitated, sighin' then slumpin' audibly into his office chair.

"You're asking a lot of me, Irina. When this is all over, I won't be able to stay in Entrance, let alone keep my badge."

"Oh, *dulzura,* don't you worry about that, hmm. I'm sure we can make something work."

"Cressida Irons is marrying Garro's son soon, she's an option, and obviously Loulou Garro and her twins," he said slowly, the words draggin' as he presumably thought of the implications. "Those bastards would do anything for those two or Harleigh Rose Garro."

"The one dating your son?" Irina asked slyly.

"He's no son of mine anymore."

"Good, good. Well, I'll leave it in your very capable hands, Sergeant."

"I do this…I need a bigger cut of the profits."

A rattling silence like the warnin' before the strike of a snake.

"Do you?" Irina purred.

"20%."

She laughed delightedly. "Oh, what balls you have! And what greed."

"Got nothing to live for now but myself if my wife doesn't come back, so I don't see why I wouldn't live it rich."

"Yes, that's fair." She laughed again, softer this time, just to herself. "Well, if you bring me one of the girls or those babies, I'm sure we can figure something out."

WE GOT OUT EASY. Danner walked Irina out then fucked 'round for a while 'fore he gotta call and left. I'd laid crampin' in that bench seat, ruminatin' on everythin' they'd said.

It was hard not to feel fuckin' hopeless.

Wasn't the kinda man to take anythin' lyin' down, but

what the fuck was I supposed to do? Newly patched-in, freshly crowned, and I didn't have a fuckin' clue.

We couldn't kill Danner without one or more of us going to prison, and it wouldn't absolve Zeus's guilt, so he'd continue to rot there too.

We could turn Paula and the rookie, got no doubt 'bout that, but toward what end? Couldn't put a brother on every single woman in the club so they didn't get fucked by the cops or the Ventura's, not forever.

There wasn't anythin' I wouldn't do to keep my people safe. Family were the ones who made your life worth livin', and also, the only people you'd gladly die for.

We emerged from our hidin' places twenty minutes after Danner left and ghosted outta the apartment. Bat's pale face was paler, eyes dark and haunted in his face, while Curtains couldn't keep still from the reckless, nervous energy thrummin' through him.

We all knew now just how far Danner would take his vendetta against the club.

He wanted war, and I knew the brothers wanted to give it to him, but I hesitated.

Even faced with the death of my loved ones, I paused.

No.

'Cause I was faced with the death of my loved ones, I balked at the idea of war and all its many casualties.

I kept comin' back to the principles of Machiavelli in *The Prince*, one quote ringin' out louder than all the rest.

> *"All courses of action are risky, so prudence is not in avoiding danger (it's impossible), but calculating risk and acting decisively. Make mistakes of ambition and not mistakes of sloth. Develop the strength to do bold things, not the strength to suffer."*

I knew The Fallen had the strength to suffer, we'd done it 'fore with Zeus imprisoned, Mute murdered, Harleigh Rose abused and nearly lost to us.

We could do it again.

But at what cost?

What if there was a steeper price to pay, but only one had to pay it?

And shouldn't the man to pay that toll be me? The leader, however temporary, of his people?

I was quiet as I sat in the back of the van, then kept relatively silent in church at the compound when Bat relayed the news and Priest reported, covered in another men's blood, that the rookie and Paula had agreed to turn on Danner. I kept quiet, as the quiet man thinks, and when I went home to Cressida at the end of the night, mornin' breachin' the crust of the earth and spillin' through the streets of my gorgeous home, I had the seeds of a plan sown in my soul.

CHAPTER NINETEEN

Cressida

THERE WERE times King couldn't sleep for the thoughts racing through his head. I would wake up in the dead of night to an empty bed knowing King was downstairs at the kitchen table, poetry filled pages littered across the surface and the floor, ink staining the tips of his fingers and his mouth where he'd pulled at his lower lips as he thought.

He'd once explained to me that poetry wasn't an art to him, but more like a compulsion, more like breathing than anything else, a necessary extension of himself. If he let those words build up, they congealed like soup in a cold bowl, thick and gelatinous in his head, stopping up all movement. It was only when he sat with a pen in his hand, blank paper beneath, that the words heated and flowed, spilling out the tip of the pen like blood from a vein.

I watched him from the base of the stairs the night before

our wedding, back bowed, head tipped so his face was obscured by the thick, rumpled curtain of his hair.

"Can feel you in the room with me," he muttered after a while, extending his left hand to me as he continued to furiously write. "Come here."

I went to him, padding across the cool floor naked but for the shadows moving over my skin like silk.

Four years ago, I never would have walked naked through my house alone, let alone with my partner in it, and I never would have hopped up on the table, ass to King's poetry, legs spread so I could prop the balls of my feet on his knees, exposed and aroused by it.

He was beautiful in the dark, illuminated only by the round, full moon beaming silver light through the windows to gild the ridges of his steep features in metallics. I traced a finger over his prominent cheekbone and tipped my head to the side.

"What keeps my poet up tonight?"

He stayed quiet, intensity brimming from him like a frayed electric wire. So, I picked up one of the sheaves of paper instead and softy read it aloud.

"I was born to the demons that hounded me.
They wanted my submission to their corruption like
blood ink on paper signed with my name.
I could have run,
But where is the power in that?
Instead, I became a demon myself in order to master
them all.

Own your demons."

I looked up from the page, my heart burning like coal stuck in the cavity of my throat.

"What's going on, honey?" I asked again, threading my fingers through the curls and cowlicks of his golden hair.

I need to know the problem because whatever was stalking him, I would eviscerate. I wasn't the woman I'd been before him, and I wasn't the woman I was now solely because of him. He was the flint that ignited the spark my soul needed to come into its own. I was strong enough now, if he needed me, to take on his burden, to fight those demons he spoke of in his poem. If he gave me the chance, I would fight and *die* for King…I just had to make sure if one of us ever had to be the sacrifice, it would be me and not him.

"Talk to me," I urged softly, tugging at his hair.

But he didn't speak. If anything, the static in the air increased, crackling over my skin, vibrating in the air between us.

He planted a hand on my sternum, right between my breasts and up over my heart, as he dipped his head to write another poem slanted across the bottom of a page already filled with verse. I read it upside down as he wrote, and tried not to cry.

In whatever planes of existence there are
On any star or parallel planet
You and I are together
Infinitely
Inevitably
Because nothing makes sense
In any language or any place
Without our love to decode life's purpose

There was some fierce formation moving through him, a weather system that could only be withstood and not evaded. He was an artist, a poet, a soul so tender and overfilled with emotion that sometimes the only thing that could soothe it was a cleansing tempest rain.

So, I stopped asking questions and only offered myself, my body and my spirit, to him by lying back on the poems scattered like dry leaves across the tabletop. He moved instantly, so powerfully I was almost frightened by his verve.

Not because he would physically harm me, but because there was such exquisite beauty to the words that spilled from the wounds he opened up within himself that I felt almost afraid of their grandness, fearful the way an acolyte might be when facing their God.

He started at the base of my collarbone, the felt tip of his silver pen soft and ticklish against my skin as he swirled the words across my flesh. I fought to keep still and silent as he owned me with his prose. He punctuated the completion of each poem with a kiss to the place he ended it, lips pressed to the underside of one breast and the tip of the other, the hollow cast beside the peak of my hip bones and the jut of my pubis before it gave way to my sex.

I was his canvas, his muse, both helpless laying prostrate over the table and endlessly powerful because all that creative beauty was bound up in a gorgeous man who was bound up, somehow, in me.

He didn't stop when my front was covered from breasts to toes, a poem written across my arch and tucked up under my heel. Instead, he stepped back, breathing heavy, almost panting, and painfully aroused, his cock jutting up to his belly button, where precum pooled like ink.

But his arousal and my own, pooling between my thighs and staining the pages beneath my bottom, smearing the ink with my wetness, were inconsequential next to the raging authority of his muse.

He caught me by an ankle, locked pale eyes with my own, then *flipped* me. I spun with the momentum, turning myself onto my belly so that my back and ass were exposed to his pen.

A poem down my spine, verses caught on each vertebra,

the rest branching out from my shoulder blades like wings formed by words. I felt divine, exalted by him, elevated by his worship and the ways he used words to pin down those elusive feelings that moved like midnight shadows over my soul.

By the time he crested the twin hills of my bottom, his verve had lessened, the strokes of the pen languid, almost tired as he wrung the last droplets of passion from his heart and spilled them across my flesh.

Abruptly, after almost an hour of feverish writing, he was done.

He slumped in the chair and let his forehead fall to my thighs, his breath hot against my sensitive skin. We waited there, in the wake of his magic as it slowly waned, and when he moved again, I knew it wasn't the tidal force of his emotions that moved him, but the lust left in its stead.

He tugged my ankles again, shifting me across the pages until my knees hit his thighs and my ass was canted up over the side of the table, my core exposed to his burning gaze.

His nose went first, drawing a line from the crease of my cheek to the folds of my sex, then again on the other side. The same path followed with his thumb and then again with his tongue.

There was no haste, only slumberous, heavy desire that pulled us deeper, like a net trolling the floor of the sea.

I gasped as he parted my wet folds with his tongue, as he sucked at my lips and swirled his tongue over my asshole. He stilled my quivering with both big palms on my cheeks, pulling me further apart for his delving tongue and industrious nose.

When I came, I didn't groan or thrash. It felt like sliding into warm water, rolling through me like a curling wave. I gasped and softly breathed his name.

Hearing his name woke him up again, filling him with renewed urgency as he flipped me back over. I slithered down from the table like spilled honey onto his lap and braced my hands on his shoulders as he fitted me on top of his thick cock.

The ache of him sliding inside me felt so right, the edge of pain just enough to heighten the incredible current stemming from our connection.

I rode him, softly, steadily. So slowly at first it was barely a movement, just a tilt of my hips under his hands, and then faster, rocking then crashing into the shore of his hips, my pussy leaving damp trails in the sandy hair over his groin.

And the whole time, we watched each other, caught up in the visual tangle. I watched his pupils blow wide, obliterating the normally icy blue gone liquid with lust. Loving how his lids grew heavy and his cheeks went flush as I churned faster and faster, wringing my own pleasure from him.

And just when I felt the crest of my climax lapping at my hips, he crushed my breasts against his chest, a hand pressing me faster over his cock, the other wrapped around the back of my neck so he could haul me close and kiss me.

"She tastes like fresh brine," he murmured against my lips as I moved faster and faster still. "Like sea water. I'll ride her softly, rockin', like an incomin' tide." He paused to sink his teeth into my neck, and I broke apart, shaking and gasping over him, clutching his mouth to me with a hand on his neck and the other twined deep in his hair. I felt the kick of his cock inside me, the hot spill of cum against the entrance to my womb, and I cried out at the intensity of our shared climax.

As I rode it out, he whispered the rest of his poem in my ear, "And even when she ebbs after the crest, I know she'll flow back to me again."

He pulled away, framing my face in his big, strong hands, his own features suffused with aching tenderness. "The sea always returns to kiss the shore."

He kissed me then, lips soft, tongue a lullaby soothing me from the ecstasy of my orgasm.

I wanted to ask him what was haunting him, what demons lurked in his soul and stole his sleep, but there was something so fragile in the big, strong man who loved me that I didn't push it. Instead, when he stood up, our mouths still fused, I wrapped myself around him and let him carry me to our bed where he made love to me until the earliest hours of the morning when he finally fell into a deep sleep with a small smile on his gorgeous face.

IT WAS STRANGE, maybe, to visit a prison on your wedding day, but I wouldn't have had it any other way. The girls, Benny, and I spent the morning in the cabin getting ready, drinking champagne, and laughing about the antics of our men, but the levity flattened like stale beer when we got in the car to visit Ford Mountain Correctional.

I wore my dress.

Rainbow and Benny begged me not to because they feared the visit would ruin it, but Loulou and Harleigh Rose had been particularly quiet about it. I knew it was because they understood why I wanted to wear it, and they approved, but they didn't want to pressure me because it was my day.

What Rainbow and Benny didn't understand, because they couldn't as non-members of The Fallen, was that it wasn't just my day.

It was King's too.

And The Fallen's.

I was, after nearly five years, finally, legally and spiritually, becoming a member of their family.

So, I wore the dress even though the prison guards gave me odd looks, and I had to carefully traverse the dank halls holding the train of the gown aloft.

It was worth it just to see Zeus Garro's face when they opened the door for me, and I walked into where the telephone banks were.

He was unutterably handsome, but not at all like King's perfectly carved and symmetrical beauty. Instead, Zeus was rough-hewn and textured, made of wood instead of his son's granite, warm and alive in a way that begged touching and holding. That great, beautiful face grew even more beautiful as he took me in, standing there in the dress I would wear to marry his son.

It was almost entirely lace, and a thin, gauzy chiffon that was sheer enough to cast the hint of my body beneath it but covered me from mid-shoulder to my feet where it ended in a small, but whimsical train. It made me look, I thought, as if I'd wandered through an enchanted forest and got caught up in silken webbing like some ethereal being, some fairy goddess. With my hair done up in waves and braids with a gold clip like a wreath of ivy sitting at my crown, I hoped I looked as magical as King's love made me feel.

"Fuck me," Zeus mouthed at me, eyes shining silver, wet with happiness.

I beamed at him, a smile so wide it hurt, but still, I pinned it to my face so he would know just how much it meant to me that he approved.

When I sat down and lifted the phone, the first thing he said was, "Lookin' at you like that makes me wish I'd been patient enough to give Lou a proper walk down the aisle. Women like you two are meant to be seen like this."

"When you get out," I suggested. "You could have a vow renewal and do it up properly?"

He laughed, but it was broken and bruised. "Wanna spend time with my babies and woman when I'm outta 'ere. Don't need anythin' distractin' more from 'em. Was just nice to imagine for a second."

"I'm sorry you're missing this," I said, cutting through the fat to the heart of it. "I'm so sorry that I could cry. I really wanted to do this with you there. I wanted it with my whole heart."

His smile was weighted with sad appreciation. "Yeah, Cress, I know it. Thing is, and you hold this closer than your bouquet when you walk down that aisle, I'm with you there even if I'm locked up 'ere, yeah? I'm gonna lay in my bunk, close my eyes, and picture it all as it goes down. You in that fuckin' stunner of a dress, King lookin' like some kinda biker prince waitin' for you with a smile that could light up the dark. All our family there smilin' like loons, high on all that love in the air… yeah, you can bet I'm there with you even if I'm locked up 'ere."

Tears warmed the backs of my eyes like elements on a stove as I struggled not to lose it at the beauty of his words.

"You know, King's the poet in this family, but he got his enormous heart from you," I told him. "I've never known two men kinder or lovelier than you."

"Don't go spreadin' that 'round, we got reputations to uphold," he teased.

I rolled my eyes. "All anyone's got to do is take one look at your behemoth self and they'll run terrified, don't you worry. Anyway, I'm happy to keep the secret. It makes me feel even luckier to be one of the only souls who knows the truth."

We looked at each other for a long minute, the silence like velvet between us. This man had looked out for me since the moment his son took an interest. He'd been my fake boyfriend, my best friend, my mentor, and now, he would be my father-in-law. It was difficult to give words to the kind of relationship I had with him because we were a modern family of jumbled ages and roles to play, but when it came down to it, Zeus meant more to me than I could ever say.

I tried to convey that through my eyes as they glazed with tears, tried to write all those emotions in words on the screens of my irises so that he might read them and understand.

"Yeah," he muttered, seeing them there, getting it as he seemed to have gotten me from the very start, even when I didn't get me. "Yeah, Cress, I know it. Gotta love for you that's pure as your good heart, and gotta say, for my boy? No one less than you would fuckin' do."

A sob ripped like torn Velcro from the lining of my throat.

"Gonna mess your face up," he warned me, but he was smiling because I was too.

"I can fix it. Honestly, I'm barely wearing any makeup because I knew I'd cry." I sucked in a deep breath like a drowning man given one last chance at life, trying to settle the chaos of emotions in my belly. "I just want to say one thing, and then I'll go. Lou's outside waiting for a minute to talk before we head home, but this, right now, is what I really wanted to say to you."

I breathed deep through the crush of feelings threatening to cave in my throat, and when I could find my voice again, I said, "I thought about asking my parents to the wedding. It was…hard not to, even though I hadn't spoken to them in years. I even reached out, you know, just to see how they were and what they thought about me getting married again." I laughed wetly. "They weren't thrilled, to say the least. But it was good, in a way, because I got closure. I realized that even if I did have them in my life, they would be a pale imitation of the real family I've found with the Garros and The Fallen. It's not my dad that I wish could walk me down the aisle to the man of my dreams that I'm going to spend the rest of my life with. It's you."

Zeus's head dropped between his shoulders, his gaze trained on the linoleum counter as if it was infinitely interesting. But I heard the hiccough in his breathing, the wetness at the back of his throat as he tried to swallow his tears.

"I asked Hannah to make me this." I moved my hair off my breasts to reveal the small badge I had sewn into the right top side of my dress. "God of Thunder," I read. "So that even though you'll be there in our hearts, like you said, I can still carry a piece of you down the aisle with me just as I would if you were free to walk with me."

His hands went to prop up his head as he shook it, shoulders hunched as he let the emotion work through him. It was such a vulnerable moment for the great and terrible Zeus Garro, and I was humbled that my words meant so much to him.

When he looked up at me, finally, his cheeks were dry, but his eyes were wet and red. His voice, when he spoke, was like wet gravel under tires. "Outside'a Lou and all her gifts to me, gotta say, this is the best present I ever got."

"Me too," I agreed.

Then we smiled at each other again because we were hurt, yes, enraged even at the injustice of this day and the fact they wouldn't grant him a pass to the wedding, but we had learned through all our trials and tribulations as a family that you took happiness when it came and you clung hard and fast to it.

So, we smiled, and when I finally left, it was the sight of Zeus I took with me, beaming proudly like a father, warmly like a friend, and full-on loving me like only a Garro could do.

CHAPTER TWENTY

King

"CAN YOU BELIEVE I'M FUCKIN' nervous?"

Nova scoffed as he adjusted The Fallen custom cufflinks I'd had made and had given to the groomsmen for the wedding. "Like hell you are. Never known a man more set and willin' to wear the noose."

"That's the thing, isn't it?" I admitted, leg bouncin' with nerves as I waited beneath the arch of blossoms and ivy at the end of a walkway strewn with white petals in our backyard. "Wanted this since I was eight, and don't care it makes me sound like a fuckin' girl. Always knew if I could only find the woman for me, I'd love her fiercely and forever."

"So, what's the problem?"

I let out a sound halfway between a sigh and a growl as I raked my hands through my hair. "It's just, fuck...can you tell me you've never wanted somethin' so much that when you actually got it, the prospect didn't fuckin' terrify you?"

Nova stopped his fussin' and locked eyes with himself in the mirror. A strange expression seized him, one I'd never seen before, somethin' like yearnin' muddied up by regret.

"Nah," he admitted softly. "Can't say I have."

"I know it," Lion Danner said even though he'd pretended not to be listenin' as he strummed his guitar, practicin' the song he'd sing for Cress walkin' down the aisle. "Honest to God, I feel it every day bein' with Rosie."

"Afraid to lose her?" Ares asked from the front row of seats where he sat and pumped his legs back and forth while he read from *Paradise Lost*, tryin' to get the passage he wanted to recite perfectly memorized.

"No," I said slowly as the pieces shifted and settled in my chest. "It's not fear of losin' her. That's a fear we all got 'bout everyone we love. It's the fear of happiness itself. What happens to the dreamer after the dream becomes reality? Does it go on bein' a dream forever, or do you inevitably fuck it up?"

Nova rolled his eyes and slapped me on the shoulder. "Bro, seriously, only you'd get so damn melancholy and metaphysical on your weddin' day."

I shrugged under his hand 'cause it was true, though, I wasn't melancholy, not exactly. How could you not be contemplative on a day like today? I thought of the night before, the creative stupor I'd been in as I feverishly covered Cress from breast to feet in ink. There was somethin' eatin' at me that had nothin' to do with the weddin' and everythin' to do with finally bein' king of The Fallen and knowin' what leadership and loyalty really meant.

"You mean like what happened to Adam and Eve after the fall?" Ares asked, his eyebrows screwed up as he considered my quandary.

"Yeah, bud, kinda like that."

"I think," he said carefully. "They lived happily ever after."

Nova snorted, and Ares scowled at him as if mortally wounded by his lack of belief.

"Happily-ever-after doesn't hafta mean nothin' ever goes wrong," he argued, small fists clenched. "It means you love each other through everything, the good and the bad." He paused, hestitatin' 'fore lookin' at me. "Just like what it means to be family, right?"

Fuck, but I felt my heart in my throat as I stared at the little man with the old soul sittin' there in a black suit with a patch on the breast that said 'Best Man.' Mute would'a stood up with me in that role, and I'd been hesitant to ask anybody to fill it if I couldn't have him.

But in strange ways, I thought fate had given us Ares to help ease the loss of Mute in our lives. We all needed someone with a slow tickin', somber soul like those two to keep us honest and grounded.

Like the nine-year-old did to the group of grown ass men surroundin' him now.

"Yeah, exactly like that," I agreed.

"I'm a dick," Nova admitted with a grimace. "Seems sometimes I don't know how to stop. Sorry, bro."

"No need," I assured. "But you might wanna do some thinkin' in that pretty head of yours, Booth, and see 'bout why it is you're a dick more often than not. Seems to me, a happy man'd have a harder time actin' like an ass."

"Oh, fuck off," he muttered, and I laughed at him 'cause it was impossible not to.

There was a rough throat clearing behind me, and I turned my head to see Wrath Marsden at the edge of the stage, hands shoved in his pockets, lookin' like he'd lost 'bout twenty pounds since his accident, since Kylie's murder, but the fact that he was actually outside the trailer we'd got for him to convalesce in was enough of a miracle for one day.

"Hey man." I walked to the edge of the stage and offered him my hand to hoist him up. "You gonna join us?"

We hadn't found Wrath after everythin' went down. One day, we thought he was dead, and weeks later, he'd shown up in our kitchen one morning, just sittin' at our table, lookin' like a real-life zombie drinkin' a cup of our coffee. Cress had burst into tears as she threw herself into Wrath's lap and he'd let her sit there, even held her as she cried. But I had seen the apathy in his eyes, the dull metallic sheen of his cold heart turned mechanical with loss, and I'd known Wrath had returned from the dead a different man.

Still didn't know what had happened to him, but if there was one thing I recognized, it was the look of demons lurkin' in a man's eyes, and Wrath's were full of 'em.

With Kylie gone, Cress and me were the only two souls he had left he could turn to now that his club was disbanded, and we'd done it without a word of contention. That same day, I'd gone out with Lion and his truck and brought back an Airstream so Wrath could have his own place on the property.

I'd asked him to be a groomsman one night when I'd found him on the back patio smokin', but he'd just given me a blank look, snuffed out the stick, and left.

Apparently, that had meant yeah.

He stared at my hand, face completely unanimated by any emotion, eyes flat, dead grey-blue stones, like slate. And then his hand was in mine and I was leverin' his weight up on stage with me and the brothers standin' with me.

Nobody liked him, outside'a Lion who had his own bond with him after takin' down the Berserkers, but I didn't care.

They'd come 'round, and if they didn't, and I told 'em even a hint of Wrath's story, they'd get it and get him. The Fallen were named so for a reason; not one'a us was without our tragic stories.

Seconds later, cars started pullin' into the drive, parkin'

along the road leadin' down to our cabin, nerves hittin' me again like a batterin' ram.

"You ready?" Harleigh Rose called as she walked up the path. Honest to God, I forgot her question immediately 'cause she looked so damn pretty.

She'd always been a beautiful girl, and she'd grown into a beautiful woman. It was the bane of Zeus's and my existence as she got older, but now, I was happy as fuck she'd wound up with the one man I could trust to take care of all that loveliness. 'Cause I knew, the way most people didn't, that H.R. was soft and sweet as an unfurled rose at the heart, under all those thorns. Lion would always make sure she kept that tenderness and that it remained safe from harm.

Lion stood then, mouth open, eyes blown to black by the sight of her.

"Prettiest flower in the whole fuckin' garden," he promised her as she stepped up into his arms and let him kiss her.

She pulled away with a smile then bit his bottom lip playfully. "Thorniest, too."

"Don't I know it," he muttered drily.

I laughed, drawin' my sister's attention. She cocked her head as she took me in then grinned like a loon. "You look fuckin' dapper, King."

"If I look dapper, then you look like a princess," I countered with a raised brow.

She pursed her lips. "MC princess then."

"Dapper rebel then," I retorted.

She laughed, lighter than I'd seen her in years, then bounded up the three steps to the small stage we stood on to hug me so hard it took my breath.

"Easy," I whispered, even as I wrapped her up tight and breathed in the floral scent that somehow suited her. "Try not to break my back 'fore my weddin', yeah?"

She burrowed her nose into my chest and sighed so heavily

it felt like a cleansin'. "Love you, big bro. You know that, right? Even if I'm a brat half the time."

"Only half?"

"King…" she warned, tiltin' that streaky blonde head back so we could lock eyes. "I'm bein' serious."

"So was I." I grinned then let it drop off my face as I cupped the back of her head and kissed her forehead. "In all the hardest times of my life 'fore Cress, it was my love of you that kept me goin'."

Instantly, her cerulean blue eyes, our mother's eyes, went wet with tears that trembled on her lower lids. "Cress'll be pissed you made me cry and fucked up my makeup."

"Nah." I hugged her again 'cause it was rare over the last few years she'd let me do that, show her affection easy and often as I pleased. "Wish Dad was here," I admitted into her hair.

She squeezed me. "Me too."

"Okay, enough huggin' and cryin' and all that crap," Boner bellowed as he walked up the aisle clappin' his hands. "This is a biker weddin', ain't it? Let's fuckin' well act like it then."

"No more tears," I promised him as I let H.R. go with one last hug. "Swear it."

Only, half an hour later, when the dozens of black chairs strewn over the lawn in a small clearing at the side'a our property were filled with Fallen brothers, family, and friends, I started regrettin' my promise. Seein' the faces of the people who'd been instrumental in my life smilin' and eager to witness me marry the love'a my life moved me in a way that felt like lava wakenin' in my gut, floodin' through my system so hot it felt I was bein' burned alive. Old Sam from the record shop was there, old friends from Entrance Bay Academy, and even older friends from Entrance Public, all the Old Ladies sittin' together already cryin', and their men tryin' hard not to be moved by the moment but failin'.

It was a lot to process for a man with an admittedly sensitive heart who felt too much for himself and too often for others. The very air felt thick and sweet as honey with happiness and a degree of relief that the day was finally—even after everythin' that had happened—here.

And then the bridal party came.

Benny and Carson together, the only men, linkin' arms and beamin' like proud fathers.

Rainbow then Tayline, walkin' to the rhythm of "The One" by Kodaline as Lion strummed it on his guitar, accompanied by Eugene who played on a giant piano that'd been a pain in the ass to drag out on the grass.

Then Harleigh Rose in all her glory, wearin' a black dress with her yellow hair flowin' down her back.

Loulou came next, her cloud of moonshine waves like a halo as she glided toward us, her face serene and so beautiful it made my heart ache to think Z was missin' out on the sight of her like that.

The song changed to "Love Me Tender" by Elvis, and I swallowed thickly as I spotted a flash of white through the trees, and Cressida rounded the corner.

My nose itched with the burn of tears as I looked at her, alone and proud, gorgeous in a way that literally shook me, my hands tremblin'.

She was a fairy tale come to life, like somethin' outta a dream. The dress was sorta sheer, highlightin' the movement of her sweet form through the webbin' of lace, and it hung over her shoulders precariously like one puff of wind would expose her. With all of her hair done in a fancy mass of waves and braids, her heart stoppin' face done up just enough to make her eyes fuckin' *glow*, and her mouth a deep, crushed berry colour that begged tastin', I didn't think I'd ever seen anythin' or anyone more beautiful.

Struck by her, quaked by the force of love that moved

through me and fucked my equilibrium, I was unprepared for the playful wink she shot me as she drew close.

Laughter bubbled up through the fault lines within me and erupted. I laughed long and low as she grinned at me and started to walk up the steps, only, I decided as she did that I didn't want to wait one more fuckin' second to hold her. So, I lunged forward and took her arm as she climbed the last step. Surprised, she paused and tipped her head to look up at me then lost her train of thought to somethin' she found in my face.

So, we stared at each other, suspended on the edge of the stage, locked in each other's gaze.

"Knew the moment I saw you across Mac's Grocer parkin' lot you were the one for me," I whispered just for her. "Knew it like you were made from me, for me, and you were just slot-tin' back into place inside me. Adam's rib returned to him."

Those huge whiskey eyes warmed and went wet as she stared up at me with that expression I lived for, the one that said I was her hero and her fuckin' haven, her bad boy with a good heart that beat just for her.

"I can hardly breathe for loving you right now," she admitted.

"It'd be a shame if you died on our weddin' day," I joked, but I felt the same.

My heart beatin' too fast and too hard in my chest as if it was tryin' to break free to get to her.

"If you could tear your eyes away from each other for one fuckin' moment, Priest can marry ya," Nova called out, and a ripple of laughter worked through the crowd.

Cress blushed, the dusky rose sweepin' over her cheeks and chest so that I just had to reach out and feel it under my fingers 'fore I tucked her into my arms and led her to Priest.

It shocked us both, I think, when we turned to look at the man who would marry us, an ordained minister despite his detestation of religion, and found him *smilin'*.

Not his rare, closed-lipped expression of evil delight that was more like a bloody smear across his face than a smile, or the even more unusual faint tip of his lips to the side that marked genuine pleasure, but a teeth bared, fairly soft smile that made him look almost human.

"You're smilin'," I noted, in case he wasn't aware.

The smile broke under the force of his frown as he glared at me. "Was, yeah."

"King," Cress hissed. "You ruined it!"

Priest looked at her, and the smile came back to his eyes. "No ruinin' today, Cress. Don't believe in marriage or much else 'sides. But today, I believe in you and King enough to join the two of you, and fuckin' proud to do it."

Cress's lips trembled. "Thanks, honey."

He nodded and began the more formal ceremony, but I tuned him out 'cause Cress was lookin' at me. My heart was beatin' too hard and too fast, and I felt sick and fuckin' dizzy 'cause never in my entire twenty-three years had I conceived of a happiness so big as this.

"You got somethin' to say to each other, say it now," Priest finally said.

And it was my turn.

My turn to somehow find the right words for the emotions in my chest that defied reasonin'. I was a poet, not because I wanted to be, but 'cause it possessed me, compelled me, as if the words were magic and I the wand that harboured them.

In the chaos of my overly full, riotin' heart, it was no wonder that poetry was the only way I could hope to express myself.

There was a desert in my mouth and a storm in my skull, a tossin' sea in my gut and a strain on my soul. But somehow, I found the words I wanted—no—needed to say to my woman 'fore I made her mine.

"I found love when I was eight

Pressed petals the colour of blood
Hidden between the pages
Of a book I was too young to read

Again,
At that awkward time
When my voice lacked depth
Then suddenly
Fell to the bottom of a well
That signaled maturity and I thought
"Finally, I am old enough to love."

But by fifteen, I had seen only wraiths,
Lust like brass when I would have gold
Infatuation thin as gauze and just as easily torn

At eighteen,
My half-formed soul felt fallow
My dreams withered to husks and tumble weeds
I was old enough for first love, they said
But my heart yearned for that and more

They couldn't have known what would happen
That same year
When I saw you across a parking lot
How my heart would age a decade with each beat
And the hollow cage of my chest would be at once so filled

In a second, I was found.
Too young, too old, too every single thing at once
Because with you I was made and unmade
Everything was possible because of you
Yet nothing was necessary
Because my ten-year journey

For the other half of my soul
Was done.
And that was all I ever wanted."

She was cryin', great, big tears that rolled down her face like diamonds. I caught one on my thumb.

"I was hungry my whole life. Just ravenous. Voracious for somethin' with a name I hadn't yet found. It wasn't until I met you that I knew I was famished for love'a you and it wasn't until our first kiss that I knew what it was really like to be satisfied and at peace. Cress, babe, you are the bone of my bone, light of my fuckin' life, and I won't let one day for the rest of our long lives go by without tryin' and probably failin' to express to you just how much you mean to me."

"King," she sobbed, droppin' the bouquet of nearly black red roses to our feet so she could press her hands to my chest. "How can I possibly hope to follow that?"

"You don't have to say anythin' if you don't want to," I soothed as I ran the edge of my fingers down her wet cheek. "Know you love me the same."

"I do," she promised as if pleadin' with me to understand. "I need you to know that I would fall from grace again and again if it meant living in sin with you. Honestly, I never knew how much was enough to ask for in my life until I met you, and since then? I've never thought to ask for anything else."

And then, 'cause I couldn't stand it for one more fuckin' second and it was a biker weddin' in a forest with a murderer as our officiant so fuck the conventional, I dragged Cress into my arms and kissed her.

I kissed her like her mouth was the only possible way for me to assuage the wild hunger I felt for the taste of her flesh in my mouth, her body under my hands, her heart tied to mine through our chests by some invisible and unbreakable chain.

Distantly, I was aware of Priest sayin' his final words and

the entire crowd stampedin' to their feet to roar their congratulations at us.

Nova wolf whistled, Boner pelted the stage with blossoms he plucked off the stems of the arrangements beside his chair, and Maja danced with my twin siblings in the aisle.

I broke apart from my girl, raised our joined hands, and called, "Fuck yeah!"

Cress laughed and repeated back with the crowd, "Fuck yeah!"

It was later, not much, but the sun was kissin' the edge of the horizon, paintin' the sky with all the colours of my passion for my wife.

My wife.

I kissed her deeply, twinin' my tongue with hers so I could suck the wine from it and feel her moan vibrate against my teeth.

Had her pressed up against a tree far enough from the party ragin' 'round a massive bonfire in the clearin', affordin' us privacy yet close enough to hear the strains of "Devil's Backbone" throbbin' through the air.

"Fuck me, my wife is sweet," I growled as I broke the kiss and stared at her swollen, damp mouth.

Cress gasped as I rucked up her dress with one hand and

tugged her hair back with the other so her mouth opened for me to plunder again. Finally reachin' the end of the fabric, my hand drifted up her thigh, over the smooth silk stockings and lace tops until I hooked her leg up and wrapped it 'round my hip, leavin' her exposed and pressed against me.

"Need you so much," she murmured, eyes blown to black with desire as I dragged my thumb back and forth over the satin coverin' her sweet pussy. "Please don't tease me, King. Not now. I need to feel you inside me."

"First time I'm gonna fuck my wife, I'm gonna take my time," I told her as I ran my nose up the arched line of her throat and sucked at her pulse point just to feel it race against my tongue.

I was filled with an almost heathen-like possession, the savage desire to rut with my wife after claimin' her in front of friends and kin. My blood was hot, scorchin' through, bubblin' in my belly, like some active volcano 'bout to erupt. My cock twitched at the idea of spillin' inside her tight cunt, givin' her my seed for the first time as my wife.

She was hot through the tiny panties coverin' her sex, leakin' through the fabric as I pressed over her clit again and again with firm strokes. Her head lolled back against the tree, hair catchin' on the rough bark, a flush spillin' down her chest like wine.

I ducked down to lick the hot skin and taste that blush for myself, needin' to devour every inch of her, a victory feast, a glutton with his reward.

"King," she gasped so pretty. "Please, more."

"Fuck, you make me so hard when you beg. Tell me what you want," I demanded, slidin' my thumb tantalizingly just under the edge of her underwear.

"Your fingers inside me. Your cock inside me. I want to be filled up by my husband," she groaned, an edge of frustration in her tone as her fingers tightened on my shoulders and she began to writhe against my hand. "Fill me up."

A low growl worked loose from my chest, her words unlockin' the beast that lay at the heart of me, chained to the floor of my gut, but freed by the ferocity of our passion.

Her sweet thong snapped off with one tug.

Hikin' her leg higher over my arm, I propped her ass in a palm and made quick work of my fly with my other hand. Never been so hard, thick and puslin', already damp with precum as I notched just inside her snug pussy.

I paused there, our breath churnin' hot between us, her eyes glazed with frustrated desire only I could soothe. I wrapped my free hand 'round her throat, not tight, just gentle pressure, just to feel every single one'a her reactions, the moans vibratin' against my palm, the pulse beneath my thumb.

I wanted to fuckin' *own* her as I took her for this first time.

"Mine," I growled, even my voice bestial. "Mine forever, Cress."

"Yes," she hissed, tryin' to grind down on my cock. "And you're mine."

"Always," I grunted then thrust straight home, stretchin' her tight, wet folds open and seatin' myself to the balls.

Instantly, she quaked, pulse flutterin' under my hand, eyes squeezed shut in painful pleasure.

"Fuck me, so beautiful," I told her as I started to move, long, slow glides out to the tip and savage thrusts back to the base. Needed her to feel every inch of me, needed to feel every inch of her ripplin' 'round me, suckin' me deep. "You gonna come for me, wife?"

Her breath hitched in her throat and she tightened 'round me like a wet velvet vice. "God, yes, King, yes."

"Your King, babe, your King. Say my name when you come for me," I growled through gritted teeth as I powered into her clutchin' heat, as I felt her draw tight as a bow in my arms then release with the suddenness of a loosed arrow, sex floodin' over my cock, arms tight then lax and shakin' 'round me.

"King, King, King," she chanted like a siren lurin' me against the rocks, and with one last primal groan torn straight outta my throat, I crashed against her, breakin' open in her hold, comin' and comin' so hard I felt outta my head with it.

"God, I can feel you," she panted, arrowin' a hand between our bodies so her fingers could frame where the base of my shaft met her swollen lips. She played in the stickiness there then squeezed my cock hard enough to wring one last rope of cum from me. "Love the hot, wet feel of you coming inside me like that."

"Such a dirty girl under all that class and lace," I praised as I licked her neck, hummin' over the salty taste of her on my tongue. "Could drown in you, I'm not careful."

"So drown," she told me, clutchin' me tight when I would've moved away to clean her up. "Drown in me, and I'll drown in you."

Her sex rippled 'round me again, and I groaned, drained, but not satisfied. Ignorin' her gasp, I dropped to my knees on the grass and propped one'a her long legs over my shoulder.

"King!" she gasped, slightly scandalized even though I'd seen her sweet pussy a thousand times before. "What're you doing?"

I ignored her, leanin' my cheek against her inner thigh as my shoulder spread her legs and my fingers played in her wet, sloppy sex. It was hot as fuck to watch our combined cum leak outta her pink pussy and run down the inside'a her leg.

She squirmed, uncomfortable with my examination, but I could see the way her clit throbbed and the long muscles in her thighs twitched. She was turned on by the shame, hot with the thought of me checkin' out what was mine.

"So pretty filled up with my cum," I murmured, tracin' my tongue up the tender skin of her inner thigh.

She even smelled hot, the heat of her like the sun against my upturned face.

"King…" she whined, half plea and half protest.

Then her hands went to my hair and twisted in the curls, holdin' on instead'a pushin' me away.

"Gonna eat you like this, Cress babe," I warned her, tongue flickin' at the delicate seam between her leg and sex. "I'm a grown man, and I'm still fuckin' starvin'."

My mouth sealed over her pussy, tongue in her folds, lickin' up the hot cream as she writhed under my ministrations, gaspin' and moanin' so loudly I wondered if someone might come to explore the animal amid the trees makin' so much noise.

The idea of bein' found with my mouth pressed to my woman, drinkin' from her, devourin' her, only made my cock hard again, achin' steel droolin' precum on my abs. I fisted myself, pumpin' slowly to take the edge off while I made Cress come apart over my tongue, her juices runnin' down my chin.

Drunk on the taste of us, drugged by her orgasms, I made quick work of bringin' her to climax again, addin' my fingers to the mix so I could press on the tender spot at the front wall of her tight cunt.

"Fuck, God, King, I can't take anymore," she shouted, legs shakin' so badly, I propped the other leg over my shoulder and pinned her harder to the tree, supported entirely by my mouth, my shoulders, and the bark at her back.

"You'll take it," I growled, blowin' cool air over her heated sex, gut clenchin' at the beauty of her swollen folds exposed for me. "You'll take it, and, Cress, when you come again, want you to thank your husband."

And just like that, one more wet, long, suck at her pulsin' clit, and she was comin', quakin' apart in my arms like a poorly built house collapsin' inwards. I held the pieces of her and slowly, achingly, put her back together again with soft kisses to her pubic bone and thighs, soothin' hands strokin' down her sides.

"My sexy wife," I praised. "My dirty girl."

She lolled her head against the tree and peered down at me as I carefully put her feet to the ground again. Her tongue ran a path across those plump lips as she saw my cock strainin' obscenely out'a the placket of my suit pants.

"Come on me," she whispered, eyes dark as a black hole suckin' me into their depths. "Come on me so I can wear you for the rest of the night on my skin."

"Fuck, my girl loves it dirty," I grunted as I surged up, her virginal white dress wrapped in one fist, the other wrapped 'round my dick as I jerked it brutally.

She watched, holdin' me close by the shoulders but far enough away she could see the angry red crown of my cock start leakin' down my fist. I took a moment to smear my hands across her wet sex, collectin' her cum to lube the glide of my hand over my dick, and she sighed longingly, like the sight was the best she'd ever seen.

"Love your cock, King," she murmured in affirmation, lickin' those lips, lids heavy from the weight of her desire, absolutely wrecked by passion. "Can't wait to feel your hot come on me."

That did it.

With a restrained roar, neck arched back, tendons strainin', my balls seized, and I came. Bent my head in time to see the first burst of seed land on her bared belly, the second on her smooth pubic bone, the third a hot splash against her clit.

"Fuck me," I grunted as I shuddered and pulled the last drops from my sensitive cock, watchin' them drop to the grass.

Collapsin' against her, careful to keep our groins apart, I fisted a hand in her hair and kissed her. She moaned, lappin' sweetly at my tongue to share the taste of us.

"Beautiful," I told her, overwhelmed by her perfection.

"The way you give yourself to me, Cress, gotta say, nothin' sexier, nothin' more sacred to me than that."

She smiled, and it was a sweet, almost shy thing that made my heart ache with the beauty of it. "Only ever for you."

"Fuck yeah," I agreed, possession and primal pride surgin' through me. "Only for me ever again."

We grinned at each other like drunkards, like loons liquored up on love and life. Felt so happy it seemed sinful, like God would reach down from the sky and strike me dead for bein' so content and fulfilled on an excess of each one'a the seven sins.

"Better get back before they send someone looking," she whispered. "Even though I'm tempted to stay out here together like Adam and Eve in their garden, alone and naked."

I laughed. "Adam and Eve didn't end so good, babe. Let's not liken ourselves too much to them, yeah?"

I helped her right her dress after one last look at the cum dryin' on her belly and fixed the masses of disarrayed curls that tumbled all over her shoulders and back. She tenderly tucked me back in my pants, did up my fly, a nun at service tendin' to her shrine, then we linked hands to walk back to the party together.

Only when we started walkin' did we notice the lack of human noise over the music. Concern slivered down my spine like a serpent in the grass, and with a quick look at Cress, we broke into a light jog.

When we stopped in the clearin' 'round the fire, everyone was still there, but nothin' was good.

"King Kyle Garro!" Javier Ventura crowed as he stepped forward into the light of the flames wearin' a tuxedo, arms spread like a host welcomin' his guest. "I hear congratulations are in order."

CHAPTER TWENTY-ONE

King

JAVIER VENTURA WAS the man behind the curtain, the puppet master who had pulled the strings of every single villain we'd been up against for the last five years. He was the west coast leader of a Mexican cartel, and he was the kinda vicious you could *feel*, an aura of evil intention that waxed the air 'round him like pollution.

He'd only grinned at us, waitin', as we stepped closer. I tracked the goons encriclin' the party, guns at brothers' backs and temples, Bea caught in a headlock, one'a the babies, Angel, held by a thug who stood beside a silently sobbin' Loulou.

Fuck.

Somehow, I'd known this day wouldn't go off without a hitch. People were at their weakest, most vulnerable when celebratin' and happy. It was why, historically, so many dramas had gone down at weddings.

And now one was goin' down at mine.

"Don't remember sendin' you an invite," I said coolly, gently movin' Cress behind me 'cause I didn't even want the motherfucker's eyes on her.

He laughed happily and shrugged. "Must have gotten lost in the mail. That Canadian Post really is tragic."

"What're you doin' here?" I asked, unamused.

I saw Priest try to move closer to Bea, Sander edgin' nearer to Loulou, and resolved to let Javier run his mouth until they could get into position.

"So impolite!" He turned to eye Loulou and scowled. "You were always so much better mannered than these biker heathens. Should've stayed with your father and stayed a good girl, Louise."

"Fuck. You" she snarled, spittin' at him even though he was outta her reach.

He laughed again, a hyper yip like a hyena.

And just like a hyena, I was sure he was the kinda animal that ate all the way through the bones of his victims.

"I'm here to have a little chat, or should I say, facilitate one," he continued, claspin' his hands behind his back, a businessman at a meetin'. "You see, the Staff Sergeant doesn't take kindly to you harbouring his wife."

"She stayed with us of her own violation."

"Then why isn't she here tonight?"

"She has Alzheimer's," Lion stepped up to growl. "It wasn't a good day for her."

"Not a good day, not a good day…hmm. Well, I think it's safe to say it won't be a good day for you lot either if you don't come with me and have that little chat."

"Like hell," Bat snapped from behind Javier.

"Really, gentlemen, it's obvious I've caught you at a real disadvantage." Javier gestured widely to the dozens of his men holdin' the party up at gunpoint. "I don't think you have much of a choice in the matter. Let's not ruin this joyous day with bloodshed, hmm?"

My mind raced, tryin' to find a solution to this problem. No, not a solution, nothin' so cut and dry. I had to think the way Machiavelli would, like a fox needin' to outwit the trap, a lion to scare the hyenas circlin' my pack.

And I knew what to do like Satan himself had sent the serpent to whisper in my ear.

I jerked my chin up at Javier. "Fine. You wanna talk, we'll talk, but you leave now, and I'll meet you at a neutral location."

"What's my guarantee you'll show up?" he asked, clickin' his tongue like I was some naughty boy. "No, I think I'll escort you there myself, but I have no problem with you picking the spot."

"He's not going alone," Cress said, steppin' 'round me and beside me. "I'm going with him."

"Like hell you are," I muttered, tuggin' her into me and leanin' down to press my forehead to the side'a her head. "Babe, can't think straight when you're in danger. Don't ask me to take you."

"I'm your queen," she protested. "I belong with you and go where you go."

"We each got our own battles to fight here. Need you to stay back and be strong, keep everyone calm like you do. Can you do that for me? Be strong until I get back?"

Only, I didn't tell her I had this weight in my stomach, heavy with hooks sunk deep in the walls of my gut, tellin' me I might not get back at all.

Cress seemed to sense my anxiety and turned fully into me, ignorin' the goons and the villains to focus her fuckin' gorgeous brown graze on me. She cupped my face, traced my cheekbones with her thumbs, and breathed in deep and shaky, just to smell me.

"I love you," she said fiercely, eyes brimmin' with diamond tears. "I meant what I said, I would fall from grace a thousand times over if it meant living in sin and beauty with you. I need you to come back to me, okay, honey? I need you to *live*, so don't do anything crazy, okay? Nothing gallant or brave. This isn't a storybook, and you don't need to be some valiant king who sacrifices himself for his country, okay?"

When I didn't say anythin', too busy memorizin' every single inch of her face, she shook me, voice sharp as a threatenin' knife at my throat as she repeated, "Okay?!"

"Okay, babe, okay," I soothed.

Then I drowned the lie with a kiss like a tidal wave, a kiss to crush her fears and replace em with the power of all the love I felt for her. I poured it between her lips, hopin' it would sow some eternal seed in her heart that would bloom forever no matter what.

"Love you, Cress," I mumbled against her lips. "Love you enough to tear the world apart for my girl with the whiskey eyes."

"Promise me you're coming back," she urged as I pulled away. "Promise me, King. Swear it to me, or I won't let you go without me."

I tucked a long curl behind her ear and gave her my cocky grin. "I swear it, babe. We'll have our honeymoon in Alaska if it's the last thing I do. Now let me go, yeah?"

"Okay," she whispered, hands tremblin' as she let go.

"Bone of my bone," I reminded her as I stepped toward Javier. "Of me, meant for me."

"Bone of my bone," she echoed, and then I turned my back on her 'cause I couldn't stand watchin' her cry.

"Touching," Javier said with a slow clap. "Really touching."

"It's our fuckin' wedding day," I bit out. "And you're forcin' me to leave my wife behind."

"She could come," he said slyly.

"He's not goin' alone," Nova called out, pushin' against a thug to step forward only to be hit over the head with the butt of a gun so he crumpled to the ground.

"Ah, it's you." Javier's mask slipped for a moment and his true, demonic face shone through as he glared at Nova. "If I were you, I'd stay silent so I don't turn my attention on *you*. Now." He turned back to me with his smooth grin. "Pick one person."

"Wrath," I called immediately, ignorin' the murmur of shock that pulsed through the brothers at the fact I hadn't chosen one'a them.

He was behind me somewhere, yet I knew the moment he stepped forward 'cause Javier's eyes narrowed as they traveled the length and size of the man.

"A big boy," he said with a laugh. "Though I doubt Danner will be intimidated."

"Not 'bout that." And it wasn't.

It was 'bout the fact that Wrath was the only man there who knew what it felt like to lose the love'a your life, and therefore, the only one who could begin to understand my plan.

"Whatever the reason, shall we go? Who knows, maybe you'll even be back in time to cut the cake!" He laughed warmly, as if we were best friends and this was his party, then turned abruptly and stalked toward the GMC SUVs parked in a line at the mouth of the driveway.

Wrath moved into place behind me and followed.

If they could, The Fallen touched me as I went by 'em, callin' out to me when they couldn't, just my name, until a soft echo of it lingered in the air.

King, King, King.

"Where to, Mr. Garro?" Javier called over his shoulder.

"The bluffs off Back Bay road, turn right on to Wildwood."

"Oh," he said with a cheery laugh. "How atmospheric."

We got into the back of one'a the SUVs, the door held open by Javier himself who grinned then slammed the door in our faces as soon as we were seated.

I acted quickly, whippin' out the phone they hadn't bothered to take. The man I needed to help execute my crazy plan was at the weddin', so I could only pray he'd get outta there like a bat outta hell and find a way to help me.

"You knew this was gonna happen," Wrath muttered, his dead eyes the colour of lead as he stared at me. "You're gonna do somethin' I'm not gonna like."

I flashed him a smile. "Might not come down to that, but listen good and don't interrupt. Don't know how much time we got."

CHAPTER TWENTY-TWO

King

"WANTED to talk to you man to man," Staff Sergeant Harold Danner's voice came from behind me, but I didn't turn around.

I was looking out at the ocean, tryin' to brand the sight of the Pacific rolled out like black velvet tossed with silver fragments from an over full moon into my memory banks.

I had a feelin' I might not survive the night. And if that was the case, I wanted every last moment spent breathin' to be as full of beauty as it could be, even while in the presence of SS Danner who was pure evil incarnate.

I'd been out on the cliff for thirty minutes already, Wrath waitin' with Ventura's thugs off to one side, long after Javier had departed himself. It was clever, him leavin', and I got the sense he never stuck 'round for long, especially when somethin' bad could go down. It no doubt lent itself to his longevity as a crime boss.

"Yeah? Want to confess your sins, Danner?" I asked mildly,

even though I was filled with anger.

It wasn't hot and volatile, rushin' through me like a drug the way it had before.

No.

Like a volcano after the eruption, my lava had cooled to dark, impenetrable rock.

I would not be moved or shaken off the course I'd set by petty anger, not when the lives of the ones I loved were in danger and the man threatenin' them was so close at hand.

"If we're talking about sins, boy, it's you who should repent," Danner called out, deliberately keepin' a decent distance between us. "You want the chance to come clean, I'm sure I can work with the prosecutor to cut you a deal. Maybe we could even put you in the same cell as your daddy."

"You ever worry 'bout heaven or hell?" I asked, stickin' my hands in my pockets and tippin' my chin to the star strewn sky. "Worry 'bout what level of hell they might put you in when you meet your maker?"

Danner's laugh was cold. "No. I don't. I'm the one on the right side of the law."

"Can't hide behind your shades of blue in death. Can't even do it well in life, Harold. You think you've got justice on your side just 'cause you're a cop, and you think I've got sin on my side just 'cause I wear a leather cut. Goodness is in action, not position."

"Pretty speech," he bit out, clearly frustrated by my philosophisin'. "But I came to make a deal with you so you won't see any more of your family punished for their crimes or the crimes of the ones they love."

I dragged in a deep breath of the sweet fuckin' clean and salted air through my mouth then expelled it in a gusty sigh, bracin' for what might happen next.

'Cause I'd found an answer to my question of what price I was willin' to pay to stave off war.

And like any good leader, I'd chosen to fall on my sword

rather than slip in the blood of my Fallen brothers and our families.

When I turned to finally face Danner, it was with my hands wrapped steadily 'round the cold weight of a gun.

He stepped back, eyes blown wide with shock, hands up in benediction. "Woah, woah, son, no need for the gun."

One'a the reasons I'd asked Wrath to come with me.

The man was always carryin' concealed weapons, even to my fuckin' weddin'.

"There's a need," I said calmly as Danner held up a stayin' hand to Officer Ormand and the lingerin' Ventura goons. "You've been holdin' a gun to my head and the head of the club for years. Wanted you to see how it felt."

"You used to be a good kid. I'm learning that there is no escaping criminal genes, though. You've got anarchist written in your blood."

"I've got Garro blood, and yeah, a little chaos in my heart, but I'm a rebel with a cause. And right now? That cause is gettin' you to back the fuck off from my family."

There was a thin line between sacrifice and sheer martyrdom, and I hoped like hell this was it, drawn in black beneath my feet. In that moment, I understood Joan of Arc and Socrates, Dumbledore from *Harry Potter*, and Winston from *1984*.

I understood that there was nothin' in death as fearsome as the thought of livin' without those you love, 'cause fear and love were two sides of the coin of every man's existence. And the chance I was takin', the choice I was makin', was love over fear.

So, I held my gun steady, even when Danner whipped his Glock out from its holster and took a threatenin' step toward me.

"Drop the gun, King, and let's talk about this like civilized men."

"You put my father in prison outta sheer fuckin' hatred.

Been tormentin' my brothers and their families, even put your hands on my woman. The time for talkin' is over."

"There's a way out of this for you. I came today to make a deal. You and three of your crew confess to charges of racketeering, money laundering, drug possession and distribution, while the rest of you disband your criminal enterprises, and we don't have to do this anymore."

"Why the fuck would I agree to that?" I asked, steppin' a little closer to the edge of the cliff at my back.

"Because it's the right thing to do. Because you know you're putting your family at risk, running that club the way you do. You don't want to see your new wife put away for being associated with your crimes, do you? You don't want to see anything bad happen to Loulou Garro or her babies because you got tangled up in the wrong crime syndicate."

"Not turnin' my back on my family the way you have, Harold," I told him, voice like an open trap. I needed his anger, needed him foolish and reckless and filled with so much hatred for me that he wouldn't care 'bout the witnesses at his back. "Susan's mind is deteriotatin' and you still treat her like shit. Lion Danner's the most decent copper I know, yet you still spent his entire life beratin' him."

"I love Susan," he barked, his gun risin' up, trained right on my chest. "I love her, and she left *me* because she's got a soft heart, and she couldn't take my passion for justice, for my career anymore."

"This is not justice. What you got is a vendetta that's corroded you to your core. You don't even see the man behind the cut now, you just see a demon straight outta hell."

"Maybe I should send you back where you came from?" he suggested, takin' another step toward me, just a handful of yards between us.

I laughed. "Be my guest. I'd rather die on my feet fightin' you than live on my knees in fear of *you*."

There was a distant rumble like the roll of thunder 'fore a

storm. Harleys were comin'.

Danner looked over his shoulder at the tree obscurin' the road then cursed. "Jesus Christ, King, drop the fuckin' gun."

"Not gonna drop it, Danner, unless you confess you murdered Riley Gibson. How'd it happen anyway? I know he was headed to the station to make a call down to Van PD bout corruption in the force here…did you catch him? Seize the opportunity when you saw it to kill a cop who wanted you locked up and also put away the man you've hated for decades for that very crime?"

"Shut. Up." Danner grounded out, his eyes wet, dark pools in the low light under the bright super moon.

"Was it an accident?" I asked, mild curiosity somehow an insult in my tone. "Did you hear him informin' on you and lose it?"

"I said drop the goddamn gun and shut up, Garro," Danner shouted, so crazed he didn't notice the roar of pipes had stopped, didn't turn to see Cyclops and Axe-Man appear outta the dark, their weapons raised and trained on him as they drew closer, obscured from Ventura's goon squad by shadows.

"You don't drop the gun, I'll shoot you. You're directly threatening the life of an officer. I'm well within my rights to end you!" he yelled, a crazed edge to his voice as the situation frayed out beyond his control.

I assumed that if he didn't deliver me and mine to the Venturas, he was dead. Maybe—I could almost hear him thinkin'—if he killed me now, it'd be enough to appease 'em and garner that extra percentage of payout money.

I laughed, filled with the giddiness of rebellion, high on the fumes of the loomin' tragedy, surprised by how hyper I felt at the end.

Maybe it was 'cause I'd lived a good life, the best life, with near on five years beside a woman I'd dreamed of my entire existence.

Maybe it was 'cause I knew, if I died, that I'd do it with our love like celestial dust in my veins so even when my body went, our story would be immortalized in the stars.

This was my one chance to get Danner put away. The one solution I'd come up with and the only one I could live with. Or die with.

If Danner murdered me, he'd go down for it. With the witnesses in place, it was as sure a thing as it could be.

And if Danner went to prison, with the rookie cop and Paula to testify against his other crimes, Zeus'd be free.

Never thought much 'bout dyin'. I was still a young man by anyone's standards, only twenty-three and healthy with it. My lack of curiosity 'bout death stemmed more from my life-long exposure to it more than anythin' else. Had a father who killed his uncle in a church parkin' lot when I was a kid, sent to the clink for half a dime. There'd always been guns in my house, in The Fallen clubhouse, and guns worn on the hips of the men who hung there. Learned to shoot when I was five, how to defend myself usin' the stick limbs of a twelve-year-old boy's body, and how to use a knife like a fuckin' extension of myself when Priest rolled into my life and taught me his deadly craft. Mostly, I knew death 'cause it stole my best friend, my fuckin' brother in everythin' but blood, when we were still kids, still filled with hope and piss and a shit ton'a vinegar.

So yeah, I wasn't unfamiliar with death, but it wasn't somethin' I'd ever worried 'bout for myself. Never thought of it until now, and, to be fuckin' honest, I never coulda known I'd be facin' down death's door with no chance to escape it. Suppose some would argue there was a choice, that there's a choice to be had in all things.

Only, I'd counter there was no other decision to be made for me in that moment. Dyin' meant my dad would be free, my girl would be safe, and my family would be whole.

How could I do anythin' else, but die?

For them.

Yeah, that's exactly right.

So, I stood on the edge of that cliff that had been my place, a kinda special settin' for so many of the greatest fuckin' moments of my life, and I stared down the craggy wall of rock droppin' into even more sharp rocks and the churnin' ocean below, and I braced myself while Danner's rantin' shouts escalated to the point of no return behind me.

There was pure evil at my back, and 'fore me, only a chasm that represented an empty future without any'a the people I loved.

Shoulda been a sad moment, maybe, somethin' like a tragedy. But as I heard the cock of the gun and the hard spit of the bullet from the chamber somewhere behind me, I couldn't muster up a tear 'cause I was only filled with hope.

Hope that my sacrifice would ensure the happily ever after I'd once promised my wife.

I'd found what I loved, and I was only too willin' to let it kill me.

On that beautiful cliff under an all-seeing moon over grass seeped in memories, King Kyle Garro was shot and plunged over the edge to his tragic death.

CHAPTER TWENTY-THREE

Cressida

THERE WAS no party after King left.

How could you have a wedding reception without the groom?

Instead, everyone but The Fallen and their families went home. The ones left funnelled into our small house, packing it to the gills, the smell of leather and perfume thick in the air as we chatted quietly and drank the whack ton of booze left over from the half-finished party. Everyone was doing their best to have fun, to keep the atmosphere light, yet there was still solemnity in the air, like a fantastic last meal before an execution. We were gorging ourselves on good company, good food, and good drink, but I just couldn't shake the fact that King was with our enemies with only Wrath at his back.

I didn't understand why he had chosen the ex-Berserker as his second. Wrath was a good man straight down to his toes, but he might as well have been broken at every bone from the trauma of losing his Kylie. He barely functioned, living in the airstream at the edge of our five-acre property, not leaving it for days at a time.

And he was a good guy, yes, but he wasn't King's best friend. No one could ever replace Mute for my man, but there were brothers he considered family and good friends, Bat like an uncle, Priest and Nova two of his closest comrades.

So why?

The question lodged under my consciousness like a sliver, casting its pall on the entire night.

I felt better, mildly, when an hour went by and Eugene, Cyclops, Buck, and Axe-Man went out for a ride, circling around town in case they caught sight of where Ventura and King might have gone.

Still, it was good to be with my family, even without the two centers of our wheel, Zeus and King. I spent most of my time holding one of the twins, loving that Angel smiled at everything as if the world existed only for her entertainment, and laughing that Walker was the yin to her yang, scowling and brooding like the four-month-old was already a Byronic hero. I teased Loulou about it, jokingly calling the grumpy baby a true little monster, but she wasn't offended. Instead, like the biker queen she was, Loulou leaned forward to kiss his frowning brow and whispered, "My little Monster."

Lysander, too, stayed close in a way I found comforting, surprisingly, instead of ingratiating after so much time apart. He was stalwart, this hulking presence like a vassal serving his lord. It was a strange relationship, like he was serving penance to me for his mistakes, but I was biker enough to realize that was the only way for him to earn back my trust. At one point, I laid my head on his iron thigh where he sat on the arm of the couch beside me, and he hesitated for one brief, aching, moment before he stroked my head.

There was fun stuff, too, because no biker party was ever boring.

Boner got wasted in a game of Edward Forty Hands with Lab-Rat, the man who tested every single strain of weed the brothers produced and drank everything and anything that could have possibly given him an artificial high, then promptly challenged him to a game of darts. His first three tosses landed darts in the wall, a cushion and almost in my cat's damn tail so I took his last turn, making the only 3 shots by him to actually hit the board.

Maja challenged Hannah, Lila, Cleo, and Harleigh Rose to a dance off, and I almost busted my gut laughing at the way Hannah twerked like a hip-hop dancer despite being sixty plus years old.

It was good.

It just would have been so much better with Zeus.

Incomparably better with King.

And time was ticking on. I could feel the hands of the clock move with every beat of my truculent heart, reminding me that one, two, three hours had passed, and King still wasn't home.

No one said it was going to be okay, and I appreciated that. They knew better than I did, after years of the life, not everyone came home.

I hoped to God King wouldn't go the way of Mute.

And then a phone rang, barely audible under the roar of music, laughter, and constant chatter, but my ears were on alert for any vibration or repetition of sound that might be a ringtone.

It wasn't my phone.

There was something in that—in the fact that my phone wasn't ringing—that caused my heart to turn over in my ribcage, so painful I actually gasped and clutched at my chest, thinking maybe, momentarily, I was having a genuine heart attack.

The room went so quiet, I could hear the buzz of the sound system under the Led Zeppelin song before someone swiftly turned it off.

"Yeah," Bat answered, standing up from off the ground where he'd been playing with his sons.

I didn't breathe, I didn't want to move even an inch, as if my suspension made a difference to the news I'd receive from that damn phone that wasn't mine.

Sander was beside me, hand on my shoulder, Lou to my right on the couch holding both of her babies, Harleigh Rose between my legs on the ground. Later on, I would think about how my family had surrounded me and how that meant something, but at the time, there was no solace to be had.

When Bat listened to whoever was on the other end of the phone and, as if in slow motion, turned his head to look in my eyes, his black gaze impenetrable, his expressive mouth straight as a flatline, everything around me faded away.

Because I knew.

Not that King was dead, but I knew that Bat was going to say he was.

A part of me swiftly moved into denial because I hadn't felt his death, and it seemed important that I would have. He was the bone of my bone, an intrinsic part of my soul. If he'd died, wouldn't there have been a seismic shift in my universe? A crack in the crust of earth at my feet, at the very least? A red sun, a swarm of locusts, a fucking cataclysmic apocalypse?

Not nothing.

Never nothing.

But I knew.

King was dead.

And when Bat moved through the crowd to crouch at my side and placed a hand on my knee, I didn't even hear his voice through the roar of blood in my ears. I only saw his mouth move to form the words.

King is dead.

And then?

Well, I didn't remember anything after that.

CHAPTER TWENTY-FOUR

Zeus

SHE CAME to me like a ghost, a spectre of herself as if she was the one who'd died that day. Didn't help she still wore her gown, once fuckin' gorgeous, now tattered at the hem and streaked with mud, the flowers in her hair as dead as the look in her eyes. Never seen misery so personified, not even in the mirror when my Lou was sick and dyin', not even when I'd told my own daughter she was no longer any kin'a mine, not even on all the many grievin' faces of the folks at Mute's funeral.

Nothin' in all the hard years I'd spent on livin' coulda prepared me for the sight'a Cressida Garro come to tell me our boy was dead.

She said it straight, voice strong as cold steel.

"King's gone. He's gone." As if he'd just upped and abandoned us. Seein' my frown, she'd sucked a sharp breath in through her teeth and squared her shoulders so straight they must'a ached. "He's dead."

Each word was a bullet in the chamber of her despair

slackened mouth, and they hit me with such fuckin' force I flinched 'fore I could even begin understandin' what the words coulda meant.

'Cause there was no way in any kinda hell that God'd take two sons from a man in a single lifetime.

No way He'd join two soulmates, give 'em a taste'a bliss then condemn one to death and the other, worse, to a life without their other fuckin' half like some twisted version of Adam and Eve with their apple.

But I believed it, even though every cell in my body rebelled against it 'cause'a the look'a her sittin' there across from me in a provincial penitentiary.

The look of a woman who'd had half her soul ripped away. The look of a woman made inhuman from loss. The look of a woman, I knew in my fuckin' bones, would never again be more than a ghost.

"Danner Senior," she went on in a hollow voice, each word an empty shell casin'. "He did it. Lured…" Her first hiccough over his name, the name I'd given 'im in the manner I'd given 'em to my other children, a name he'd grown in to. "Lured King to the cliffs and shot him in the back."

Rage swallowed me whole like the mouth of some great and awful beast, sharp teeth shreddin' through my guts, crunchin' through my bones 'til they were dust on the back'a my numb tongue. Felt like I couldn't move 'cause my skin would split with the force'a the demolition roarin' through me.

If I moved an inch, I'd end up locked behind bars for fuckin' life, 'cause the next person I saw, I'd kill outta pure black fury.

"Danner killed my boy," I echoed. My voice wasn't dead like hers 'cause my heart was temporarily shielded from the misery by the purity of my wrath. My body sent the message to my brain: I only had to find and murder Danner to right this egregious fuckin' wrong. Like some kinda magic, Danner's black blood on my hands, drippin' wet to the ground, would resurrect my firstborn like Adonis reborn from Apollo's tears.

"They're going to arrest him—Danner—for what he's done. He fled after the shooting, but every single Canadian chapter of the club, and the cops, are looking for him, and when they find him, he's done. Hutchinson tipped off the Internal Affairs Department to Danner's previously sketchy track record and they've opened up an investigation into his past…including the murder of Riley Gibson. Paula Jones is willing to testify that she was the one who stole your gun from the clubhouse, and a few of the cops Priest got cozy with before… well, *before*, have also flipped on Danner."

She dragged in a deep breath like a drownin' woman, gulpin' it down to fill the empty void inside'a her.

She'd been a wife for only a matter'a hours 'fore she'd become a widow.

The wrongness of it twisted up my guts like coiled barbed wire. I pressed my hand to the glass window 'tween us, needin' more than anythin' to comfort her 'cause I was already a lost cause, and I needed to do *somethin'* or I'd go outta my skin.

After a long hesitation, her glazed eyes vacant like a dead fish, she tilted forward and pressed her forehead to the glass over my hand.

"You're going to be free, Z. There were witnesses to the shooting, and now that they're actually doing something about Danner's corruption, there is no way you won't be acquitted for Gibson's murder. You getting free? It's the only fuel in my tank right now. Knowing my beautiful father-in-law will get out of this horrible cage," she whispered in a threadbare voice that fucked with my anger and set it to crumblin'. Then she turned those big, whiskey coloured eyes my son'd always loved so fuckin' much up to mine with her face up against the plexiglass, and I lost my breath to the catastrophe of sorrow in her gaze.

"We don't even have his body," she wheezed through the

tight squeeze of tears in her throat. "He went over the cliff and he was lost to the sea."

A crater opened in my chest, in the space I assumed my heart might'a previously been, and yawned open with painful alacrity, devastatin' my insides.

Fuck me.

Could life really be so fuckin' unjust that the best man I knew would die at the hands the worst kinda man I'd ever met?

"He looked so beautiful," she breathed, tears smearing against the glass, catching in her eyelashes like diamonds. "In his suit…you should have seen him, Zeus. He looked exactly like an angel cast down from heaven. All that gold hair in the afternoon light, it was like a halo." A moan rumbled through her throat, pure agony. "I held that beautiful face in my hands and stared into those arctic ice eyes, and I swore I'd love him forever."

Her eyes fluttered closed, and a tsunami of tears erupted from the pressure of her pressed lids, wetness streamin' down the glass like rain.

"That was only yesterday," she mouthed more than said aloud. "Yesterday, I held him in my hands."

Her head angled down to look at the hands in question then she slowly raised 'em to the glass so I could see the twin scars on her palms, the tattoo of the Queen of Hearts on the inside'a one finger and the gold ring 'round another. She offered 'em to me, the last place she'd ever touched my son, as if I could somehow feel that last touch through 'er.

The last time I'd touched my son had been four months ago when they'd locked me in 'ere.

So, I pressed my hands over hers and my forehead against hers on the glass, and together, just for a moment—'cause a moment was all I was gonna give myself 'fore I got my shit together and figured out how to slaughter Danner from inside'a this concrete hell—I closed my eyes too and cried with her.

"He was the very best of us," I grunted as the tears fell, so hot they scalded down my cheeks and pooled like fresh wax in my beard.

"He can't be dead," she begged, her dead eyes reawakening to turn crazed, Dr. Frankenstein's experiment gone wrong. "He can't be dead. Please, Zeus, he just…he just *can't be dead*."

"Cress," I said, but the word was broken. "If he's dead, it's only on this earth. You gotta know he's gonna be 'ere every day so long as you and me and all the hoards'a people who knew and loved him still live."

"It's not enough."

Fuck me, 'course it wasn't. But how was I supposed to comfort a woman with a shattered heart when my own was crumblin' all 'round the edges, threatenin' to cave in, too?

Suddenly, she shifted, pullin' back from the glass and wipin' a hand under her nose to clean herself up. I watched as brick by brick, she carefully collected herself until the Cressida I'd first met, prim and proper as a buttoned-up tweed suit, sat 'fore me.

It was fuckin' scary, and I wasn't afraid to admit it. Watchin' her act like that reminded me of Priest after he'd come to us from his own crazy heartbreak.

He'd never recovered genuine emotions, not really.

"Lou is here," she told me with an anemic smile. "I'll send her in."

"Cress," I called, 'cause even though she was sittin' right there, she'd gone again. "I got you, yeah? We all do."

She looked off into a distance only she could see and smiled softly, in a way that made it an expression of pain. "This time, I got you. We'll see you out of here soon, Zeus."

She knocked on the glass once then turned and walked to the door where the guard stepped up to let her out, taking her arm like some macabre father leading his bride down the aisle.

She didn't look at me again 'fore she left, but I knew the vision'a her with dead eyes in that white dress would haunt me until my dyin' day.

Cressida

I'D INSISTED on going to tell Zeus myself. First, I'd suggested it, then, when I was met with worried expressions, I'd demanded, and finally, when they'd protested, I had pulled on a tendril of the smoking wrath bubbling volcanically in my gut and screamed at them to take me to see Zeus fucking Garro.

Someone, probably Lou, had called Lysander and my boys after we'd had our interviews with the police in the early morning of my wedding night, and it was him, Benny, Carson, and Ares who had driven with me to Ford Mountain Correctional to speak with Zeus.

Telling Zeus had been the one solid thought in the sea of

grief that threatened to suck me into its undertow, and I'd clung to it with an almost religious sort of fervor, but now that I had completed the task, there was nothing left to anchor me.

"Back home, princess?" Sander asked, his big body looking fairly ridiculous folded behind the wheel of my small Honda Civic.

"No." I didn't want to go back to the home I'd shared with King. I didn't know what I would do there, alone with my grief and the ghost of our memories stalking my every step. There was a small, not inconsiderable part of me that considered burning it down so I'd never have to step foot in it again.

The pile of wood was no home without my King, and I knew it wouldn't be ever again.

Sander met my eyes in the rear-view mirror where I sat holding Ares's hand. "Where to then? You could stand to eat. Wanna stop by Honey Bear Café and get one'a those fruity coffee drinks you like?"

"I'm not hungry." Though, I was. Just not hungry for food. Hungry for King, for the feel of the air in the room when he entered it, electric like the hum of live wires, and his big hands on my body, gentle and rough only when I needed them to be. I was hungry for his gorgeous face, just to see it animated again, his nostrils flaring with breath, his eyes so like ice with their beautiful cracks and fissures of pale blue colour lit from within with some secret mirth.

It wasn't a hunger that would ever be satisfied with anything less, and I wasn't stupid enough to believe otherwise.

"Where to then?" Sander tried again, sharing a look with Carson in the passenger seat.

"The clubhouse," Carson suggested. "Why don't we check in on the clubhouse? Maybe start planning the funeral?"

"No!" I snapped, doused with the icy water of reality. "No funeral. Not now."

"Cress…." Sander started, but stopped when I cut my glare to his in the rear-view mirror.

"No. No funeral. We don't even have his body." I'd been robbed of the opportunity to stare at him even one last time, even waterlogged from the Pacific and scored through with a bullet. "Zeus is still fucking incarcerated, and I won't have him missing King's funeral. Not when he's missed so much already..."

"Okay," Ares agreed immediately, his huge brown eyes glowing with compassion as he held my hand tightly in both of his own. "Let's wait for Zeus."

I smiled woodenly at him.

"You don't have to smile for me," he whispered, leaning close to tilt his head against my shoulder. "Know what it's like to not want to smile."

I rolled my lips between my teeth to seal the sob that wanted to break free. Instead, I ran a shaking hand over Ares's soft, springy curls and held him to me. Benny squeezed my other hand and mirrored Ares's expression so that I was bracketed by the two sweetest boys I knew.

"Let's go to the clubhouse anyway," Carson suggested, and I knew it was killing him that he couldn't help me, not really. He was a man of action, not words, and there was no action to take against my grief. "Maybe there's been news about where that motherfucking Danner Senior fled to."

He meant it innocuously, probably. Just venting his anger for his friend's murder, just thinking being at the clubhouse would help me heal because it was where King grew up. He didn't mean for it to ignite in my belly like flint struck over the kindling of my helpless fury.

Danner.

The bastard who'd murdered the best man that had ever lived.

He was still free. Still somewhere out there living and breathing when he should be *dead*, or at the very least, locked up forever.

Suddenly, I had an anchor to ground me in that raging sea of grief again.

I didn't say anything, though. Not when we pulled through the gates and parked in the lot. Not when we all shuffled inside, heavy and slow with sadness. Not even when we pushed through the door of the clubhouse and found every single brother littered across the surfaces of the space like crumpled garbage, useless in their sorrow.

It was only when I spotted Priest, standing in the far corner by the window, alone with his arms crossed, eyes to the front lot as if prepared for an assault, that I let that excited fury brew.

I stalked through the room, ignoring everyone else because I didn't see anyone else, not with my tunnel vision locked on the one man who could help feed my dark hunger instead, hunger that was taking shape and name.

Vengeance.

Priest's eyes immediately cut to mine and the intent in them, the calculating, artic rage in them, made my breath catch because it nearly matched my own.

I knew before I even asked what his answer would be.

"That piece of shit SS Danner is still free." I planted my fists on my hips and jutted my chin in the air, daring one of the brothers to stop me. "I want to help find him, and when we do, I want to kill him."

"Cress," Buck stood up from his stool at the bar and frowned at me. "Woman, I know you're grievin' but that is straight up *not* how this shit works, ya get me? This is club business, and we got no use for a woman in it."

"Fuckin' right," Heckler muttered.

"Oh, fuck off," Boner exploded, shoving up from the couch. "You really gonna stand there and tell King's fuckin' *widow* she can't get the retribution she deserves? That motherfucker murdered her man."

"No shit," Buck bellowed, stalking forward so he and

Boner were toe to toe. He was thicker through his barrel chest, with a big square head and meaty hands, but Boner was one long line of lean muscle, and I didn't know what would happen if they came to blows. "You think I don't know my brother, a man like a grandson to me, was fuckin' killed? I want vengeance as much as any'a you! But a woman's got no place here, 'specially not one like Cress."

The room rumbled with low chatter and murmurs of protests and agreement, but I stepped forward, the air instantly going dead quiet.

"A woman like me?" I mused in a voice I didn't even recognize, one that was as cold as the barrel of a gun and just as cocked to deliver something deadly. "A woman like me. What kind of woman is that, huh, Buck? Are you talking about the woman I used to be, before I loved King? The prim and proper, judgemental, scared off her ass Cressida Irons? Because I haven't been her for four fucking years, and whatever's still left of her inside of me? It's dead. I have no softness left, no class for the sake of classiness or morality just to colour inside society's line. That went comatose years ago, and now, after this, this *horror*, there's none of that left.

You want to know what kind of woman I am, Buck? I'm the kind of woman that would carve open her own chest right now just to show you the empty cavity where my heart used to be. And then, bleeding and hollow, I'd be the kind of woman who'd take that same knife and stab it through Harold Danner's goddamn eye sockets for taking away the only man I'll ever love. And you know what I'd do, the kind of woman I am now? I'd *laugh* while I did it because I'd know it was the only joy I'll ever feel again."

My face was twisted up into something grotesque, a snarl and sneer together in perfect disharmony.

"Don't cast me out," I beseeched as I looked from Buck to the other brothers in the room. "I've fallen from grace, but I thought I had a home here, with my Fallen family. When I need you now, are you really going to prove me wrong?"

The silence was thick and reeking, filled with discomfort, banked anger, and conflicting ideas. It was the silence King had told me about after every chapel he'd been to since he'd been taken on as a prospect. It was the silence that came between action and inaction, between stagnating and evolving.

Even after everything, the club wasn't so good with change.

And a woman asking to get in on their action was too radical even for the rebels. I knew it instantly, as if defeat had a taste, and it was in the air.

My shoulders rounded and all that hot air rising from the flames in my belly cooled then settled into dust and ash.

"Right," I said, the word leaking from my mouth like blood from a wound. "Right then. Fuck you all very much."

I turned on my heel the train of my wedding dress dragging behind me as I pushed through the doors into the waning spring sunlight. Benny, Carson, and Ares leaned against my car, but the second they saw me, they stepped forward and each of them enfolded me in an embrace.

Tears streamed down my cheeks, but I only noticed when Benny sweetly rubbed them away with his thumbs.

"Wait there a second, Cress," Buck called from the doorway of the clubhouse.

A low growl worked itself up Carson's throat, and he stepped forward with his teeth bared. "No, you fucking wait *there*. She came to you for help, and it's obvious you turned her away."

"You don't know what she's askin' for," Bat protested, but he did it tired, running a hand over his face and up into his hair as if he wasn't convinced of his own argument.

"I don't give a fuck. Someone you love comes to you for

help when they're so lost to grief they can't see straight, you don't turn them away without a bloody good reason."

"You want her to go to jail after all this?" Buck growled.

Carson stilled, then turned to look at me. His eyes were hard, but his mouth softened as he saw me wrapped up in Benny and Ares. He turned back to the crew gathered on the stairs and shrugged. "I'm thinking after everything that's happened, it'd be good to give her the chance to make her own choice about what she's got left to live for when the love of her life's been ripped away."

He turned back to us and barked, "Get in the car. We're goin' back to our place."

We got into the car, but I didn't remember doing it or the drive to their small bungalow off Main Street. I was in a fog as Benny drew me a bath, as he and Carson talked about whether one of them should sit on the toilet with me so they could make sure I didn't do harm to myself. Apparently, it was decided that Tayline and Rainbow, who arrived at some point, would sit with me, reading to me.

I thought they read from Paradise Lost, but I only guessed that because one line resonated like a struck chord in my head and wouldn't leave my thoughts.

"How can I live without thee, how forgo
Thy sweet converse and love so dearly join'd."

CHAPTER TWENTY-FIVE

Cressida

I WAS ready that night when they came for me. The night as dark as ink spilled across the town, no moon to illuminate the way, clouds veiling the stars of their shine. I sat on Benny and Carson's front step in black jeans and a black, long-sleeved tee, King's hunting dagger affixed in its leather sheave to my belt. Benny and Carson were in bed, wrapped up in each other and softly snoring while Rainbow and Tay dozed in the guest bedroom in the same bed I had pretended to go to sleep in. I was betting they wouldn't wake up. It had been a long, awful two days for everyone, and they'd been there for me through all of it without much sleep.

So, I waited on the front stoop and tried not to focus on the acute throbbing pain in my chest that radiated throughout my entire body like a strobe light.

It didn't take long past midnight for them to come.

The familiar rumble of motorbikes grew to a muted roar as six Harleys rounded the corner of the small cul-de-sac and parked at the curb. I was off the step and moving toward them before they could even take their helmets off.

Nova was at the lead, handsome face transmuted by wrath and sorrow. "Ridin' with me."

We didn't have to talk about it, about why he, Priest, Curtains, Boner, Axe-Man, and Cyclops were there in black in the dead of night, about why I'd been waiting there for them.

They got it, me, and what had to be done.

They were showing me in the way bikers could how much they loved me.

Enough to make me an accessory to their crimes.

Even though pain blasted through my chest as I zipped up my leather jacket and swung a leg up to climb on the back of a bike that wasn't King's, I did so quickly, needing to feel the road beneath me, riding toward a future bright with violence.

"Tight, Queenie," Nova ordered as I wounded my arms around him. "Not a joy ride."

No, it most certainly was not.

We roared off as a group, Nova riding in front with the rest fanning out behind us, a formation of leather backed geese. I held tight and stayed quiet, letting the rush of wind drown my thoughts, letting the bite of cool air replace the harsh ache of mourning.

It took about an hour to get down the mountain to the bright lights and pale skyscrapers of Vancouver, and then only a few minutes more to navigate the streets to the warehouse district where we parked in front of a seemingly abandoned storage unit.

"Behind me, do as I say," Priest told me, stepping forward to take point.

This was his gig, the darkness and the night, the violence and the blade. Priest was the club's enforcer not because of his size, though he was tall and packed with lean muscle similar to King, but because his mind was full of shadows and his soul haunted by demons who whispered to him loudly enough to drown out the guilt of the sins he'd committed for the club.

I nodded, boots clipping against the pavement as I followed the brothers into the echoing warehouse.

Two men stood in the center of the space, both big, wide across the chest, cloaked in shadows that made them seem like living nightmares. But I felt no fear as I looked at them, only relief and gratitude because somehow, Wrath and Lysander had found *him*.

Him. The man who had ripped apart my world without so much as blinking.

Him The man disguised by the wings and blue of justice who was secretly so much worse than the 'bad' men he chased after.

Harold Danner sat in a chair with the seat taken out of it, his naked ass perched on an empty frame, hands bound from shoulders to wrists behind his back so tightly, his shoulders jutted out like stubs where wings once might have stood. There was a massive gag in his mouth, dirty fabric stuffed so far down his throat, I could see the swell of it in his bruised neck. He was filthy, a little bruised up, but otherwise basically unharmed.

A thrill of dark delight warmed my belly at the knowledge that would soon change.

I came to a stop in front of him, close enough to see the hatred burning up his eyes, to see how far gone he was to the evilness that had corroded his soul.

"Where was he?" I asked, not recognizing the cold, hollow tone of my voice, like empty shell casings falling to the concrete.

"Met with a guy I know does forged passports," Sander said. "Wrath, the club, and me all put out feelers to our contacts, and this one pinged. Picked him up from a shitty hotel on East Hastings."

An unfeeling laugh escaped me like acrid smoke as I

addressed the murderer stuck in the chair. "You thought you could escape the wrath of The Fallen? Always thought you were better than us…tonight, I guess, we'll prove to you just how wrong you were."

"Cress," Sander started softly, drawing my gaze to find him helping Priest set up a table filled with implements of torture. "You sure about this?"

"This… this…" What did I call the being that murdered King in cold blood? There were no words horrible enough, scalding enough on my tongue as I fought to say them that represented the depths of his villainy. "This animal killed King, and in doing so, he killed *me*. He's been trying to kill the club for years. He deserves so much more than this, but at least I can make sure he suffers some of the agony he's forced on us."

Sander sighed, but Priest nodded, getting it because part of him was just as dead as parts of me.

"Gotta find out where he kept his doctored documents and payouts," Curtains said. "King, uh, King and some of us broke into his house, but he didn't keep any'a that stuff layin' 'round there. We need it, we want to get him put away for more than just murder."

"We need it to prove he killed Riley Gibson," I said. "I know."

"You start," Priest allowed, walking to me with a glimmer of metal in his hand. I swallowed at the sight of the blade-tipped brass knuckles he unfurled in his palm. "Get him warmed up for me."

I stared at the weapon, flexing my fist, wondering how I'd be able to leash the anger and its toxic violence once I'd given into it for even a second.

"I want to kill him," I admitted through my teeth, the burning desire to feel Staff Sergeant Danner's blood on my hands almost vampiric, as if I needed it to live, to sustain me.

Priest's cold, strong hand took my own and he carefully

fitted the brass knuckles over it. When he was done, he shocked me by palming the back of my head and bringing my forehead to his so all I could see were his dark and stormy blue eyes.

"Death is quick," he murmured, and I noticed the slight accent that leaked through his words sometimes. "It's bein' left on earth to suffer for our sins that's the real hell. We take our pound'a flesh now 'cause we need it. We deserve it. Penance for his sins against us. Balm to our fucked-up souls. We take it ruthless and savage to let the beast in us breathe."

My blood hummed, and to my shock, my mouth watered, as if vengeance had a taste, and it was delicious.

"In the end, it's worse to leave him broken and alive enough to feel his wrongs every day for the rest of his miserable existence, locked up with men who he put in lock up himself. Might not even last long inside," he admitted. "But better to put him through the shame of it than kill him quick."

I flexed my hand open and closed, testing the weight and the feel of the weapon. I knew it was Zeus's preferred method of torture because I'd seen his collection of brass knuckles in his house, and I got why. I'd be able to feel the pain I inflicted on Danner echoed back through my hand like a barometer of justice meted out.

"Does it get better?" I whispered to him, even though I knew the answer by the ghosts that haunted his eyes at all times.

He paused, grimacing. "Not a liar, never wanted to be, and can't lie to you now. You'll suffer all the days'a your life. That's why we gotta match his sufferin' to yours, so he can wear half the burden of it."

I nodded, slanting my head so I brushed my cheek against his and pressed a kiss to his lower jaw. "Thank you for not lying."

His nod was curt, a muscle jumping in his throat, but I

knew it was good emotion that pained him, and it alleviated just a bit of my own ache.

"Now," I said, striding forward so that I loomed over the cop that had killed my King. My smile was stretched and branded into my face, hot, distorted, smoking with heat. "I'm going to beat you to within an inch of your pathetic life, and then, if you don't tell me where you've hidden your deceits, I'm going to let Priest take that very last inch away."

When Danner didn't move or blink or mumble behind his gag, I took it for what it was—a morbid invitation—and cocked back my arm the way King and Priest had taught me to, and began my systematic dissimilation of Harold Danner the moment my brass covered knuckles tore through his cheek and crushed against his bones.

PRIEST TOOK over when my arm shook too badly to continue, but I sat on the ground at Wrath's feet and watched The Fallen enforcer at work. It was bloody, gruesome even, and I now understood the horrifying purpose of tying Harold to a chair without a bottom, having watched Priest beat his exposed balls blue with the end of a heavy, tied hemp rope.

Cyclops tended to my sliced, raw knuckles, dabbing at the cuts with vodka poured from a skull flask on his belt, wiping up the streaks of the cop's blood that trickled down my forearm with the edge of his Harley Davidson tee. I wasn't close to Tayline's Old Man, he'd always been too distant, too into Tay and nothing else, but I knew that would never be the same after this. You couldn't watch a man beat another nearly to death, until the victim sobbed and wailed like a newborn, without forming intractable bonds with each other.

He held my hand when I was done, dwarfing mine in his palm.

It took three hours for Priest to get him to the point of agony where his secrets spilled from him like so much confetti, littering the air with his sins.

We didn't rejoice.

Instead, cold as automatons, we cleaned up the mess—Boner with the bleach, Wrath burning the bloody towels—and hog-tied the comatose former Staff Sergeant before throwing him in the trunk of Sander's stolen SUV. It was still dark enough, quiet enough, for Wrath and Sander to drop him off at one of the downtown police stations and get away unnoticed.

The rest of us got back on the bikes and made our way up the mountain.

I was the first one off the bike at Lionel Danner's ranch property, climbing down from Nova's Harley to open the gates then opting to run by foot to the corner of the acreage where a massive willow tree wept in the middle of a field.

There was a heart carved into the bark, the initials HD & SH embellished within it. Harold Danner and Susan Hobbs, his wife. I didn't allow myself to dwell on the murderer's love for his wife because it would've made me soft.

And I was nowhere near soft now.

Only hard shell over hollow innards.

I dropped to my knees under the sweet carving and started to dig.

The rocky earth cut into my already sore, bleeding hands, but I barely felt it. Beneath this soil lay Zeus's salvation, and in the storm of my selfish mourning, that was the only objective keeping me anchored.

The men arrived, boots thumping, chains rattling, and then Axe-Man was there with a shovel and we were digging together even though I probably could have stopped.

My breath caught and shattered on the hard edge of a sob as my fingers wrapped around the lid of a steel box. Priest was there then, and Cyclops, prying it out of the ground with me, but yielding it to my hold once it was free.

My hands trembled so badly, I couldn't even fumble with the lock. Nova took it from me gently, placed it on the ground, and produced his flashy ivory handled gun to shoot the lock off before returning it to me.

I sucked in a deep breath and pried the lid off.

A gun sat in the middle, so innocuous, just an object, but it was the key to everything, the same model as Zeus's gun, a cop's gun, and the weapon that killed Riley Gibson.

My eyes burned so badly, I couldn't see the faces of the men around me as I lifted my head to look at them and say, "He's free. Oh my God, Zeus will finally be free."

CHAPTER TWENTY-SIX

Cressida

A MONTH WENT by in the blink of an eye, and all I was, was sorrow.

Now that the evidence had been found to clear Zeus's name, Mr. White had set the ball rolling on getting him released. I'd had this image of him getting out the next day after finding the gun and the box of documents hidden at Danner's old ranch home, but the law didn't work like that. Still, with nothing left to rally against, waiting for Danner to be processed and prosecuted and Zeus to be let free, I succumbed to my internal injuries and went into a kind of coma.

I knew the passing of the days by the people who were scheduled to keep me company.

Lou every weekday afternoon with the babies, except for Thursday when she went to the Autism Center to work.

Harleigh Rose on Mondays, Wednesdays, and Fridays,

often with Danner in tow who played his guitar for me until I cried. I think they thought tears were good for me.

Maja and Hannah on Thursdays, sometimes along with Cleo and Lila, trying to make me laugh, but if a funny bone could break, mine had, and I never did.

Zeus on Saturday. Every Saturday, I'd go to him for the full length of his visiting hours, all three of them. He'd talk and talk about King, and it was the only day I really spoke and remembered what the sound of my own voice felt like in my ears. We talked about King as if he was alive, and it was the only good I found in any days that followed his passing.

The brothers took turns, too, less organized, one or more of them 'poppin' by' because they were bored, in the neighborhood, had nothing to do. I didn't believe them, and they didn't care, even when I didn't talk. They just put old movies they knew I loved on the TV or read to me, badly, aloud from books they'd never once opened.

But like I said, a month went by in a blink of an eye, and all I was, all I remember of that time, was sorrow.

CHAPTER TWENTY-SEVEN

Zeus

PRISON'S NOT SOMETHIN' a person gets used to. Doesn't matter how many years ya spend there, not how many times a man's in or outta the place, prison always weighs on the body in strange ways, like the air against your skin durin' an electrical storm. At all hours, you could feel the wrongness of bein' imprisoned in a six and a half square metre concrete cell with hundreds of other men who've committed any number of despicable crimes for a variety of honourable and dishonourable reasons.

You felt like cattle, the kind kept on the massive ranches in the southern United States where it's cheaper to let 'em die'a heat stroke than install air conditioning in the barns. It felt industrial and animal in a strange tandem that just equalled somethin' *wrong*.

I hated that wrongness and the feel'a it on me like I'd never get clean of it.

Took years after I got out the first time to rid myself of that current on my skin, and only when I met Lou did it truly disappear.

As I let the guards strip search me one more fuckin' time then collected my meager belongings, I worried that the wrongness would haunt me again on the outside. That I'd meet my babies for the first time and the connection wouldn't sink in my heart 'cause the electromagnet pulse of prison would cancel it out. That I'd hold my woman and love my woman yet not be enough 'cause there I was, a demon fresh outta hell, and she was everythin' angel.

I carried that worry like a fuckin' boulder on my shoulders as I waited for the gates to open so I could walk out into the lot and greet my family, save one beautiful, irreplaceable soul. There was nothin' in the world more important to me than bein' there for my family, and through our hardest time yet, I'd been sequestered outta reach, unable to offer the comfort and support they needed.

It fuckin' killed me, and with that pain came shame. I was ashamed even though I'd done nothin' wrong 'cause I hadn't laid a hand on Riley Gibson. That was somethin' else prison was good at doin' to you, rapin' your soul so all you felt was guilt and shame and wrongfulness, even when it wasn't warranted.

So, I was worried as the concrete doors parted to reveal a hoard'a people clustered in the parking lot 'round a dozen cars and even more Harleys.

And then, eyes sweepin', sweepin' over faces so fuckin' dear to me, my gaze settled on the pair of true-blue eyes I'd been yearnin' for, and everythin'—the guilt, the shame, the sorrow, and the wrongfulness—just fell away dead at my feet.

Couldn't even move with the force'a it all passin' through me. I just stood there while my Lou started forward, breakin' into a sprint the way she had as a girl in a parking lot full'a bikers shootin' at each other, just bookin' it toward me like I was the only thing that could save her.

And fuck, but I knew she was the only one who could save me.

My arms opened on instinct, and I caught her easily as she hurtled through the air to wrap her entire body 'round mine, like vines 'round a tree.

Fuck, fuck, fuck.

I braced as emotions crashed through me with the force of tsunami waves.

Relief, joy, and love so fuckin' big in my chest, I thought I'd burst as I planted my face in all'a Lou's thick, fragrant silk hair and just fought to breathe through the mess of emotions ragin' through me.

Her hands clutched at me, movin' over my hair, my neck and back, up over my cheeks, until she pulled my face outta her neck and held me still to rake her wet, velvet gaze all over my features. Tears streamed down her cheeks, her eyes so blue against the flushed cheeks they looked otherworldly.

I fisted a hand in the back'a her moonbeam hair and planted my forehead against hers just to feel her sweet breath against my face.

"My Lou," I said, voice mangled and rough with tears I wouldn't shed.

"Zeus," she breathed then choked on a sob that set her entire body to shaking. "Oh, God, Z. My love, my guardian monster, my man."

I sealed my mouth over hers, unable to last a moment more without her taste on my tongue. She cried hard into the kiss, but her arms squeezed me as tight as she could, her breasts so soft against my chest, her tears wet and salty over my lips. I wanted every inch'a her against every inch'a me 'cause I knew she was the only fuckin' thing that would rid every particle of that prison cell from my skin.

"Love you so much," she mumbled against my mouth, one hand brushin' over my beard then over my mouth as if she was attemptin' to memorize the feel'a me. "Love you so much more than any words I could think to say to you."

"You don't gotta say anythin'," I assured her, tucking her head against my neck so I could hug her tight. "I got you just like I always got you and I'm not fuckin' leavin' ever again. You hear me?"

"I hear you," she muttered between pressin' kisses to my neck. "I've always heard you."

"I know, little girl," I said, 'cause I did. The kinda connection we shared wasn't somethin' that could be put into a box with words. It lived in us, just as it had lived in us since I saved her as a kid, and it would live with us until the day we died.

"The babies," I said to her, my eyes moving over her hair to the crowd giving us a moment a few yards away. My gaze found 'em quick, two bright blond heads'a hair, one held by my girl, Harleigh Rose, and the other by their Aunt Bea. "Fuck me, they're big."

Lou laughed through her tears as she pulled herself outta my neck and smiled into my face. She'd never looked so goddamn beautiful as she did then, beamin' into my face like I was her fuckin' hero. "You'll never believe how gorgeous they are, Z. Just like their Daddy."

"If they're beautiful, it's all you," I said as I started forward, eyes pinned on my kids. "Can't wait to meet 'em."

"I tell them about you every day," she promised. "Their big, badass daddy with a heart purer than gold."

I just squeezed her closer under my arm, my voice robbed by the sight'a the babies I'd been robbed of seeing for the first six months of their lives.

It was obvious who was who, even as identical as they were. Walker was decked out in miniature biker fashion, a black AC/DC shirt worn under a leather jacket and little boots on his feet. He was silent, massive blue eyes already pale like mine and King's, wide and watchful as I approached him. His sister, on the other hand, babbled away in a high, bright voice, one plump hand fisted in Harleigh Rose's tee and the other reaching out for 'er mama and me. She had a scowl on her gorgeous face, and her darker blue eyes flashed like the inside'a a flame, like she was irritated with us for taking so long to get to her.

My heart rocketed against my ribs, threatenin' to break 'em.

"Fuck me, but they're fuckin' perfect," I said as we stopped before 'em. My voice was ragged and torn with the emotion cloggin' up my throat, but no one called me on it.

"Hi Daddy," Harleigh Rose greeted softly, almost as if she was afraid I'd disappear if she shouted. "We missed you something crazy."

Still clutchin' Lou on one side, I opened my other arm so she could slot herself into my other side, breathin' in a deep drag'a that floral scent of hers, rememberin' how that very fragrance had gotten me through my first stint in the can.

"Missed my baby girl," I told her as I kissed her forehead. "Missed ya more than I can say."

I tried not to focus on the obvious lack of my son in the group, but I could feel it in the lopsided beat of my overfull heart. Still, I had to be strong for 'em all, at least durin' this first reunion.

Later, alone with my woman and my kids, I'd suffer.

Annoyed with her lack of attention, Angel let out a shrill shriek and hit me in the chest with her little fist.

I burst out laughing.

When I'd recovered, tears gathered in the corners of my eyes, all three'a my girls were lookin' up at me with straight up adoration that felt like a shot of Canadian whiskey to my gut, warm and fuckin' heady.

"Got another impatient little miss on my hands, don't I?" I

asked Angel as I ran my rough, scarred knuckle over the petal soft curve of her cheek.

Never seen a more beautiful baby, and that was the truth. Harleigh Rose'd been cute as fuckin' could be, but there was sheer perfection in the red, curvy mouth and the huge, long lashed eyes of this golden, curly haired baby girl. I felt my heart constrict as we made eye contact, and I realized my future would include being wrapped 'round her tiny, dimpled finger.

"Goner just at the sight of you," Lou murmured, fingering a lock of Angel's golden hair. "Just like her mama."

"She's a smart girl, so it goes without saying she'd love you right off," H.R. reasoned as she pressed her nose into my chest and cuddled closer. "She knows she's got the best damn dad in the whole fuckin' world."

"Could film this shit and sell it to the Hallmark Channel," Nova called out as he pushed off the side'a Lila's VW bug and sauntered forward, snaggin' Walker from Bea as he did so. "'Bout cried watchin' you guys, really, I did. But I'm thinkin' it's time to bro down for the men here who're too insecure to shed some manly fuckin' tears."

Lou and H.R. laughed wetly as they struggled through their tears, Nova's typical nonchalance breakin' the heavy silence in the lot, everyone rushin' forward to exchange hugs and backslaps with me. I held Walker in one arm and Angel in the other, Lou stuck to my side like a tattoo I'd never remove as I talked to my brothers, their women, and the rest'a our family.

Only when everyone was casually crowded 'round me, talking over each other and movin' 'round each other in that way we did, did I notice the one person who hadn't come forward yet.

She stood off to the very left of the lot, her ass on the hood of her modified pink Honda Civic, arms wrapped 'round her legs, chin to her knees. It was a posture I'd never seen her in, bent and broken like it was a permanent thing. Her normally glossy thicket'a golden brown hair was lank and pulled into a messy bun, her clothes swallowin' her both 'cause they were obviously King's and 'cause she'd lost a fuck ton'a weight she didn't have to lose in the first place. Ares was with 'er, standin' in front and to the side'a her like a miniature sentry. The sight'a him like that reminded me of Mute, reminded me of King, the two fuckin' incredible souls we'd lost that would'a done exactly the same for that woman.

Lou caught me lookin' and sighed. "I don't know what to do anymore, Z. She just…she just can't get it together anymore."

"Can't blame her," Harleigh Rose said from the circle of Danner's arms, tippin' her chin to say her next words to the man holdin' her. "I wouldn't get over you, not ever."

Danner dipped to press a kiss to her upside-down mouth, and I blinked away the image as I looked away, not needin' to see my baby girl in the arms of a cop, even if he was one'a the good ones.

"How bad?" I asked.

Lou bit her lip, but it was Priest, lingering to our right with Bea and her mum, who surprised me by sayin', "Me bad, brother. Me when I first came to ya."

"Fuck," I muttered, closin' my eyes against the memory'a Priest, barely a man, cut up like someone'd tried to make him into ribbons, eyes more haunted than the battlefield of the Somme.

He'd wanted to die, that boy.

And now, apparently, Cress did too.

I kissed Angel and blew a raspberry on Walker's neck that resulted in a husky giggle 'fore I passed 'em off to Loulou who propped 'em on either hip like a fuckin' natural.

"I got 'er."

She smiled at me, that secret kinda smile that was like a

hand reachin' through my chest to clutch at my heart, remindin' me it beat just for 'er. "I know it."

I tipped my chin up at her then took off across the asphalt. None'a the brothers tried to stop me, which let me know just how fuckin' bad off Cress must've been.

When I was a few feet out, Cress still hadn't raised her head, but Ares stepped forward, forehead creased and arms crossed.

It was a physical warning, to be gentle with her, to treat her with care, or I'd have him to answer to.

Fuck me, but no grown man should be moved to fuckin' tears so many times in under an hour.

I cleared my throat and offered him a grin. "Ares, buddy, you gonna give your ole man a hug?"

He hesitated, eyes flickerin' as he tried to decide between bein' a kid or a man in that moment. But he was only nine, he had a whack ton'a time to grow up and not a whole lotta time left to give in to the tenderness'a youth, so I made the decision for him.

Dropped to one knee and opened my arms.

He was in 'em in three seconds, little body wrapped up tight 'round my own.

I clasped the back of his head and held on tight. When Ares gave ya affection, it wasn't somethin' to squander.

"They missed you," he whispered in my ear, his thick Spanish accent somethin' I hadn't even realized I'd craved until I'd heard it again. Seemed to me, I'd left five kids on the outside, Ares included.

"Missed them. Missed you," I admitted.

"Were you scared?"

"Nah, not of anyone inside. They were all scared'a the big, bad Zeus Garro," I teased as I pulled back to look at his face.

He grinned slightly. "Everyone should be scared of you."

"Not you," I reminded him. "Not them." I indicated the

family gathered in the parkin' lot'a the prison like it was your average fuckin' family reunion.

"Nah," he agreed. "You're a teddy bear for us."

The laughter felt good in my throat after months of disuse, so I laughed even harder just to feel it move through me. "Yeah, kid." I ruffled his hair and stood up. "Great big teddy, that's fuckin' me."

His big grin faded as I looked over him at Cressida, and he said quietly, in a voice more fearful than I'd ever heard from him, includin' when we'd found him lost and alone squattin' in my cabin. "Please, help her."

I tipped my chin at him and squeezed his shoulder as I moved past and finally arrived in front'a my son's girl.

She stirred, liftin' her head so those long lashed, pretty as hell brown eyes met mine. They weren't so pretty then, though. In fact, they were fuckin' dead.

"Z," she said on a tremblin' breath. "Don't touch me."

I cocked my head. "Gotta give my girl a hug."

"You touch me now," she warned. "I'll shatter like a glass in your hands, I swear."

"Teach," I said gently, but she just shook 'er head.

"I'm not a teacher anymore," she reminded me like she always did. Then she opened her palms and looked down at 'em as if surprised to find 'em empty but for the scars Fallen enemies had put there. "I'm not anything anymore."

"You fuckin' *are*," I growled. "You're my daughter-in-law, my wife and oldest daughter's best friend, you're the owner of the best fuckin' bookshop in the nation, and one'a the best fuckin' women I've ever known. You're *everythin'*, and just 'cause my boy isn't 'ere anymore to fuckin' prove it to ya every single fuckin' day in the way only he could, doesn't make it any less true, yeah?"

Ares moved closer, takin' up Cress's hand and shootin' me a look that said he wasn't hot on my aggressive stance.

"You remember when Loulou was sick? How crushed up

inside you felt? How you felt like you couldn't even breathe?" she asked. "I can't breathe, Z. I can't freaking breathe without him. Do you understand? I. Cannot. Breathe."

She started gaspin', tryin' to swallow back the tears that permanently haunted her.

"I'm touchin' ya," I warned as I reached out to pull her into a hug.

I could feel the bones in her body, achingly close to the skin, and I wondered how much she was eatin', sleepin', then decided she'd be babied by Lou and me until we could get 'er properly sorted out.

Despite her warnin', she didn't cry when I held her. Instead, in a voice'a pure agony, she whispered, "I'm so angry, Zeus. So angry, I can't breathe. So sad, I can't breathe. Air doesn't do anything for me anymore except make me cry every time I take it in."

"So cry," I said. "Cry as much as ya fuckin' want, Cress. We got arms enough to hold ya and hands enough to dry your face whenever you're done. King didn't just give ya his heart, you get me? He gave you all'a ours, too, and there's a no return policy. You gotta let us love ya now, even when the thought'a love makes you want to wail in agony. You gotta let us do that, yeah?"

She sniffed and held perfectly still, not embracin' me, not even breathin' for so long I almost shook her, and then she moved. Slowly, like a newborn calf discoverin' its legs, Cress moved her body 'round mine and hugged me.

I felt her tears soak into my shirt and let out a breath that rattled my fuckin' lungs with relief. "We can mourn 'im together, ya hear?"

"I won't ever get over this," she said with such spiritual certainty I wondered if mournin' King might become her religion.

"Me neither. We can mourn him together every day for the rest of forever."

"Promise?" she asked, a hairline fracture in her ironclad control.

"For us, babe..." She shuddered at the use of the endearment King had so often given her, but I forged on. "King'll never die."

CHAPTER TWENTY-EIGHT

Cressida

IT WAS A GORGEOUS SUMMER DAY. The sky was cerulean blue over the brilliant green of the frequently watered grass, and the air smelled of freshly churned earth and the sweetness of damp flowers. The late summer blooms were just starting to disintegrate, littering the streets with pale masses of sunburnt petals that gathered like snow drifts. One spiraled through the air over my head as I scanned the masses and masses of black-clad gatherers collected at First Light Church cemetery to celebrate the life of King Kyle Garro.

There were over twenty chapters of The Fallen, from all over North America and as far as the United Kingdom, who had come out to mourn the loss of the prodigal heir to The Fallen MC empire, and not one of them seemed unaffected by his passing. There were even some clubs represented that were technically unaffiliated with The Fallen, but shared no bad blood with the club, and had come to show solidarity over losing a brother and high-ranking member of the organization.

It should have given me comfort, the sheer amount of human lives King had positively impacted, to see how many grieved for him. It was unfair, and I tried to focus on that, but I had never felt so possessive of anything in my life. My grief was all I had left of him. I didn't want anyone to empathize with me. It was wrong, but I hated them for their attempts to do so because there was no possible way they could understand what it was like to lose the very essence of my soul. I'd handed my heart to King and let our love mold my life like clay into something so much *more* than it had been before.

Now, I was left a hollow, broken vase with nothing to fill it.

How could anyone understand that?

I could only withstand the comfort of Lou and Zeus, because they truly understood, having lost both King and Mute, and Harleigh Rose because she had nearly killed her own love in order to save him. Ares, too, because although he had never divulged his secrets to me, there was a great and terrifying turmoil in his young gaze. And Wrath, who was still so mired in mourning over Kylie that I wondered if he would ever recover. It wasn't often people were given priceless gifts to know how it felt when they were irrevocably lost. I both pitied and treasured each of those who understood. It was my one small comfort.

It was Lysander who stood at my side like a sentinel, massive body inflated in a physical threat warning anyone who came to pay their respects not to fuck with me. He didn't offer me a shared sense of grief since he hadn't really known King, not properly, but he offered me the kind of raw tenderness only a brother can gift, constant physical affection and knowledge, although he might not know how to voice it, that he'd be there for me until the end of time.

Rainbow, Benny, Carson, and Tayline were in a little half-moon at my back, not talking or touching, just standing in a show of support that made my heart ache a little less fiercely.

The brothers made a tight circle around the gaping hole in

the ground where King's empty casket would be laid to rest, as if guarding it from the eyes of people there not privileged enough to see it. As if that wound in the earth represented the wound at the center of each of us. The brothers were animal in that way, in the way of not wanting their vulnerabilities exposed for fear that someone might think it stood for weakness.

They stood with just inches between them, silent and dry-eyed, but they were mere echoes of their normal selves; their bodies wan and aching with stillness, their features smaller and more refined when separated from their usual grins and glowers. It wasn't raining, but they all seemed water-logged with grief, bloated with the tears they'd never shed in front of others.

These were men who were not unused to suffering, bearing it the way soldiers did, stiff lipped and tightly coiled around the emotions that threatened to overtake them.

I loved them acutely as I looked on them, wishing King was there to take their emotional baggage in the way he had a knack for. I wished he would climb out of that hollow casket and sling an arm around Bat as he teased Nova about his latest conquest. Those bleak expressions on their faces would break open like sunlight after a storm.

But King's magic was dead, gone with him to the grave, and I had no sunlight to offer them in his stead.

Zeus did his level best to break through the heavy crush of silence and morbidity hanging over our heads when he took the podium. I tried to listen to his speech through the rush of blood in my ears, to focus on his beloved face and not that yawning black hole in the ground, and finally his words sunk in.

"King would'a wanted it sunny," Zeus started, smiling with his mouth and not his eyes. "He would'a wanted it like this, 'cause he was a man who saw everythin' good in the world. Born with rose tinted glasses, that kid, lovin' life and everyone he met 'til they proved 'im wrong, and then, if they did, he just cut 'em out and went on his merry fuckin' way. He…" He paused and looked down at his empty hands, trying to find words there for the enormity of the emotions in his big heart. "He was just the best'a us. Can't even take the credit really, kid basically raised 'imself and his sister, grew to be a man 'fore he could even grow facial hair." Everyone laughed, but the sound was bruised, misshapen.

"Grateful to everyone for comin', for sharin' in this with us, 'cause we got a metric fuck ton'a grief, and it needs help bein' carried. That said, I'm glad to carry the weight'a it for the rest'a my life 'cause King was so fuckin' worth lovin' and knowin'. Feels like anyone who didn't know 'im was robbed, so good a man he was, so fuckin' beautiful, I gotta say, to have in your life.

Not gonna stand 'ere and lie to ya. The death of a son? Not somethin' I'll ever recover from. Death'a two sons? I'll be walkin' half-dead 'til the reaper comes callin' for me one day. I got my Lou and my babies, my Harleigh Rose, my brothers, and the rest'a our family to get me through, but I also got this, and I wanna share it with you so maybe you can breathe a little easier…"

Zeus looked up and directly into my eyes, his silver gaze pinning me like stakes to the ground. I couldn't move or speak, transfixed by the power of emotion shining in his rugged face.

"His whole life, King only wanted one fuckin' thing, kid you not, an eight-year-old with intent, he was. He wanted one thing, and that one thing was the love of a good fuckin' woman. Well, we can breathe easier knowin' King found that in his wife, Cressida." His voice cracked and rumbled like the ground about to break open during a quake. A sob bubbled up in my throat and lodged behind my voice box as he thumped his chest over his heart. "He found what he loved, and I gotta believe, he's restin' easier knowin' he'd had four fuckin' wonderful years livin' out that dream with 'er. And I'm 'ere to say to 'im, if he can hear me in heaven or wherever the fuck only the very best'a people go, that all'a us are gonna take care of his woman, of his life's purpose, until the day we all join him in the afterlife."

Z ripped his rage from mine like tearing off a bandage, and I flinched at the loss of his balm over my torn heart. He stepped out from the podium and moved slowly, achingly, over to the table holding the coins Bat made for Fallen funerals, big silver dollars stamped with the Fallen symbol on one side and a reaper on the other. They were payment to the ferrymen or God or Satan, whichever deity might need paying in the afterlife, to ensure their brother got safely to his resting place.

Z picked one up, held it aloft for everyone to see, and called, "King Kyle fuckin' Garro, may the best of us rest in peace."

"King Kyle fuckin' Garro," everyone echoed, a rough roar of mostly male voices so loud they seemed to tremble the earth.

He tossed the coin atop the coffin then moved to me, standing so tall I had to crank my neck back to maintain eye contact. I kept it, though, because these days, my eyes said more than I was capable of communicating with words. It seemed King had owned all the good ones, and now that he was gone, so was my love of language.

"You ready to get up there, teach?" he asked softly, not touching me because he respected how fragile I was.

I didn't want to be there, let alone want to speak, to purge even an ounce of the feeling inside me because sharing it seemed like setting it free somehow, and I wanted to hoard every single ounce of King I could bear to hold inside me.

But it was King who'd taught me how to be strong, and part of that was tending to the souls who cared for your own. The people swathed in black and congregated in the cemetery like a murder of ravens deserved to hear me speak about

King, the person who'd loved him best and had pledged to love him forever.

So, I nodded curtly, accepting the touches on my back from the friends who supported me, and let Sander and Wrath escort me to the podium then flank my sides as if I was the President of the United States with her security detail.

Honestly, it felt good to have such pillars of strength beside me.

"King brought me to life." I laughed weakly, having prepared a speech but unable to remember a lick of it even though I'd been a teacher for years, and I was used to public speaking. I shrugged weakly and went with it. "It sounds so trite, but it's true. I saw him across the parking lot of Mac's Grocer, and my entire universe shifted, my perspective radically rearranged, and suddenly I was someone else. No, not even someone else…it was like finally, I was *me*. All the bullshit of my life, the social mores and puritanical values forced on me by my family, were purged by the sight of a man-boy leaning on a motorcycle like it was his throne and the blacktop his kingdom. I knew in that moment that I would give anything to rule by his side, but I never could have known that dream would come true. I never could have known just how many times I would be called to pay the price for it."

I opened my palms to the group, the red web of scar tissue in the center of each hand like painted bullseyes.

"I never could have known that loving King would make me strong enough to withstand anything that came for us, and so much did. I gave up everything I'd ever known for him, and in exchange, he gave me an entirely new world. One we would rule over together. In the end, only death could tear us apart, and even then…" I choked on my sob, trying to block out the tears that broke through the crowd like rain from storm clouds at the provocation of my words. "Even now, King will never be dead to me because he lives inside me so vividly. King Kyle Garro was so alive that he could bring even my dead soul to life, just as I know he brought life and joy and so much happiness to the broken souls of so many people gathered here for him today."

My hands shook as I took the folded piece of paper from my pocket, and it was only when I leaned over the podium to smooth it open and wet landed on the page that I realized, despite my best efforts, I was crying.

"King was such a dichotomy. He was goodness and sin, sharp and sweet, a dream and a nightmare all wrapped up in one gorgeous package. Sometimes, I think, the depth of his own mind and heart confounded even him, as he would have to spend long hours sussing it out in his journal. Even though he didn't share his words with most people, he was a beautiful poet. I want him to live on for all of you just as vibrantly as he will live on for me, so I had his poems printed into books." I paused as Harleigh Rose and Ares moved through the crowd, handing out copies of the black covered book embossed with a crown. "I called it King of Iron Hearts because King might not have been Prez of the Fallen, but he was the emotional sovereign of the group. And I'm no poet, not like him, but I added some of my own words to it because I needed a way to express just how irrevocably and unequivocally I loved my husband."

I sucked in a deep breath and made eye contact with Z who tipped his chin up at me, lending me his strength so I could go on.

"I, well, I want to read you one of those poems now because there isn't a more poignant way to express exactly how I feel having to say goodbye to the man who made my existence a life worth living.

No Goodbye

You never said goodbye
And you always did before

At the door to our house before
Work with a kiss I felt in my toes.

You never said goodbye
And you promised me you would
When the day came that we went
To sleep holding hands
Knowing
That we would not wake up again.

You never said goodbye
And now I can't help feeling
That this isn't a goodbye for good.

That one day when I am sitting in the kitchen
You will come in carrying apples and tell me to
Bake you a pie like I did that very first day
We were in love
I'll have flour in my hair and juice on my cheek
That you'll lick off with laughing lips
And everything will have been
As it was before
When you were still here."

I LOOKED up at the crowd, but there were tears so thick in my eyes they obscured my vision like funhouse mirrors. Taking a deep breath, I dashed the back of my hand over my eyes and blinked to clear my sight.

I needed to see them as I said this last goodbye. I needed witnesses to bear the weight of the sorrow in my bones as I stepped away from the podium and walked to the edge of the grave where King's chrome casket sat inside the earth.

I collected one of the coins in the basket on a table beside me and flipped it in my fingers as I stared down at the empty casket and wished, just for a moment, that I would be buried there too.

"'The mind is its own place, and in itself can make a heaven of hell or a hell of heaven,'" I quoted from Paradise Lost. "But it was you who made this place a heaven on earth, and it will, never be the same now that you've fallen."

I tossed the coin into the pit, watching as it tumbled over the smooth surface then fell into the dark soil.

Lou and Harleigh Rose were beside me in the next instant, wrapping their arms around me as they collected their own coins and prepared to drop them in.

"You were king of my heart long before you were anyone else's," H.R. whispered as she white-knuckled the coin and stared with unseeing eyes into the pitted earth. "You kept me safe even when I didn't want to let you. Love you big bro."

Lou leaned in to me heavily as she breathed deeply through her pretty tears. "This is the second man I love that I've had to put in this earth…my only consolation is that now they're together."

She tossed the coin in then pressed a kiss to my head before going to Z, who stood off to the side looking hollow and dazed with grief.

One by one, the brothers stepped up to toss their own coins and say words about their fallen brother. Then family went. Lila cried so hard, Nova had to step forward to take her under his arm and usher her away from the grave, and Bea held her mother's hand so tightly, it was a wonder she didn't break bones.

I watched them and their grief gather like a great wave off in the distance, and as more and more people emptied their sorrow into the grave, I felt it loom over me, threatening to consume me.

"You're stronger than you know," Sander told me, somehow sensing I was about to break.

"We're almost there, Queenie," Wrath said, stepping close so his hulking shoulder pressed into my side. "Give it a few more minutes and then it'll all stop."

God, but I wanted it to stop.

Witnessing how many people loved my man was not soothing. It was like a thousand javelins all impaled through my chest, fixing me to the spot even as I bled out all over my feet.

Slowly, *finally*, the ceremony was over, and Zeus stepped up to invite everyone back to the clubhouse for the reception.

I didn't move and no one made me. A few of the brothers rounded out the circle of loved ones, barring me from well-wishers, and they finally all dissipated. Only then did the club leave, each brother touching me in some way as they departed, trying to fill the emptiness in me with their love.

"Gotta say it," Buck grunted as he clamped a meaty hand over my shoulder and dipped his head down to look me in the face. "We had a bad go of it the last few months with Z locked up, butted heads 'cause I'm an old dog not likin' new tricks… but fuck me, Cress, I loved that kid like he was my own. Ya gotta know how sorry I am that he might'a died not knowin' that."

"Oh, honey," I said, overcoming my own selfishness for long enough to wrap the burly, older man in a tight hug. He smelled of gasoline and leather, and I was thrown back to those early days of loving King when he'd gotten Buck to drive me to and from work on his huge Harley. "Whatever your issues were lately, there wasn't a day that passed that King didn't love and respect you. He just…he just wasn't the kind to take intellectual differences personally. You *have* to know he loved you."

Buck cleared his throat compulsively a few times, trying to clear the tears. "Yeah, yeah, I guess I knew that. Just needed someone to say it, ya know?"

"I know," I said, because I did. King had loved me with

everything he had, but now that he wasn't here, I had no one to tell me that. No matter what, knowing something and having that same thing said to you were two very different things.

"Come on, old man," Nova said with a watered-down version of his signature movie star smile as he collected Buck and moved him away. "Let's go drink away our pain."

"Only thing to do," Buck agreed as they walked over to the last dozen bikes parked on the grass beside the street.

"We'll meet ya there," Zeus offered as he stepped close to my side and palmed the back of my head in one big hand in order to curl me into his chest for a hug. "You stay 'ere as long as ya want, yeah?"

"I'm staying," Ares pipped up, crossing his arms and planting his feet like a little General.

I'd forgotten the mechanics of a smile, but I would have, seeing that, if I'd had it in me to try.

So, Ares stayed, along with Benny, Carson, Nova, Wrath, Lysander, and Priest. They stayed as I sat at the edge of King's grave, watching with bowed heads as I watered the wound in the earth with my tears. When I was done, eyes swollen so painfully I could barely blink, they didn't say anything as I rounded the pit and grabbed the shovel pinned in the excess dirt. They didn't even blink when I started digging, tossing the black soil onto the metal casket, wincing then sobbing at the hollow *thwack* it made against the empty coffin.

Instead, Sander disappeared for a while then returned with more shovels, and together, the eight of us laid King to rest in his grave.

When it was done and covered, I collapsed on the soft surface, exhausted because I hadn't slept or eaten much in weeks, but relieved because I'd been the one to see his death through to the end.

One by one the men lay with me, heads angled inward so

we fanned out like a wheel. Each of them touched me somehow except Wrath, Ares with his hand in my hair, Nova with a leg draped over one of mine, Benny the other, Carson with his head pressed to mine, Sander with his hand cupped under my head, and even Priest, unloving, unfeeling though they said he was, reached over his head to gently palm my cheek.

I wasn't sure how long we laid there for, only that it grew dark and so cold I shuddered as Sander picked me up and carried me to Benny's car to take me home.

A patient, lingering photographer captured a shot of us like that and printed it in the next day's *Globe & Mail* with a title that went viral: "*Even rebels mourn the fall of a King.*"

CHAPTER TWENTY-NINE

Cressida

LIFE WENT ON, but it did so with a limp, an obvious lopsidedness to everything in my life. Nothing was the same after the fall of King. For the third time in my life, I felt colossally changed, my DNA altered by the tragedy so I felt like an entirely new human being. Loving him was the backbone of my existence.

How could I ever move on without him?

I still worked at Paradise Found with Benny and our small crew of staff every weekday, drinking my dirty chai lattes and gabbing with people over books. I still lived in my little cabin even though it echoed with a silence that rang in my ears at all hours of the day and night. I still listened to Elvis just to feel the pain flare open again in my chest, listening until the tears that no longer flowed freely, ran down my cheeks, purging enough of my sadness to help me breathe a little easier each day.

But I did not go to The Fallen compound.

Hephaestus Auto was also the home of too many memories, King striding toward me in a bright white tee and grease smeared jeans, smile wicked, confidence cocked like a weapon aimed at my heart.

I avoided the clubhouse and his bedroom there where he'd first told me he loved me. That he'd rip apart the world if it wronged me.

It was too much.

So, the brothers came to me, circling me like carrion over a carcass, always lurking and hovering. They meant well, I knew that, but as the weeks turned into a month after the funeral and more time passed, their concern started to chafe.

No amount of biker men could account for the loss of my biker poet.

It was as simple and profound as that.

The depth of my sorrow poisoned me like arsenic, making me wan and anemic, nauseated and unwilling to eat. Although it wasn't intentional, I was wasting away physically, and I thought it was cruel of them to point it out as often as they did. How could I keep food down when my gut constantly tossed like the sea? My body was a storm in itself, chaotic with constant tension and bone-deep grief.

I think they worried that I'd kill myself, but honestly, I didn't think about that. I was broken in a way I knew could never be fixed, but I didn't want to die. Not yet.

King had told me something profound when Mute died that stuck with me even through my darkest days. Even though he loved his brother enough to want to follow him to the other side of the veil, he knew that Mute wouldn't accept him there if he went before his time.

If Mute couldn't live, King would do it for him.

So, no suicide, and some days, I even mustered smiles and genuine conversations that felt like band-aids over bullet holes. It was a start, though, and I was determined to succeed.

I was lucky to have so many people in my life that loved me, and I tried to focus on that.

Eventually, the veil of grief began to part like the winter fog banks dissipating under a spring thaw, and that was when I began to notice the details again.

The sound of Loulou's raspy laughter as she watched Zeus play with their babies, tucking each tiny human in either arm as if they were footballs. The way Harleigh Rose oriented herself around Lion whenever they were in the same space, even if they weren't talking to each other. How Nova seemed unduly irritated and interested simultaneously in a newly single Lila, and how Lysander always hesitated before he touched me, even after weeks of seeing me nearly every day, like he was a stray cat worried I'd hit him just when he got comfortable in my space.

I noticed, too, painfully, little things King had left behind.

An inscription in the copy of *The Prince* I'd given him when he patched into The Fallen, "*'Never attempt to win by force what can be won by deception', and what deception is too great a price to pay for freedom?*"

A guidebook I didn't remember buying about Alaska, pages circled in red, inscriptions running up the margins in King's cramped cursive. I spent hours reading it, running my fingers over the annotations, dreaming about visiting Sitka where we had once planned to go on our honeymoon.

One day after I'd picked up Ares from school and he was doing his homework in the kitchen, he even pointed out the massive X King had crossed with the silver felt pen over Sitka on the old globe that sat on our sideboard.

The fog cleared further when my thirty-first birthday rolled around, and I realized for the first time that I was a widow.

I didn't want to celebrate, but Loulou had packed up the twins and Ares and arrived with a lopsided cake she and Harleigh Rose had made themselves, their men following with tender hugs and eager smiles, Nova and Bat, Priest, Sander, and Cyclops with Tayline and Rainbow after that. Benny and

Carson were already in the house, having let themselves in through the side door so I could wake up to the smell of bacon cooking in the kitchen.

Breakfast was nice, and the cake for lunch was ugly but delicious, even though I couldn't keep any of it down.

I had just flushed the toilet, eyes burning with tears and stomach still churning when Lou appeared in the doorframe, her full lips rolled under her teeth.

"Please, not another lecture on taking care of myself," I moaned as I slapped the toilet seat down and washed my hands. "I'm not bulimic, and I'm not suicidal for the last freaking time."

"No," she agreed slowly. "I don't think you're either of those things."

I splashed cold water on my face then frowned at the sight of myself in the mirror, shocked that I'd lost so much weight in my face, repulsed by the dead look in my eyes.

My gaze found Loulou's in the reflection, and I felt my lip roll under into a pout I couldn't control. "Look at me."

"I am," she said softly. "I do."

"I can't go on like this," I admitted, staring down at my hands as they trembled, noticing my wedding ring was too loose around the base of my finger.

"I know, babe." She stepped farther into the bathroom, closing the door on the voices downstairs. "I can't say I've gone through what you're experiencing, but in some ways, I have. Zeus being locked up, yeah, but also, once, for a while, I was convinced I was dying and that I'd have to leave Z behind. You have to know, from that point of view, that neither King or I could ever rest easy knowing our loved one was suffering so much while still living."

I nodded, a tear dropping to the basin. "Sometimes, I think I'm getting a little better…and then I don't."

"It'll take time," she soothed, stepping up behind me to wrap her arms around my waist, both of her palms flat on my belly. Her eyes were soft, but somehow stern the way only a mother's could be as she held my gaze in the mirror and said, "Think it's more than mourning that's got you in such an emotional tailspin, Cress. And I think you know it."

She splayed her hands open across my stomach, and I watched her, swallowing through the sudden desert in my throat.

"How long have you known?" I croaked.

"A few weeks. There's no reason you shouldn't be keeping your food down. At first maybe…when you were crying so hard you made yourself sick. But not now. Have you been to the doctor?"

I sighed, my hands sliding over Lou's so we both pressed against the life inside me. "Yeah. It's too soon to tell the gender, but he or she is healthy."

"You need to take better care of yourself," Lou scolded gently. "You're growing a *life*, Cress."

"Life after death," I agreed. "I think it must have been the night before the wedding or even in the forest hours before he died."

"A parting gift from God, maybe," she suggested, propping her face on my shoulder, rubbing her cheek against mine.

I snorted. "I believe in Satan more than God at this point."

"From fate, then."

"Yeah, maybe." I shifted my gaze up to hers again. "Have you told anyone else? Zeus?"

She hesitated, brow furrowing as she sensed a shift in my intensity. "I wanted to make sure before I told him. He's going to be so excited. Everyone will be."

I shook my head. "No, Lou, I don't want them to know. At least, not yet. I need to go away for a spell, try to get my head on straight. If I'm going to be a single mother to King's baby, I want to be a good one, the *best* one I can be. I need some time away from this place before I can do that. It's like living in a haunted house."

"So move," she suggested immediately, arms tightening around me as if she physically couldn't bear to let me go. "Come live with Z and me, or we can find you a new place closer to town."

"No. I need a vacation, and before you say you or H.R. or Ares or whoever will go with me, I don't want that." I dragged in a deep breath and felt strong for the first time in a long freaking time as I said, "I knew you'd all come to me today so I thought it would be as good a time as any to tell you. I'm going to take King's Harley on a road trip up the coast to Alaska. It's where we were supposed to take our honeymoon, and I just have this feeling I need to go there in order to get closure."

"A feeling?" She frowned. "Cress, I really don't think a long road trip on a motorbike you barely know how to drive is a good idea when you're pregnant and mourning."

I shrugged, but my eyes were hard on hers. "I don't care. I'm a literature student, a book lover, when I see signs, I believe they should be followed."

She sighed, closing her eyes as she hugged me tightly. "You helped me in high school when I needed a friend, so I'll stand up for you now when the brothers try to crush this plan under their heels, but I really, really hope you know what you're doing."

"For the first time since King died, I feel excited about something."

"Okay, then, okay." She blew a strand of white blond hair out of her face and smiled. "You tell them that, they won't be able to say boo about it."

Oh, they said boo. Zeus stood up so fast, he knocked a chair over, breaking the leg in the process, and Nova shouted so loudly, Ares had to cover his ears. Z almost demanded they call a church meeting as a club to vote on it, but I reminded him I was a woman and not a member, not even really an Old Lady anymore.

"You insult me again by sayin' that, Cress, I get you're hurtin', but I won't forgive ya," he'd growled, stalking over to hold me by the shoulders. "Long as I'm on this earth, you'll be loved by me and cherished by me, ya hear? You're family. Fuckin' *nothin'* changes that."

"Okay," I agreed, because I hadn't meant to imply otherwise, but I'd grown clumsy with my words, not used to talking much since the accident. "But then as my family, you need to respect my decision to go. The funeral, it was…nice, but it didn't give me closure. I never got to say goodbye to him, and I need to try to find a way to do that."

"Yeah," he'd finally said, searching my eyes, his own turned as soft as grey clouds after unleashing a storm. "Yeah, don't like it, but I'll find a way to be at peace with it if that's what you need."

"It is."

He'd nodded, and the rest of my friends reluctantly followed his lead, even though they each tried to sway me otherwise over the course of the evening.

I had fun that night, though, relishing it in a way I hadn't since King's loss, knowing it was my last night with them before I left. I played with a grumpy Walker, who everyone had officially started calling Monster, and a giggling Angel. I listened to Ares read to me from 'This Side of Paradise' by F. Scott Fitzgerald before he fell asleep in my bed, staying for a sleepover because he didn't want me to be alone on my birthday.

Sander didn't say anything about my leaving even though I could feel his despair. We had just reconnected, and it had been like two magnets meeting, straight back to the closeness we'd shared growing up yet doubled because of the way he'd supported me through my grief. When everyone left with kisses and some tears and a dozen promises for me to call them every day, he lingered awkwardly by the door.

So, I'd gone to him, wrapped my arms around his hard waist and pressed my cheek to his chest. "Love you, big brother. Thank you for…everything."

There was a heart-wrenching moment of hesitation and then his big arms were around me, squeezing me so tightly, I almost couldn't breathe.

When he spoke, it was in my hair, his lips pressed to the top of my head. "Know you gotta lotta people you can call if you need anythin', but I hope ya know, Queenie, that I'd be honoured to be the first person you reach to for help if you need it. Nothin' on this earth I wouldn't do for ya."

"You've never called me Queenie before," I said, pulling back just enough to look up into his handsome, weathered face. "I thought I was your princess."

The green in his eyes glowed as he smiled a little, secret smile and bumped my chin lightly with his fist. "Doesn't seem so fittin' anymore. Woman I got in my arms is every inch a queen."

I sucked in a sharp breath through my teeth, trying to shore up the tears in my throat.

"No one stronger than you," he assured me. "Why do you think your man called you his Iron Queen? Gotta spine of steel, Cress, it's held you strong through everythin' so far, and I doubt it'll let you down for the rest. You do what you gotta do to heal, and then you come home to us soon, yeah? You've gotta whole fuckin' town rootin' for you here."

I hadn't thought of it that way, but it was true. I knew I had the Garros and The Fallen, but I also had the citizens of Entrance, most of them at least, especially now that so many of the corrupt police were in the process of being put behind bars.

Danner's sentencing trial was set to begin in a week, and I wanted to be gone before then. I wasn't a witness, so I didn't have to testify, and I didn't think I could survive the news crews and worried townsfolk showing up at my house again.

So, the next morning, after making one last apple pie for breakfast, eating it straight out of the oven with Ares, both of us blowing hard on our forks to cool the molten fruit, I dropped him off at school and made one more pitstop before I hit the road properly.

I hadn't been back to the cliff top since the incident. It was the sight of my nightmare come to life, and it felt cursed like the sight of some ancient burial ground.

But I needed to see it.

So, I swung my leg of King's bike and staggered as I tried to maneuver the heavy weight, still not completely used to the thing even though King had taught me to ride it countless times. The trail was dry, the flowers long dead from the sun roasting them through the summer, and there was already a nip in the air that said our Indian summer was over and winter was around the corner. I hugged my backpack to my chest to ward off the chill and held my breath as I finally entered the clearing over the bluff.

It was gorgeous.

I could picture King and Mute sitting on the terrifying edge, shooting the shit. Could see the exact spot we'd made love after he proposed to me and the place we'd tussled, laughing and naked in the long grass off to one side.

It was a location full of memories, all the good ones now crushed by the weight of a single tragedy.

I moved slowly across the space until I stood on the precipice. The wind rushed over me with eager hands, tugging at my clothes and hair, igniting a shiver down my spine and stinging my eyes, but I kept them open. I wanted to memorize the texture of the froth-tipped ocean, the exact shade of its metallic sheen under the low hanging sun. I wanted to remember the exact angle of the curve in the bay and the height in metres from the top of the cliff to the rocks below.

Eyes to the view, I dug through my bag and produced the glass bottle I'd prepared days ago. There was a poem inside, one of many I'd found myself writing just to feel a connection to King, just to purge myself of even an iota of the pain clogging up all my pores.

He is not dead.
I love him, and I wear him in my heart.
So.
He is not dead.
I know him, and I live out his days in my head.
So.
He is not dead.
I am still alive, but half-formed because he is not here also.
So.
He is not dead.
Because if he was, I would be too.
The stages of grief: denial.

It wasn't about creating something pretty, so I hadn't cared to cast a critical eye to the verse. I just needed to get it down on paper, to make it a tangible thing I could touch, because maybe then, I could find a way to conquer it.

I pulled back my arm with the bottle in my hand then hurled it with all my might out into the sea, watching as it dropped, spinning, tumbling, green in the yellow sunlight over the blue waves. I'd assumed it would crash on the sharp teeth of rocks jutting up at the base of the cliffs, but it landed much farther out, settling with minimal fanfare in the waves.

I paused, mind suspended like a sprinter set before a race, braced to explode into movement.

And then, dangerously, I wondered.

I thought back to the wedding after everyone had left except for The Fallen and family, trying to recall who was there, searching frantically through them in my mind's eye, grateful that years of teaching had given me a gift for remembering faces.

No Eugene.

King's uncle, Kylie's keeper, The Fallen's secret harbourer.

I knew Buck, Cyclops, and Axe-Man had arrived at the bluff minutes before Danner shot King. They were testifying in court next week, and they'd all been altered by the experience, muted somehow.

But Eugene hadn't been with them.

My heart started racing, and I broke out in a cold, prickly sweat that made me itch from nose to toes.

I fumbled with my phone until I found his number and pressed the green call button.

"Cressida?" he asked immediately, probably surprised to hear from me because we hadn't been tight since King passed, and I was starting to question why.

"Eugene, I decided to go…rowing off my property, and I got stuck in a riptide that took me way too far out to sea. Could you bring your boat around and pick me up? I'm too exhausted to get back myself."

It was early, and Eugene owned a bar, so he'd probably been sleeping, but immediately he said, "Hold tight, and be careful not to get too close to those rocks. I'll be there as soon as I can."

I stared at the phone long after it had been disconnected, then finally put it in my backpack and sat on the cliff to wait. My blood felt fizzy in my veins, treacherously carbonated with a hope I hadn't felt in weeks.

I stared down the edge of the cliff, calculating the drop to be somewhere around a hundred and fifty feet, and wondered idly, if it was too far a jump to survive.

Not so idly, I decided I didn't care.

When I spotted Eugene's small powerboat rounding the

point, I stood up and started to take my clothes off. Not all of them, just my heavy jeans and my leather jacket.

I waved at Eugene as he drew closer, knowing he was probably scared out of his mind seeing me at the edge of the cliff.

Or maybe not, which proved what I'd been too frightened to articulate, even in my thoughts.

I thought about the leap I'd taken when I'd decided to be with King, how much blind faith I'd had in him and my feelings for him, and how I'd been rewarded tenfold for taking the chance to fall for him.

And I'd fall for him again.

Any time, any place, any way I could.

"I love you," I murmured into the wind before I sucked a deep breath into my lungs, coating them with needed oxygen, and then…

I jumped.

EPILOGUE

King

I'D ALWAYS BEEN able to find solace in nature. It might'a been my poet's heart that found the complexities of the earth profound, echoes of my own thoughts and emotions hidden in the movement of the trees and the achin' crash of waves across the shore. I'd picked a good house, a little one, on a cliff just outside'a Sitka, Alaska, where the trees stood as watchmen at my back and the ocean unraveled like a rumpled carpet at my feet. There was beauty in so much of this place, and it was one'a the reasons I'd settled on it, but it did little to soothe my desolate soul.

The woman I loved had eyes like the forest floor, dappled in golden daylight, dark with evergreens and light with spring frost. I got lost in the woods behind my house and imagined I was gettin' lost in the depths of her eyes.

The sea, the sky, and the eternal sunlight of an Alaskan summer reminded me of her, too, and I wrote poem after poem 'bout the way she haunted me, but nothin' could purge the sorrow from me.

So, I lived. If you could call it that. Chopped wood, fed the fire at night, read book after book, always returnin' to *The Prince* and *Paradise Lost* 'cause she'd loved those best, and at night, in the darkest hours, I thought of her while I held myself in my palm and spilled across my chest. Went to the store, bought groceries, ignored the look of the red-haired cashier who wanted me too much, and went home to do it all again.

It was borin' as hell, but in the moments when I'd almost gotten on the shitty second-hand Harley I'd bought to fix up, itchin' to head back to Entrance, I reminded myself that Zeus'd be home with his babies 'cause of my sacrifice.

It was only a matter of time.

And Eugene kept me updated, sendin' old school post-cards through the mail filled with his cramped, chicken-scratch writin' I only had a hope of decipherin' 'cause I'd made furniture with him for years and knew his hand.

Danner'd disappeared after my 'murder', but turned up some days later, hog-tied and beaten to a bloody pulp, on the steps leadin' to a Vancouver police station.

Now, seven weeks later, he was finally on trial for murder, corruption, assault, and more. I had no doubt Mr. White's firm would put him in the metaphorical ground where he belonged.

It wasn't right of me or fair, but I'd been hopin' over the last weeks that Cress would've made sense of the clues I'd left her and found me. With the help of Uncle Eugene, I'd left a trail of breadcrumbs, some poems well placed, a hint on the globe, an email in her inbox advertisin' a vacation in Sitka. She still wasn't with me, and I had a feelin' I'd done a gross disservice to her grief. Even just parted from her as I was, knownin' she wasn't dead, I felt half sentient without her.

I sighed gustily then laughed, thinkin' of my Cress and how often she sighed dramatically, even when she didn't mean to be passive aggressive. Closin' my eyes, I gave up on the poem I'd been writin' and flopped back to the grass. The warm sun glowed tangerine behind my lids, and the soft caress of the ocean breeze moved like velvet over my cheek.

"I imagined you in a heaven looking something like this. Warmed by the sun, easy with death, writing in your journal."

Fuck, but I missed her voice. It was a smooth alto that pealed like bells when she laughed. It was almost what I missed the most, her laugh, and makin' her do it while she stood in my arms, frothed over with mirth.

"Never knew when I joined you there I'd be as angry with you as I am now."

I frowned, 'cause in none of my imaginings was my babe mad at me. A second later, a hot splat landed on my cheek and rolled into my ear.

It was not raining.

My body stilled, bloated with a hope so big it seemed I would fuckin' burst if I so much as opened my eyes.

But I did.

I had to.

And when I opened 'em, I saw the most beautiful sight I'd ever seen in my fuckin' life, includin' the day Cress walked to me in a dress caught like dew on her skin durin' our weddin'.

'Cause she was there, gilded by the sun, drippin' hot rain on my face, eyes awash with tears and pain and relief so acute I felt it like a knife in my chest.

She was there.

"You're lucky I love you so goddamn much," she whispered through the pressure of tears in her throat as she cupped my face and ran a thumb along the edge of my cheek. "You're lucky I've spent the last forty-eight days begging and praying to God for even one last look at your face. You're so lucky." A sob rolled through her painfully thin frame. "You're so lucky you're alive so I can't hate you for leaving me."

"Cress," I murmured, leanin' up to bring her down on top of me then rolling over so she was pinned to the grass and her tears ran tracks down to her ears. "My Cress, my love, my Queenie, don't hate me. Fuck, if you hated me, it'd be worse than any kinda death."

"You left," she hiccoughed. "You left. You left. You left."

"Do you get why?" I asked softly, ready for whatever reaction she might have 'cause I deserved it.

I *had* left her, so alone and so obviously broken. Her beauty was dimmed by the grief she wore in the bags beneath her eyes, in the awful hollow of her thin cheeks and the jut of her sharp bones beneath her skin.

The urge to cry wrapped like a hand 'round my throat as I looked at what I'd done to her in order for all of us to survive and thrive in the long term.

"I don't care why," she cried, shakin' her head back and forth even as she clutched at me, knuckles white in their hold against my tee, legs locked over the backs of mine. "I don't *want* to care why. I want to hate you because I thought you were *dead*. I thought I would never hold you like this, never touch your haloed hair, kiss your mouth or speak our secrets forehead to forehead in the middle of the night."

She lost the rest of her words to tears, cryin' so violently I worried she'd choke. I sat up and tugged her into my lap so that she could wrap herself 'round me like chains, lockin' us up tight. She seemed to find solace in that, cheek pressed to my pulse, then a kiss there, then tongue, eatin' at the beat of my heart through my skin, needin' to feel each movement of my blood to ascertain I was truly alive.

"I'm here, babe, I'm here," I chanted brokenly as she cried.

She sobbed for a long while, until there were no more tears in her ducts, until she was so purged of sadness she felt lighter, almost hollow in my arms, completely empty.

I vowed then and there, I'd only ever fill her up with love and beauty for the rest of our long lives.

"Made you a promise a long time ago, that no matter what pain and ugliness I brought to your life, I'd bring you double that in sweetness and beauty. Know right now it seems all I've given you is the hurt and the bitterness, but you give me a shot at it again, Cress, babe, I promise you, there won't be a day that goes by you won't feel just how much I love you. Just how much I *live* for you. And you know, you gotta know, I'm a man who makes a promise, I'd die 'fore breakin' it."

"But you did die," she murmured tiredly as she rested on my shoulder. "You died, and I had to realize what it was like to live without you. That's the punishment God should have given Eve, to live separate from Adam, to walk the earth alone, because *that* is what hell is, King. To be alone without you."

"Never again," I swore, so desperate for her, I couldn't stop touchin' her, my hand in her thick, silky hair, lips against the satin of her cheek, kissin' the faint lines formin' from laughter at the edge of her big, tired eyes. "You hear me? Did what I did for you even though it doesn't seem like it. Did it for you and our family. We were never gonna be safe with Danner stalkin' us. Never."

"I know," she whispered, finally pullin' away to look me in the eyes, hers stale with old pain. "I found him. I found him and beat him for what he did to you, and when I did, I saw how little he cared about what he'd done. He wouldn't have stopped hunting us until we were dead or in prison. I know… I know you sacrificed so that everyone else wouldn't have to."

"Forced that sacrifice on you too," I acknowledged. "Can't tell you how sorry I am for it, babe."

"It was living hell," she admitted weakly, her fingers carvin' through my hair compulsively, almost as if she thought I'd disappear if she didn't keep hold of it. "But you're alive. *Alive.*"

"My smart girl, findin' the clues I left for you."

"Honestly, I didn't put it all together until I was about to go on a road trip to Sitka alone and stopped off at the cliff. I tossed a bottle in the ocean and when it didn't shatter, all the pieces of the puzzle just clicked together. Just to make sure, I called Eugene, and he brought the boat around before I jumped."

"What?" I growled. "Are you fuckin' kiddin' me? Why the hell did you jump?"

"Relax," she said with an eye roll, her sass a feast for my gluttonous soul. "I obviously survived, though, Eugene about killed me himself when he pulled me into the boat."

"It's a fuckin' risky jump, Cress. It was a last resort, not a fuckin' adrenaline sport. You're lucky Eugene was there with the boat or you coulda been lost in the current or crushed by the rocks."

"Eugene," she said darkly, lips twistin' at the sour taste of his name. "The ultimate secret keeper. Such a bastard for helping you and not telling me."

"Babe, it happened in an instant. Wasn't exactly sure what would go down or when, but I planned it with Wrath and Eugene just in case. No way I was gonna let Dad rot in prison for a crime he didn't commit, let my baby sister and brother be without a father like I had for too long. No way I was gonna let that motherfucker keep threatenin' you. Not that kinda man, babe."

"I know," she pouted, so damn pretty I had to suck that lip into my mouth. "But you could have told me."

This was the crux of it. If she couldn't forgive me for keepin' her in the dark, she'd be lost to me forever.

The thought sent my euphoria crashin' through the floor of my gut.

I sunk my fingers in the thick hair over her ears and held her perfect face close to mine so all she could see was me.

"Babe, you think I haven't been livin' each day in a world of pain not bein' with you, knowin' how much *more* pain you must've been in, thinkin' I was gone to you forever, you'd be so fuckin' wrong. But how could I have told you any quicker? No way you coulda gone through with the funeral and everythin' convincin' enough to make it believable."

"There was a part of me that didn't believe you were dead. You didn't *feel* gone, you know?"

"Yeah, I know, Cress." I angled my forehead against hers and breathed her in so the essence of her infused my lungs, charged through my blood, and filled me up with her light. "Can't say I made the best choice, just the only one I saw to be taken at the time. Soon as I could get word to you without bein' obvious to anyone keepin' an eye on you, I did."

"You did," she agreed, so tired now that her eyes kept closin' and takin' too long to open again. She propped her head on my shoulder and curled up like a kitten. "I don't know if I forgive you entirely for what you did. I'm going to wear the scars on my heart for the rest of my life, and I'm probably never going to be able to let you out of my sight again. But I love you. It seems so complicated, but when it comes down to it, I love you, and I want to be with you. I don't care in what country, on what planet, in what year, under what circumstances. I'm yours and you're mine."

"That's it?" I asked, voice cracked right in half by the force of her words.

"That's it," she mumbled. "I'll probably be mad in the morning again, and the morning after that, and maybe after that for a long time to come, but you're patient, and you'll take it so I can purge it. Eventually, all that's left will be love and no more pain. I'll forgive you, it's just going to take time."

"How can you be so fuckin' perfect?" I breathed, shocked and humbled by the woman I was honoured enough to call my wife.

"Not perfect, just yours. Bone of your bone," she said, plantin' a hand against my ribs. "Made from you, for you."

"Yeah, babe," I agreed then lifted her head to gently lick open her mouth and take my fill.

When I broke away, she was smilin', eyes so soft a brown they looked velvet. "So, this'll be our home until we can go back?"

"We always wanted to come here," I said in answer. "Seemed a good place to hide until Danner went away for more than just my murder."

"Any place is good as long as you're in it. I'm serious about never letting you out of my sight."

"I'm good with that," I told her, kissin' her again, rollin' so she was on her back and I could move my hands over her body, feel the form I'd only been able to touch in my dreams.

When my hand skirted up her sweater over her stomach, she stopped me, pressin' my palm flat to the slight curve.

I watched as her eyes filled with tears again and she whispered, "Was going to name him King if you were really gone, but now, we're back to Prince."

Happiness like nothin' I'd ever known carbonated my blood and kicked like adrenaline through my heart.

"It's not the same as being at home," she admitted with a warbled smile. "But I brought some family with me."

I kissed her 'fore the last word was even fully formed, eatin' it off her tongue, holdin' her so tight she could feel my bones through my skin, the race of my heart against her breasts, the relief and sadness and euphoria movin' through me.

"Love you more than my life," I said against her mouth.

"Yeah, honey, I think you proved that."

And then, like I hadn't done in months, like I hadn't done since I'd last seen her glorious fuckin' face, I threw my head back and *laughed*.

And Cress?

She did it with me.

The end.

Thank you so much for reading *AFTER THE FALL*!

Inked in Lies (The Fallen Men, #5) is coming next!

If you want to stay up to date on news about new releases and bonus content join my reader's group or subscribe to my newsletter!

Need to vent?
Join the After the Fall Spoiler Room!

If you loved King's poetry, check out *King of Iron Hearts*, the poetry collection I wrote in the voice of Kyle Kyle Garro!

If you loved reading about King's romance with his prim and proper ex-teacher Cressida, you'll love his father, Zeus Garro's taboo love story! Discover what happens when the Prez of The Fallen MC saves the life of the mayor's daughter and their lives become entangled for good…

A Top 40 Amazon Bestseller…

"Taboo, breathtaking, and scorching hot! I freaking loved WELCOME TO THE DARK SIDE."—Skye Warren, *New York Times* bestselling author

One-Click WELCOME TO THE DARK SIDE now!

Turn the page for an excerpt…

Welcome to the Dark Side (The Fallen Men, Book #2) Excerpt

I was a good girl.
I ate my vegetables, volunteered at the local autism centre and sat in the front pew of church every Sunday.
Then, I got cancer.
What the hell kind of reward was that for a boring life well lived?
I was a seventeen-year-old paradigm of virtue and I was tired of it.
So, when I finally ran into the man I'd been writing to since he saved my life as a little girl and he offered to show me the dark side of life before I left it for good, I said yes.
Only, I didn't know that Zeus Garro was the President of The Fallen MC and when you made a deal with a man who is worse than the devil, there was no going back…
A standalone in The Fallen Men Series.

Prologue.

Welcome to the Dark Side Excerpt

I was too young to realize what the *pop* meant.

It sounded to my childish ears like a giant popping a massive wad of bubble gum.

Not like a bullet releasing from a chamber, heralding the sharp burst of pain that would follow when it smacked and then ripped through my shoulder.

Also, I was in the parking lot of First Light Church. It was my haven not only because it was a church and that was the original purpose of such places, but also because my grandpa was the pastor, my grandmother ran the after-school programs, and my father was the mayor so it was just as much his stage as his parents'.

A seven-year-old girl just does not expect to be shot in the parking lot of a church, holding the hand of her mother on one side and her father on the other, her grandparents waving from the open door as parents picked up their young children from after-school care.

Besides, I was unusually mesmerized by the sight of a man driving slowly by the entrance to the church parking lot. He rode a great growling beast that was so enormous it looked at my childish eyes like a silver and black backed dragon. Only the man wasn't wearing shining armour the way I thought he should have been. Instead, he wore a tight long-sleeved shirt under a heavy leather vest with a big picture of a fiery skull and tattered wings on the back of it. What kind of knight rode a mechanical dragon in a leather vest?

My little girl brain was too young to comprehend the complexities of the answer but my heart, though small, knew without context what kind of brotherhood that man would be in and it yearned for him.

Even at seven, I harboured a black rebel soul bound in velvet bows and Bible verse.

As if sensing my gaze, my thoughts, the biker turned to look at me, his face cruel with anger. I shivered and as his gaze settled on mine those shots rang out in a staccato beat that perfectly matched the cadence of my suddenly overworked heart.

Pop. Pop. Pop.

Everything from there happened as it did in action movies, with rapid bursts of sound and movement that swirled into a violent cacophony. I remembered only three things from the shooting that would go down in history as one of the worst incidents of gang violence in the town and province's history.

One.

My father flying to the ground quick as a flash, his hand wrenched from mine so that he could cover his own head. My mother screaming like a howler monkey but frozen to the spot, her hand paralyzed over mine.

Useless.

Two.

Men in black leather vests flooded the concrete like a murder of ravens, their hands filled with smoking metal that rattled off round after round of *pop, pop, pop*. Some of them rode bikes like my mystery biker but most of them were on foot, suddenly appearing from behind cars, around buildings.

More of them came roaring down the road behind the man I'd been watching, flying blurs of silver, green and black.

They were everywhere.

But these first two observations were merely vague impressions because I had eyes for only one person.

The third thing I remembered was him, Zeus Garro, locking eyes with me across the parking lot a split second before chaos erupted. Our gazes collided like the meeting of two planets, the ensuing bedlam a natural offshoot of the collision. It was only because I was watching him that I saw the horror distort his features and knew something bad was going to happen.

Someone grabbed me from behind, hauled me into the air with their hands under my pits. They were tall because I remember dangling like an ornament from his hold, small but significant with meaning. He was using me and even then, I knew it.

I twisted to try to kick him in the torso with the hard heel of my Mary Jane's and he must have assumed I'd be frozen in fright because my little shoe connected with a soft place that immediately loosened his grip.

Before I could fully drop to the ground, I was running and I was running toward him. The man on the great silver and black beast who had somehow heralded the massacre going down in blood and smoke all around me.

His bike lay discarded on its side behind him and he was standing straight and so tall he seemed to my young mind like a great giant, a beast from another planet or the deep jungle, something that killed for sport as well as survival. And he was doing it now, killing men like it was nothing but one of those awful, violent video games my cousin Clyde liked to play. In one hand he held a wicked curved blade already lacquered with blood from the two men who lay fallen at his feet while the other held a smoking gun that, under other circumstances, I might have thought was a pretty toy.

I took this in as I ran toward him, focused on him so I wouldn't notice the *pop*, the screams and wet slaps of bodies hitting the pavement. So I wouldn't taste the metallic residue of gun powder on my tongue or feel the splatter of blood that rained down on me as I passed one man being gutted savagely by another.

Somehow, if I could just get to *him*, everything would be okay.

He watched me come to him. Not with his eyes, because he was busy killing bad guys and shouting short, gruff orders to the guys wearing the same uniform as him but there was something in the way his great big body leaned toward me, shifted on his feet so that he was always orientated my way, that made me feel sure he was looking out for me even as I came for him.

He was just a stone's throw away, but it seemed to take forever for my short legs to move me across the asphalt and when I was only halfway there, his expression changed.

I knew without knowing that the man I'd kicked in his soft place was up again and probably angry. The hairs on the back of my neck stood on end and a fierce shiver ripped down my spine like tearing Velcro. I didn't realize it at the time, but I started to scream just as the police sirens started to wail a few blocks away.

My biker man roared, a violent noise that rent the air in two and made some of the people closest to him pause even in the middle of fighting. Then he was moving, and I remember thinking that for such a tall man, he moved *fast* because within the span of a breath, he was in front of me reaching out a hand to pull me closer…

A moment too late.

Because in that second when his tattooed hands clutched me to his chest and he tried to throw us to the ground, spiraling in a desperate attempt to act as human body armour to my tiny form, a *POP* so much louder than the rest exploded on the air and excruciating pain tore through my left shoulder, just inches from my adrenaline-filled heart.

We landed, and the agonizing pain burned brighter as my shoulder hit the pavement and my biker man rolled fully on top of me with a pained grunt.

I blinked through the tears welling up in my eyes, trying to breathe, trying to *live* through the pain radiating like a nuclear blast site through my chest. All I saw was him. His arm covered my head, one hand over my ear as he pulled back just enough to look down into my face.

That was what I remember most, that third thing, Zeus Garro's silver eyes as they stared down at me in a church parking lot filled with blood and smoke, screams and whimpers, but those eyes an oasis of calm that lulled my flagging heart into a steadier beat.

"I got you, little girl," he said in a voice as rough and deep as any monster's, while he held me as if he were a guardian angel. "I got you."

I clutched a tiny fist into his blood-soaked shirt and stared into the eyes of my guardian monster until I lost consciousness.

Sometimes now, I wonder if I would have done anything differently even if I had known how that bullet would tear through my small body, breaking bones and tender young flesh, irrevocably changing the course of my life forever.

Always, the answer is no.

Because it brought me to him.

Or rather, him to me.

Get it now for FREE on Kindle Unlimited!

I knew the moment I finished writing Lessons in Corruption that King and Cressida deserved more story.

Even though there is an eight-year age difference between King and Cressida, they were both still so 'new' to living at the end of their first book with so much growing and life left to live. In After the Fall, I wanted to explore not what it means to fall in love, but what it means to *stay* in love with your chosen partner every single day. It means sacrifice, compromise, passion and logic, endurance and spontaneity. It means prioritizing your loved one and showing them how much you love them every moment you can because life is short and fragile. I wanted to explore the little intimacies of life with an established couple that are so beautiful and so underappreciated in romance because we are usually all about the journey of getting to 'I love you' instead of what it means to live those words every day after first saying them.

A note on *Paradise Lost* and *The Prince*; both characters are consumed by their love of literature, so it was only too natural and important to weave these two important works into the narrative. If you haven't read them, I highly encourage you to do so!

Now, on to the crew who keeps this boat afloat.

Allaa, I wish I had better words to describe what you mean to me. You are my spiritual twin, my sister, my friend, and my confidante. I love you unspeakable amounts and appreciate the role you play in my creative process more than I could ever say.

Michelle, thank you for stepping up for me, for always supporting me and loving me as if you were born to do it. I admire you and love you to the depths of my soul.

To my sunshine, Annette, your positivity and love bring light to my life every day.

Sarah from Musings of a Modern Book Belle, thank you for being my cheerleader, my critic, and my friend. You always make me a better author and your friendship makes me a better person.

Kim BookJunkie, thank you so much for working with me! Your patience, resolve, and understanding have made this crazy process so much easier on me. I hope I didn't give you too many grey hairs, and I cannot wait to get you to edit for me again.

Jenny from Editing4Indies, you are my saviour. Thank you for polishing this manuscript from a diamond in the rough into a polished gem.

Candi from Candi Kane PR, you make releases ten times less stressful and any author knows that's worth everything. Thank you for your endlessly hard work on my behalf and for providing me with essential advice. I love you so much.

Najla Qamber from Najla Qamber Designs, is the only woman I have ever worked with on a cover. She is my wizard and the creator of all my gorgeous graphics.

I love thanking my Review Team because without them, the good word of Giana Darling wouldn't spread nearly as far and wide.

Giana's Darlings, each and every one of you mean so

much to me. Thank you for giving me a loving, supportive corner of the internet to call my own.

Ashlee, you are such a badass Slytherin, and I am so grateful to have your creativity, friendship, and humour in my life. The day we became friends is a day I will always be grateful for.

Ella, my love, your strength and friendship inspire me every day.

To Sarah Green, the newest addition to my inner circle but someone who I feel as if I've known forever. Thank you for punctuating my day with your witticisms and stories. I love you so much and can't wait for you to visit.

I have so many friends in this amazing community that I cannot possibly pay tribute to all of them, but you all know who you are, and you know how much I love you.

There are countless bloggers who made this release shine like the North Star in a sky filled with innumerable book releases, and I'm so grateful to each one of you. My most special thanks has to go to Jessica @peacelovebooksxo, Lisa @book_ish_life, Ashlee @ashob1229, @b.b.lynnreads, @insanebooklover, @krysthereader, @totallybookish28, @gianadarlingfans and @kerilovesbooks for always sharing and supporting my posts.

To my sister Grace. This book is for you because I wouldn't be here without your lifelong support and encouragement. Thank you for always wanting me to be exactly who I am inside.

To Fiona and Lauren, you two have provided me with enough solace, adventures, laughter, and love in this decade plus that I've known you two to last me a lifetime, , and it thrills me every day to know we have so many more decades of fun and friendship together. I can't wait to one day dedicate a book to Mrs. H and Mrs. A, because that's obviously going to be one of my wedding presents to both of you!

To my Armie. It seems ridiculous that we've only known

each other for three years, yet we have enough shared memories to last a lifetime. You make each day even more beautiful to me simply by existing.

My Albie, I've never singled you out in my acknowledgements before, but of all my boys, you are the most worthy of my gratitude. Thank you for putting up with my needy, moody cat-like behaviour and for being my best friend since middle school. I can't image how much poorer my life would be without you.

As always, to the Love of My Life. In every book I write, I try to find the words to explain how deeply one person can love another. In every book, I fail to bring to life the complexities of a love like ours. I'm so grateful that I have a lifetime to try to do justice to that emotion and commitment. You inspire me every day.

OTHER BOOKS BY GIANA DARLING

The Evolution of Sin Trilogy

Giselle Moore is running away from her past in France for a new life in America, but before she moves to New York City, she takes a holiday on the beaches of Mexico and meets a sinful, enigmatic French businessman, Sinclair, who awakens submissive desires and changes her life forever.

The Affair

The Secret

The Consequence

The Evolution Of Sin Trilogy Boxset

The Fallen Men Series

The Fallen Men are a series of interconnected standalone erotic MC romances that each feature age gaps love stories between dirty-talking, Alpha Males and the strong, sassy women that win their hearts.

Lessons in Corruption

Welcome to the Dark Side

Good Gone Bad

A Fallen Men Companion Book of Poetry:

King of Iron Hearts

The Enslaved Duet

The Enslaved Duet is a dark romance duology about an eighteen year old Italian fashion model, Cosima Lombardi, who is sold by her indebted father to a British Earl who's nefarious plans for her include more than just sexual slavery… Their epic tale spans across Italy, England, Scotland and the USA across a five-year period that sees them endure murder, separation, and a web of infinite lies.

Enthralled (The Enslaved Duet #1)

Enamoured (The Enslaved Duet, Book 2)

The Elite Seven Series

Sloth (The Elite Seven Series, #7)

Coming Soon

Inked in Lies (The Fallen Men, #5)

AhiL (Dante's Book)

ABOUT GIANA DARLING

Giana Darling is a USA Today, Wall Street Journal, Top 40 Best Selling Canadian romance writer who specializes in the taboo and angsty side of love and romance. She currently lives in beautiful British Columbia where she spends time riding on the back of her man's bike, baking pies, and reading snuggled up with her cat, Persephone.

Join my Reader's Group
Subscribe to my Newsletter
Follow me on IG
Like me on Facebook
Follow me on Goodreads
Follow me on BookBub
Follow me on Pinterest

Milton Keynes UK
Ingram Content Group UK Ltd.
UKHW020946260524
443151UK00012B/219